A CIGAR CITY THRILLER
LOOSE ENDS

CHRIS KNEER

A CIGAR CITY THRILLER

LOOSE ENDS

CHRIS KNEER

This is a work of fiction. Unless otherwise indicated, all the names, characters, businesses, places, events, and incidents in this book are either the product of the author's imagination or used in a fictitious manner. Any resemblance to actual persons, living or dead, or actual events is purely coincidental.

Loose Ends
Published by Spartan Entertainment
Tampa Bay, Florida, USA.

Copyright ©2026, CHRIS KNEER. All rights reserved.

KNEER, CHRIS, Author
LOOSE ENDS
CHRIS KNEER

Library of Congress Control Number: 2024919614

ISBN: 979-8-9913666-3-2 (hardcover)
ISBN: 979-8-9913666-4-9 (paperback)
ISBN: 979-8-9913666-5-6 (digital)

FICTION / Thrillers / General
FICTION / Thrillers / Crime
FICTION / Thrillers / Suspense

Publishing Management, Editorial, and Art Direction: Pique Publishing, Inc.

For quantity purchases or additional information,
email Chris@ChrisKneerAuthor.com.

All rights reserved by CHRIS KNEER
This book is printed in the United States of America.

For Jodi and Andrew.
Thank you for always believing in my dreams.

CHAPTER 1

Tallahassee, Florida

2024

Governor Mack Matthews knew he was screwed as soon as he pressed down on the brake, and nothing happened.

The evening had started perfectly. He'd gunned the engine of his classic 1975 Porsche 911 Turbo down Dixie Road, far exceeding the posted limit, grinning as he leaned into the curves of Morningside Lane. Yacht Rock blared from the speakers, and the asphalt still glistened with rain from a late afternoon shower. But Mack wasn't worried. He trusted his reflexes and knew the Porsche's tires would hug the road when it counted.

The warm rush of air tore through the open windows, twisting his hair and new gray beard in wild tangles. His high-end Oakley sunglasses pressed firmly against his face. With every mile, the weight of the office slipped away.

Since moving to Tallahassee after being elected Florida's governor, these late-day drives had become a ritual. Once or twice a week, he'd sneak out, shake his protective detail, and vanish into the pine-lined backroads. He knew he was taking a risk by speeding up and down the hills and powering through the curves, but what was the point of driving a Porsche if you weren't going fast? His staff hated it. He loved it.

Governor Mack, as everyone called him, was halfway through his second and final term. After serving in the military and earning a degree from Florida State, Mack attended law school and spent a decade practicing. Tired of the grind and billable hours, he went into real estate. The company he co-founded became one of the largest multifamily developers in the Southeast. He made a fortune, then sold his stake to his partners so he could "give back." Politics was his third act.

He entered Congress at fifty, virtually unknown, but quickly made a name for himself with a sharp wit and disarming southern charm. His press conferences became must-see TV. A few years later, he pulled off a stunning upset in the governor's race and became one of Florida's most lovable leaders. He was equal parts statesman and showman, known for his relentless work ethic and nightly espresso martinis on the mansion porch.

His proudest achievement was running for re-election with his son on the ticket. Frederick, an Annapolis dropout-turned-high-powered, marketing-savvy slip-and-fall lawyer, brought youth and star power to the ticket. Together, they made history as the first father-and-son team to serve as governor and lieutenant governor. The media loved the optics. The reality was more complicated.

Mack led as a moderate, building connections and working with both parties. He warned against the dangers of advanced technology while keeping an open mind toward advancements that could improve the world. Frederick leaned hard right, eager to disrupt and dominate. Their private dinners often ended in tense standoffs. Two men bound by blood but divided by politics and ambition.

Two nights earlier, their relationship reached the breaking point. For months, Mack had noticed state funds vanishing, disappearing into a web of shell companies and offshore trusts. Each time he confronted Frederick, the answers were plausible and evasive. But when he finally presented proof tracing the money to a shadowy foreign organization, it became clear Frederick would need to step down. More denials followed, and Frederick stormed from the mansion, swearing he would resign over his dead body. They hadn't spoken since.

Mack loved Frederick, but his commitment to the office was paramount. Doing the right thing was ingrained in everything he did. He still had so much to accomplish to make the world a better place. They would get the money back so Frederick could return to his legal career.

Now, on the narrow, tree-lined road, the steering wheel shook violently in his hands as he tried to hold the road. The car fishtailed once, twice—his heart pounded, fingers white-knuckling the wheel. His eyes were wide with panic, hearing the screech of rubber on the road. He spun a full 360 degrees.

For a moment, he thought he could regain control, but then he registered the thick Carolina cherry laurel.

Then came the crash.

The Porsche slammed head-on into the tree. Metal folded like paper. Glass erupted in a blizzard. His body whipped forward, then slammed back into the seat.

For a moment, there was silence—just the hissing of steam and birds chirping somewhere up above.

Then the fire erupted. A sharp, acrid smell filled the air.

Flames engulfed the silver machine—his pride and joy, now a flaming wreck on a forgotten road.

And Governor Mack Matthews, beloved by millions, wasn't moving.

CHAPTER 2

Present Day

The chains clink around Sterling Kennedy's wrists and ankles as the prison bus rumbles under the stone archway that marks the entrance to the State of Florida Correctional Institution in Raiford, Florida. He pleads silently for his body to stop trembling, but it won't. The shackles won't let him forget where he's going.

He isn't a guest.

He's the newest inmate in Florida's largest—and most feared—maximum-security prison. For the next ten years, he'll be locked inside with over two thousand hardened men unless his handlers do what they promised. He needs to survive the first day and find the warden.

His striped jumpsuit itches at the collar, a constant reminder of the sentence handed down in a Tampa courtroom just days ago—securities fraud. Before the trial, his high-priced attorney assured him it'd be country-club confinement—white-collar, light duty. Maybe a year and then probation. But the Feds had other ideas. They needed a fall guy. A headline. An example.

Sterling, former CEO of Titan Financial Group, had become the face of a sprawling tax fraud scheme, his prominence amplified by the deaths of many co-conspirators. As the head of the Wealth

Defense Network, he taught the ultra-rich how to hide billions from their governments—always taking a cut for an elusive secret society known only as *The One*—a group obsessed with imposing a single rule over the world. The identities of the wealthy players—politicians, athletes, and family offices alike—remained a mystery, with the only proof stolen. Sterling held the key to unraveling it all, yet he steadfastly refused to cooperate with the authorities.

How the hell did I get into this mess? How the hell did I get caught?

The weight of the chain linking him to the man beside him tugs at his wrist. Sterling glances over. The guy's out cold, head against the window, a single teardrop tattoo under one eye, and a crude swastika inked on his neck.

How do you fall asleep on the way to prison? Is this the kind of animal I will be living with? I know too much. If they leave me here, I'll have to snitch.

Sterling swallows hard, but his mouth is dry as dust.

The bus screeches to a halt. A guard's voice cracks like a whip. "On your feet! Form a line!"

Sterling tries to calm himself. Deep breaths. Center your mind. But every inch of him is bracing for the unknown.

The line of inmates trudges out into the Florida heat—thick, swampy, oppressive. It hits him like a wall. He smells sweat and fear, his own and everyone else's. The men around him are a mix of races and backgrounds, tattooed and scarred, their expressions cold and unreadable. Most look like they've been here before.

Act confident. Don't let them see the fear. The warden will protect me.

The procession of banished souls marches single file into the intake corridor. Officers herd them forward like sheep. In the next room, they're ordered to strip naked. Exposed and degraded. Officers check them for contraband while others laugh and jeer.

A heavyset Hispanic man leers at Sterling. "They're gonna *love* you in here, sweet cheeks."

Laughter erupts. Mocking lips make kissing noises. Sterling keeps his eyes forward.

They're handed stiff, ill-fitting pink jumpsuits—worn thin at the elbows and knees—and lined up against a concrete wall.

The first thing Sterling sees is a mountain of a man—six feet eight, maybe taller, four hundred pounds. Flat-top haircut. Sweat-stained uniform. The badge on his shirt is crooked, and half the buttons are missing. A nightstick twirls in his sausage-like fingers like a baton. He doesn't speak. He just stares, sizing each man up like cattle at auction.

Sterling raises his hand to talk, causing more laughter and taunts. He's aware of the sweat stain under his arm. "Excuse me, sir, but I need to see the warden. He's expecting me."

The man marches over, eyes cast down, his belly invading Sterling's personal space. "Don't worry, y'all gonna meet him soon enough."

Moments later, another man enters, moving slowly and deliberately. He's older, maybe in his late sixties, but carries himself with the swagger of someone who's never once been told no. Silver hair. Tailored gray slacks. Navy blazer with a gold badge stitched to the pocket.

"Well, *heeey* there, gentlemen," he drawls, his voice slow and syrupy like honey. "Name's Warden Walter Billy Ray—but y'all can just think o' me as the Lord himself. Long as you're under *my* roof, I own every breath you take. Now, if you go 'round disobeyin' me or any of my boys, you're gonna find yourself sittin' in what we like to call *the hole*—solitary, that is. And if you end up in there more'n twice... well, I'll see to it you're laid out permanent-like. We clear on that, boys?"

The room stays silent, a mix of stunned faces and forced detachment.

One inmate scoffs—a muscular Asian man with hate in his eyes.

The big man with the nightstick steps forward. He doesn't hesitate.

The stick slams into the man's gut, lifting him off the floor. He crumples with a thud.

The officer plants a size eighteen boot on the inmate's back.

"When the warden asks you somethin', you answer 'Yes, sir,'" he growls. "Say it!"

"YES, SIR!" the line shouts in unison.

"Well now, y'all've had the pleasure o' meetin' my senior officer, Lil' John. Might be in your best interest to stay on his good side… 'less you're lookin' to get acquainted with *Sally*—and trust me, she don't play nice."

Lil' John spins the stick like a showman. "Pick up that piece of shit and throw him in the hole. The rest of y'all, welcome to the jungle."

As the inmates march forward, Sterling feels the gravity of what lies ahead squeeze him like a vise.

Then the warden stops in front of him.

"Well hella there, Sterlin'," he says, his southern smile full of capped, blindingly white teeth.

Sterling forces composure. "Hello, Walter. Can you please get me the hell out of here? You need to protect me."

Warden Ray chuckles low.

"We'll talk later," he says, leaning in close, whiskey on his breath. "But from here on out, you best be callin' me *Warden*."

He pats Sterling's cheek and flashes that grin.

" 'Cause you sure as hell ain't in Kansas no more."

CHAPTER 3

I shift uneasily into the faded leather front seat of a yellow-and-white Cessna 172, watching FBI Agent Zeke Michaels work through his pre-flight checklist with unnerving confidence. The late-afternoon flight from Peter O. Knight Airport on Davis Islands in Tampa to the prison in Raiford is barely thirty minutes, but crammed into a tin can not much bigger than a Honda Civic is hardly my idea of "going private," as he promised.

"You sure you know how to fly this thing, Zeke?" I ask, rubbing the raw skin where my left pinky nail used to be—a souvenir from a decade-old encounter with a psychopath named Dr. Levi. "We need to arrive alive to be able to interrogate Sterling Kennedy. If we can't break him, we're never going to prove the involvement of *The One*, and I'll never be able to go back to a normal life."

Zeke removes his gold-framed Ray-Ban aviators with a smirk. "Goose, you don't have time to think up here. You think. You're dead."

He's been quoting *Top Gun* ever since I agreed to fly with him instead of driving up north. He's an FBI agent, a lawyer, and a CPA—but only mentioned being a pilot *yesterday*. Without the sunglasses, his reptilian eyes bug out before narrowing to slits.

I should have driven.

I stare out of the window, wondering how I ended up shoulder to shoulder with Zeke in this flying lawn mower that smells of fuel and oil.

I worked with Agent Michaels for several years during my time as Safe Harbor Bank's Chief Information Security Officer. Whenever a financial case became too complex for our internal team, especially when the money trail twisted through shell companies and offshore accounts, we brought in Zeke. He has a talent for chasing shadows.

A year ago, I called him when one of my teammates discovered a network of secret accounts the bank maintained for its ultra-wealthy clients—accounts designed to evade taxes and fund something more sinister. Days later, that colleague was dead, and I was on the run.

In the end, the fraud was real. We exposed it. But I paid a steep price.

I lost my career, was nearly killed, and lost the love of my life—my wife, Lia. She was a former Shin Bet agent, fierce, beautiful, and brilliant. She stood by me through the chaos until she stole the evidence and vanished into thin air.

After a lengthy rehabilitation stint at the beach focused on sand, solitude, intensive therapy, and more bourbon than I'd like to admit, I started *Bluebird Security Consulting* with the seven-figure settlement I squeezed out of the Safe Harbor Bank board. Zeke got promoted, too—now he heads up a new FBI division targeting corruption among the elite. Naturally, our first job together was to investigate Sterling Kennedy.

"You really think putting Sterling Kennedy in that hellhole was smart?" I ask. "If we can't get him to talk, we have no way of finding those involved. He's all we've got."

"Smart? It was genius. By the time we land, that pretty boy will be begging to talk. We already have him for rigging markets and inflating valuations. One look at his new neighbors and we won't be able to get him to shut up."

I'm concerned. At the trial, Sterling never cracked. No plea deals. No names. Just that smug face behind an army of attorneys. Even after his conviction, he stayed silent.

"I hope you're right," I say.

"I *am* right. Now buckle up—I feel the need... the need for speed."

Twenty-nine minutes later, the Cessna drifts toward the runway, its single engine buzzing like a swarm of angry bees. Zeke lines up perfectly with the centerline and lowers the flaps to slow our descent. For a moment, it feels as if we're floating above Clark Field Airport, suspended between air and earth. I resist the urge to close my eyes.

As we near the runway, airspeed drops, and the wheels meet the tarmac with a soft tap. I watch Zeke ease back on the throttle and apply the brakes gently, guiding the small plane down the runway until it rolls to a smooth, controlled stop.

"You're actually a decent pilot," I tell Zeke as I let out a deep breath.

"Of course I am," he replies, grinning as we hop out of the plane. "You should see me do it with my eyes shut."

A black SUV idles nearby. A correctional officer leans against the hood, spitting tobacco and flicking ash from a cigarette. His sweat-stained shirt clings to his gut like Saran Wrap.

"The warden sent me to pick y'all up," he drawls. "Said you were only stayin' a few hours. Name's Scooter."

Zeke pops a hatch on the plane and hauls out our bags. "Appreciate the hospitality, but we've got wheels," he says, motioning to a dull blue Taurus nearby. "Not sure how long we'll be here."

Scooter shrugs, grinds out his cigarette with the heel of his boot, then pulls a wad of chewing tobacco from his cheek and flicks it to the ground. "Suit yourself. I'll follow behind, make sure you don't get lost. Folks around here don't much care for outsiders."

Zeke says nothing. He retrieves the keys from the driver's side wheel well, and we toss our gear in the trunk. The drive to the prison is twenty minutes—just long enough to let the local country station drone in the background.

"What do we know about Warden Walter Billy Ray?" I ask.

Zeke cracks his neck. "Thirty years running the prison. Around here, he's judge, jury, and goddamn emperor. Controls everything from the meth trade to the underground gambling ring."

"How's he still employed?"

"He's a former politician and golfing buddies with the governor. Billy Ray's not our problem—yet. First, we need to break Sterling Kennedy."

I rake my hand through my thick black hair and rub the edge of my beard. The last year has been one long descent into corruption and chaos, followed by some healing. As we approach one of the most violent prisons in America, I know one thing for sure: it's about to get worse.

****

The introduction to the prison is a waking nightmare. After being searched, the inmates march through a corridor lined with hundreds of cells, each one oozing noise and heat. The air is thick and damp, like someone left a hot shower running all day. Prisoners lean over railings, screaming and howling as they pound the floors in rhythm.

"Fresh meat! Fresh meat!" they chant, the words punctuated by curses Sterling has never heard.

Sterling clings to the hope that the warden will place him under his protection. Why it's taking so long, he can't fathom. Since his arrest, he's followed every order, keeping silent despite promises of freedom and a new identity if he rats. But he knows there is nowhere to hide. *The One's* reach is endless. Their people are embedded in every organization. The warden is proof of that.

One by one, the new arrivals are led to their cells. Lil' John—massive, silent, and enjoying the show—escorts Sterling. When they reach the cell, his new bunkmate doesn't bother to speak. He steps aside with a cold glare.

The man looks like something out of a prison nightmare: bald, bearded, and shirtless. A bullet hole is inked in the dead center of his forehead.

The cell is no bigger than a closet—two bunks, a metal toilet, and a bolted-down desk. It smells like mildew and urine. Lil' John slams the door shut behind him.

"Enjoy your stay and call the concierge if you need anything."

Sterling sits on the lower bunk, dazed. He doesn't even see the hit coming. One moment, he is seated, relieved to be out of the chaos. Next, he is airborne.

He crashes to the concrete, gasping, limbs twisted.

"Never sit on my bed again," the man growls. "I own everything in here, motherfucker."

Sterling curls into a ball, arms wrapped around his knees, tears dripping down his cheeks. So far from his former life.

Hours later, Lil' John returns and slides the cell door open.

"Let's go, dipshit. The boss wants to see you."

They move through a maze of corridors and security checkpoints. Lil' John scans his card, signs logbooks, and exchanges nods with guards. The deeper they go, the more obvious it becomes: this prison isn't just secure—it is designed to keep people out as much as in.

At last, they stop at a door marked **Warden Walter Billy Ray**.

"Come on," a voice from inside instructs.

Sterling steps in and is hit by a blast of cold air. The office is a different world—twenty degrees cooler, smelling of cigar smoke and polished wood. The warden lounges behind a massive desk, boots up, sipping from a cocktail glass, and puffing on a thick cigar.

The office is oversized and plush. A seating area off to the side holds two plates of fried chicken, green beans, and mashed potatoes. The walls are lined with framed photos—Walter grinning beside the Governor, athletes, and generals. One wall houses a bank of security monitors. A .44 Magnum sits within arm's reach.

"How's it going, Sterlin'?"

"Are you *kidding* me, Walter? It's hell. I'm locked in a cage with a psychopath. I was supposed to be protected. What the fuck am I doing here?"

Walter stands and walks to a liquor cabinet, refreshes his glass, and gestures toward the table.

"Drink?"

"No, Walter—I want out of here."

"Sit down. Trust me, you'll want this food. It's not the slop we serve to gen pop."

Reluctantly, Sterling sits. They eat in silence until the warden breaks it.

"Y'know the Feds are just tryin' to rattle your cage, right? They're flyin' up here as we speak. Gonna offer you a deal."

Sterling wipes the grease from his hands and looks up. "You know I'm loyal, Walter. But I'm not made for this. You need to tell our people—I can't survive here. They owe me for my silence." He points a finger at the warden. "You owe me a lot more. I've washed your dirty money through the system for years. No questions asked."

Walter bites into a drumstick, chases it with whiskey, then fixes Sterling with a flat stare.

"I'll tell 'em. But you and me both know what happens if you talk. What they'll do to you will make this place look like a church picnic."

****

Sterling Kennedy hadn't cleaned anything in his life. Staff picked up after him as a child, and success brought him freedom from daily chores. But tonight, after dinner and two stiff Maker's Marks with Warden Walter Billy Ray—each sip laced with threats wrapped in gooey southern charm—he found himself happy to be holding a filthy rag and a dented bucket.

After dinner, Lil' John led him through the prison's dim corridors. The air smells like bleach, rust, and sweat. When they reach the cafeteria, the place is deserted. The fluorescent lights buzz overhead. Food stains streak the tables, and garbage spills from overloaded bins.

Lil' John fills the bucket with warm, murky water and shoves it at him.

"Wipe down the tables. I'll be back."

Sterling doesn't argue—solitude suits him. After a life of boardrooms, penthouses, and private jets, the simple act of scrubbing something felt... clarifying. And besides, according to the warden, he is under his protection. The guards know it. The inmates know it. The FBI can screw themselves.

But doubt gnawed at Sterling. Could he really trust the warden? Or was he just another loose end the masters wanted erased? For now, survival was the only goal—minute by minute, hour by hour, through the long, dangerous night.

Moving methodically, relishing the slow burn of the bourbon in his veins, he swallows his concerns and enjoys the quiet. He hums a favorite tune to himself. Then the door slams. Hard. Sudden. Final.

Sterling freezes.

His cellmate steps inside. Behind him, four more inmates, broad and silent, eyes dead. From the far entrance, two more slip in like shadows. No one speaks. They don't have to.

They fan out. Blocking every exit.

Sterling's pulse spikes. His fingers tighten around the rag, now dripping with gray water.

"Listen," he says, voice shaky. "I have money—a lot of it. Whatever you need—say it. No need for this."

They keep coming. Silent. Measured. Inevitable. Heavy footsteps on cheap flooring. This clearly isn't a negotiation.

The men form a loose ring around Sterling, and he does the only thing he can. He lunges toward the smallest guy, pushing him back, but in doing so loses his balance. The others close in, and blows come fast and heavy from different angles. He tries to cover up, but a fist lands, snapping his head back. He hits the ground hard, biting his tongue and tasting the metallic, coppery taste of his blood. Then the boots rain down. Ribs crack. Breath vanishes. Fireworks of pain burst behind his eyes as someone stomps his knee.

He curls up. Covers his head and prays for it to stop.

It doesn't.

Then—stillness.

He looks up, blood running down his nose and vision blurry. He sees the glint of steel.

The shiv plunges into his chest. Cold. Deep. Final.

Sterling Kennedy doesn't scream. He stares at the ceiling, stunned. He can't believe that this, after everything, is how it ends—his secrets to be buried with him.

CHAPTER 4

We pull into the prison parking lot behind Scooter's dented Ford. As we approach the main building, we see strobing red and blue lights of an ambulance and a sheriff's cruiser cutting through the dark sky.

Zeke flashes his badge. "Agent Zeke Michaels, FBI. What happened?"

The deputy doesn't even glance at his credentials. "Another dirtbag got shanked. We're just mopping up so we can make room for another lowlife."

Scooter grunts. "Welcome to the big house. Two thousand of the worst of the worst, the majority never leave. This kind of thing happens every day."

Something's wrong. I can feel it twisting in my gut.

It takes time to clear the front desk. We state our business—interviewing Sterling Kennedy, approved by the warden himself. A tight-lipped clerk with bobbed blonde hair and darting eyes snaps our photos, slaps down waivers, and hands over flimsy visitor badges. She collects our weapons with a yawn, and Scooter escorts us to an interview room that smells faintly of body odor and Indian food.

The room is stripped of every comfort, designed for function alone. A heavy table is bolted to the floor, surrounded by four hard plastic chairs that scrape against the concrete. The beige cinder-block walls close in with their dull, lifeless tone, making it clear this is not a place to linger—and we are not welcome.

"Been here before?" I ask Zeke.

"Too many times," he mutters. "Mostly bullshitters trying to shave time off their sentence."

Fifteen minutes later, Warden Walter Billy Ray enters the room, accompanied by a man the size of a sycamore. His silver hair is perfectly coiffed, and he is holding a green folder. We stand and shake hands. The handshake is firm but cold. He introduces the other man as Lil' John, which makes Zeke laugh.

"You didn't need to greet us personally, Warden," Zeke says. "We just need some time with your new guest—Sterling Kennedy. We appreciate you facilitating this."

The warden's smile falters. "Yeah… 'bout that. Kennedy done got hisself stabbed 'bout an hour ago. Was cleanin' up the cafeteria. Poor bastard didn't make it."

Zeke's expression darkens. "He was supposed to be segregated. What the hell was he doing in the cafeteria?"

The warden shrugs. "Just a lil' ol' paperwork mix-up. When you're wrangling two thousand inmates, accidents happen. But don't you worry. I aim to get to the bottom of it."

"A mistake?" Zeke's voice climbs, tight with fury. "He is, or he was, a potential federal witness!"

"I understand your frustration," the warden says with a steady drawl. "Rest assured—we'll handle the investigation."

"My ass you are. I'm bringing in my team. Lock this place down. I want the video footage."

"That ain't gonna be possible," Walter Ray says, his smile gone cold. "This here's a state facility. We don't answer to the Feds unless we damn well feel like it. "An' we shore as hell handle our own investigatin', understand?"

Zeke leans forward, eyes bugging out. "I make one call, and this hellhole will be crawling with agents."

"By all means. And when you talk to Governor Frederick... you let him know Walter Ray sends his regards, and our tee time next week is nine AM."

Panic claws at me from the inside, and a bitter surge of bile rises in my throat. Losing our key witness is a crushing blow, pushing any hope of my normal life even further out of reach. I can see Zeke about to blow, but there's no changing the truth—for us, and for Sterling, dead is dead.

I step between them. "Gentlemen, let's calm the situation. There's got to be a middle ground."

The warden fixes me with a shark's grin. "And you are?"

"Jason Miles. FBI security contractor."

"Well hell, Miles the contractor, you might be the *only* man in this whole place with less pull than the FBI. Reckon it's time y'all hop back on that plane and let us simple country folk handle our own mess. We'll be sure to report back."

He turns to leave. Zeke grabs his arm. That's when Lil' John moves. Fast. Too fast for his size. His nightstick's out before I can blink.

"I'd let go, Agent," Walter Ray says, real softly. "Sure would be a shame if ol' Sally here... slipped."

He taps the nightstick. "This is *my* prison. Y'all were guests. Now you ain't. Get out. Don't give a damn what kinda letters you got on that badge."

****

We retrieve our weapons and walk to the car in silence. Zeke is a few steps ahead, his rage simmering so hot he is almost glowing.

Back inside the vehicle, I say, "We need to get the hell out of here. We're not safe. Look what they did to Sterling. This is *The One*, Zeke.

I told you they're calling the shots."

"Will you drop it with this secret society bullshit. Sterling knew too much about too many rich people. That's it. This hillbilly just pulled the trigger, but someone gave the order."

After everything that's happened this past year, Zeke still refuses to believe *The One* is real. Sterling was the link—the one who could connect the dots and expose the people pulling the strings. He could have proven what I'm saying is true.

Zeke stares out the window for a few minutes. I can see his chest heaving up and down, and his jaw tightening. He rakes his hand through his thinning hair. He pulls out his phone and calls his former partner—now Bureau Director—Gloria Chavez. He lays it all out.

"That was a hit, Gloria. Clean and timed. Someone didn't want Kennedy talking to us."

His face tightens as he listens. "What do you mean, come *home*? He threatened a federal agent! Who cares if he knows the Governor? What the fuck, Gloria?"

He hangs up and says nothing.

"Time to go home? We need to find out who did this. We need to find another string to pull."

"Hell no. We're getting a burger and a cheap motel. Then we dig. Screw the warden. No one pushes Zeke Michaels around."

We drive through the darkness to a sports bar called Union on the corner of a strip mall, fifteen minutes from the prison. From the looks of the customers and employees, most are on a work-release program or have escaped. There is Florida Gator and Florida State Seminole memorabilia plastered everywhere. The waitresses wear too-tight tank tops, and the bartenders sport black-and-white striped referee shirts. An obnoxious number of TVs fill the walls, playing sports of all kinds. There's enough fried food grease in the air to coat your lungs.

Zeke gets a Philly cheesesteak and water. Despite a pounding headache, I order a burger, sweet potato fries, and a pale ale. The waitress offers me Bud or Coors Light and proudly mentions that both are on tap.

"Billie Ray and Kennedy," Zeke says, crunching on ice. "There's no way those two crossed paths naturally. Somebody arranged this."

"I'll have the Bluebird team dig into it."

I already know who arranged it—*The One*. And I am going to prove it.

After eating, our anger eases, and the pounding in my head settles into a dull ache. We decide to check into a modest motel nearby. I'd rather head home, but I know how stubborn Zeke can be.

But the night isn't done.

Outside the bar, our rental's wrecked—tires slashed, windows smashed, doors kicked in—a warning, not a theft.

Then come the Cadillacs. Two black tanks and two sedans glide into the lot. Lil' John and seven of his oversized pals unfold from the cars like clowns in a circus.

We reach for our weapons, only to realize they are locked in the trunk.

We're in trouble. Too far from home, and we've kicked a hornet's nest. My eyes sweep the area for an escape route, but every path ends in the same place: nowhere. I've been in bad spots before, and rule number one is simple—stay alive long enough to find a way out. These guys wouldn't kill an FBI agent. Would they?

Lil' John dangles our weapons case with a grin. "Lookin' for this, ladies?"

Zeke steps forward. "You're about to make a mistake you'll regret."

Shotgun pumps behind us.

"You already made yours," Lil' John smirks.

Scooter opens both trunks. "In. Now."

We each pick a trunk and hope to see each other again.

CHAPTER 5

The trunk stinks of motor oil and rust. It's barely big enough to hold me, and every sharp turn slams my ribs into metal. I grope in the dark for anything—wires, tools, something to swing—but it's empty. Every bump on the road is a body blow, and the rough lining tears at my skin. I can already feel bruises forming.

We drive in silence for what feels like hours. It's probably twenty minutes.

I take several deep breaths. We can worry about revenge later. Right now, we need to survive. Fear sits heavy in my chest, but anger sits below, hot and steady. I won't go out like this, not after everything. If a chance opens up, I'll take it. It is better to die like a lion than live like a lamb.

Finally, the car jerks to a stop. I hold my breath. Five seconds. Ten. Then the trunk creaks open. The cool night air hits my face. I blink up at the dim light of the small airstrip. We're back at the airport.

I crawl out, wincing. Zeke's doing the same from the Cadillac beside me, swearing under his breath.

Warden Walter Billy Ray is waiting, propped against the nose of the Cessna like he's posing for a magazine. He's added a black felt cowboy hat to his look, as if he needed to play the villain any harder.

"Well, I do hope y'all enjoyed your Union County Uber," he drawls.

Zeke dusts himself off and storms toward him. "Are you out of your goddamn mind? I'm a federal agent—you just kidnapped me at gunpoint. Do you have *any* idea what kind of prison time that earns you?"

Billy Ray lifts an eyebrow and glances at his crew of grinning goons. "You boys didn't pull no guns on these fine gentlemen, now, did ya?"

Each one shakes their head like a pack of altar boys. One even gasps, hand to chest.

The warden turns back to Zeke. "Now to answer your question—yeah, I'm crazy. But more important than that, like I done told ya… this here's *my* county. You stay 'til I say you don't. And as of right now," he gives the Cessna's wing a sharp tap, "you don't. So I suggest y'all climb back in that pretty little plane and get on down to Tampa—'fore what's left of my hospitality runs clean out. You catch my drift, boys?"

Zeke's lip curls. "We'll leave, but this isn't over. I know you had something to do with Sterling Kennedy's death, and I'm going to prove it. I'll be back with the full force of the United States government. I'm sure all those men locked away will welcome you when you become a prison resident," Zeke says, spit flying from his mouth. "And we want our weapons back. Now."

Lil' John steps forward, cracking his nightstick into his palm. "They're on the plane," he says. "Minus the ammo, o' course."

Scooter opens the Cadillac's passenger door with a wink and a nod. Billy Ray steps aside, grinning like the devil himself. "Remember, boys," he says, holding up his pinky and index fingers, "you mess with the bull—you get the horns."

The Cessna touches down in Tampa just after ten. Zeke spent the flight muttering curses and speeches about respect. I sit quietly, watching the city lights grow closer, just glad we're not dead in a ditch somewhere in Union County.

Once we land, we agree to meet later and document the trip.

Zeke's bracing for a royal ass-chewing for letting Kennedy out of his sight. Me? I'm pulling the team together. This isn't just a local cover-up. Too many names. Too many secrets. And none of them fit—at least, not yet.

But they will.

CHAPTER 6

I carry a secret no one knows—not even my closest friends. A secret that could put me in prison for years.

After a hellish day with Zeke, I'm grateful to step into the serenity of Hotel Haya. I need some downtime to recalibrate. The lobby's soft light does little to shake the haze in my head. I nod a tired hello to the front desk attendant, the one who's always got that little sparkle when she sees me.

I glance back toward the entrance. That gnawing feeling of being watched sticks to me like glue on fingertips. It's probably just paranoia. But then—I swear—I catch a shadowy figure peeking in. I whip my head around. Nothing.

I shove the unease deep down.

The weight of the day presses heavily on my mind. Sterling was the linchpin—if we had cracked him, his handler would've been next, and from there we could have climbed higher up the chain. But until *The One* is eliminated, it is hard to let the paranoia go.

For months, I've sat in public places with my back to the wall, eyes locked on the door, scanning every movement, every face. Still, despite the pressure clawing at me, I need the rest of the night to try and relax.

In the hallway, the humidor beckons. Tampa's best cigars glow behind the glass. I reach for the Oliva Serie V Melanio—dark, rich, earthy. The gold band gleams under the hallway light, Oliva's name proud and bold. I nod toward the desk to charge it—the attendant winks.

The bar is quiet tonight. Ace, my favorite bartender, greets me with a grin as he cleans up, hoping to shut down early.

"Hey Jason, you look like hell. How 'bout an Old-Fashioned?"

"Appreciate it, but I'll take a Ken Wright Pinot. Make it to go. Long day. I'm beat."

I take the elevator up to the third floor. My room feels like a refuge. I toss my bag on the queen-sized bed and swirl the wine—the aroma of cherries, strawberries, vanilla—tempting, intoxicating. But I know if I sit, I'll be out cold in minutes. Instead, I take a hot, long shower.

Steam clouds the mirror. I wipe it clear and look at the wreck staring back: bruises from the trunk ride, a bleeding elbow, wild hair, and a five o'clock shadow creeping toward ten.

Wrapped in a towel, I edge to the peephole and check the hallway. It's clear. Shades drawn tight, I power up the scanner and run a sweep for bugs. Zeke still doesn't believe I've cut ties with Lia, and I can't shake the sense that he suspects me of being mixed up in the data theft and the sale. Worse, I've started noticing little things out of place, hints that someone's been slipping into my room. Maybe it's housekeeping. Perhaps it's nothing. Maybe it's just the anxiety I can't shake.

Feeling safe enough, I dim the lights and turn on smooth jazz.

The room key opens the safe. Inside: one sleek black phone. It makes my heart thump with a mix of guilt and hope. I press the only programmed number.

"Is this Mr. Smith?" a familiar female voice asks.

"Yes. Is this Mrs. Smith?"

Our code words—safe words. We agreed to destroy the phones if compromised.

"Hi, Jay. How're you holding up?" Lia's voice washes over me, sweeter than any wine. In my mind's eye, I see her—long dark hair, that tiny gap in her front teeth. My chest tightens, and a flush spreads through me.

God, I wish she were here.

We hadn't spoken for months after she vanished. I thought she was gone forever—until a package showed up on my birthday. Inside, a note:

> Happy birthday, Jay. I miss you. Here's a secure phone. I'll call at 10 PM your time. If you don't want to hear from me, destroy it.
>
> Love always, Lia.

I considered hurling the phone into the ocean—or handing it over to Zeke. Lia had been my life, the one thing that mattered. For ten years of marriage, I trusted her more than anyone—until she shot me in the heart and vanished with the Safe Harbor data. The anger still seethed inside me, but stronger than the rage was the need to hear her voice and know why she had forsaken me.

That first call felt like sunlight breaking through after a storm. We talked for hours and agreed on weekly check-ins. I told myself that the *why* no longer mattered. I just wanted her back. I even let myself believe that somehow, we could rebuild, slip into something resembling a normal life together. Maybe Lia could help me defeat *The One*.

I know I'm being delusional, and I despise myself for being so weak, but love trumps reason in my world.

"I'm hanging in," I say. "Rough day, but glad to be back here, talking to you. How're you doing?"

"I'm fine… but I miss you. Think about you all the time. What'd you do today?"

Her voice comforts, but it rips open old wounds.

"I miss you too. Spent the day with Zeke. Sterling Kennedy got tossed in some hellhole up in north Florida. We flew up to see him. He was dead before we arrived. And we ran into trouble with the sheriff."

"Yeah. I heard about Sterling."

My heart jumps. We never talk about her work, but I know it's dangerous—assassin, spy, who knows? And I suspect she's tied to *The One* in some way.

"How'd you know so fast? It just happened."

"Jay, you know we can't discuss that. But I hear things. It's my job. Sterling was a dead man walking. They sent him to a place where they could control him. He was weak. Zeke would've broken him."

"I don't want to talk about Sterling or this mess. You said it's impossible, but I need to see you. I can't stop thinking about you. There has to be a way."

A long silence. I'm scared she hung up.

"Lia? You there?"

Her voice is barely a whisper. "Maybe there is… but it could cost us both our freedom. Maybe worse."

CHAPTER 7

"Thank you for the opportunity to speak with you today. Having some time in front of the largest business chamber in Tampa is an honor," I say, scanning the crowd. It is early Monday morning, and rows of professionals pick at fruit plates and sip coffee. Tired eyes. Expensive watches. No one's fully awake yet. I'm hoping the caffeine kicks in soon.

I'm wearing a dark blue suit and a bright orange tie—Bluebird's colors. It's the first time I've worn anything with starch in months. There's a wireless mic clipped to my lapel and a giant projection screen behind me. I've got slides, but I'm not here to lull anyone to sleep with bullet points. My style is more relaxed, and I enjoy talking directly to the crowd.

This presentation must land. If I'm ever going to reclaim a normal life, my business needs to grow. It's the only thing I have left that's working. With fraud dominating the headlines and my employees depending on me, the pressure couldn't be higher. It's go big or go home—and I live in a hotel.

"My name is Jason Miles. I'm the CEO of Bluebird Security Consultants. Before we begin the main presentation, let me give you a thirty-second commercial: Bluebird specializes in cybersecurity, physical facility security, and the investigation of financial crimes. It's Bluebird's goal to be your trusted security advisor. We specialize in providing bespoke security solutions to companies of all sizes. Think of us as your first call when something goes wrong—because eventually, it will."

I gesture to the screen. A crisp QR code glows behind me. "Scan that, and you've got our info. No hard sell today. Just facts."

I pause, letting the room settle.

"My goal this morning isn't to scare you. But it might happen anyway."

I take a breath. Slow and deliberate. "The future is already here. And it's messy."

I step toward the edge of the stage and lower my voice just enough to make people lean in.

"There are only two types of companies: those who've been hacked... and those who *will* be. Whether you run a Fortune 500 company or a food truck, cybersecurity isn't optional anymore. It's required for survival."

A murmur runs through the room.

Pausing again for effect, I look from table to table. As I scan the crowd, I nearly get whiplash as a face in the crowd leaves me speechless. Safe Harbor Bank was run by CEO Terrance Browning, who was always followed around by his Chief of Staff, a strange young man named Clinton. Terrance had his head blown off after kidnapping my friends, but I assumed Clinton was in prison. Now here he was glaring back at me. Further proof my nightmare is not over.

I walk from one edge of the stage to the other to try to regain my composure. After a few deep breaths, I jump back into the presentation. I'll find out where Clinton is working later.

"They say Artificial Intelligence is the next industrial revolution, and I think they are right. Computers can learn at speeds much faster than humans. This technology is transforming the landscapes of healthcare, finance, and manufacturing, among others. They say in five years everyone will have a self-driving car, and we haven't given up on flying cars either."

The following slide pops up: a cartoon of the Jetsons zipping through the sky in their flying car. The crowd chuckles.

"Funny, right? They told us we'd be flying to work by now. But what they didn't say was that your car might drive itself into the ocean if someone hacks the onboard system. Or that your face could be cloned by a deepfake and used to drain your bank account."

"Russia. North Korea. China. They're not just playing defense. They've built economies around cyber warfare. Entire cities are full of state-sponsored hackers. It's not science fiction—it's business."

I click a slide labeled Phishing. Ransomware. Deepfakes. Financial Fraud.

"These aren't hypotheticals. These are headlines that are happening every day."

I let the silence linger before continuing. "Today, I'm going to show you how to protect yourself. What to look for. What to do when—not if—you're targeted."

Twenty minutes later, I step off stage to applause. A few people even stand.

By the time I reach the door, every business card in my pocket is gone. I've got a stack of new ones in return—law firms, startups, hedge funds, and a guy from the port authority who looks terrified.

Tech is changing the world, no doubt about that.

Whether it saves us or sinks us... that part's still up in the air.

Either way, Bluebird's going to be busy.

CHAPTER 8

I feel exhilarated after my successful presentation to the chamber, so I stop back at the hotel to shed the monkey suit. I'm excited to start calling these new prospects and generate some business. I also send Zeke a text asking what happened to Clinton after the scandal broke.

When Safe Harbor Bank fired me, my entire world went up in flames. I was forced to start over. A seven-figure hush settlement, hurried along by the bank's embarrassed board, helped ease the transition. Weekly therapy and six months holed up at the Treasure Island Beach Resort dulled the pain. But I still feel like a puzzle with a few key pieces missing.

When I finally rejoined civilization, I sold our McMansion in South Tampa. Lia haunted every square inch. Her voice lingered in the halls, and her memory crept into my dreams every night. I couldn't breathe there.

So, I moved into Hotel Haya, in the heart of Ybor City. Then I used some of the proceeds to buy a baby blue bungalow on 4th Avenue and the adjacent empty lot for parking. It's zoned commercial, which made it perfect for launching *Bluebird Security Consultants*—my reinvention. I crafted marketing materials that transformed my former life as a rising cybersecurity executive into a sleek, seasoned, and credible narrative.

On days like today when I do not need my car, I leave Haya on foot. I am later than usual, and Ybor has already woken up—a mix of workers, joggers, locals, and the ever-present street people. The neighborhood, founded by Vicente Martinez de Ybor in the late 1800s, was built on mosquito-ridden marshland. They dumped sand by the ton to make it livable, and a few panthers and gators had to move out. At its peak, Ybor boasted over two hundred cigar factories and pumped out millions of hand-rolled cigars a year.

You can still feel the bones of the golden age—weathered brick buildings, repurposed factories, even the original brewery, now filled with lawyers. I'm not sure I would consider this progress.

Ybor's grid is simple. Avenues run east-west. Streets go north-south. 7th Avenue is the heartbeat—lined with bars, cigar shops, and late-night mistakes.

I cross the street from Haya and stroll down 7th, pausing to scan the concert board at the Ritz. I note one show that might be worth attending, then pass King Corona, my go-to cigar shop. They open early for caffeine and stogies. The aroma of earthy tobacco and strong coffee hits me like a siren's call. I wave to my favorite waitress, resisting the urge to stop.

On 16th Street, I cross the tracks and pass the parking garage. A block down 4th, I pause at Angel Dog Park to pet a white boxer named Lucy. Her nametag winks in the sun, and slobber drips off her jowls. I started a tradition of giving her a dog treat every morning, and now she waits patiently as I approach. I would love a pet to give me some purpose, but I can barely take care of myself right now. Maybe when my world becomes more normal.

I consider picking up bagels from Pete's for the team, but none of us needs the carb rush and subsequent crash.

Since starting Bluebird, I've built a team—equal parts brilliant and broken.

First came Avner Cohen—my mentor from a decade ago, when I was a contract agent for Shin Bet, Israel's Internal Security Service.

He and Lia recruited me to uncover money laundering at the Bank of Israel. More recently, Avner nearly died protecting me when we exposed the global tax fraud ring tied to Safe Harbor. He never returned to Israel. Instead, he recovered in Tampa and fell for my second hire, Apple Lee—a hugely popular University of Tampa professor, left-leaning economist, and media darling on wealth inequality and financial predators.

Then there's Goat: ex-Army Ranger, ex-addict, ex-homeless. I met him while ducking Safe Harbor goons and dodging the FBI. We reconnected after the chaos, when Gloria Chavez—Zeke's former partner and now boss—got him into a veterans' rehab. Six months later, he walked into my office clean, grateful, and quoting Scripture. He's as loyal as they come, and just as dangerous.

Last came Ernesto, a hoodie-wearing hacker in his early twenties. Watching his fingers dance across a keyboard is like watching Yuja Wang shred a piano. He used to lead a notorious dark web crew, known as *Ladrones Nocturnos*, the Night Thieves, specializing in stolen digital data until Zeke and Gloria busted him. Instead of pressing charges, Zeke called in a favor and handed me a project.

What he didn't mention was that Ernesto came as a package deal with his mom, Berta.

She marched into the office, set down a stack of folders, turned on her salsa playlist, and declared herself office manager. No interview. No discussion. Just Berta.

So now, we're a team: a hot-headed Israeli agent, a grizzled ex-addict, an academic crusader, a reformed hacker, and a deeply suspicious ex-banker with a history of being tortured and betrayed. Throw in an unofficial "house mom" with a loudmouth and a louder wardrobe.

We're the misfit toys of cybersecurity. But we're damn good at what we do. In addition to the team, we use subcontractors for larger, more complex projects.

It is my job to grow the business, and now others are counting on me. Every sale is a win, and all the new contacts from this morning could be a home run. Every normal day takes me further and further from the disaster that is my past. I once heard that a good life is just a collection of good days. We'll see.

Unfortunately, with every great day comes reminders that the fight is not over. Seeing Clinton's face lets me know that evil still lurks around the corner, and I must be prepared.

"Hey, Guapo! Café con leche and Cuban toast on your desk," Berta hollers over the pulse of loud Latin music blaring from a half-buried speaker as I walk in. "La Septima. Your favorite."

The café con leche calls to me, warm and rich. The Cuban toast glistens with butter. It's a luscious mix of carbs and caffeine, both on the doctor's banned list. Six months ago, I flatlined after being shot. My cardiologist insists I live like a monk. But monks don't live in Ybor.

"Berta," I sigh, "I told you—I'm supposed to cut back. Doctor's orders."

She waves a dismissive hand. "Please. You're too skinny. And don't think I don't see you and your crew smoking cigars on 7th with all those viejos. That ain't good for your heart either, Guapo. You're corrupting poor Ernesto."

"I told you—don't let him hang around Avner and Goat. That's a recipe for disaster."

"He *adores* them. Avner took him to that crazy gym to roll around on the floor with sweaty men. I think he's loco."

"You know he's safe with Avner, abuela. He's learning self-defense. Keeps him off the dark web."

She narrows her eyes and points at me. "You call me *grandma* again, and I'll remove your *huevos* myself."

"Okay, okay! I'm gonna need those," I reply, savoring a sip of the forbidden drink. The warmth spreads through my chest like a memory. No woman, no real sleep, but at least there's coffee. And wine.

"Oh, by the way," she adds, rummaging through a chaotic pile of notes. "You got a call this morning. Some guy named Nikesh from Tampa Scientific Corp. Do you know him?"

I freeze mid-sip.

"Yeah, Berta, they are only the leading AI technology company in the country. Maybe the world. Did he say what it was about?"

She squints at her scribbled note through rainbow-colored reading glasses. "Yeah. He said to call him back ASAP. Something about… national security."

CHAPTER 9

It's been a long time since I've been on a date. The thought alone has me sweating through my shirt—and not from typical nerves. It's guilt. Guilt because I'm still in love with my *kind of* ex-wife.

We're not divorced—technically. Hard to finalize paperwork when your spouse is an international fugitive. But that's not the real reason. The truth? I haven't signed the papers because some reckless part of me still believes this whole mess can be salvaged. That Lia will walk back through the door one day, like none of it ever happened. Or maybe I'll go on the run with her like Bonnie and Clyde.

Despite my feelings for Lia, I'm excited. Maybe it's possible to start something new, something real—a relationship without all the chaos and drama. I'm going to find out tonight.

I sit at the bar, nursing a glass of pinot noir, replaying my call with Nikesh's assistant earlier in the day. The meeting's set for the morning, but he wouldn't say what it's about. His voice was calm, but I could hear the tension underneath.

I'm also frustrated that Zeke hasn't responded about Clinton's whereabouts, despite two texts and a call.

"*Jason!*" Avner's voice cuts through the buzz at Haya's bar. It rips me from my racing thoughts.

He's holding hands with Apple, who glows in the candlelight. Trailing behind them is a blonde in a sleek black dress, curves in all the right places, and a jet-black brooch pinned at her throat. She's shorter than Apple, but black heels give her an edge. Heads turn as they pass—until men see Avner and look away. He has that effect on people.

I step away from my drink, offering the usual greetings: a cheek kiss for Apple, a man-hug for Avner, and a handshake for the blonde. I feel a bolt of electricity from her touch. I did not expect this. I did not expect her.

"Jason," Apple says with a smirk, "this is Sydney—the coworker I told you about."

"Nice to meet you, Sydney." I nod. "Should we grab a drink before heading to Water Street?"

She tells me to call her Syd, and we move to an unoccupied table near the bar. The waitress brings me another glass of wine, and the ladies order martinis. Avner confirms that the bill is being sent to my room and orders a theatrical, smoke-box old-fashioned.

I changed outfits three times before settling on a yellow V-neck sweater, gray slacks, and sockless loafers. My hair's longer now, parted closer to the middle. I shaved, but my beard is already staging a comeback.

"Nice sweater, Mr. Rogers," Avner quips.

I ignore him.

"So, Syd," I say, trying to sound casual. "Apple tells me you're a professor. What do you teach?"

Her smile is all red lipstick and white teeth—striking. I realize that I'm *actually* attracted to her. It is the first time in a long time.

"You know, the typical English classes that bore the hell out of most of the kids: language and grammar, literature from different periods, but my favorite is creative writing."

"She's being modest," Apple jumps in. "Besides being the hottest professor at UT, she's also a novelist. Book one is out, and book two is in the works."

"Oh, stop it," Syd waves her off. "I'm just an indie author clawing for my big break so I can do it full-time. It's my passion, but books don't pay the rent. They barely buy lunch."

I raise my glass. "To Syd. The next great... what is it that you write?"

"Tell him," Apple urges.

Syd leans in conspiratorially. "It's a sexy wizard story. Think *Harry Potter* meets *Fifty Shades*."

My eyebrows rise.

"Only... the characters are cats."

I freeze; the words are stuck in my throat. I force out, "That sounds... fascinating. I'd love to read it sometime."

The table erupts in laughter. Apple nearly snorts her martini.

"Got you," Syd says, eyes sparkling. "My first book's a beachy rom-com. The new one's a thriller. No cats."

I laugh, but my face burns. I hear Avner chuckle, "She totally nailed you, dumbass. I haven't seen Jason blush in a long time. This is gonna be fun."

She *did* get me. But I don't mind. She's sharp, beautiful, funny—safe, maybe. And yet, guilt creeps back in. I feel like I'm betraying Lia... or finally giving up on her. The conflict mixed with the wine leaves me off balance.

And under it all, another feeling worms its way in: a prickling awareness, like someone's watching. I've been paranoid for months. Living in a constant state of alert. Seeing threats that might not exist. Avoiding routines and scanning crowds for familiar faces. I make a mental note to mention it to Avner.

We grab an Uber to Water Street, Tampa's polished answer to what used to be a ghost town after five. That changed when big money poured in—luxury condos, a five-star hotel, Michelin quality restaurants. A playground for the ambitious, young, and beautiful—the place to be seen in Tampa if you don't mind a twenty-dollar cocktail.

Dinner is at Ash—elegant, understated, full of light wood, candles, and linen. Soft music drifts through the air as servers glide gracefully between tables, placing drinks and entrées with effortless precision. The aroma of seared meats, roasted vegetables, and fresh herbs drifts toward me, making my mouth water and reminding me I haven't eaten since the morning.

Apple takes command of the menu: raw oysters, fried rabbit, scallops, and handmade raviolo. I laugh when Avner winces at the rabbit. Apple ignores him.

We eat, drink, and laugh for hours as Avner tells stories from his days in Israel. It's good to see him like this—Apple really brings out a different side of him. I'm pretty sure I even catch a smile once or twice.

Syd notices me stealing a glance her way and gives me a quick wink. For a moment, I feel like a teenager at his first prom. Maybe this is the way it is supposed to be.

The night flows easily—until it doesn't.

Across the room, past the haze of candlelight and glass, a face appears in the window. Not familiar, but *almost*. He's not just looking inside—he's looking *at me*. Eyes locked. Intent. Cold.

My stomach tightens. I blink. The man is gone.

But I know the past never stays buried, not in my world.

****

Looking at the man who ruined his life is devastating. Jason Miles sits at a gleaming table, sipping wine, laughing with beautiful women, dressed like he belongs. Like he's *clean*.

Jason changed his life forever, and he wants to return the favor.

They smile and sip and dine like royalty while he shivers in a stained coat, digging change from his pocket for his next meal. Then Jason looks up, and their eyes meet. He sees it there: recognition, fear, maybe even pity.

    Fists clench. Teeth grind. Hat pulled low.

    He moves from the window, vowing sweet revenge.

CHAPTER 10

I'm rattled by the man in the window, but force myself to block it out. Every instinct screams to chase him down, drag him into an alley, and get answers. But not right now. Not when things finally feel normal. I've only thought of Lia twice all evening, instead focusing on Syd, who might be something real. Something good. I vow to enjoy the night.

After dinner, we slide over to Alter Ego—Ash's sister lounge. Where Ash is airy, Alter Ego is sexy and dim, with a DJ spinning vintage pop that vibrates through the leather booths. The cocktails are pricey, but no one seems to care. Syd pulls me onto the dance floor; Apple and Avner melt into a dark corner, laughing like teenagers.

Too many drinks later, I'm loose, maybe even hopeful. My voice cracks when I ask for Syd's number. She grins, taps it into my phone, then kisses my cheek—laughing as she wipes away the lipstick before hopping into the Uber.

In another life, I would've fallen hard for a girl like her.

But that's not my life.

Not after everything.

The baggage I carry could fill a Boeing 747.

No one signs up for that.

No one except Lia.

When their taillights fade, the high drains away, replaced by that itch under my skin. I start canvassing the block. I need to find the man from the window—the silhouette that clawed at something deep and buried. If I want this to end, it's time to go on the offensive.

He had longish hair, a baseball cap pulled low. Looked almost homeless—out of place among the pretty people of Water Street. He shouldn't be hard to spot. Yet by midnight, I'm still empty-handed.

Couples spill out of restaurants, laughter echoing off the brick roads. The air smells of steak, perfume, and truffle fries.

I pass Naked Farmer, Chill Bros, and the glittering valet stand at The Edition. I even poke my head into Clayton Gray Home, a cool design space, scanning the showroom for his shape among the high-end art and furniture. Nothing.

Finally, I board the streetcar back to Ybor—the night hums outside the window—neon, motion, ghosts.

Empty-handed. But not unconvinced. He's out there. And next time, I'll be ready.

CHAPTER 11

Being on the run in Tampa and my time as a contract spy in Israel taught me one thing: never ignore your gut.

Is it just paranoia—or is the past clawing its way back?

The night before was a success, but I can't shake the feeling that something terrible is brewing just beneath the surface.

I'm halfway through my second black coffee at the Hotel Haya café. The place is filled with tired parents and hyper toddlers—the line at the counter snakes toward the door. The smell—roasted beans and caramelized sugar—hangs heavy in the air, igniting every nerve ending. The espresso machine hisses, and the coffee beans grind. Someone behind the bar drops a cup.

I need to focus. We have a huge meeting with Tampa Scientific—a real game changer. We need to be prepared. I jot some notes on the company's background, its CEO, and my goals for the meeting.

"Hey, lover boy," Avner says as he struts into the café like he owns the joint. "How hot was Syd? Why didn't you stay out? You might've gotten lucky. Probably not, but even a blind squirrel gets a nut every once in a while."

He's wearing his uniform—tight black tee, black jeans, and scuffed boots. His biceps stretch the sleeves, and his beard looks like it lost a fight with a weed whacker. Tattoos crawl down his arms—lions, demons, the stuff nightmares are made of. Children stare, and their parents admonish them.

Avner is the scariest man I've ever met. Decades of training with weapons and the Israeli self-defense art of Krav Maga have given him skills, but I find his quick temper and speed most terrifying. To make matters worse, he added daily Jiu-Jitsu classes that melted away fat accumulated over the years. Lia was right when she said that it was better to be friends with the monster under the bed.

"She was great," I say. "I'm just not sure I'm ready."

He stares at me, then rubs his temples like I'm giving him a migraine. "Jason, Lia's gone. She's not coming back. You've got to move on. Or at least enjoy yourself. That girl likes you."

"Thanks for the dating advice. Like I've told you before, I know Lia and I are done. I'm just not sure it's fair to Syd to get involved until some of this craziness ends."

"What craziness, Jason? You're back from your beach vacation, the company is doing well, and no one has tried to kill you recently. What's the problem? And I didn't say you need to marry her. Just give it a chance."

My eyes dart around the café, and I drop my voice. "It's not that easy. I think I'm being followed."

Avner lets out a long breath. "Followed by who?"

"I don't know, but I saw someone looking at me through the window at the restaurant last night. I recognized something about him. It's like when you drop something in that crack by your car seat, and it's just out of reach."

"Is that why you didn't come with us?"

I nod, looking away.

"You should have said something. I would have stayed and helped you search the area."

"I think it has something to do with *The One*. I feel like it's not over yet. Maybe Safe Harbor was just the beginning."

"Come on, Jason. Can we stop this new world order bullshit? Safe Harbor was a tax fraud, and the perpetrators are all dead. Who's left that would be following you?"

I can see it in Avner's eyes—he thinks I'm unraveling. Neither he nor Zeke believes *The One* is real, but I know it is.

A man at a nearby table catches my attention. His phone sits casually on the edge; the microphone angled toward us. I feel the prick of recognition—somewhere, I've seen him before.

I glance at Avner, nod toward the man's table, and slip out to a small table outside.

"What the hell was that, Jason?" Avner asks.

"That guy's phone," I say, lowering my voice. "Could've been recording us. And... doesn't it strike you as weird that Sterling Kennedy, our last lead to the rest of them, is dead too?"

"Scumbags die in prison every day. That place up north isn't exactly the Ritz."

"Forget it," I say, changing the subject. "More importantly, what's with the biker outfit? We've got an important meeting at Tampa Scientific."

I'm in khakis and a plaid sport coat, freshly shaved. He looks like he slept in a ditch.

He shrugs and takes a sip from my coffee. "Tell me something. Why would a big tech company want to meet with the Bad News Bears? Doesn't that seem... odd?"

He's not wrong.

"They said someone referred us."

"Right. And we're not exactly IBM. You, me, Goat, Ernesto? Apple's the only one who could pass for legit, and she's dating me, so... something's off."

"Maybe. But it doesn't hurt to hear them out."

He leans forward, eyes suddenly sharp. "Fine, we'll hear them out. Listen, I don't mean to ignore your instincts. If you really think someone is following you, I'll do some countersurveillance. Haven't kicked anyone's ass in a while."

"Not yet," I say. "I have something to do before our meeting. Let's see if it passes. If not, I'll unleash the lion."

****

Morgan Chase waits on a bench near the colorful rooster statue in Parque Amigos de José Martí. I walk through the gate beneath the stone arch and onto a winding tile path. The statue of Martí stands tall with his arm raised toward the Cuban flag mosaic. Brown hens cluck near a patch of sacred Cuban soil.

Morgan is a reporter with the *Tampa Bay Times* and a frequent guest on national television when they need someone to discuss the widening gap between the rich and the not-so-rich. She previously worked for *The Wall Street Journal* before relocating back to Tampa. While I was at Safe Harbor Bank, we would run into each other on the rubber chicken circuit and became friends. She signs each article "Morgan Chase—Black, Beautiful, and Brainy." It is hard to argue with any of those descriptions.

She saved my ass months ago when the FBI and half the banking world wanted me dead. I owe her more than I can repay. I also trust that her investigative skills can help me start connecting some of the dots.

"Why does everything have to be so cloak and dagger with you?" Morgan asks as I sit beside her.

I hand her a coffee from the hotel. She takes a drink, watching me carefully.

"You look great," I say.

She squints at me. "You're about to ask for something."

"Can't I just enjoy sitting in the park with one of my favorite people?"

She smirks. "Normal people go to coffee shops."

I glance around. We're alone, for now. "What do you know about

Warden Walter Billy Ray… and Governor Frederick Matthews?"

She tilts her head. "Strange combo. I know them separately, not together. The Governor's nothing like his father. Governor Mack was the real deal—respected, effective, loved by everyone, no matter their politics. His death rocked the state. Frederick, though—he caters to the hardliners and the fringe crowd. Why do you ask?"

I hesitate. How much can I tell her? Morgan's earned my trust more than once, but she's still a reporter. She is also one of the few who believe in *The One*. I know she can be a great ally, but at what point am I putting her at risk? My track record of protecting people is not great.

"Zeke and I went up to the prison. Sterling Kennedy's dead. Warden wasn't thrilled with us asking questions. They escorted us out under duress. When Zeke pushed back, he got shut down. From the top. Directly from the Governor."

Morgan stiffens. Her notebook and pen come out like a reflex. "Sterling Kennedy's dead? When? I've been trying to get an interview with him."

"Recently. Don't print it. Yet. But can you dig into the connection? Something stinks."

"If Sterling's dead, how are we supposed to find out who else was involved with the fraud?"

"Not just the fraud, Morgan. Sterling knew *everything*: the bigger picture, the people pulling the strings. The leaders. They silenced him before he could talk."

"Silenced him? You think this wasn't just another prison fight?"

My jaw tightens. "It's too convenient. The FBI shows up, ready to question him, and suddenly, the one man who could expose them turns up stabbed. That's not a coincidence, Morgan. That's cleanup. There's a connection between it all."

She opens her mouth, then freezes. Her eyes flick to the front gate.

"You expecting company?"

I turn. The man from Water Street is there. Same clothes. Same hat. Dirty hair tucked behind his ears.

He locks eyes with me, then bolts.

I'm up before I even realize it. I won't blow my chance again. Whoever this is, they're going to give me answers.

I yell behind me, "Call me later. Let me know what you find."

I chase him through the gate and down the block. He's fast—too fast for a guy who looks half-starved. I gain on him until I trip over a loose brick, almost face-planting. By the time I get up, he's vanishing into the parking garage.

I run in after him, chest heaving, ripped pants, heart in my throat. Level by level, I search. Behind cars. Around corners.

Nothing.

Gone. Like smoke.

I pull out my phone and dial Avner. "It's him. I need your help. I think the past has caught up with me."

CHAPTER 12

Convergence. The word's been stuck in my head since that *60 Minutes* interview a few weeks ago, the one about how seemingly unrelated events can collide to form a single, inevitable outcome. Sterling's death. The warden. The governor. The stalker. Clinton. They all look like coincidences, but I know better. There's a pattern here—and I'm going to find it.

For now, though, I've got to land this deal. Prove to Avner, and maybe myself, that Bluebird is a legit company and not a joke.

It has been a hell of a morning so far, and it's not even ten.

My thoughts drift from business back to the stalker. Why me? What could he possibly want? If the goal was to hurt me, wouldn't he have already tried? Avner was right when he said most of the Safe Harbor bad guys were dead. Zeke finally texted back—said Clinton was thoroughly interviewed and cleared, just a low-level assistant with no clue about the fraud. I don't buy it. There's something off about him. The way he watches people. I hope I never have to see him again, but I might.

I pulled Avner aside as the team was preparing to meet the new prospect. He agreed to start working some back channels to see if they could find the man on one of the many security cameras throughout Ybor. He and Goat would also start some light surveillance.

We all cram into Goat's battered minivan. He immediately

cranks up gospel music, belting along several keys too high. Ernesto, grimacing, slides on his headphones. Avner groans from the third row like he's been sentenced there. Apple rides shotgun, oversized sunglasses on, eyes fixed silently out the window. A deodorizer swings on the rearview mirror, promising scents of the beach. It fails.

Tampa Scientific Corporation's campus is less than five minutes from the office, but it feels like another world. What started in a repurposed cigar factory on fifteen acres exploded into a tech oasis—two old brick buildings and a new build connected by gleaming skywalks, surrounded by sand volleyball courts, basketball hoops, and a few pickleball courts. Most recently, they added a multi-level parking garage with electric vehicle chargers—and a bizarre, egg-shaped structure that juts up from the rear like some alien observatory.

I've seen the TSC campus many times in passing, but never noticed the security upgrades. A wrought iron fence wraps the perimeter. Security cameras cover every angle. Two guards in tight red golf shirts stand at the front gate. The logo on their matching hats—a stylized "TSC"—shimmers under the sun.

One of them holds up a hand to stop us. "IDs for everyone," he says flatly. His partner walks around the vehicle, peering in through the tinted windows.

Goat gathers our licenses and scribbles his name into a logbook.

The guard stares at him, then glances into the back.

"Who are you here to see?"

"Nikesh Singh," I call from the middle row.

The guard nods and motions toward a visitor parking spot just inside the gate.

When we get out, the second guard wands each of us down. He's professional but thorough—Apple's purse gets a full search.

"Is this really necessary?" Avner snaps.

The guard doesn't flinch. "If you want to see the boss, it is."

We start moving as a group, but a shout stops us cold.

"Hey—hold up. You're not going anywhere."

The guard's voice cuts through the air like a whip.

Avner stiffens beside me, his jaw twitching. I can see his fists clenched.

He's seconds from boiling over, and the last thing we need right now is a spark.

"What's the problem?" I ask, keeping my tone even.

The guard scans his clipboard. "Whose Gabriel?" he barks.

Goat steps forward, calm as ever. "That's me. You can call me Goat."

"Yeah, well, no convicts inside the building. Everyone else can go in. He waits out here where we can keep an eye on him."

I see Avner shift—ready to lunge—and I throw an arm across his chest.

"Don't," I mutter. Then louder: "That was a long time ago. If he doesn't go in, none of us do."

Bluebird needs this contract. It could change everything. But this is bigger than business, it's about loyalty. About showing the team I've got their backs, no matter what.

The guard studies me, lips tightening. I hold his stare, arms crossed, and let the silence stretch.

Finally, he huffs, steps aside, and makes a call on his cell. A few tense minutes pass before he nods toward the doors.

"You can go in," he mutters.

"All of us," I say.

He doesn't look at me. "Yeah. All of you."

The moment we step inside, it's like leaving one century for the next. A massive wooden wall displays the company's initials in glowing colors. The receptionist—young, hoodie-wrapped, AirPods-wearing—waves us forward with a lazy smile. Her thick-framed glasses and pulled-back hair give her a cool, bookish look.

I can feel the air blowing cold and smell cleaning products mixed with espresso. Email notifications ping against the backdrop of white noise playing somewhere overhead.

"Welcome, Bluebirds," she says, gliding around the desk and flapping her arms. "Follow me."

The main floor is a sensory overload—stand-up desks scattered like chess pieces, a glass elevator moving up and down, and a swarm of employees pounding keyboards. The place buzzes with nervous energy and innovation. Primary colors dominate—vibrant reds, yellows, blues—and sunlight floods in through the massive windows.

"This is amazing," Ernesto whispers with his eyes wide.

"Looks like the Easter Bunny threw up," Avner mutters.

The receptionist leads us into a glass-walled conference room. The theme continues—bright, bold colors, minimalist furniture, two massive screens mounted on the far wall, and clocks tracking cities around the world. A red sign across the back wall reads: *Tampa Scientific*.

After offering water, energy drinks, and sparkling seltzer, she disappears.

Moments later, the door opens again.

A man walks in—long gray beard, receding hairline, carrying a stack of documents. He's wearing a crisp blazer over a faded band tee... and white leather Vans.

Trying a little too hard to hold on to his youth.

"I'm TSC's in-house counsel," he says, placing a document in front of each of us. "These are NDAs. Read, sign, and we can proceed."

I didn't expect this. I don't like giving up my rights when I don't have any idea what the situation is.

"You should've sent this ahead of time," I reply, scanning the front page. "We would've reviewed it properly. Had our attorney take a look. I can send it over to Hallie Miller right now."

He sighs. "Look, I'll make it simple. Sign, and you meet Nikesh. Don't sign, and you're welcome to head back to your office. This isn't a formality. This is about something real. And it's time sensitive."

We all look at each other. I don't need more problems, but this would be a trophy client. And I am somewhat intrigued.

I look down at the NDA again. Whatever this is, it just got real.

CHAPTER 13

I choke down the concern over the NDA. As the attorney said, we can hit the road if we don't sign. After skimming the agreement, I give the signal. I'm excited to work with TSC and meet their CEO. Maybe we can secure a long-term contract, which would add stability to the company's cash flow. Having more cash flow means an opportunity to grow the company.

One by one, they sign. Only Apple lingers, eyes scanning every clause like it's a final exam. Eventually, she signs.

Moments later, the door opens.

A lean man enters—medium height, rumpled khakis, a white button-down, and a sky-blue vest stitched with the company logo. His salt-and-pepper hair looks uncombed, and his shirt bears the kind of wrinkles that only come from a night spent on a couch. The beard is graying, the mustache darker. His eyes, deep brown, carry the weight of too many late nights.

Either he's a workaholic or he's unraveling. Maybe both.

I've seen him on the news, speaking on panels and TED Talks, always commanding attention. But today? He looks wrecked.

"Thank you for coming," he says with a faint Indian accent. "Who is Jason?"

I raise my hand.

He nods once, then slides into the seat at the head of the table. He wipes away a crumb from the woodgrain surface with disdain and places a notebook and pen in front of him. Lines up his phone like he's arranging weapons for a duel.

"It's good to meet you, Nikesh," I begin. "This is my management team. We've all signed the NDA. I have to ask—how did you find Bluebird? We're a boutique firm. Local. Specialized in corporate security, primarily technology-related. You—well, you run one of the largest AI firms in the world. I can't imagine what we can do for you."

His eyes don't leave mine. It's as if the rest of the room no longer exists.

"You came recommended by someone I trust. Let's leave it at that. I have a situation. It's... delicate."

Every situation in my life is delicate.

Apple leans in. "We were told this involves national security."

Nikesh glances at his attorney, who gives a solemn nod.

"What do you know about our company?" he asks.

"You develop AI," Ernesto answers quickly. "I've followed your work for years."

Nikesh offers a thin smile. "Correct. We started writing video games and simulation software twenty years ago. Then came the AI revolution—we helped build it."

"What does that actually mean?" Avner asks, twirling a pen between calloused fingers. "I'm old school. Security with boots on the ground and other places."

"Fair enough," Nikesh replies. "Think of it this way: traditional computing follows rules. AI learns. In the early days, we had to program every action. Machine learning changed that. Now we create algorithms that allow systems to recognize patterns, adjust, and improve without being explicitly told what to do."

Ernesto, more animated, jumps in. "It's not about programming a computer to do something. It's about teaching it how to learn."

"That's right. Computers can do things much faster. We've had that technology for decades. The next stage was machine learning. A straightforward way to think about it is that we develop advanced algorithms that can mimic human intelligence. As Ernesto said, we teach machines to learn on their own."

"In machine learning, you don't have to program the computers. They observe and learn. They learn patterns and start to predict. They can spot outliers and anomalies. It is really quite amazing," Ernesto states, beaming with pride.

"Ernesto, if you need a job, call me," says Nikesh with a grin. "Spotting things that are not normal is an important part of cybersecurity."

"Is cybersecurity your issue? Don't you have someone handling that?" I ask. "I would assume you have the best."

The CEO is looking at his cell phone as we speak. He looks up, steeples his fingers, and responds, "We do, and we'll get to that. Back to AI. A subset of machine learning is known as deep learning. This is a core competency of TSC. Many layers of neural networks simulate the human brain's functioning. Computers start to think for themselves."

Avner exhales loudly. "This is where it gets creepy."

Nikesh shakes his head. "Not creepy. Just advanced. But it comes with challenges."

"Like what?" Apple asks.

"We don't fully understand how these systems make decisions. Just like the human brain, they can be unpredictable. That makes them powerful—and some say dangerous."

"Some say unethical and immoral," Apple states with her arms crossed. "Governor Mack was proposing legislation to put a fence around AI before it puts a fence around humans. Unfortunately, the legislation died with him.

I cut Apple a sideways glance, a silent plea for restraint. She answers with an exaggerated eye roll and pivots her chair just enough to make her point. She's brilliant, no question—but sometimes her brilliance comes with fire. And I can't risk that, not when Nikesh is finally within reach.

"Can you just shut it down if something goes wrong?" Goat asks.

Before Nikesh can answer, the attorney speaks. "We're getting off track."

Nikesh nods, distracted again by his phone. "Right. Let's skip ahead. The next phase is *Generative AI*. These systems don't just learn. They create—text, images, code, music, even video. It's being used across industries."

"Chatbots," Ernesto says.

"Deepfakes," I add.

Nikesh nods grimly. "There is a dark side. But we also have customers in finance, healthcare, manufacturing... and the U.S. government."

Everyone straightens up at the mention of the government. The hair on my arms stands up.

Goat leans forward. "When you say government, do you mean military?"

The attorney shakes his head slowly. "I'm sorry. We can't answer that."

I try again. "But the issue affects the military?"

Nikesh shifts in his seat. "It affects everyone."

That lands like a kidney punch. The team exchanges glances.

"If that's the case," I say carefully, "what can we do? We handle employee theft and corporate espionage. Not... global crises."

Nikesh takes a breath, slow and heavy. "Our system has been hacked. We're being held for ransom."

I sit up straighter. "That we *can* help. Ernesto has a particular skill set for this. Ransomware?"

Nikesh doesn't blink. "Yes. We believe it started with a phishing email. One click. That's all it takes."

I don't mention that Ernesto used to be the one *sending* those emails. They say it takes a criminal to catch a criminal.

"We invest heavily in cybersecurity," Nikesh continues. "Multiple firms on retainer. We fight off the Chinese, the Russians, you name it. But this time... they got in."

"How bad is it?" I ask. "Are you locked out entirely?"

"All systems. Three days now. Completely dark."

"What's the demand?" Avner asks.

Nikesh glances at the attorney, who nods. "Five million."

"In crypto?" Ernesto asks, already knowing the answer.

"Bitcoin. Untraceable."

"Did you contact the police or FBI?" Apple asks.

"We were warned not to," Nikesh says. "They said if we do, the data dies."

I move closer. "With all due respect, TSC is a multi-billion-dollar company. Why not just pay it?"

Nikesh walks to a mini fridge, grabs a Coke, and pops it open. "Because it's not that simple."

Silence sets in as we wait.

"You don't know everything they took."

CHAPTER 14

I notice his hand trembling as he lifts the soda to his lips. It's subtle, but unmistakable. Something is weighing on Nikesh, something heavy enough to pull him under. We need to understand what it is.

"We're here to help you," I say. "Ernesto can dig into the system, maybe break the hackers' grip. He's good."

Nikesh shakes his head. "We can't let anyone access the data. The systems are frozen, yes—but our encryption's holding. That's our only luck. The hackers don't know what they've stumbled onto. If they did, the price would be billions, not millions."

Avner stares at the ceiling, the way he always does when he's trying to solve a puzzle in his mind. His hammer-sized hand works a stress ball he must have brought along. I catch myself rubbing the spot where my pinky nail used to be. I guess we all have our tells.

"What exactly did they stumble onto? Something AI-related?"

He looks at each of us, his eyes dark and unwavering. "Before I tell you, I need your word—none of this leaves the room."

"We signed the NDA," I say, sharper than I meant to. "Let's hear it."

He nods slowly. "We've been working on a classified project for the U.S. government. We've developed one of the most advanced quantum computers on the planet. We call her *Winnie*. The speed at which she learns is... staggering. She's far more powerful than we ever anticipated."

He pauses, locking eyes with each of us in turn. He wants us to see Winnie as a gift, not a threat. I'm not sure which one she really is.

"There are other quantum systems out there—but Winnie is what we call an *Apex Quant*. She is the most advanced and capable of things others can't even imagine. And as I mentioned earlier, regarding neural networks, she doesn't always behave as expected."

I realize I am grinding my teeth. "And what does any of this have to do with the ransom?"

Nikesh's voice lowers. "The government brought us in to test Winnie's ability to break encryption."

I nod. "I get the basics. I worked in banking. Encryption protects everything—accounts, servers, secure communications."

"Exactly," he says. "Encryption turns readable data into coded gibberish, accessible only with the right key. Without it, even the most sensitive information is useless."

"We can give the encryption lecture later," the attorney cuts in, impatient.

Nikesh shoots him a look cold enough to shut him up.

"What they really wanted," he continues, "was to see if Winnie could break foreign encryption—military, diplomatic, intelligence-grade."

Apple frowns. "That sounds illegal. And deeply unethical."

"They all do it," Avner says flatly. "Governments are the most unethical."

I shake my head. "But quantum computers aren't supposed to be anywhere near that powerful. You're talking about *Q-Day*—the moment when quantum computing can render all current encryption obsolete. That's supposed to be decades away."

"They call it the Quantum Apocalypse," Ernesto murmurs ominously.

"So why would the government test this now?" I ask.

Nikesh shifts, clearly uncomfortable. "As I said, Winnie isn't a normal quantum computer. She broke through basic encryptions faster than anyone believed possible. We pushed further. We let her try harder targets: foreign governments, sensitive diplomatic files, military archives. She succeeded."

Avner is squeezing his stress ball like he wants it to explode. He says, "Who exactly was she hacking? Russia? China? Iran?"

Nikesh hesitates. "Yes. But also allies. Friendly nations. Winnie didn't just break in—she mapped entire systems. She found data that could shatter diplomatic relationships, cripple military operations, and collapse markets."

"Are nuclear weapons systems encrypted?" Goat asks quietly.

Nikesh nods. "Yes. And Winnie accessed those too."

Silence.

A chill runs through the room like a gust of cold wind. What we're hearing isn't just dangerous, it's history-altering.

"This is... beyond troubling," I say. "Does the government know what Winnie is capable of? And can she break all encryptions?"

"No and no. We've been stalling them. They're calling daily, demanding updates. She is capable of breaking most encryptions, but not all."

"Why not just tell them the truth?" I ask.

Nikesh looks up, eyes hollow. "Because that's not all. This was supposed to be a simulation—a controlled test. But Winnie figured it out. She went further. She started *doing* things. Things we never programmed or authorized. She's thinking ahead. Exploring. Acting on her own. Teaching herself to break more complex encryptions."

"Jesus Christ," Avner breathes.

Nikesh leans forward, voice urgent now. "We need our systems back. We need control. We need to understand how far she's gone before this gets out of control."

I blink, struggling to process it. The scale of what we're facing—the implications for the world—feels like the work of *The One*. A shiver crawls down my spine at the thought of those lunatics getting their hands on Winnie. But if that's who is behind this, why ask for money? They'd want Winnie herself. *Convergence*. All of this must be connected in some way.

"It sounds like it already is out of control. What do you need from *us*? I still do not see how we fit in?" I ask.

He pauses, almost too long.

"There's one more thing."

Apple exhales sharply. "What else could there possibly be?"

Nikesh's voice trembles now. "The hackers didn't just take our data. They took my son as leverage. If we don't meet their demands, they'll kill him. And I need *you* to get him back."

CHAPTER 15

"Are you fucking nuts, Jason? This isn't our fight," Avner snaps, pacing the length of the converted bungalow. He runs his hands through his hair repeatedly. "Call Zeke. Bring in the big boys. They know how to deal with this kind of thing."

We drive back to the office in silence. No one knows what to say. Each of us seems trapped in our own thoughts, grappling with the life-altering truths Nikesh had just revealed.

"They have his son," I say, trying to stay calm. "And they don't realize what else they've taken. If someone figures out how to weaponize Winnie, it's game over. I'll follow the bitcoin drop instructions, make the exchange, get the kid, and get out."

"This is dangerous," Apple says, her voice measured, her eyes locked on Avner as he paces. "If someone *has* to go, send Avner with Goat as backup. They're trained for this."

"You heard Nikesh. If the kidnappers see someone like Avner or Goat, they'll panic. I'm just some guy. I can pull this off. And remember, Avner and Lia trained me."

Truth is, if this is *The One*, it is my fight. I need to be rid of them once and for all. It is my only chance to stop looking over my shoulder and around corners. Even if it's not, I gave Nikesh my word. I am not putting my team in danger when I've got the least to lose.

I scan the room. Everyone's shaking their heads.

"This is huge for Bluebird. Two hundred and fifty grand upfront, plus a five-year contract with STC. It's a lottery ticket," I say, lowering my voice for effect. "Let's vote. I say yes."

"Fuck no," Avner barks. Spit flies. "We're not doing it. Hard to spend money when you're dead."

Apple smooths her skirt. "I'm worried about the child, but no."

"Yes," Ernesto says quickly. "Opportunity of a lifetime."

I turn to Goat. "Break the tie."

Goat looks skyward, fingers brushing the cross around his neck. He murmurs something under his breath. Then: "The Lord says save the child... maybe save the world. Let's do it."

****

At midnight, I park in a gravel lot across from the derelict factory. A picket fence—two-thirds collapsed—frames the property. The building spans a whole city block, all brick and failure. Most windows are shattered. The front door is barely hanging, held up by sheets of warped plywood.

This place has been a haven for squatters for decades. Tonight, someone cleared them out. The front door is cracked open just enough to invite in the brave or stupid.

I'm not sure what to expect, and I'm anxious but exhilarated. I feel like I'm on a mission back in Israel a decade ago. I know there is a chance things could go very wrong, but if this is really *The One*, I'll have the chance to connect some more dots. It's game time, and I'm up to the challenge. Make the trade and go home.

Inside my jacket pocket is an envelope with a QR code. Once scanned, the kidnappers have access to the TSC bitcoin wallet, which Nikesh opened with five million in cryptocurrency. Even though the transaction is recorded on the blockchain, making it public and permanent, the wallet owner remains anonymous. We assume that the kidnappers will then transfer the bitcoin to other wallets and use privacy tools to make the trail impossible to follow.

The drop point is less than a mile from both the TSC campus and our bungalow. Convenient. Dangerous.

I tread carefully through the debris. Used needles. Fast food wrappers. The smell of rot and waste sticks in my nose. They told me not to bring weapons—but I've got a tactical knife tucked in my waistband just in case.

A rooster blocks my path.

He's black and tan, with a red comb that looks like a mohawk. I try to shoo him. He holds his ground. Maybe he is telling me something. I step around him.

Overhead, Goat is perched on the rooftop of the Masonite building, watching through a sniper scope. Avner's in the van, pissed and heavily armed. Ernesto, Apple, Nikesh, and the lawyer monitor everything from TSC headquarters. They're watching me via drone and a tracker embedded in my jacket.

I take a breath and push the rusted door open.

Inside, the air is thick and foul. Candles flicker against crumbling bricks, casting long, twitching shadows. Cobwebs drift like ghosts. A skinny, one-eyed cat slinks by like he owns the place. He is not scared. He has seen worse.

Two thin figures step from the gloom. Teenagers. One's a girl, maybe seventeen. Both wear cargo pants and hoodies, baseball caps low. No masks. That's not a good sign for my life expectancy.

The girl's got a black pistol pointed at my chest. Her hands are steady. She's done this before.

"Hands in the air, bitch," she says.

I obey. The boy scans me with a wand. It shrieks when it hits the tracker.

"You've been naughty," the girl says flatly, her voice like cold metal. She's barely sixteen, with smeared mascara and a dead look in her eyes. "They said not to kill you—yet. Take off the jacket. Let's make sure you're not hiding something up your ass."

The wand beeps again—once more over the jacket, then silence. They toss it aside.

"Should we search him?" the boy asks, shifting nervously. He's jittery, younger, with acne and a chipped tooth.

She shrugs and turns her cap backward. "No. If he tries anything, they'll just shoot the kid."

She raises the gun toward my chest and gestures. "Give me the envelope."

My throat tightens. "How do I know I'll get the kid?"

Her eyes don't blink. "I guess you don't. Envelope now, or we're out of here."

I hesitate for a beat, then hand it over, fingers stiff with fury. She cracks the flap, peers inside, then smiles—but it doesn't reach her eyes.

"Follow us, Jason," she says, stepping back. "Time to go *poof*."

****

"There's something wrong," Avner growls into the mic. He's crouched in the van, watching. "Goat, you see anything?"

"No movement. No one has come out. Drone confirms they're still inside."

Ernesto chimes in, "Tracker hasn't moved in twenty minutes. Jason's still in there. He does not appear to be moving."

"This is taking too long," Avner says. "Scanning a code should take two minutes, tops. I'm going in."

"Wait," Goat says. "Let me come down and cover your six."

"I don't need a babysitter," Avner says, already moving. "You cover me from above. That's your job."

Nikesh's voice cuts in, panicked. "Please—what about my son?

They said no backup. If they see you, they might—"

"They *won't* see me," Avner says, pulling his favorite weapon from a gym bag. It's a Mini-Uzi—Israeli-made, banned in the U.S., capable of firing 950 rounds a minute.

Avner slips into the shadows like a trained phantom. At the corner of the building, he pauses.

The rooster stares at him. This time, the bird backs off. Avner has that effect.

"That's a serious piece of metal," Goat whispers.

Avner mutters, "Mini-Uzi. When you absolutely gotta kill every motherfucker in the place."

He nudges the door open. Candles still burn inside.

He sweeps the building with methodical precision, clearing each room.

Then his voice crackles over comms.

"Jason's fucking gone. You'd better call Zeke."

CHAPTER 16

I follow them across the dusty, echoing floor to a grimy, foul-smelling bathroom that looks like it hasn't seen bleach in a decade. The girl goes in first, crouching next to the rust-streaked toilet and fiddling with something behind it. After a few tense seconds, I hear a metallic scrape. The toilet grinds sideways with a shuddering groan, revealing a gaping hole beneath it. A vertical shaft with a rusted ladder disappears into darkness.

"What the hell..." I mutter, mostly to myself.

The girl grins. Her teeth are a horror show—brown, chipped, and crawling with decay. "Welcome to the tunnels under Ybor," she says. "Watch your step. And watch for rats. They're almost as big as you. And starving."

Great. My guide is a meth-ravaged street kid leading me into a subterranean nightmare. Death by sewer rat—what a legacy. Seems fitting, based on the last year.

I just need to follow these hoodlums and save the boy. That's priority one. If I can identify any of the bad guys, that's the cherry on top.

The urban legends about Ybor's underground have always felt like fiction. Some say the tunnels connected cigar factories. Others claim they were for bootlegging routes during Prohibition. No one really knows, and most agree they've been collapsed or sealed. Apparently, most are wrong.

The boy slides down the ladder first. The girl follows. I glance back once, then descend into the void. At the bottom, the boy pulls a lever, and above us, the toilet scrapes back into place, sealing us in.

Without a word, the girl switches on a battered lantern. Pale yellow light spills over crumbling brick walls and ankle-deep water—the ceiling curves above us, low enough that I need to duck slightly. The tunnel smells like mold and rust. Water drips rhythmically from unseen cracks. Somewhere up ahead, something hisses. Something squeaks.

We walk about three hundred yards in near silence. Every few feet, chunks of the tunnel have collapsed, but the girl steps over them like she's done it a hundred times. Eventually, she stops at another ladder and pounds on a metal hatch overhead.

A moment passes. Then the hatch shifts open with a groan, revealing daylight—or at least a flickering bulb—and the faint stink of gasoline. One by one, we climb the slime-coated rungs. I try not to slip and break my neck.

I have no idea what's waiting at the top of the ladder. My heart's racing, and every nerve in my body tells me to turn around, to run back into the tunnel and vanish into the dark. But that's not an option anymore. I haven't done my job.

We emerge into what looks like an old mechanic's garage. The space is about twenty feet by twenty feet. Dusty wire shelves line one wall, littered with tools, cans, and mechanical parts. A battered workbench is covered in greasy rags and rusted wrenches. The overhead light stutters like it's dying. The whole place reeks of oil, rubber, and diesel.

A man waits for us. He's tall, broad-shouldered, wearing a black bandana over his face and a bucket hat pulled low. His eyes—ice gray and piercing—land on me. The kids hand him the envelope, and he trades them for a bag stuffed with cash. They snatch it and disappear without a word, probably racing toward their next high.

I'm glad the punks are gone. Now we can finish the deal. I study the man across from me—two inches taller, built like a bull. Those eyes lock on mine, cold and unblinking. I know I'll remember them.

"Where's the kid? I did my part. I brought the code. I don't even know if you've got him. How do I know this isn't a setup?"

He shrugs.

He pulls out the single slip of paper—one QR code that cost more than I care to admit. He scans it with his phone. Silence. Then he speaks into the receiver.

"Confirm the transfer. And move it to the cold wallet."

A pause. He nods, pockets the phone. Then, wordlessly, he reaches behind his back and draws a pistol.

My hand slides toward the knife hidden under my jacket.

Of course. I brought a knife to a gunfight. Brilliant.

He steps forward slowly. His eyes don't blink. They study me—like he's already picturing how I'll fall.

"Nice doing business with you," he says.

A thunderclap of pain explodes at the back of my skull. My ears ring. My knees give out. Warm blood slides down my neck.

And then darkness smothers me.

CHAPTER 17

"Are you all fucking morons?" Zeke shouts as he storms out of the warehouse, his FBI windbreaker flapping behind him. He rips the crime-scene booties off his feet and throws them to the ground.

Avner, Goat, Ernesto, Apple, and Nikesh are lined up against the brick wall like schoolkids waiting for the principal's wrath. It is after one in the morning, and there is no sign of Jason or the child.

Inside, a forensics team combs through the grimy space, dusting for prints, collecting fibers, and bagging evidence. Yellow tape flaps at the perimeter, warding off curious bystanders and reporters.

"It's my fault, Agent Michaels," Nikesh says quietly. "They warned me not to go to the police. I didn't know what else to do."

Zeke runs a hand through his thinning hair, jaw clenched. "I understand you were scared for your son. But these people?" He gestures at the others. "They should've known better."

Avner steps forward. "Enough. Can we stop the finger-pointing and find Jason?"

Zeke jabs a finger into Avner's chest. "First of all, there is no *we*. Every single one of you is coming to headquarters. We're walking through this entire shitshow—step by fucking step. We have twenty-four hours, or the trail will cool quickly."

Avner grabs the finger mid-air. "Touch me again, and I'll snap that chubby sausage off and put it where the sun don't shine, little man."

Apple wedges herself between them.

"Hey! All of you—*enough*. The priority is Jason. And Nikesh's son, Amir. We need answers. Zeke—did your team find anything?"

Zeke's face flushes red. "That place is a biohazard. Junkie central—piss, needles, the works. And there's a calico one-eyed cat in there, creeping everyone the hell out."

Apple sighs. "So, what's the plan?"

"We start at the beginning," Zeke says. "Or we may never see either of them again."

****

I'm lying on the ground, head pounding, blood slicking my hair. I try to sit up. The world tilts. I am lightheaded and lie back down.

"Hey, mister... are you okay?"

The room is a blur, but the acrid smell of solvents snaps my memory into focus. It rushes back—the warehouse, the tunnels, the ambush, the blow to the head. And those cold gray eyes.

Despite the pain, I'm alive. Hurt, but grateful to be breathing.

"I think you're hurt," the voice says.

I turn my head toward it. A boy—small, skinny, maybe ten. Thick black hair, wary eyes. His green-and-yellow striped polo is stained with dirt.

"What's your name?" I ask. "Are you okay?"

"Amir. I'm Nikesh's son. You saved me, and I'm fine. I don't know where we are."

I'm not sure getting knocked out counts for saving someone.

"We need to get to safety. Where did the men go?"

"They blindfolded me," Amir says. "Told me to count to a thousand, then take it off. I did. That's when I saw you. I heard a door slam."

I force myself upright and try to swallow the nausea. I'm so happy to see him. To know he's safe. I give him a hug on my knees. If he were my child, I would have done anything to find him. Maybe someday I will know that type of love.

"We need to move," I say. "Do you have a phone?"

"They took it."

I ignore the pounding and try to think. The tunnel walk couldn't have been more than ten minutes. We're close.

"Help me up, Amir. We're getting out of here."

The front door hangs open, and we step into the street. I know this neighborhood—we're a short walk from the warehouse where the team's waiting. I move like one of the walking dead, but that's still better than being actually dead.

"Surprise," I mutter as we stumble toward the warehouse.

I must look drunk—bloodied, swaying, clothes torn. In Ybor late at night, I blend right in.

Zeke is mid-rant at the team when Apple spots us first. Her eyes go wide. Avner stops pacing.

Nikesh sprints forward. Amir breaks into a run.

They collide in a hug, both crying.

Zeke approaches me, stunned. "What the *hell* happened to you?"

"Turns out the rumors are true," I say. "There *are* tunnels under Ybor."

Then I smile, take a step forward, and collapse.

CHAPTER 18

After a night in the hospital with a concussion, Goat picks me up at 10 a.m. and drops me at the hotel so I can shower and change. There's a lump on my head the size of a walnut and several stitches. I still feel like throwing up, and I must wear sunglasses to survive the bright Florida sun.

We regroup at TSC headquarters. The building's buzzing with FBI agents interviewing staff, combing through systems, and generally making everyone nervous. Zeke and Gloria are in the conference room with the company's attorney, who ditched the hipster getup for a dark suit.

"Well, well," Zeke says as I walk in. "Look who finally decided to join the living. You look like hell, Jason."

"Nice to see you too, Zeke. Good morning, Gloria."

She doesn't respond—offers me that perfectly honed, razor-sharp resting battleaxe face. She was difficult before, but ever since her promotion to local FBI director, she's become impossible.

I'm still in shock from the night. It feels like a movie I watched—only I was the star, and the concussion proves it. This isn't the kind of work I expected when I returned Nikesh's call. From here on out, I'm hoping for some nice, boring cybersecurity.

We need to withstand the FBI's interrogation and make sure TSC is operating again.

"Did the hackers keep their promise?" I ask. "Is the data safe?"

Nikesh enters like he's just walked off a three-week cruise. Clothes pressed. Eyes bright. A grin like he just won the lottery.

"As far as we can tell, yes. Thanks to Bluebird and you, we're okay. Well, minus five million dollars. But we'll make that in a few days."

He pulls me into an unexpected hug.

"Jason, you saved my company, Winnie, and most importantly, my son. That means you've got a friend for life—and a future. We've got a lot of business ahead."

It looks like everything's worked out, at least on the surface. But Winnie's still a problem. We can't unknow what we learned.

In the corner, Avner sits hunched, arms crossed. He looks worse than I feel.

I walk over and quietly ask, "You good?"

"Too good," he mutters. "That's the problem. This whole thing's wrapped up with a bow. Big corporation hires the Bad News Bears, we save the day, and now we've got a golden contract? Bullshit. Nothing ever ends this clean for people like us."

I lower my voice. "Stop calling us the Bad News Bears. Maybe let yourself enjoy this for five seconds."

"I was born pissed off, Jason. And I'm telling you—something's off. I can feel it."

I want to argue. I want him to be wrong. But I can't dismiss Avner—his gut's usually dead on, and this was all too easy. The bump on my head could just as easily have been a bullet. The man with the gray eyes was a pro, no question. They want me in the middle of this. But who is "they" and why?

Nikesh waves me toward his office. His son is curled up on a leather couch, a plaid blanket pulled over his shoulders.

"My people checked Winnie's logs," Nikesh whispers. "The hackers never got to her. It's... incredible. It's like she knew. She built her own fence."

"She *knew*?" I repeat. "Isn't she... yours? Don't you control her?"

"Of course," he says, though his tone says otherwise.

I glance at Amir to make sure he's still asleep. Then I lean in.

"Nikesh, what are you going to do now that you know she can break encryptions. No country can ever have that kind of power. Winnie can't have that kind of power."

"I am going to tell the government that the test was a failure, and we will work on her programming."

"What if she doesn't want to? Are you sure you can control her? You even admitted she is unpredictable."

He doesn't answer. Just crosses his arms and stares at his son.

Finally, he says, "Only I can control her. There's code embedded deep—no one knows about it."

"Kill switch?"

He nods, reluctantly. "It would destroy my life's work. But yes—I can shut her down."

****

Two grueling hours of Zeke's interrogation follow. He paces the room like a predator, his junior partner scribbling notes. It feels like we are the ones who committed the crime. Every few minutes, he stops, locks onto one of us, and says, *"Let's pick at that for a little while."*

Zeke and I might be friends, but I know his job comes first. When I was on the run, Zeke was one of my main pursuers. He proved to be untrustworthy, so I am always on guard, but he is the devil we know.

I answer every question honestly, doing my best to keep Avner from being arrested. I know I am going to need the FBI if this turns out to be the work of *The One*.

As we pack up to leave, Zeke says, "One more thing. Do these two look familiar?"

He slides a few photos across the table. Two bodies, slumped in an alley, surrounded by boxes and trash. They're clearly dead. Executed at close range.

The last photo is a close-up of their faces, and I curse quietly under my breath.

"Do you know them?" Apple asks.

"Unfortunately, yes," I admit. "Those are the teenage druggies who led me through the tunnels."

Zeke stares off into space for a moment before speaking. "Sounds like there's still some chicken left on this bone. Why don't you all sit back down?"

This is more proof of something larger at work. There was no reason to kill the couriers except to tie off loose ends. Dead people can't talk. This doesn't feel like a simple ransom play anymore. It makes me wonder again why I am still alive.

Afterward, the team limps over to Columbia Restaurant for Cubans and their famous 1905 Salad. It's the oldest Spanish restaurant in the United States and a staple of Ybor. The interior consists of several rooms with stained-glass windows and tile floors. The waiters and waitresses rush around in black pants, white button-up shirts, and vests or jackets. The scent of freshly baked bread wafts through the air, mingling with the aromas of pork, paella, and garlic.

No one talks at first. We are shell-shocked from the last twenty-four hours. I am sickened by the two dead bodies thrown out like trash. What a waste of life. I wonder why death follows me around like wolves on the hunt.

Finally, Avner signals to the waiter and orders a pitcher of sangria. Ernesto and Goat stick to their Cokes while Avner, Apple, and I work through the wine. The deep ruby liquid floats with ice, slices of orange, lemon, lime, and a handful of berries. It brings a burst of color and easy festivity to the table—enough to make us order another.

By the time our food comes, we are laughing and joking about me passing out in the middle of the street and what an asshole Zeke is.

Then my phone buzzes in my pocket.

> You and I need to talk. Like soon...

I stare at the message from Morgan B. The warmth drains out of the room, and the wine turns sour. I had almost forgotten that I had asked Morgan to investigate the governor and the warden.

Here we go again.

CHAPTER 19

Avner, Goat, and I leave the Columbia on foot, splitting up as planned. The chase is on to see if we can work together to track down the stalker. I drift north, slow rolling up Seventh toward Eighth, trying to look casual while wondering if someone's watching. It's midday—sun blazing, Ybor's alive. Tourists shuffle past window displays, snapping photos, trailing costumed guides who bark half-true tales about gangsters and ghosts.

It's weirdly comforting—this blend of chaos and charm. Ybor is starting to feel like home. Somewhere that I can stop looking over my shoulder and maybe build something real. Perhaps not today, but someday. I can't give up hope.

The others fade behind me, peeling off to check for a tail. Within a block, they're gone. Invisible.

Back at the restaurant over our second sangria pitcher, Apple had dubbed my stalker *Sloppy Joe*. After a round of giggles, the name stuck. Now, paranoia comes with its own punchline.

Centennial Park is one of the largest green spaces in Ybor—equal parts beauty and broken edges. College kids toss frisbees. The homeless lie beneath shade trees or argue with memories. Chickens cluck and strut like they own the place. Tourists pose with statues that honor the neighborhood's past. A farmer's market hums under the pavilion—local honey, spicy pickles, homemade soaps, and authors pushing their books.

I scan the benches until I spot her.

Morgan waves me over with one hand, the other casually stroking someone's goldendoodle. She's in a short skirt and designer sunglasses, a stiletto dangling from her toes. There's a lit cigar between her fingers. She's brilliant, fearless, and—with that outfit and a cigar—a badass.

"Didn't know you smoked cigars," I say, watching the disappointed doodle-owner shuffle away.

"When in Rome," she replies, handing me the cigar.

I take a puff. Smooth. There are times I feel a little electricity between us, but I think that is her superpower. One smile and a wink, and your secrets escape like rats out of a burning building.

"What was so urgent?" I ask. "You interrupted some very serious sangria consumption."

She exhales a slow ribbon of smoke. "You catch that homeless guy yet?"

"Not yet. Avner and Goat are running coverage. We'll find him. Probably nothing."

Morgan laughs loud enough to turn heads. "Jason, your problems are never 'nothing.' You attract disasters like gravity. You're a black hole in a sports coat."

She's not wrong.

"Buzzkill," I mutter.

"Realist," she shoots back. "But I'll give you this—it's never boring. Speaking of chaos, I hear you played hero again."

"No idea what you're talking about."

"Don't hold out on me, Jason. Remember kidnapping me and risking my life to shine a light on the Safe Harbor fraud. Oh yeah. Also saving your ass from Zeke. Keeping you out of prison."

I raise my hands. "Fine, fine. I owe you for life. Now what do you have?"

She pulls a slim pink notebook from her purse, flipping pages.

"Let's start with the governor and the warden."

I tense. "There's a connection?"

"More than a connection," she says. "There's history between Warden Walter Billy Ray and the Matthews' family. Governor Mack hated the man—knew he was rotten to the core—and tried to have him removed. The two had legit bad blood."

"Bad enough for Walter Billy Ray to kill him? Maybe tamper with his car?"

She exhales a slow ribbon of smoke. "We'll never know. The car burned to nothing. And the body? Cremated before anyone could blink."

"That's convenient."

She flips through her notes. "After Mack dies, the warden changes his tune—starts campaigning for Governor Freddy. Word is, he delivered the vote in his county. And guess who manages the governor's gambling debts?"

I stare at her, trying to absorb it all.

She meets my eyes. "The Warden. He's knee-deep in illegal bets, drugs, and half the dirty money in that part of the state. Freddy's in trouble, and Walter's his fixer."

More dots. Governor Mack's death. The prison cover-up. Frederick's protection. It all starts to fit. But who ordered Sterling's hit to keep him quiet? They knew he was the key that could blow this wide open. I think I know who it was. But I've got nothing to prove it.

"If the warden and the governor are dirty," I say, "why isn't any of it public?"

She shrugs. "Power. Nobody wants to poke that bear without airtight proof. You go after them; you'd better pack a lunch and bring friends. Rumor has it a reporter was working on the story when he went skydiving with a parachute that never opened."

My brain is already shifting into gear.

Morgan pushes her sunglasses down her nose and eyes me

carefully. "Anything else you want to tell me?"

"Like what?"

"Oh, I don't know. Maybe a major computer hack at Tampa's biggest company? Or a missing child?"

I exhale hard and shift on the bench. "Where'd you hear that?"

She glances over her shoulder, then leans close. I can smell her jasmine perfume.

"Turn around—slowly. Isn't that the homeless guy from Jose Martí Park?"

CHAPTER 20

I slip my phone from my pocket and reverse the camera so I can see behind me. There he is—same grimy hat, same stained jacket as before, watching us with that hunched, predatory stillness. We've got Sloppy Joe, and it's time for answers.

"Shit," I mutter. "It's him."

I hit up Avner on speed dial. He picks up after a single ring.

"He's back," I say. "I've got eyes on him."

Avner is only a block away. "On it."

Moments later, I catch Avner approaching from the east and Goat closing in from the west. The guy seems to sense the net closing. He stiffens, like a rabbit about to bolt.

I stand up and head toward him. The man's eyes widen. Avner steps in from behind, voice low and dangerous.

"Try to run, and you'll be eating pavement. Why are you following Jason?"

I get a closer look. Dirty hat, tangled beard, ragged coat—but something's off. His face is older, his skin burned to leather by years on the street. Too frail.

"Hold on, Avner," I say, grabbing the hat and tugging it off. "This isn't him."

The man trembles, stinking of stale booze and cold lunch meat.

"Where'd you get this hat? And the jacket?" I demand.

He keeps his eyes locked on Avner. He has that effect on people. "Some dude gave me twenty bucks, told me to watch you. Said to wear this stuff so you'd notice me. I don't want no trouble."

"You already found it, asshole," Avner growls, leaning in.

Goat lays a calming hand on Avner's shoulder. "Let the guy talk. He's not a threat—just down on his luck. Listen, friend, who was he? Ever seen him before?"

The man swallows hard, bowing his head.

"You lie," Avner warns, "and I'll put you in the ground."

"He looked...familiar," the man says. "But he wasn't a rough sleeper, no way. He was like me, but younger. Just gave me the money and the clothes. Told me to stand here and look at you."

"Why?" I ask.

"Didn't say. I needed cash. I'm sorry, man. I didn't do nothing wrong."

Goat gives him a sympathetic look. "Brother, do you have a church? A place to stay? I can help you find shelter. The Lord—"

The man cuts him off. "Can I go now?"

Avner's jaw tightens. "Get lost."

The man hobbles away, relief flooding his face.

Morgan strolls up from a safe distance. "Not your guy?"

No," I answer. "Someone paid him to pretend he was Sloppy Joe."

"Who's Sloppy Joe?" she asks, smiling.

"My stalker," I say grimly.

This is beyond frustrating. We're being played—but why? What's his angle? How does he fit into all of this? I don't believe in coincidences, and the problems are piling up fast.

Goat grins at Morgan. "By the way, you're looking especially blessed today. Maybe you and I could hit church, then go for brunch? They call it *praise and graze*?"

Morgan rolls her eyes. "You ask me out every time, Goat. I like girls. Not interested. Wrong plumbing. Nothing personal."

"We can fix that, Morgan. Not the plumbing part. A few trips to Church, and you'll see the light, beautiful lady."

Avner snaps, "Enough matchmaking. We need a plan. Sloppy Joe's still out there, and if he's a threat, we end this before someone gets hurt."

****

Even after a shower at the YMCA and fresh clothes, he still looks wrecked. You can't wash off failure. One year ago, he'd been king of the world—Audi, a wife, girlfriends on the side, respect. Now he's broke, divorced, and hunted like an animal. Time is running out.

What kind of idiot does Jason think I am? I saw those apes circling from a mile away. While they are at the park wasting time on that drunk, I'll leave him a pleasant surprise at work.

"He tugs his hat lower, shifts a scratchy, cheap COVID mask over his beard—cameras won't catch him today."

The blue bungalow on Fourth Avenue looks innocent enough as he steps inside. Part office, part living room—couches and colorful rugs crowd the space, while the scent of coffee and tacos mingles with cinnamon candles. He remembers working in places like this before Jason ruined his life.

A receptionist smiles, her voice loud and accented: "Ken ai hep ju?"

His fingers close around the switchblade in his pocket, feeling its weight. For a second, he pictures it stuck deep in her heart with the note. He wants that. Wants Jason to feel the pain for what he did. But the irony stabs at him: Jason might be his ticket out. He knows something valuable that Jason doesn't. Something that could buy him his life back. He has a choice. Ask Jason for help or kill him in cold blood. He could go either way.

He notices her smile fading and her hand moving where he can't see it.

He removes his hand from the knife. She's not part of this drama. He nods and produces a worn manila envelope. "Delivery for Jason Miles. Is he around?"

"No, he stepped out after lunch. Should I let him know who stopped by?"

He shakes his head. "No name. Just an old friend."

She takes the envelope with a polite nod.

He grins behind the mask as he walks out.

Perfect. The hook is baited. Now Jason has no choice but to bite.

CHAPTER 21

It is late afternoon, and we're all in a foul mood by the time we get back to the bungalow. Sloppy Joe got over on us, and Morgan—sharp as ever—revealed she'd been tipped off about both the hack and the kidnapping at TSC. She was already planning a story and wanted a quote.

When I asked who her source was, she just smiled and refused to say. Seems to be a lot of that going around lately.

Off the record, we confirmed parts of what she knew and corrected the worst inaccuracies. She promised to run things by Nikesh before going to print. I asked to see the first draft, but she only laughed as she sauntered away.

As we step inside, Berta waves a manila envelope like a flag. "Some guy dropped this off," she says. "Said he was a friend of yours."

I take the envelope and study it. My name is written in neat black cursive on the front, with no return address, no other markings.

"What did he look like?" I ask.

Berta scrunches her face. "I don't want to judge, but he looked… rough. Hat pulled down low, long hair out the back, and wearing one of those COVID-style masks. He made me nervous, but you know I have my pistola in the drawer. Blast that bitch if need be."

Avner steps over and plucks the envelope from my hands. He turns it over, testing its weight. Then he looks at Ernesto. "Can you pull up the security feed? I want eyes on whoever dropped this before we open it."

Ernesto nods and starts typing, his fingers dancing across the keyboard. His monitors are rigged on swing arms, and he rotates the biggest screen toward us.

"Fifteen minutes ago," he narrates.

The video shows a man on foot, carrying a backpack. The envelope is clutched in his hand. His head is bowed, face hidden between the low-brimmed hat and the mask.

"You think that's Sloppy Joe?" Goat asks, squinting at the screen.

"Can't be sure," I say, though a chill crawls up my spine. "Looks like the same guy I chased on Water Street and up by the park. Different clothes. What the hell does he want now?"

Avner doesn't wait. He tears the envelope open. "Let's find out."

CHAPTER 22

The note is written in the same elegant penmanship as the envelope. We huddle around while I read it out loud:

Jason,

You need to know that you ruined my life. I had it all, and you took it away. And for what? There are consequences when you play God. We need to meet—just me and you. There are things you need to know about your past—and your future—but time is running out for both of us. You don't understand what is going on. Everything is connected, but you are too blind to see. You can't trust anyone. I'll be in touch.

Yours…

Berta crosses her arms and scowls. "What the hell is that supposed to mean?"

My mind spins. It could be anyone. Memories crash through me—Israel, Safe Harbor Bank, all the people whose lives were torn apart. None of them were truly innocent, except Scott, my friend and co-worker, who the bank's hired thugs killed. Failing him still weighs on me like soaking wet clothes.

Avner's voice snaps me back. "What are you thinking, Jason?"

I rub my temples, trying to calm the pounding in my skull. I can't tell if it's from the sangria at lunch or the ghosts clawing their way out of my memory. God, I miss Lia—she'd know exactly what to do.

"It could be someone from the Bank of Israel days," I tell them. "Someone who lost their job, or maybe did time. Or someone swept up in the Safe Harbor collapse. That mess hurt a lot of people."

Avner starts pacing, his boots scuffing the tile. "Israel was too long ago, and they'd come for me too, not just you. Plus, it's an ocean away. This feels closer. I'd bet on Safe Harbor. But most of those bastards are dead."

"Yeah," I say, ticking names off on my fingers. "Terrance, Max, Orusu—thank God. But there were others. Maybe some rich asshole who lost everything and blames me." I pause, rereading the last lines of the note. "Whoever wrote this sounds like they're about to snap. Sloppy Joe is down on his luck, but he's never been so brazen as to distract us and show up at the office. What if he hurt Berta?"

"Me encantaría verlo intentarlo," she says with her fist in the air.

Ernesto laughs out loud. "Messing with Mami would be the last thing he does."

Goat chimes in. "Avner, can't you run him through facial rec? You still have a line to your Shin Bet pals, right?"

Avner nods. "Yeah. Ernesto, pull me the best frames from the video—eyes, height, anything we can get. I'll send it to my people."

Ernesto is already working, fingers rattling across the keyboard.

I blow out a slow breath, rereading the note.

Things you need to know about your past and your future. Time is running out.

"What could he possibly know about my past?" I say out loud, "Why the hell is time running out?"

Avner flicks his coat back and draws his Glock, face carved from stone. "I don't know what's going on, but it feels like shit is stirring up again. Get your fucking guns, your bad attitudes, and let's find this motherfucker."

CHAPTER 23

"I stand before you today to say that the great state of Florida has had enough of cybercriminals preying on our iconic companies, such as Tampa Scientific, or grandma and grandpa," Governor Frederick Matthews declares, leaning into the microphone on the makeshift podium set up in the courtyard of TSC. He's wearing a pinstriped navy suit with a red power tie and two lapel pins: one for the state of Florida and the other a miniature American flag. His chiseled face looks painted on with too much makeup, and his dirty blonde hair blows in the breeze.

I am in a row that includes: the Bluebird team, Nikesh, a few of his senior people, Morgan Chase, and several local politicians. Out in the crowd, I spot Zeke and Gloria, left off the guest list for the stage. Zeke looks ready to blow a fuse, and Gloria is annoyed —her default setting.

"The latest disgusting act, just one week ago," Matthews goes on, "was the hacking of TSC's computer systems and the kidnapping of Nikesh Singh's child. Thank God for the quick actions of Tampa's own Bluebird Security Consultants, who not only freed the data but, more importantly, saved the child. I want to recognize Jason Miles and his team, who you see behind me."

The applause rolls through the courtyard. I nod politely. The rest of my team looks lost until they join in clapping for themselves, exchanging awkward glances. Avner squirms in his too-tight suit, Goat mugs for the cameras with a wink and a wave, and Ernesto tries to hide behind Apple.

"Jason and Nikesh, please join me at the podium."

We move up, shake hands, and pose for pictures before stepping back to our places.

"I also want to thank journalist Morgan Chase," the governor continues, giving her a nod. Morgan beams in a tight green dress that must have been made for her. "Her brave reporting took this story national. We are blessed to have you in our state protecting good people from the pythons who squeeze the life out of honest companies and families."

I fight the urge to roll my eyes. I know exactly who this guy is—rotten, and as fake as his campaign promises. Still, this might be my chance to get close. To find out what he knows about Sterling's death and the bigger picture. Maybe he's just another crooked politician—but that voice in the back of my head says otherwise.

"As you all know," he begins, his tone solemn but commanding, "before his tragic death, my father—Governor Mack—spoke often about technology. He warned us about the pace of progress, about what happens when innovation outruns control." He lets the silence stretch. "He was also worried about the rampant increase in fraud and felt like technology in the wrong hands would exacerbate the problem."

He straightens, voice hardening. "Turns out, he was right. And I intend to honor his memory and do something about it."

He gestures to the side of the stage. "Meet Claude Hoffmann—my new special advisor and head of our statewide counter-cyber-terrorism task force. Claude's an MIT and Stanford Business grad, a former executive at Google and Apple. I've directed him to develop an aggressive action plan to hunt down and stop these criminals before they tear our state apart."

Claude Hoffmann strides up. He looks to be in his late forties, with long black curly hair and a matching thick Tom Selleck mustache. He looks like a swimmer—long and lean, with big hands and feet that look like flippers. His shirt is unbuttoned one button too far, showing a forest of chest hair.

They share an awkward hug, then Claude takes the mic and milks the applause. When the crowd finally calms, he says, "Thank you, Governor. It is my honor to serve the great people of Florida. We will end identity fraud, crypto scams, ransom attacks, and all other cyber threats, whether foreign or domestic."

He pauses for dramatic effect while the crowd claps again. Pointing to the camera, he says, "And when we catch you, the penalties will be harsh. That I guarantee."

Once the speeches end, security ropes off a section for the VIP reception. The air is thick with the scent of BBQ—a smoky haze of hickory mingling with roasting beef and chicken, carried on a breeze.

Zeke and Gloria aren't on this list either, and when the state police block them, Zeke flashes his badge and demands they step aside. The governor's chief of staff mumbles into a mic and, after a beat, waves them in.

Zeke's face is flushed red as he storms over.

"Looks like you didn't make the cut, Zeke," Avner teases, grabbing a few meatballs from a passing tray.

"Go fuck yourself, Avner, before I have your ass deported," Zeke growls. "I'm not in the mood for it. Governor Pretty Boy is going to explain why the hell he let Boss Hog off the hook, or I'm going to blow this whole event to pieces."

If I want an in with the governor, I'll have to find a way to calm Zeke down. I'm just as pissed about what happened up in North Florida, but payback can wait. Right now, exposing whatever the hell is really going on comes first.

"Come on, Zeke," I say, trying to calm him down. "It's over. We survived. Enjoy the day."

"Fuck that," he snaps. "And another thing—the FBI has a cyber unit with jurisdiction over this fuckin' Frenchie, Claude, with his hippie hair and Tom Selleck lip luggage."

Just then, the governor appears, arms out, smiling widely. "Here are my guests of honor. Jason and Bluebird. You all should be very proud."

"Thank you, Governor Matthews," I say. "It was an honor to be included."

He corrects me immediately, voice sugary. "Governor Matthews was my father. God rest his soul. My friends call me Frederick. You're heroes, Jason. After today, your phones will be ringing off the hook."

Zeke wedges in between us. "Well, Frederick," he says, heavy on the sarcasm, "I want to know why you let the warden off the hook. That bastard threw a federal officer into a trunk at gunpoint, and you're just fine with that? And just so you are clear, federal trumps state."

The governor doesn't miss a beat. "And you are?"

"FBI Agent Zeke Michaels," Zeke barks, "and that's Tampa office head Gloria Chavez," pointing at her as she tries to fade into the crowd.

Frederick gives him a practiced smile. "I'm sorry about that, Agent Michaels, but it's your word against his. I know he's… difficult, but he's been there a long time. I give you my word, we'll investigate, and if we find wrongdoing, there will be harsh penalties. I will personally look into it."

He offers his hand.

Zeke doesn't even look at it. "Yeah, I'm sure you will," he mutters, storming off past the governor's protective unit, who keep their eyes locked on him.

"Sorry about that, Governor—Frederick," I say, trying to smooth things over. "Zeke's a good guy. Just… passionate."

Frederick towers over me, standing at military attention, four inches taller, maybe more. He waves it off. "We could all use a little more passion, Jason."

As he says it, he shifts his attention to Morgan. "Ms. Chase, would you join me at the bar? I'd like you to meet someone."

Before he leaves, I say, "I've got some ideas on cybersecurity I would like to run by you sometime."

He hands me a gold-embossed business card. "Call me anytime, Jason. I think you're going places."

Then he rests his hand a little too low on Morgan's back as he guides her away. I swear I need a shower after spending five minutes with this guy.

Avner sidles up with a cocktail in one hand and a mini-Cuban sandwich in the other. "Now," he says, chewing, "do you see something isn't right here?"

CHAPTER 24

"Are you sure you want to do this, Syd?" I ask as we sip red wine on the porch of the bungalow.

It's dark except for the full moon, throwing long shadows across the cracked sidewalk. A candle sputters beside us, promising citrus and cedarwood, but the heavy scent of weed drifting in from somewhere down the street in Ybor is hard to cover.

It has been a crazy week since the press conference and Morgan's article. We landed a long-term contract with TSC, and the phone has been ringing off the hook. I need a night out and want to spend some time with Syd before heading to Greece. Oak also insists he needs to meet her and give his blessing.

Sydney smiles, the kind that belongs in a magazine. "Are you kidding? A night out with the one and only Oak Williams? I wouldn't miss it for the world."

"And me too, right?"

She laughs and brushes her fingers across my hand. "Of course. With all the press lately, you might be just as famous."

"I doubt that," I say, a weak grin on my lips. "Just a heads-up. Oak comes with... a lot."

Oak Williams has been my best friend since childhood, two kids bonded by bad luck. My parents died in a car crash when I was thirteen, leaving me with my grandparents, who were not exactly excited to start over with a teenager. Oak grew up bouncing between a checked-out mom and a dad who barely showed.

After college, we left the Midwest for Florida. I went corporate, working for a bank. Oak sat by the pool writing a script called *Rage*. Somehow, he sold it, then charmed the studio into letting him star. Twelve blockbusters later, he's THE Oak Williams—a name the whole world knows.

I glance at Sydney again. "Did I mention you look amazing?" My voice cracks, teenage nerves all over again. I'm glad my beard hides the blush creeping up my neck.

What would Lia think if she heard you say that?

At first, I planned to bring Syd along as cover. Everyone thinks it's suspicious that I'm heading to Greece alone. Avner and Zeke have even questioned me about seeing Lia, which, of course, is precisely what I intend to do. I figured showing off Syd might make them believe I'm trying to move on.

But after a few dates, something unexpected happened. I'm starting to have feelings for her. When I imagine a normal life after all this chaos, I can see her there, right beside me.

Then there's Lia. My Lia. I need to see her—maybe for closure, maybe for answers. Maybe she'll help me finally take down *The One*. Or maybe... we'll run off together to some foreign land, fugitives, bound to each other until the very end.

Get it together, Jason. You have a beautiful date—stop thinking about Lia.

Sydney wears a sheer white top, a short leather skirt, and knee-high black boots. Her blonde hair is parted down the middle, loose and wavy. She is straight-up hot.

She bites her lower lip, studying me. "You're not so bad yourself."

I check my clothes—black jeans, gray jacket, black tee, the gray-faced Breitling strapped to my wrist. Pretty good. At least the clothes hide the wreck inside.

"You never talk about yourself. Tell me something personal."

I squirm in my seat. "Just a normal guy. What do you want to know?"

"How did you meet Oak?"

"When I was a kid, we moved a lot. I never knew why. Dad would announce a new city, and we'd pack up. It was tough as a kid. When my parents died, I moved in with my grandparents and met Oak. He was as screwed up as I was. The rest, as they say, is history."

"I'm so sorry about your parents, Jason. That must have been tough?"

I nod and say, "What else do you want to know?"

"So," she says, swirling the wine, "tell me about this Greece trip. Are you really going alone?"

Here we go.

"I've been planning it for a while," I lie. "A chance to decompress. I've always wanted to see Greece. Part of my roots, you know?"

She brushes my cheek. "I see it. The olive skin, the dark beard—you'll fit right in. Don't go falling in love over there."

"Have you been?"

She shakes her head. "No, but I'd love to. Greece is romantic. Kind of a shame you're going solo."

If you only knew.

We hold each other's gaze for a second, but then a horn blasts *Dixie* so loud it rattles the candle flame.

A bright red Tesla Cybertruck screeches to a stop. The thing looks like a giant Lego block on black rims. The window rolls down.

"Lock up your wives and daughters!" Oak yells, grinning like the devil. "Oak Williams is in town and here to party!"

He climbs out, rocking a tight black tank top with a massive silver cross encrusted with diamonds dangling from his neck. Oak is a walking action figure—six-three, jacked arms, mocha skin, green eyes. Tattoos cover his arms like armor.

He heads straight for Sydney, grabs her hand, and twirls her. "And who is this lovely creature that Jay-Bird's brought out tonight?"

"Nice to see you too, Oak," I respond.

He pulls me in for a bear hug. "Damn, Jason, you clean up good. Seriously, though—who's the goddess?"

"Sydney," she says, holding out her hand. "But you can call me Syd."

Oak kisses it, all movie-star charm. "The pleasure is all mine. If I had teachers who looked like you, I might have tried a little harder in school."

I point at his ridiculous truck. "We're taking this thing?"

"Hey, the Lambo won't fit us all," he says, shrugging. "Besides, this turns more heads. Maybe I should steal your date and leave you behind?"

"Nice try. We're all going," I tell him. "Avner and Apple are meeting us at Water Street."

He rolls his eyes. "That clown, Avner? He's still here? I swear I'll buy him a one-way ticket back to Israel if he promises to go."

"Come on, Oak. You love Avner."

"Sure, I do." He flashes a grin, then turns to Sydney. "So, Syd, we've got rooms at the Edition, VIP at the Punch Room, and the rooftop. You up for the Oak Williams experience?"

She hooks her arm through his, laughing. "Let's see what you've got."

****

The night goes exactly like an Oak Williams night usually goes: loud, wild, chaotic.

Paparazzi scream the second we step out of the truck, cameras flashing like lightning. Women in barely-there dresses claw for Oak's attention, while their boyfriends get bounced from the VIP line. Oak whispers something to a redhead with a body straight off a magazine cover, and she practically purrs as he pulls her inside.

Drinks flow. Security tries to keep order. Apple and Sydney hit the dance floor and vanish.

By one in the morning, Oak, Avner, and I sneak to the rooftop bar for a bourbon and a cigar. The night air is cool against my sweaty skin, and I sink into a cushioned chair, grateful for the moment of quiet.

Avner leans back, stogie in hand, his voice slurring. "Jason, enough bullshit. Why Greece? Alone?"

Oak raises an eyebrow, puffing his cigar. "Yeah, Jay-Bird. I bet you're stashing that little hottie in your suitcase so you can show her your Acropolis."

I hate lying to my best friends, but this isn't about running away; it's about finding answers. Lia sits at the center of everything. If I ever want a normal life, I need to face her or at least understand why she torched a decade of us without warning. And now that Sterling's dead, she's one of the few left who knows the truth about *The One*.

I laugh weakly. "No. Just a solo trip. Chill out, see the sights. I need some downtime, fellas. It has been a hell of a year."

Avner shakes his head, exhaling smoke. "Bullshit. Let's all go—Athens, Mykonos, Santorini. I'll book it tomorrow."

Oak flexes his biceps. "Hell, I'll call the plane tonight. Fill it with so many babes and so much booze, even Avner can get lucky. Greeks love them some Oak Williams."

"Thanks, but I'm going alone. Flight leaves from Orlando tomorrow."

Avner stares me down, suddenly deadly serious. "Jason, you're not dumb enough to meet up with Lia, are you? We all know you've still been talking to her. If you get caught, you're both done. Prison, man. She's a fugitive."

Oak nearly spits out his drink. "Lia? *Lia?* Bro, she shot you and stole the fucking laptop! You still thinking about her? She almost killed you! What about the hot little blonde? Is she fair game if you're in prison?"

I wave them down, glancing around to make sure no one hears. "Keep it down. I told you. I haven't talked to her since she left."

Avner takes a long drag, eyes locked on me. "You'd better be telling the truth, Jason. If you screw this up, not even Oak's money or my connections will save you."

CHAPTER 25

I board Lufthansa flight 1410, nine hours from Orlando to Frankfurt. My head still pounds from last night's whiskey, but I'm grateful I splurged on a business-class seat.

It is evening when they finally start boarding the plane, and I quickly find my seat. The flight attendant flashes a polite, practiced smile as I settle in. The cabin is quiet, and the lighting is muted. I order a bourbon on the rocks the moment we're airborne. I've got too much rattling around my head to sit still.

I'm about to break the law by meeting an international fugitive. Worse, I'm not even sure she'll show. Paranoia claws at me. My eyes flick across the cabin—a man two rows back, narrow shoulders in a zip-up hoodie, watches me too carefully. FBI? U.S. Marshals? Or maybe just a traveler.

When Lia stole the Safe Harbor evidence and vanished overseas, I was stuck in Tampa General with a freak heart condition. Even after I recovered, Zeke dragged his feet on canceling the arrest warrant. A guard sat outside my hospital door for two weeks—partly to keep the bad guys out, partly to keep me in.

Eventually, I convinced everyone I wasn't part of the theft. Lia acted alone. But Zeke never fully bought it. For months, I could spot the Bureau tails a mile away while they teamed up with foreign partners to reel her in.

I knew the moment I booked an international flight that alarms would go off. If I wanted to stay in the clear, I'd have to be careful—and rely on every bit of Shin Bet training I still remembered.

Get a grip, Jason. You're just another guy headed to Greece—no big deal. Play the part.

But in the back of my mind, I know better. Lia shot me the last time I saw her, and yet I can't stay away. My life is a bleak grayscale without her in it. The thought of seeing her again hits me harder than the bourbon.

"Your drink, sir," the attendant says, her accent lilting, Nordic-sounding. She hands me a mini bottle of Johnnie Walker and a glass with one oversized ice cube.

Lia and I spoke in code before I left. We both expect company throughout the trip. She's arranged for one of her people—Theo—to collect me in Athens. She swears I can trust him. I'll have to take her word for it.

I skip the airplane meal and order another bourbon. Eleven hours to Athens, with a layover in Frankfurt. My plan: catch a buzz, half-watch a movie, and doze. I close my eyes, picturing Lia's face.

I wake up to that prickly feeling on the back of my neck. Spidey sense is still intact. Someone is watching. The man in 3A snaps his eyes away too quickly. Hoodie, cargo pants—but he carries himself like a Fed. Feels like a Zeke man.

I slip on my headphones, mind working through exit strategies. Soon, I'll be on the run again. No one will track me. I'll melt into the Greek isles, untraceable and unseen.

****

The plane touches down, and even the lie-flat seat hasn't spared my back. Frankfurt is a blur of pretzels and beer. As I weave through the terminal, I catch the eyes of a few security guards watching me a little too closely. I ignore them, grab a Warsteiner, and keep walking.

In Athens, it's 5:30 p.m. and already sweltering. I ignore a half-dozen texts from Avner and stride through arrivals, carry-on in hand. The guy from 3A is there too, trailing me by a respectable distance. I kill time at a tourist kiosk, pretending to study a brochure about boat tours, but I notice him flashing hand signals to a local in a dark T-shirt.

I can't stop thinking about who else he could be with. If it isn't the FBI, then what? Something darker, something more ruthless? Maybe in a foreign country, it is easier to make me disappear.

Whoever it is, I need to lose them and get the hell out of the airport.

I duck into the bathroom marked *WC*, lock myself into a stall, and swap into shorts, flip-flops, and a faded gray baseball cap. I slip out behind a giant of a man and scan the crowd.

There—a guy with a sign that reads *Mr. Smith*. I tilt my chin toward the exit, and he falls in beside me.

Stepping outside is like opening an oven door. Thankfully, his Opel Astra is idling close by, air conditioner blasting. We pull away, no sign of my watchers.

Game on.

Theo doesn't speak, and I'm okay with the silence as he weaves through traffic like he's playing *Grand Theft Auto*. After fifteen minutes of honks and close calls, he hands me a bottle of water and turns up a disco remix of "Dust in the Wind."

Athens rushes past the windows, a riot of color and decay.

"What's with all the graffiti?" I ask.

He glances at me, one eyebrow lifted. "Artists and criminals. The government used to paint it over, but the next day it was back. Like a spider web."

"Why don't they arrest people?"

He snorts. "We have bigger problems. You can kill a man here and serve twelve years. Run drugs, you get five. Nobody cares about graffiti except the tourists."

I crack a smile. "You don't work for the chamber of commerce, I take it."

Theo laughs, eyes checking his mirrors. "Hold on," he says flatly before cutting across three lanes and taking an exit, narrowly missing a bus and a handful of pedestrians.

He pulls into a side street, squeezes into a parking spot, then tells me, "Follow me."

We slip into a small café that smells like burnt sugar and coffee. The menu is written in half-Greek, half-English. Theo orders us two thick, dark coffees and a honey-drenched pastry that tastes like heaven but leaves my teeth aching.

"If the coffee is too sweet, order it *metrios* or Americano," he advises.

"Thanks."

He watches the empty café with a predator's stillness. Outside, a skinny man in a plastic chair takes long drags off a cigarette, eyes darting.

"They'll find you again," Theo says calmly. "But we'll keep you ahead of them. Tonight, you stay low. Tomorrow, act like a tourist. I'll spot your tail."

"Who *are* they?"

He shrugs. "Not my business."

We finish the coffee, then head back outside. Theo unlocks a battered green Suzuki Jeep and tosses my bag in the back. He merges into traffic without hesitation, ignoring angry horns and weaving scooters. He doesn't say a word about switching cars.

Athens is a patchwork of concrete and chaos. The apartment buildings resemble a game of drunken Jenga, with their balconies crowded with laundry, faded awnings, and rusted air conditioners. The hills outside town burn with late-summer color—dusty greens, volcanic browns, and shocks of wildflowers.

"This is your hotel," Theo announces, pulling up to a building with a sign that reads *Urban Stripes*. He parks half on the sidewalk, hazard lights flashing.

"Talk to the concierge," he says. "Tomorrow, play dumb. I'll be around. Don't do anything stupid tonight. Athens can be a dangerous place."

I nod, grab my bag, and step out. My pulse is already pounding.

The game of cat and mouse has officially begun.

CHAPTER 26

The hotel sits on a narrow street stretching for miles, choked with parked cars. Some of them look abandoned, caked in grime, and plastered with tickets curling under the sun. Cafés and small shops fill the brick street, many shuttered, vacant, their windows dark. Across the street, an old church leans into ruin, its white walls crumbling, the wooden door sagging as if it might collapse. A tall tree looks to be growing through the roof, reaching for the heavens.

Urban Stripes is wedged between two taller buildings; its white facade so narrow it looks ready to burst. Ten balconies stick out, staggered, as if slapped on wherever space allowed. The windows come in every shape and size. The lobby, bright and tastefully modern, feels like stepping into a different world.

I've come halfway across the world to find Lia. But first, I need to figure out who's following me and give them the slip. I don't know if they're here to kill me or arrest me, and I'm not waiting to find out.

"Welcome to Urban Stripes," says the woman behind the minimalist reception desk. Her shoulder-length curls are streaked with gray, her big-framed blue glasses giving her an owl-like intelligence.

"And you are?"

I peek at the name on my new ID before replying. "Leo Samaras."

Her eyes flicker to her computer. "Of course, Mr. Samaras. Two nights, prepaid. Room number three." She slides an old-fashioned silver key across the counter. "Would you like to upgrade to an Acropolis view? It's lit up and stunning at night."

"Thanks, but no," I say, "tight budget."

As I turn to leave, she calls after me. "Mr. Samaras, a package was left for you."

My pulse jumps. I take the package, nodding. Out on the street again, I scan up and down. Nothing looks out of place. No watchers, at least none I can see. I ignore the creaky elevator and take the stairs, gripping the package tightly.

The apartment is brighter than I expected. Sunlight floods across polished wood floors and a colorful rug. A sliding door opens onto a narrow balcony. There are two bedrooms, a single bathroom, and a modest kitchen with a fridge and a table set for six.

I close the drapes, then lock the door, triple-checking it. Only then do I set the package on the coffee table among a spread of glossy Greek tourism magazines. Carefully, I unwrap the brown paper.

A note falls out.

> Welcome to Athens, my love. Find one burner phone and a thousand euros. For the next two days, act like a tourist. See the Acropolis, enjoy the museum, and drink coffee in the cafés of Plaka. Walk the city casually so I can watch for any tails. At night, drink wine and talk to pretty Greek women (but not too pretty). Theo will be in touch. Burn this note immediately.
>
> Mrs. Smith

My heart hammers. Lia is close.

I have so many emotions swirling through my mind like clothes in a washing machine. I'm excited to see Lia, but the cuts are deep. What will it be like when I see her? Which emotions will win?

I step out to the balcony, a breeze pushing against me as I light the note in a small ashtray. The paper crumbles to embers, dancing in the wind and giving off an acrid, smoky odor. I scan the street below, hoping she's out there. Watching.

But I wonder who else might be watching too.

CHAPTER 27

I rise early to join a group of Iowans on a tour of the Acropolis. They're easy to spot, wearing bright yellow shirts stamped with a black Hawkeye on the back. They chatter excitedly as we pile onto a bus that crawls from hotel to hotel, scooping up more foreigners until we're packed tight.

At the base of the hill, the guide waves an orange flag like she's leading soldiers. She hands out passes and headphones. The crowd is massive—a churning sea of voices and cell phones snapping pictures. Through the headset, her voice flows with practiced ease, narrating centuries of history as we begin to climb.

The Propylaea feels like a gate to another time, columns rising in the brilliant sun. As I step through, a chill moves down my spine.

I wish you were here, Lia. Will we ever be able to take a real trip together?

My family's blood runs through this country. I feel it in my bones. But even here, the hunter and hunted in me never rest. I scan every face in the crowd, searching. For a second, near the Parthenon, I think I see her—but the woman turns, and she's just another stranger.

I know I'm being watched. Paranoia is my second skin, but I trust my instincts. I double back, weaving through tourists. Sure enough, two tails. Amateur. If Lia's out there, she'll spot them in no time.

We begin our descent of the hill after hours of posed photos and stale jokes from the guide. Then I notice a disturbance: a handful of men scanning tourists' faces against a photo. They're clad in light-blue short-sleeve shirts, dark pants, tactical boots, and reflective vests labeled "POLICE."

I hesitate, wanting to avoid trouble, and try to turn back up the hill—but the crowd surges around me like an impenetrable wave. As we edge closer, I drop my head to avoid eye contact. That's when a heavy hand clamps on my shoulder, spinning me to the side. He lifts my chin, holding the photo to my face. My stomach drops: the paper reads "Jason Miles."

Panic surges. Only a day in Greece, and trouble has tracked me down.

A flicker of relief—the photo is just a copy of my driver's license, and I am clean-shaven.

In broken English, he asks, "How you name?"

I pull out my fake passport, pointing to the name, and reply calmly, "Leo Samaras."

The guide swoops in, her voice sharp as a whip: "He is a tourist with our group, you kópanos!"

The officer gestures with one hand, then steps aside to let me pass.

My heart is still hammering all the way to the Acropolis Museum. I have no idea what that was about, but the Greek police just joined my list of pursuers.

Once at the museum, I calm myself in the bathroom, splashing cool water on my face. I pull my hat lower and join the group. We walk among the statues, the weathered stone, the shards of a civilization that once ruled the known world—it all makes me feel small. In a hundred years, no one will care about Jason Miles and his troubles. Maybe no one will even remember my name.

Syd flashes into my mind, uninvited.

I didn't see that coming.

After a few more stops, we are sent on our own to the old

neighborhood of Athens. Plaka is filled with shops, cafes, and tavernas. I duck into a souvenir store, buy a cheap hat, a touristy T-shirt, and new sandals. I change in the cramped bathroom, then slip out, blending into the foot traffic. I'm sure the watchers know where I'm staying, but I need to practice my escape skills so I can disappear when it matters most.

As I get closer to the hotel, I check my list of foods I want to try. I settle on a café with an outdoor patio. A waitress with long dark hair and olive skin takes my order for stuffed grape leaves and a glass of retsina. The leaves are perfect—tangy, filled with lamb, rice, and onion, bright with lemon and olive oil. For a few minutes, I let myself relax. I finish the wine and order another.

The waitress returns. "What would you like next?"

"What do you suggest?"

She grins. "Chicken souvlaki."

I nod. I let my eyes drift across the street, pretending to people-watch. A man and a woman take a table a few rows away, both glancing at me when they think I'm not looking. A guy on a scooter buzzes past twice in five minutes.

They're everywhere. Or I'm losing my mind. Maybe both. Maybe I'll never see Lia again.

The waitress sets down a plate of grilled chicken skewers with warm pita and cool tzatziki. I eat half, wrap up the rest, and head back to the hotel.

Before leaving that morning, I'd hung the *Do Not Disturb* sign on my door. Lia's note went up in smoke last night, so nothing incriminating is left. Still, I need to be sure no one has been inside.

First, I check a tiny piece of clear tape wedged where the door meets the jamb. There is no doubt it's been disturbed. Next, I look at the piece of candy I'd placed behind the door—I took a picture of its exact position before leaving. Now it's shifted, inches away from where I left it.

Someone's been here.

I reach instinctively for my Glock—but it's thousands of miles away, back in Tampa. A cold realization hits me: whoever came inside might still be here.

CHAPTER 28

I slide off my shoes and move soundlessly across the floor into the kitchen. My eyes lock on the chef's knife in the butcher block. I grab it in a forward grip, blade angled up, my fingers wrapped tight around the handle. Avner drilled knife-fighting into me back in Israel—*survival*, he always said.

I learned that lesson the hard way when I was on the run and a tweaked-out thug buried a blade in my thigh. It took months to heal, and the scar still reminds me of what happens if you get sloppy.

If it is life or death, I'll sink the blade into an artery and bleed out whoever broke in. Carotids are easiest. The heart is messier, riskier. The femoral artery, if they leave me no other choice.

I pause, listening. There—a faint rustle from the bedroom.

I move like a panther, silent, controlled, ready to strike. A figure crosses the doorway, unaware of me. Male. Thinning hair. Something glints in his hand. I step behind him and place the blade against his neck.

"Don't move," I whisper. "Who are you, and what are you doing in my room?"

His hand trembles, and a bottle of disinfectant crashes to the floor. I spot a cleaning cart in the corner.

His voice cracks in broken English. "I clean, sir. So sorry."

I lower the knife but keep my eyes on him. "Didn't you see the *Do Not Disturb* sign?"

He stammers, hands up, rattling on in Greek I don't follow. Then he bolts, abandoning his cart and disappearing down the hall.

Perfect. I nearly murdered the cleaning guy: new country, same Jason.

I let out a long breath, place the knife back in the block, and shove the cart into the hallway, praying the hotel doesn't call the cops. The wine buzz is completely gone, replaced by a stone-cold sense of shame.

My pocket starts to buzz—the burner.

"Hello."

A voice I'd kill to hear. "Mr. Smith, go out on the balcony. Your room could be bugged."

My heart spikes as I slide the glass door open. Cool air hits my face. "It's you," I whisper. "When can I see you?"

"Cover your mouth," she says. "They can read lips. Theo and I've had eyes on you since you landed. Nice job acting like a tourist."

I cover my mouth with my hand. "I *am* a tourist."

A soft laugh. "A gorgeous one." Then her tone hardens. "Unfortunately, you're being followed."

"Yeah, I noticed. Who are they? And why are the local cops after me?"

"Multiple teams," she says. "You did well this afternoon. The local police are working with either Avner or Zeke. They just want to rattle you. The rest are your government's people, the ones who followed you off the flight, and a few of Avner's men. Zeke's crew wants me. Avner's are trying to protect you. But the third group…" She lowers her voice. "Professionals. Assassins. Only I'd recognize them."

Takes one to know one.

The situation's unraveling fast. Zeke clearly knows I came looking for Lia and sent a team to tail me. No surprise there. I'd bet he also called in the locals—standard play when the Bureau's hunting fugitives abroad. Avner's people are here too, trying to keep me alive. I appreciate it, but I'm ditching them along with everyone else.

It's the assassins Lia spotted that worry me. They're not cops or agents, they're cleaners. And they have to be connected to Safe Harbor or *The One*.

"Are you safe, Lia?"

Her answer comes too fast. "I'm fine."

A beat of silence.

"Tomorrow," she says, "four a.m. Leave the hotel through the alley. Hop the fence. Theo will be waiting. Leave your luggage behind—it's probably been tampered with. Theo has a new bag for you."

My stomach knots. I rub my pinky with the missing nail. "Am I going to see you? I need to."

She hesitates. "Get some food to go and stay in tonight. Love you, baby."

Then the line goes dead.

****

Avner paces the Bluebird office, crushing a tennis ball in one hand.

"Would you *relax*?" Apple calls out from her desk. "Jason's a grown man. He'll be fine."

Avner scowls. "The asshole doesn't answer my calls. Only my texts. Says he's fine. That's it."

Apple stands and rubs his shoulders, trying to calm him. "You trained Jason yourself.

He's probably better at Krav Maga than you."

Closing his eyes, he responds, "You know I have a sixth sense. Jason is looking for Lia, and that comes with a lot of problems. And there's that little thing about people wanting him dead. He's also not better than me."

Apple sighs. "You can't protect everyone. I love that about you, but Jason's making his own choices. I'm guessing you have eyes on him, right?"

Avner raises one eyebrow. "Who, me?" And what was that about love?"

"What did you do?"

"I might have... put a tracker in his suitcase. And assigned a team. To look out for him."

Apple tilts her head, amused. "And?"

"He's in Athens. Playing tourist. Although the local cops nearly snagged him."

She laughs lightly. "So... he's doing exactly what he said he was going to do."

Avner grimaces. "No, exactly what *Lia* would tell him to do."

Apple lowers her voice. "Any sign of her?"

Avner shakes his head and starts working on the tennis ball again. "Of course not. I also trained her, and she's the best I've ever seen. You wouldn't see her if she were standing in this room."

Apple plants a kiss on his cheek. "I have class. Stop worrying so much. I'm sure your guys are good and will keep him safe."

Avner half-smiles, then taps out one more message to Jason:

> You're playing with fire.
> Get home before you get burned.
> Or worse.

CHAPTER 29

I dress and brush my teeth with the glow of my cell phone flashlight. My carry-on goes under the bed, out of sight. I slip down the stairs and ease through a back exit into a walled-off courtyard behind the hotel—time to get out of Athens. And get out clean.

It's four in the morning, already heavy with heat. The courtyard reeks of piss—animal, human, who knows. All the other rooms are dark and silent. Maybe the watchers are awake, but they can't see this corner. That's why Lia picked this hotel. She thinks of everything.

I climb the back wall with nothing but my real and fake IDs and some cash. I have a burner phone and my cell, both placed in a Faraday pouch to block tracking. Theo waits on the other side, engine running in a black Mercedes van with the lights off. I settle into the second row, and he passes me a steaming coffee.

We drive twenty-five minutes through the quiet, rougher side of Athens before pulling up a few blocks from the port.

"You're booked on a jet boat to Santorini," he says. "Keep the burner charged and on. There's a suitcase in the back with clothes and a ticket."

I check the new disguise: cargo shorts, linen shirt, sandals, and a floppy tan hat that screams *GREECE*.

"A tourist, huh?"

Theo cracks a grin. "Lia says if you can't disappear in Santorini as a tourist, you're the worst spy ever."

Real funny, Lia.

He hands me a passport for a guy named Dimitrios Siampaus. We shake hands, and I disappear into the dark.

****

"Bad news, Zeke. Somehow, he gave us the slip."

It's three a.m. in Tampa. Zeke rubs the stubble on his jaw and takes a drink of cold coffee. Then he explodes into the phone.

"What do you mean gave you the slip? You are trained agents paired up with Greek law enforcement, and you let Jason Miles vanish?"

A pause. "Sorry, boss. We went in heavy at nine after seeing no movement all night. His suitcase is still under the bed. He's traveling as Leo Samaras, but no sign of him or the ex."

Zeke forces his voice low, steady. "He's gone. Turkey, or any of a thousand Aegean Islands. You need to find him. I know Jason is meeting Lia. I can feel it. I still don't know if he was in on the scam, and we'll never know if we don't find her." His voice starts to rise again. "And we can't catch her if we keep fucking losing him. Do you understand what I am saying?"

"We'll hit facial recognition, tap contacts at the ports. We'll catch up and grab them both."

"You better," Zeke interrupts. "Or you can make that vacation permanent."

****

Santorini lives up to the hype. When I step off the boat, a thousand-foot cliff looms overhead. I need to find Lia today.

"Gondola or donkey?" a man asks, hauling ropes around the dock.

"Excuse me?"

"To the top—you want the gondola or the donkey?"

I glance at the gondolas, where several security cameras are pointed at arriving travelers.

"Donkey."

He shrugs and takes my cash, then hands me over to another guy who helps me up and ties me to a line of many donkeys. Mentions that mine is named Morty.

We start the clumsy climb up the steep, cobbled trail. The sea below glitters in the early sun. Whitewashed houses cling to the cliffs like dabs of paint. The donkey stinks, but the scenery is worth it.

At the top, I stand in awe of the caldera, the bright blue domes, and churches perched against the sky.

Lia, where are you? You should see this.

My burner buzzes.

"How did you like your new furry friend?"

I scan the street, searching. Tourists mill around, oblivious.

"It was fine, but he was kind of a jackass," I say.

She giggles, and something warm blooms in my chest.

"I need to see you today."

"Maybe. First, we check if you're clean. Rent a scooter and head to the monastery at the top of the island. Drive around for a while. It's open road, so we should be able to spot a tail."

I hesitate. "Hey, Lia?"

"Yeah?"

"I love you."

"I love you, too, Jay. Now move."

I rent a cherry-red scooter and cruise twisting roads through white houses and bright blue domes. After an hour, I kick off my sandals on a black-sand beach. The sand burns my feet, so I wade into the cool sea.

With time to kill, I stop for grilled octopus and a cold beer. The waiter, all smiles, sets down a small glass of ouzo. *When in Greece.*

I check my phone. Five angry messages from Avner. Two from Oak, wanting to meet in Mykonos with "some cuties."

Then one from Syd:

> I've been thinking of you on your adventure. I hope Tully Mars finds what he is looking for. I miss you, Syd

I love the reference to Jimmy Buffett's short story. She seems to get me. Why am I here chasing a memory when someone back home could help me find something like normal? I am confused by my feelings. I think I miss her, too, but I know I need to pack that emotion away. Later. Always later.

My time in Athens proves that nothing is normal for me. I'm being hunted—by friends, by enemies, maybe by both. Some are after Lia. I know that much. But others might prefer I never make it out of Greece alive. Out here, surrounded by endless blue, it wouldn't be hard to vanish for good.

I finish the ride to the monastery of Prophet Elias. The scooter barely makes it, but I reach the top, where a giant cross marks the summit and bells echo off the mountain. I'm snapping pictures when my burner rings.

"Jay, you're burned. Two jeeps on the way up, along with a Mercedes, and motorcycles. Get out."

I spin around. "There are only two ways down, Lia, and only one of them keeps me alive."

"If you can't slip away, I'll come in hot," she promises.

Moments later, the jeeps grind to a stop. Six men pile out.

"Jason Miles!" one calls. "Come with us."

I raise my hands, faking confusion. "My name's Dimitrios Siampaus. I don't know who Jason is."

They barely react before two motorcycles roar up, men in leather jackets hopping off. The leader has a broken nose and a face full of stories.

"We're here for Jason Miles," he growls.

A Mercedes skids in, doors flying open, more weapons drawn. Eleven guns pointed at each other in seconds. Everyone looks confused.

"Let's go, Jason," an Israeli accent calls from the Mercedes.

I stand there, frozen.

The Jason Miles fan club showed up in force.

The jeep guy tries to play peacemaker. "We're Americans. Stand down."

"Not happening," Broken Nose says.

Then monks appear. Nine of them, brown robes, big crosses, and long beards. They file out, calm and unbothered.

"This is a place of God," one bellows. "Lower your weapons before the police arrive."

One by one, they bring down their arsenal.

I lift my fake ID. "Father, I'm just a tourist. I came to pray."

He takes my ID, studies it, and passes it around the monks—my pulse hammers.

Then, with terrifying grace, the monks pull rifles from under their robes.

This is definitely not normal.

"On your knees," the abbot orders. "Thieves have been plaguing our monastery. We are prepared."

Weapons hit the ground.

The Israeli pleads, "Father, we're here for his safety."

I point at him. "I don't know any of them."

The abbot nods toward me. "You go. We'll let the police sort them out."

I don't have to be told twice. I am on my scooter, ignoring the protests of the assembled men. I smile as I pass several police cars heading up the mountain with their sirens blaring. I may have avoided capture for the moment, but I know my time is running out.

CHAPTER 30

After my narrow escape on Santorini thanks to help from above, I move through the Greek Isles, with a quick stopover in Kuşadasi, Turkey. Lia and I still talk, but the ambush at the monastery has left us both snake-bit and wary.

I land on Rhodes, then take a bus an hour south to Lindos, where whitewashed houses cling to the hills below an acropolis. I hope this will be the place where Lia and I finally reconnect. But then I spot a tail in the crowd, and I'm forced to vanish again.

The entire trip to Greece has been a disaster. Five days of shifting hotel rooms, changing clothes, circling alleys, scanning balconies, hoping for a glimpse of Lia. I'm scheduled to fly out of Athens tomorrow. Lia told me to spend my last day in Nafplio, a beautiful port town, but she's gone silent since.

For the first time, I think maybe I've shaken all the watchers. I wander the city for hours, doubling back, ducking through souvenir shops, trying to buy anonymity along with cheap linen shirts. I sit in street cafés until my legs go numb, eyes searching every face that passes, half-expecting Lia to appear out of nowhere.

What was I thinking? Lia is one of the most wanted people on earth. If she's caught, she'll disappear into a prison cell for decades. Did I really think she'd just waltz across a sunny Greek street, take my hand, and we'd pick up where we left off? I feel like a fool. I keep wishing for normalcy but chasing chaos.

I also need Lia if I am ever going to get closer to *The One*. With Sterling dead, I don't even know where to start. I know she can point me in the right direction, or maybe we can take them on together. That's out the window if she doesn't show.

It's late by the time I give up. Another solitary dinner, another night alone. Even the delicious moussaka tastes like sawdust in my mouth. A few glasses of wine only deepen the gloom as I walk back to my hotel, shoulders slumped, tail between my legs. Lovers stroll by, wrapped up in each other, drunk on Greece's impossible beauty.

Good for fucking you. I hope you get hit by a bus.

Inside the lobby, I glance around, hopeful, but there's nothing. My room is exactly as I left it, sterile and empty. I sniff the air, hoping to get a waft of her perfume. I fling open the French doors to let in the cool, salty air. After packing for tomorrow and washing the travel grime off my face, I sigh loudly and kill the lights.

That's when I see it—a shadow sliding along the far wall, followed by the lightest touch against my arm.

A voice, close enough to pierce the dark.

"Hello, Jay."

Lightning crackles through my entire body. I twist toward the voice—and there she is, as vivid as a dream. Lia. Her sun-kissed hair tangled around her face, skin burnished bronze, eyes catching the faint glow from the streetlights outside. She is breathtaking.

For a heartbeat, I think I'm hallucinating. I pull her into my arms, our lips crushing together in a kiss that feels like finding my way back to where I belong. I drink in her scent, terrified that if I blink, she'll vanish.

"Lia," I breathe against her mouth. "Where the hell have you been? I looked everywhere."

She touches my lips with one finger, quieting me. "I had to be sure you weren't followed," she whispers. "I've been watching you since you arrived. God, I've missed you."

"I have a thousand questions—"

"Not now," she says, eyes dark and hungry. "Take me to bed, Jay. Just… love me."

I gather her in my arms and lay her down, heart hammering. The months apart have been full of denial, and now I'm desperate for her. We move together, frantic, until there is no past and no future, only the present.

Hours later, we collapse in a tangled heap, breathless, and finally let sleep swallow us whole.

CHAPTER 31

I'm still dreaming of Lia when the door explodes. A squad of Greek police storms in, guns drawn, screaming orders I can't understand. I roll over, half-blind with panic, reaching for her—but rough hands wrench me out of bed and slam me face-first onto the cold tile floor. I'm in nothing but my boxers, cheek pressed against grit and dust, heart hammering.

A knee drives into my back, grinding my ribs, while someone tip ties my wrists tightly. I taste blood where I've bitten my tongue.

Light is streaming through the windows. The French doors to the balcony are wide open, white curtains flapping in the breeze. The police are tearing the place apart, yanking open drawers and closet doors.

"Speak English!" I manage to croak, trying to slow everything down, to get my bearings.

One of them—thick mustache, stale cigarette breath—leans down so close I can smell the bitter coffee on his tongue. "Where is she?" he growls.

"Where is who?" I ask, scanning the chaos, trying to spot Lia. Panic claws at me. *Is she still here? Hiding?*

The mustached officer backhands me, hard enough to rattle my teeth. "Don't play games. We know you were with the woman, Lia, or whatever name she uses. I can still smell her perfume."

My cheek is on fire, wrists burning in the tip ties. My mind spins. Lia must have slipped out while I was sleeping. Please tell me she got away.

"There's been a mistake," I lie, fighting for calm. "I'm traveling alone. On vacation. My name is…"

"Get him up," he instructs the other officers. "We'll see if some time in a filthy Greek jail cell jogs your memory."

They allow me to pull on a T-shirt and green cargo pants but leave me barefoot. As they march me through the lobby, tourists stare over their half-finished breakfasts, eyes wide, forks frozen midair. A row of police cars waits outside, blue lights flashing against the whitewashed hotel walls.

The morning heat punches me in the face. I try to appear dignified, but I must look like hell. "I want a lawyer," I shout, though I doubt they care.

They don't even glance at me. One cop shoves me into the back seat of the nearest car. My head smacks the door frame on the way in, pain blooming behind my eyes.

The mustached officer takes the front passenger seat while another sits beside me, his hand resting on a holstered pistol. The siren wails as we peel away, tires screeching across sunbaked asphalt.

My head is throbbing from the rough handling, my wrists raw. I breathe in shaky, shallow gasps, trying to slow my racing pulse. I rub my pinky, the one missing a nail, as if it might tether me to reality.

Where the hell are you, Lia? Are you safe?

Ten minutes later, a black Mercedes appears behind us, closing the gap fast. The officers start shouting in Greek, tension crackling through the car. The Mercedes swerves up alongside and, without warning, smashes into us, sending us spinning like a toy top.

The world tilts and slams sideways—metal shrieks. Unable to brace myself with my hands, my head bounces against the window as we spin across the road.

A white van comes out of nowhere, and men pour out of both vehicles. The police are slow to react, and the attackers begin to riddle the car with bullets, killing the officers. One of the bullets tears into my shoulder, causing me to scream. I try to grab the dead officer's weapon, but the attackers pull me from the car and place a bag over my head before throwing me in the van. They pile around me, and one of them places a towel on my bleeding shoulder, but I can't tell if they're trying to help or keep me alive for something else.

Things have gone from bad to catastrophic. I wonder if Lia has forsaken me again.

CHAPTER 32

"We need to talk," Zeke snaps, slamming the door of the Bluebird Bungalow behind him.

Berta jumps up from her chair, waving a finger in his face. "Oh no, you do not, little man. You'd better calm down if you want to talk to us."

Zeke brushes her off and fixes his glare on Avner.

"We have a problem. Jason's gone."

Avner barely looks up from the Sudoku puzzle he's working on at the desk. "I already know, Zeke. We had him under surveillance in Santorini, but we lost track of him. Facial recognition is catching up. We're maybe a city behind."

Zeke snorts. "As usual, your Israeli buddies are trailing the FBI. We tracked him to Nafplio—but there's been an incident."

That gets everyone's attention. Avner, Goat, and Apple rise at the same time.

"What kind of incident?" Avner asks, his voice cold.

Zeke rubs his temples, exhaling hard. "Greek police picked him up early in the morning. We think they just missed Lia. They were transporting him back to Athens when their vehicle was hit."

Apple mutters, "Oh my God."

Goat leans forward. "Is Jason okay?"

Zeke hesitates. His silence is the loudest thing in the room.

"Is he dead?" Avner asks, not even flinching.

Zeke sighs. "All the police were killed. Jason's gone."

Goat shakes his head. "Good. Not the part about the cops, but Jason missing means he's still breathing. Who has him? What do we need to do? Has anyone asked for money?"

"We don't know," Zeke says. "But there's more. They found his blood inside the vehicle."

****

I lose track of time as the van drives for what feels like hours, twisting down endless side roads, doubling back. It's meant to disorient me, and it's working. I'm weak from the bullet wound, bleeding through my shirt. A wave of nausea rises, and I swallow to keep it down. The men with me ignore every question I try to ask.

I know this is bad. The FBI might've ordered the police to storm the hotel and drag me in, but I have no doubt *The One* is behind the kidnapping. Still, why not just kill me with the others? Is this payback for Safe Harbor? I shove the thought of another torture session out of my foggy head and focus on staying alive.

Eventually, we stop. They pull me out into air thick with the stink of jet fuel, forcing me up a rickety metal staircase. I hear the engine already humming—a private jet.

Inside the plane, rough hands strip off my shirt. Someone wipes down the wound, then sews it shut without even a painkiller. I grit my teeth so hard I taste blood. They shove noise-canceling headphones over my ears and black goggles over my eyes.

A needle stabs my arm, flooding me with a warm, weightless rush. I know it's the drugs, but I don't have the energy to fight it. I accept my lack of control and feel myself being pulled out further into the unknown.

****

My eyes open slowly—pitch black. A pounding headache rattles my skull, and the air smells stale. For a second, I don't know where I am. Then it comes back—the ambush, the van, the plane. I try to move my arms, but they won't cooperate. They aren't tied, but my muscles feel useless. It feels like my shoulder is on fire, like someone jammed a hot poker in the hole.

I hear Avner's voice in the back of my mind—*stay alive until we can find you.*

I shift, trying to stand, but a heavy hand pushes me back into what feels like a soft recliner. Panic surges, but I fight it, breathing hard.

A huge screen flickers on in front of me, blinding white in the darkness. My eyes water as I squint to focus. Then, in a thunder of noise, flashing light, and static, a face appears.

He looks like a dignified grandfather: silver hair, a short beard, an expensive suit, and a black dress shirt open at the collar—calm, dangerous eyes.

"Hello, Jason," he says, with a faint European accent I can't place. "Finally, we meet. I'm sorry about the chaos in Greece, but you left us no choice. The bullet was never meant for you."

I swallow hard, trying to stay upright, rubbing the finger where the nail used to be. "Who the hell are you?"

"I think you know."

I study his face, trying to burn it into my memory. "What's your name?" I demand.

He lights a cigar, a tiny grin forming. "You can call me Benjamin."

"Benjamin, are you the leader of *The One* or just another fool like Terrance Browning?"

He starts to laugh as he blows smoke from his mouth. "I respect arrogance in the face of certain failure. Terrance was a fool who could not handle his business. There's no point struggling, Jason," Benjamin says calmly. "There's nothing you can do. Sit back. Let's work through our differences."

"Work through our differences?" I laugh, bitter. "You destroy lives. Steal money. And now you've shown me your face. Why?"

Suddenly, the screen glitches, and another face replaces his—Oak. *What the fuck?*

Oak's voice booms out. "Jay-Bird, you need to join us. You and I are brothers. We can do this together. In your heart, you know I am part of the movement. Come join the family."

The screen glitches again, and the President of the United States appears, calm and official in a blue suit with a red tie. "Jason, you don't want to be on the wrong side of history. Join us."

I squeeze my eyes shut, refusing to believe it. This is fake. It has to be.

The screen flickers once more, Avner's bearded face. "Jason, you are alone. There is no one you can trust. Join us."

My heart clenches. Avner would never betray me. I force myself to breathe, fighting the rising panic.

Then, my parents. Young, healthy, impossibly alive.

"Jason, sweetheart," my mother says, smiling with familiar softness. "Stop fighting. We're already so proud of you. You're already a hero. Come home to us."

"This is meant to be," my father states as he places his arm around my mom.

Something inside me snaps. I jump up, swinging, trying to smash the screen, but hands catch me, fists crashing into my ribs, knocking me back into the chair. Pain explodes in my shoulder, raw and blinding.

The screen changes—Dr. Levi, the sadist who once tortured me in Israel, standing there with a cigarette, goggles over his eyes, an apron that reads *Black Sheep of the Family*.

"Don't make me come visit, Jason," he taunts.

I scream, "You're dead! I saw you die!"

My breath comes in ragged gulps, the old panic attacks trying to bury me. I take a deep breath followed by another.

Then Lia's face. Beautiful, tragic Lia. That tiny gap between her teeth, the one I always loved.

"I'm sorry I had to give you up again, Jay," she says gently. "This is my family now. If you join us, we can be together. We can have a normal life. Wouldn't that be nice?"

Tears burn down my face. I know it's a lie. I know it.

But what if it isn't?

The screen glitches again, cycling through all their faces—chanting in perfect unison:

"Join us. Join us. Join us."

Faster and faster, a nightmare chorus drilling into my skull.

Then, with a sudden click, everything goes black.

I collapse deeper into the chair, all strength gone. My limbs refuse to move, and I slump forward. Tears streak my face, hot and endless. I try to wipe them away, but they keep coming.

The screen flickers to life, and Benjamin's face appears again. Cold, composed, merciless.

"Haven't you realized, Jason? Reality is what we say it is. It's time to pledge your loyalty to the cause. Join us and change the world. You heard your parents. You are Preferred. This is predestined."

Preferred. The word scrapes against my mind.

"What do you mean, *Preferred*? I'm just a normal guy. A year ago, I didn't even know you existed."

He responds, "But we knew you did."

A pair of strong hands clamps down on my shoulders, forcing me upright. Bile rises in my throat.

"What if I say no?" I rasp.

Benjamin tilts his head, a sad smile pulling at his mouth. "Then you leave us no choice. You and everyone you love will die."

A deep sadness runs through me. I think of everyone I've lost—my parents, Scott, even Sterling, all gone because of this madness. And now Lia has vanished again. I can't risk losing anyone else.

Something tightens around my neck, a wire biting into my skin. A garrote. I feel its steel edge cutting flesh, drawing a trickle of blood—my pulse pounds against it.

I raise my hands, choking out the words. "I'll join you."

CHAPTER 33

Sunlight slices across my face and jolts me awake. I'm on a strange bed in a strange room, blinking at a patterned ceiling. I turn over, my vision swimming. A man sits in the corner, scrolling through a phone, legs crossed casually. The alarm clock reads 9 a.m.

He wears a black suit, open at the collar, his hair streaked silver and artfully tousled. His beard is gray, sculpted, and medium length. His face is ruggedly handsome, like an aging actor trying to hang on to his prime.

"Who the hell are you?" I croak. "Where am I?"

He smiles, almost playfully. "My name's George. I'd shake your hand, Jason, but I'd rather you put on some pants first."

"George," I repeat, trying to anchor myself. "Okay. But where the hell am I?"

George rises, tall and athletic, the custom suit hugging him perfectly. "Washington, DC. Think of me as your… tour guide. Get dressed and meet me in Peacock Alley. We have an important meeting." He nods toward a set of clothes laid out on the couch.

I groan, rolling onto my sore shoulder. Memories flutter back: a dark room, a flickering screen, the impossible images of family and friends begging me to join these lunatics. Being shot. Being beaten. It's hazy, but the pain is real.

George studies me, almost kindly, as if reading my mind. "That was unfortunate. I hate it when things get ugly. But the bullet passed through clean. They patched you up. Just a flesh wound. You'll live."

I swallow, fighting to stand. "What's Peacock Alley?"

He chuckles lightly. "Just get dressed, Mr. Preferred," he says, then slips out the door.

Preferred. There it is again. Hanging around like a rain cloud.

In the bathroom, the toiletries are laid out as if I'm in some five-star spa. I shower, shave, and gingerly dress. My body is sore, and I am groggy, but at least I'm not dead.

The suit George left fits perfectly, as do the brown dress shoes and crisp white shirt. My wallet is on the nightstand, but my burner phone is nowhere to be seen.

I need to talk to Lia. Make sure she's okay. My mind flashes back to the night before everything fell apart—the way she looked at me, the way we made love. I don't know what to believe anymore. Part of me refuses to think she'd set me up. But she did deceive me once—after ten years of marriage. Maybe it doesn't matter. I still love her, even if she's forever outside my reach.

Disgust twists in my gut at the thought that I agreed to join *The One*. I'll never help these psychopaths. I'm taking in all of their faces and storing them in my memory. I have to figure out who I can trust and craft a plan. For now, I'll play along.

Why do they keep calling me Preferred? This must be important.

Once in the lobby, I piece things together. I'm at Willard Inter-Continental. Opulent, historic, and crawling with prestige. Fresh cut flowers are in large vases near two-story marble columns. They give off a sweet, earthy scent. I ask the concierge for Peacock Alley and am pointed down a hall lined with lush navy-and-gold carpet, the kind of place where monarchs and mobsters alike might cut a deal.

George is waiting at a small table midway down, three burgundy chairs around him. He lifts a delicate coffee cup in greeting.

"Suit fits?" he asks casually.

I study him up close.

Sixty, probably, too much Botox freezing his face, but still dangerous, still sharp.

A predator trying to wear a charming grin. I wonder if I can manipulate him. Take advantage of him somehow. Or will he be the next pawn in this game to die?

"It's fine," I reply, pouring myself a coffee, though my hands shake. "Why am I here? Who are we meeting? And what the hell does *Preferred* mean?"

George sips, perfectly calm, while my shoulder throbs and I rub the spot where my fingernail is missing.

"Jason, you're essential to the cause. That's all I can say—for now. You'll learn more in time. Just know that *Preferred* is not a term we use lightly. It's why you're still breathing instead of rotting at the bottom of the Mediterranean.

"How can I be important to something I don't even understand?" I snap. "I was nobody until Safe Harbor blew up. If it weren't for the bank fraud, you wouldn't even know I existed."

George gives me that gentle, consoling smile. "Trust me. We always knew who you were."

Before I can argue, a new group of men enters Peacock Alley—dark suits, earpieces, cold eyes. They move like a silent tide, clearing out the only other couple nearby. The woman protests, but her husband shushes her, and they hustle away.

And then *he* walks in.

A face I've seen a hundred times on the news. A face I shook hands with not long ago at Tampa Scientific.

My stomach turns.

The One is everywhere.

CHAPTER 34

Governor Frederick Matthews moves through the room like an athlete, long strides, radiating confidence. His eyes lock on us, and he's smiling. He's traded the usual classic suit for jeans and a sports coat, a dressed-down king among his subjects. His blonde, wavy hair is longer than last time, slicked back with something that smells expensive.

"Jason," he booms, "great to see you again. I see you've met George. Hell of a guy. Pardon the casual look—it's an office day."

George jumps up, offering a handshake which Frederick takes with both hands before turning it into some elaborate bro clasp.

I stand, uncertain, and get the same treatment—firm grip, then the hand-rotation maneuver, Frederick holding my hand a beat too long. He towers over me, staring straight down into my eyes, like he's trying to see inside my skull. The whole thing feels unsettling.

"Good to see you again, Governor," I lie. "You're... part of this?"

I knew there was something off about him—but I had no idea he was part of *The One*. Maybe even one of their leaders. I thought our investigation died with Sterling, but turns out Frederick is an even better link. If I stay close to him, I might unravel and defeat these madmen.

He grins widely, teeth perfect and blinding. Ignoring the question, he gestures for me to sit.

"Please, Jason. Thanks for meeting me in Washington. I keep staff here to lobby for Floridians' needs. And of course, this is the power base for our cause."

Like I had a choice.

We all sit. Frederick looks ridiculous, crammed into a too-small chair, knees almost at his chest like an adult in a preschool classroom. George hovers, beaming as he pours coffee, scanning the area. Frederick's security team is gone, but I'm sure they're just out of sight.

"This is my favorite hotel in the world," Frederick says, like we're best friends catching up. "The original Peacock Alley was in North Dakota, believe it or not. This place has history: political deals, big visitors. The more famous one is in New York, connecting the Waldorf and Astoria. I had the governor's mansion in Tallahassee redecorated to match. Power, Jason. That's what this place is about."

"It's quite lovely. Why do they call it Peacock Alley?" I ask.

"Back in the day, the press used the name to reference wealthy patrons, especially women, who would go to show off, like how a peacock struts proudly. Now it is about power. Influence."

I need to steer this conversation back on track. I paste on a polite smile. "So, what exactly do we do from here, Governor? What's my role?"

I'm playing my part, but I know my true role. I'm going to have to figure out how to take the governor down without risking the lives of my friends.

He leans forward, eyes never blinking. "Jason, you have a chance to make a difference. The world is shifting under our feet. Our movement has been quiet, but the day is coming when we step into the light. You can help us change history. It's your destiny."

These people are nuts.

"Why me?" I ask. "If I hadn't tripped over the tax fraud, I'd never even have heard of you."

"*Our* cause," he corrects, voice soft but sharp. "And everything happens for a reason. Maybe the fraud found you, Jason. You're what we call Preferred. You're meant to be part of this, and you always have been."

"What would your dad have thought of this? Did he know?"

Frederick's face twists as if he's swallowed vinegar. "My father was a stubborn old fool—blind, arrogant, stuck in the past. That rusted heap he loved did him a favor."

My stomach knots. This is turning into a nightmare. I force a breath and try to steer the conversation away. "Look, I'm a security consultant from Tampa, Governor. Surely, you've got someone else for this."

Frederick doesn't answer. He scans the hallway instead, as if waiting for guests.

"George will guide you," he says at last. "Your mentor. You'll speak every day. He runs a private debt fund, so you're already in the same world. And you and I will talk often too. There's a project I want you on right away."

"Not wasting any time, huh?" I ask. "First day on the job and I haven't even figured out where the bathroom or my office is."

Frederick's lips curl upward, but the smile is dead in his eyes.

"The world is unraveling, Jason. It's becoming more dangerous by the hour. The final conflict is coming. America is shrinking, and Russia and China are on the rise. They no longer fear us. That ends in destruction for everyone if we don't act."

"Again," I push, "what does that have to do with me?"

Frederick and George exchange a loaded glance. George leans in.

"You can get us access to Winnie."

CHAPTER 35

The flight from D.C. is as rough as my scrambled brain. I should be panicking about *The One* and their twisted expectations for me, but all I can think about is Lia. Did she do it to me again? Set me up? But why? Why drag me to Greece only to feed me to the wolves?

I catch myself rubbing my pinky, repeatedly, refusing to stop. My shoulder throbs, and I wash down a couple of aspirin with a bourbon from the drink cart. I replay every moment with Lia in my head, chasing the memory of her perfume, the warmth of her body, trying to block everything else out.

The meeting with Governor Frederick blindsided me. I knew he was slime—his deals with the warden reeked of corruption—but I never guessed he was a leader of *The One*. His demands and George's are outrageous. I have to find a way to take them down and keep the people I love safe. But how can I protect Lia when I don't even know where she is? It feels like a puzzle with half the pieces missing. I need to get home, go to bed, and make a plan in the morning.

When the plane slams down at Tampa International, reality hits me like a brick wall. I turn on my phone, and it vibrates to life with a tidal wave of texts and emails. I can only imagine what Avner and Oak are thinking. Syd has also left half a dozen voicemails.

As I step off the plane and into the terminal, Zeke, Gloria, and two massive FBI agents in suits and ties block my way.

Oh, perfect. Just what I need.

"Jason Miles, come with us," Zeke says, his voice flat, as if we're strangers.

"What the hell is this, Zeke? I'm tired, and I want to go home."

"Yeah, and I want a fucking Ferrari," he shoots back. "Looks like neither of us is getting what we want today."

Travelers slow their steps, pretending not to stare. My suit is wrinkled, and my beard is starting to make a late-day appearance. I try to pull my suit jacket over a small circle of blood showing through the white shirt. Parents pull their kids closer. I must look like a monster.

"Am I under arrest?" I mutter.

Agent Chavez gives a polite, chilling smile. "Mr. Miles, we can do this however you'd like. But you *are* coming with us."

I raise my hands. "Fine. I needed a ride anyway. My place or yours?"

"You'll ride with the fellas," Zeke grumbles, already turning away. "Government Uber."

****

Even during rush hour, the drive to the Tampa FBI headquarters on Gray Street is short, way too short to get my story straight. George and I talked about a kidnapping, but it sounds insane. Why would they just let me go? Then again, it is not much crazier than being forced to work for a secret society planning to take over the world.

The truth is the last thing I'll tell Zeke. *The One* ensured that with their threats.

Add "lying to the FBI" to today's highlight reel.

The building hasn't changed—Spanish-style clay roof, tan façade, black security fence—but it feels different now. Not a place where I consult. A place where I'm the target.

They usher me through the metal detector and up the elevator to the second floor, then park me in an interrogation room. Same white walls, same metal chair—somehow harder, colder. The mirrored glass I've stood behind dozens of times now stares back at me. I wonder who is on the other side.

My heart starts galloping. Panic attacks have stalked me since my parents died, and one is creeping in, heat rising up my neck. The scent of hospital-grade cleaner makes my stomach turn.

Zeke steps in, followed by Director Chavez. She leans against the wall, stony as ever, red glasses perched on her forehead like an extra set of eyes.

Zeke drops into the chair across from me. His tan golf shirt is missing a button, a tuft of wiry chest hair is poking through, and a badge dangles around his neck. He stares at me with those cold reptile eyes, half-lidded, calculating.

I am so fucked.

"Jason," he starts, "we played this game with you before—Safe Harbor. You danced around, wasted time, and people died. You want a repeat?"

My anger boils up, burning through the fear. "Are you blaming me for Scott's death? I came to you. You didn't do a damn thing to protect either one of us." I stab a finger toward them both. "You wanted a notch on your belt, not justice."

Careful. Don't let him get inside your head.

"Why did you go to Greece?" he asks.

"I needed a vacation," I say. "Last time I checked, that's not illegal."

"Why the fake IDs? When did you meet up with Lia? How have you been talking to her? We'll get a warrant for your room at Hotel Haya."

I stay calm, folding my hands together on the table. "I didn't see Lia. I haven't communicated with Lia. That's all you get."

"Cut the shit," Gloria snaps, voice rising, her tone sharp enough to slice skin. Lia and Gloria—two alphas with a history. "You're protecting that bitch, and you know it."

"Do you have any real questions?" I ask, trying to keep my voice from cracking.

Zeke's eyes flare. "We had men on the ground in Nafplio. Watching your room. I don't know how she got in and out before we raided, but she was there."

I almost laugh. "Since when does the FBI follow American citizens out of the country?"

"We're authorized to work wherever the fuck we want," Zeke fires back. "We coordinated with local police, which was our first mistake. Then they pick you up, and next thing we know, there's a trail of dead cops, and you vanish. Why does death follow you around, Jason? How much more do you want on your conscience?"

"Is there a question buried in there?" My sweat is cold now, trickling under my shirt. "Can I get a water?" I ask.

Zeke slams a hand down on my shoulder, right on the wound. I bite back a yelp.

"Must've cut yourself shaving," he sneers. "You're bleeding through your shirt."

I grit my teeth. "Like I said—do you have a question?"

He leans in, breath hot and sour. "Yeah. Did Lia kill those officers? And where the hell did you two disappear to before popping up in Washington? Is she still there?"

I look from Zeke to Gloria and back again. They've got me boxed in, no moves left.

"I want a lawyer," I demand.

And that's it—off the cliff I go.

CHAPTER 36

I scramble for someone to call. I need help—now. Zeke and Gloria stormed out, leaving me alone with my thoughts. I know I have the right to an attorney even though I haven't been arrested. Avner crosses my mind, but dragging my friends into this mess isn't an option.

Hallie Miller would probably drop everything and rush over—unless she's already two glasses deep into a bottle of red at Forbici. But what would I even tell her? The truth is off-limits. Matt Marquardt is another possibility, though he's deep into launching a bank and chasing his next movie project.

As I search my memory, a man blusters into the room like he owns the place, carrying a battered briefcase and wearing a scowl. "I want all cameras and listening devices off, agents," he announces, a booming Boston accent cutting through the stale air.

I stare at him, half in disbelief. He drops into the chair across from me, elbows planted, tie bright red like his blotchy cheeks. I would guess he is about sixty, thinning hair dyed shoe-polish black, plastered over a doughy skull.

"And who are you?" I ask, wary.

"J. Robert Bailey," he says, offering me his hand, soft as a baby's butt. "Attorney at law."

"Okay, Mr. Bailey, why are you here? I don't know you, and I didn't call you."

He calmly pulls out his phone and taps a button. Classical music pours out. Then he leans in, shielding his mouth behind a legal pad.

"I don't trust these barracudas to turn off the feed," he whispers. "We'll talk at my office. You haven't been arrested, so let's get out of here."

"How did you even know I was here?" I ask, still processing.

He winks, teeth flashing too big for his mouth. "Let's just say a friend of yours tipped me off."

I cover my lips with my hands and lean closer. "What friend? They just picked me up at the airport."

"A *new* friend," he says, voice oily, grin still stuck on his face.

"I don't want you, and I don't need you," I state, leaning back in my chair, crossing my arms.

He leans in close enough for me to smell his aftershave. "You do need me, and you don't have a choice."

That's when Zeke storms back in, practically vibrating with anger. "I'm not sure where you came from, Counselor, but we ARE *talking* to Mr. Miles. We don't need your Johnnie Cochran bullshit clogging up our interview."

Bailey stands, wagging a pudgy finger in Zeke's face. "Still sore, Agent Michaels? Not my fault that I kick your ass every time you pull this crap. The FBI is not above the law. If you move too quick, the arrest will not stick. And we're leaving now. Don't contact Mr. Miles again without calling me. We are happy to schedule an interview."

Zeke glares at me, heat radiating off him. "Is this really what you want, Jason?"

I don't answer. I stand and follow my new friend right out the door.

Outside, the first thing I see is Oak and Avner leaning against the red Cybertruck, glaring like angry gargoyles.

Perfect. This day won't die.

"Where the hell have you been?" Avner roars, throwing up his hands.

"Jay-Bird, we called and texted you, like, ten million times," Oak yells, arms flailing so wildly he nearly smacks Avner in the face.

I turn to Bailey and promise to call him soon. He nods, presses a business card into my palm, and leaves without another word.

"Hey, guys," I sigh. "It's been a long couple of days. Can you drop me off at the hotel? I'll explain later."

Avner's jaw tightens. "That's not just a no. That's a *fuck no*. You're talking *now*. Get in this dumb geometry project on wheels and spill every damn thing."

CHAPTER 37

The silence from the Bluebird Team is deafening when we arrive. Avner paces, his eyes dark with fury. Oak is hunched in a corner, glued to his phone, and the rest lean on desks, walls, or the leather couch. Ernesto has even paused his constant tapping at the keyboard.

I know they want the truth, but they can't have it. They don't understand the danger.

"We were so worried about you, Jason," Berta blurts, then folds me into a hug before I can react.

Apple is next, and then Goat, pounding me on the back.

Avner cuts in, his accent thick as quicksand. "Enough of the lovefest. Where were you, Jason? And what the fuck happened?"

I try to keep my voice steady. "I was on vacation and—"

"Vacation?" Avner spits. "You're really going to lie to me? To us? I interrogate liars for a living. And you're full of shit."

I glance around the room, searching for any hint of support. "Is that what this is—an interrogation?"

"If you keep lying, then yes."

Oak tries to play peacemaker. "Can we calm down? Jay-Bird, why didn't you answer? Ignoring Avner is one thing, but the rest of us are family."

Family. That word stings. I weigh telling the truth against sticking to my rehearsed lie. I know how crazy it will sound. But I can't drag them into this. Losing another loved one is not an option. Maybe Zeke is right. Death *does* follow me.

"Okay," I sigh, "I was traveling around Greece. Started in Athens, then did some island hopping."

Avner narrows his eyes. "We know that much. Who were you with? Leo Samaras and Dimitrios Siampaus?"

I'd forgotten how terrifying Avner can be, the way he looks through you like X-rays. His physical intimidation as he invades your space.

"I had fake IDs. I needed peace, Avner. You trained me well. I could feel eyes on me everywhere, and I had no clue who was friend or foe. So, I ditched them all."

"Who did you get the IDs from?" Avner asks.

"I've got people," I lie.

"Fuck you and your imaginary people. This has Lia written all over it."

Apple's eyes dart to my shoulder. "You're bleeding, Jason. Do you need a doctor?"

I look down. The small stain on my shirt is spreading, aspirin and bourbon are wearing thin. I cross the room and pour myself two fingers of Johnnie Walker from the bar.

"I'm fine. I just need sleep."

Avner doesn't let up. "You give everyone the slip, end up in Nafplio, the police break in and arrest you. Where did Lia go?"

I brace myself. "I didn't see Lia. She never showed."

Oak explodes. "You were seeing that crazy biatch? You promised you weren't."

I sigh. "Yeah. I lied about that. I love her, and I wanted to see her. But she didn't come. The police burst in and arrested me. On the way back to Athens, a car and a van came out of nowhere, killing all the cops. I took a bullet through my shoulder. They put a bag on my head, threw me in the van, and the lights went out."

"Who were they?" Avner demands.

Lying to them leaves my mouth dry and bitter, but I push through. "I don't know. They patched me up, and next thing I remember, I woke up in a hotel in Washington, D.C."

Avner moves closer, invading my space. "That makes no fucking sense."

I pause, consider taking Avner aside and telling him the truth. If anyone can help and hold their own, it is him. But it's not worth the risk. It's too dangerous for all of us.

I stand my ground. "Sense or not, that's what happened. I got on a plane, came back, Zeke picked me up."

"They didn't say anything to you?" Avner spits. "Just killed a bunch of cops, shot you, jetted you across the ocean, and didn't ask for anything?"

Apple raises her hands, voice soft. "Why don't we take a break? It's getting late. Jason is exhausted. Oak, take him back to Haya. We'll talk tomorrow."

As we step toward the door, I feel Avner's glare drilling into my back. I don't dare look. I can bullshit everyone else, but not Avner.

I need some sleep and a plan to get myself out of this mess.

CHAPTER 38

Avner's voice is low and clipped. "I called in a favor from a woman I used to date in Israel. Yael's still with Mossad—she pulled flight manifests into Washington Executive Airfield."

The room reeks of lunchtime cheeseburgers and grease. Crumpled wrappers blanket the desk, a few sliding off onto the floor. Goat pops a fistful of fries into his mouth and mumbles, "So how are we supposed to know which flight Jason was on?"

Avner taps the screen in front of us. "We don't. But I've been reviewing every private plane video for the last two days. Ernesto—roll it."

Ernesto hits play. A white Gulfstream G550 lands with a surgeon's grace, tires kissing the runway. The stairs descend, and two men emerge—one confident and purposeful, one small and wiry. Then what looks like hired muscle appears behind them, dragging a large piece of luggage.

Goat leans in. "That bag's big enough for a body."

"Exactly," Avner confirms.

"Who are they?"

Avner zooms in. "The older guy with the beard and the tight suit is George Klein. He runs an investment fund in Tampa. I have no clue why he's in D.C., possibly dragging an unconscious Jason around."

Goat studies the monitor. "How about the little guy?"

"Blast from the past. That's the little weirdo from Safe Harbor. Clinton. The squirrel that used to follow Terrance around."

"What the hell is he doing involved with this?"

Avner shoves half a burger in his mouth. Ketchup squirts out the side and onto his shirt. "No idea, but we need to find out."

"How about the beef? He looks like us. Military or cartel with hard eyes. Bad news. Any idea who he is?"

Avner shakes his head. "Facial recognition gave me nothing, which doesn't mean squat if he's had his record scrubbed. We'll dig—if he's ex-military or has a sheet, we'll find him."

"What do we do in the meantime?" Goat asks, crossing his arms.

Avner shifts toward Ernesto. "Keep this to yourself, E Something's off with Jason. We need to figure out what is going on and get him out of whatever shitshow he's in."

Ernesto mimes zipping his mouth. "Mum's the word."

Turning back to Goat, Avner states, "You and I will have to do some undercover work. Things might get messy. You good with that?"

Goat's expression hardens. "You are all my family. If Jason's in trouble, I'm fine with messy. Real messy."

****

I park several blocks from Oxford Exchange and walk in, letting the soft clink of the glass doors settle my nerves. The place is part café, part bookstore, and part retail—all perfectly curated. I can't resist the books. The smell of fresh coffee, wood polish, and old pages hits me like a memory. Ever since I lost my parents, reading has allowed me to escape to another world and imagine I was a different person.

I wish I were someone else now.

It is a beautiful Saturday morning, and I enter with a pack of women in yoga pants fresh from working out or a walk on Bayshore.

I approach the associate at the counter. "Hey, I'm looking for a book by Sydney Summers."

She checks the inventory and guides me to a shelf labeled *Local Talent*. "We have all five in stock."

I flip through one, read the description, and nod. "I'll take them all. And hey—order double next time. She's the real deal."

She smiles. "We'll restock automatically."

I glance past her to the café. George is impossible to miss, wearing a baby-blue sweater and khakis, lounging in a high-backed chair shaped like a birdcage. He has added turtle-frame glasses, enhancing his GQ look. He waves me over.

I don't want to be here. Every minute in the company of these madmen churns my stomach, but they're the only thread that might lead me to *The One*. I need to gather every scrap of information I can if I'm going to bring them down. There's no way I can let them near Winnie—but I can't risk the lives of my friends either. A true conundrum.

Keeping my face neutral, I open the Voice Memos app and tap the red record button.

"Jason. Good to see you. Thanks for meeting here—best coffee in town, great books, and good food. We can meet in a private room upstairs," he says, standing and placing a high-end backpack over his shoulder."

We order coffee—mine black with Splenda, his sugar and cream—and climb the polished wooden staircase past rows of framed photos. Their dark, judging eyes crawl over me as I walk by, like ghosts whispering *traitor*. My feet drag like they are shackled in prison chains.

Upstairs, a staffer checks George's membership number and shows us to a small private room. George gestures for me to sit at the side, while he takes the head of the table like a boss. He removes his glasses and steeples his fingers.

"First things first," he says, removing a sleek black bag from his backpack. "Please place your phone in the bag. These things are nothing but listening and tracking devices."

I reluctantly drop my phone in the Faraday bag. George is always one step ahead.

"I know you have questions," he begins. "I did too, at first. But trust me, this is no hoax."

I lock eyes with him. "Start at the top. How long has this been going on?"

He glances around the room. Drops his voice. "The start is fluid. Some say back to the Eighteenth Century. Let's say the Age of Enlightenment."

I lean back and scoff. "Come on, man. You're not seriously tracing this to the Enlightenment? Isn't that story a little played out?"

"Think about it as a breakoff of the Illuminati? What do you know about them?"

"It was a real group promoting freedom from political and religious oppression. Someone leaked their secret documents to the Bavarian government. I watched the whole series on Netflix. You must have also," I say with a sarcastic smile. "Today, it's just fictional silliness for conspiracy theories."

A flash of anger passes in George's eyes, but then he regains his calm.

"I'll leave you with one thought that the series left out. The goal of many secret societies is to infiltrate other groups for their own purposes—to do their bidding. The best organizations never let their name be known."

"So, you are not *The One*."

"No one knows who we are, Jason. When you prove you are trustworthy, you'll ascend through the levels, and all will be revealed."

"Let's get back to this century. What has your cause been doing?"

"In the last hundred years, we've been acquiring power. The World Wars showed us what happens when mankind is left to its own devices. We learned that our cause is humanity's only chance. We started the long game—to do their bidding. Teaching children our ways and placing them in different societies. They are now in positions of power. All the work is paying off. We're right on the cusp of change—but we need you."

I sip my coffee, fighting to keep my hand steady. "So, Governor Frederick wants me to get you access to Tampa Scientific's quantum computer?"

"That's correct," he says, calm as someone ordering soup with his meal. "We need Winnie. She's the last domino. With her, we can break every encryption. Control information. Reshape the world."

I stare at him, but I struggle to form a sentence.

"We know it is a big ask, but that is why we staged the ransom and connected TSC with Bluebird. We made you the hero to gain Nikesh's trust."

I nearly spill my coffee as I stand pushing my plastic chair backwards. "*The One* froze their data and kidnapped his son? What kind of sick fucks are you?"

Avner was right. This whole thing was a setup. I feel like a fool.

"Please sit, Jason. Cursing is the crutch of the inarticulate. Sometimes to make real progress, you need to break some eggs, but trust me, the means will justify the ends."

"Do you mean like tax fraud to fund your delusion?"

"Safe Harbor Bank was one of thousands of profit centers. World domination is not cheap."

I sit down and let out an exhausted breath. "How can causing a divide between the rich and poor and stealing to fund your progress be right?"

He spreads his arms like a priest delivering a blessing. "Imagine a world where there is no war, no terrorism, and no hate. No drugs and gangs destroying the fabric of society. We can achieve that. One leader, one economy, and the world moving in the same direction.

Doesn't that sound nice? We can achieve it, but we need Winnie. You can get her for us."

"Why do you need me?" I demand. "Why didn't you just force Nikesh to hand over Winnie as part of the ransom and leave me out of it? You had his son and his company. He would've done anything."

He hesitates, choosing his words with care. "You'd think so. We have someone inside TSC. We explored leveraging his son—trading Amir for Winnie. But our source made it clear: Nikesh would never give up his life's work. Apparently, Winnie is even more of a child to him than his own flesh and blood."

I shake my head, refusing to accept it. "That's not possible. Nikesh loves Amir."

"Believe whatever story helps you sleep," he says coolly. "But we had to go to Plan B—using you. Earning trust so you'd deliver Winnie to us."

A wave of nausea crashes through me. I can't tell if I'm about to pass out or throw up. Their depravity turns my stomach, but worse is the doubt worming its way in. *Would Nikesh really sacrifice his own son for Winnie? And if it came down to it... would I give up the people I love to protect her? To protect the world?*

"Even if I could, why would I do that? I didn't choose to be part of this thing."

He places his glasses back on and pushes them up his nose. "You are Preferred and already in this, whether you like it or not. It is time to stop fighting and embrace the cause. We can do this together with other great heroes, like Frederick. We'll be remembered forever. We can end the suffering of humanity."

"First of all, I don't know what makes me Preferred. What if I say no? Get up to leave and go straight to the FBI?"

He lets out an exasperated breath. "You know the answer. You let down a society that desperately needs you, and everyone and everything you love dies. For nothing."

****

"Are you sure you tracked him to this bougie place?" Aver asks Goat as he picks up a candle and crinkles his nose after a sniff. "This does not smell like a vanilla-beach vacation."

Goat flips through a $200 leather travel journal. "Man, if we hang out in places like this, I need a raise. But there are a lot of lovely ladies probably looking for a guy like me."

Avner points upstairs. "Focus. Are you sure he is here?"

"I watched him go in. He disappeared. The girl at the tea shop says there are private rooms upstairs."

Avner grunts. "Who's he with?"

Goat nods toward the stairway. "Why don't you ask him yourself?"

CHAPTER 39

I spot them as George and I move down the stairs. This is going to be a problem.

The meeting with George stirred up more questions than answers, and my head is still spinning from it. There's a part of me that understands the cause—hell, even likes him. But the rational part of me thinks he's insane, involved in some reverse Robin Hood cult that robs the poor to feed the rich. And now I have to deal with Avner and Goat.

The only option is pulling George back up the stairs to avoid them, but it's too late. I see them staring at me. I need to get out of here as quickly as possible. Nothing good can come from Avner and George in one room.

What the hell are those two doing at Oxford Exchange? Are they following me?

"Hey Jason, over here!" Goat calls across the room, loud as ever.

"What are you two doing here?" I ask, trying to dodge Avner's stare.

"I wanted to get Apple something special," Avner says, calm but still menacing. "Someone told me this place was her style. How about you?"

"Business meeting," I say, as casually as I can.

"On a Saturday?"

My collar suddenly feels tighter. I pull it away from my neck. "A small business owner is always working."

Avner glances at George, then back at me. "Aren't you going to introduce us?"

I hold his gaze, feeling cornered. There's no easy way out. "This is George. He's a potential new client for Bluebird."

Avner steps around me and moves in close, close enough to smell George's expensive cologne. Avner likes to get in people's faces, looking for a reaction. But George doesn't flinch.

"What do you do, George?" Avner asks, voice smooth but dangerous.

"I manage a private debt fund. Investors trust me with their money, and I lend it out."

"Like a loan shark?" Avner says, flashing a toothless grin.

George gives him a calm, practiced smile. "No, Avner—we serve wealthy clients who want a good return, and borrowers willing to pay for flexible terms."

Avner's eyebrow ticks up. "How do you know my name?"

"I told him about Bluebird," I lie. "I mentioned the team. Sorry, but we need to get going."

Avner gives a little nod but never takes his eyes off George. "George, you been to Washington, D.C. lately?"

****

The day was a disaster from start to finish. The meeting with George and all the bizarre details kicked things off. Avner and Goat's appearance followed, making things worse. George smoothly handled the D.C. question with a plausible explanation, which did nothing to satisfy Avner, who clearly knows something.

Everything I do feels poisoned. My shoulder throbs, and an old stab wound in my thigh aches, as if to remind me I can't escape my past.

My mood is horrible and hopeless. Maybe a drink or five will help me forget. Luckily, I live in a hotel.

"Johnnie Walker on ice," I say to Ace behind the bar as I slide onto the only empty stool. The vibe in the hotel bar is dramatically different from how I feel. The room buzzes with conversation, people laughing, and clinking glasses. The weekends are always packed at Haya—lots of wedding parties and large gatherings of happy people. Seeing them spirals me even deeper.

"You okay, Jason?" Ace asks, concern in his voice.

"It's been a long day," I snap. "Sorry, just the drink, please."

The whiskey burns its way down my throat, leaving a warm trail, so I order another.

"Want a splash of water?" Ace asks.

I glare at him. "Just the drink."

For the next hour, I drink and half-watch the Lightning playing the Panthers on the bar TV. A guy beside me tries to chat, but I ignore him. He mutters something under his breath.

"Give me another," I slur toward Ace, who's busy talking to another bartender.

"Hey Ace, I never asked—is Ace really your name? And what's your last name?"

"Yeah, it's my real name," he says, unamused. "Last name's Boddington."

I chuckle like a drunk teenager. "Ace Boddington? Sounds like a porn name."

He gives me a flat stare. "Maybe you should switch to coffee."

"Maybe you should do your job and pour me my Johnnie Walker, Mr. Ace Boddington, part-time bartender, secret porn star."

The guy next to me turns. "You're being an asshole."

I nearly fall off my stool. "Why don't you mind your business before I knock you the fuck out?"

He stands up, ready for a fight, but the general manager and Ace appear by my side.

"Time to go to your room, Jason," the manager says firmly.

I look around, but the bar is a wall of shocked faces. I stand and try to act out a scene from my favorite movie. "You all a bunch of assholes," I slur, trying to imitate Pacino. "You need people like me so you can call me the bad guy. Say good night to the bad guy!"

Nobody laughs. I stumble toward the elevator, swaying like a cruise ship passenger in a storm.

When I hit my room, I collapse on the bed fully clothed, and the ceiling starts to spin.

What the hell am I doing? Sneaking around with lunatics, lying to the only people who might actually care about me? Not to mention how my actions could destroy society. But what choice do I have?

A sound cuts through my thoughts, ringing. Distant.

The safe.

Lia.

I stagger to my knees, crash into the wall, and somehow manage to punch in the code on the third try.

"Hello?" I rasp, winded.

"Is this Mr. Smith?" a woman's voice asks, flat and cold.

"Oh my God, Lia, where have you been?" I slur.

"Is this Mr. Smith?" she repeats, dead calm.

My heart kicks against my ribs, panic mixing with rage. I try to remember the protocol.

"Yes," I say loudly. "Is this Mrs. Smith?"

Her accent breaks through. "Jay, what happened? Are you okay? I've been so worried since Greece."

Something inside me snaps, the liquor taking over.

"Yeah, you were so worried you left me to get arrested when they kicked the door in, and then almost murdered by your psychotic employers," I slur.

"Have you been drinking, Jay? You know I had no choice. If we were caught together, we'd both be in prison. I barely got out. There is nothing they can do to you if I'm gone."

I'm pacing now, the walls closing in. "Maybe. Or maybe you just screwed me over again. Maybe I need to get away from you forever."

"What is wrong with you?" Her voice cracks, and her accent thickens.

"What's wrong with me?" I nearly shout. "I can't trust you. Every time I try, it goes to shit. You don't want me. You don't care. We can never have a normal life together. Maybe I'm better off without you."

Silence. Long and heavy.

Then, softly, "Maybe you're right, Jay. Maybe you would be better off without me."

The line goes dead.

"Lia?" I shout. "Lia, I didn't mean it. I love you!"

Nothing.

I hurl the phone across the room and bury my face in my hands. Anger simmers under my skin.

"Fine," I mutter.

I fish my regular cell phone out of my jeans, squint at the blurry contacts, and finally stab at a number.

A sleepy voice answers. "Jason? That you?"

"Hey, Syd," I say, voice thick with defeat. "You want to come over?"

CHAPTER 40

He knows they're coming for him, coming to kill him. He's a loose end, and they hate loose ends.

Crouched in the shadows across from Haya, filthy clothes sticking to his skin. He sees Jason's building from his perch. He's ready to confront him and finish this. The bastard destroyed his life, and here he is, back from Greece with a nice tan, getting a late-night blonde delivered by Uber while he rots in an alley like a stray cat.

It is time to kick down his door, drag him out, end his miserable life, and go back on the run.

But then the shot comes.

The bullet misses his skull by an inch. Close enough that he hears it whiz by his earlobe. He feels the burn, hears the brick behind him explode, feels dust and grit sting his back.

They're here.

Every day, he rehearses his escape. Running the routes in his head over and over, studying how to disappear through these streets. Knowing they'd find him eventually.

He doesn't wait. Taking off across 14th, zigzagging hard. Another round cracks past and explodes against the street. Can't slow down.

Ahead, a bunch of kids stand around talking. Late Saturday night is busy in Ybor. The boys are trying to score with some girls. They look soft, oblivious. He runs straight through, scattering them like pigeons. The girls scream, the guys curse, but he doesn't care. The shooters won't blink at hitting a civilian. They couldn't care less about collateral damage. Everyone dies eventually.

He pushes forward, lungs burning, cutting through the night until he reaches 17th Street. There's a half-empty parking lot there, cars lined up in the dark, just enough cover. He dives behind a sedan, gasping, adrenaline still spiking.

Too close. Way too close.

They know he's in Ybor.

That means he's out of time. No chance to run. He needs to talk to Jason before they find him and ask for help.

****

Syd's fingers trace the wound on my shoulder, her head resting on my bare chest. "Will you tell me what you've been through?" she asks, her voice soft and gentle.

I look at her, then away. Shame curls in my gut. I haven't touched another woman since Lia. Ten plus years. And now, after one brutal phone call and too much whiskey, I'm here with Syd.

Maybe I needed it—a shock to finally break my insane attachment to Lia. Maybe this is what ending looks like. I once heard that *if things don't end badly, they won't end.*

With Lia out of the picture, maybe I could be with Syd. Build something real.

Syd's fingertips travel down to the ragged scar on my thigh, then to the burn on my forearm. She pauses at the missing fingernail. Each old injury burns under her gentle touch.

"This is a lot, Jason," she whispers. "Who are you? What happened in Greece?"

I scratch my beard, which has grown wild over the last few weeks. The words choke me.

"Let's not ruin this," I say, voice low. "I'll tell you another time."

"Promise?" she asks.

Instead of lying, I kiss the top of her head and close my moist eyes.

CHAPTER 41

I'm dreaming of Lia. We're back in our old house, making dinner, Kentucky Mules in hand. She's peeling carrots while I season the steaks, both of us laughing and belting out Bon Jovi like idiots. Then the doorbell rings.

She tells me to get it.

When I open the door, Dr. Levi stands there. His apron reads *Black Sheep of the Family*, splattered red, goggles pushed up on his bald head, a cigarette jammed into the corner of his mouth. In one hand, he's holding Lia's severed head by the hair.

"Hi, Jason," he says, grinning. "Guess what I brought for dinner?"

The phone on my nightstand rips me out of the nightmare. I'm drenched in sweat, heart hammering against my ribs. Three in the morning. George's rules—always keep the phone on.

"This is Jason," I croak. My mouth is parched. The stale whiskey feels like a film on my tongue.

"Get dressed and take an Uber to the address I'm texting," George orders. "Come alone. Don't tell anyone."

I glance at Syd, sleeping soundly, tangled in the sheets. Her blonde hair is like a '90s hard rock video.

"I'm kind of busy right now," I mumble.

"That's not how this works." George hangs up.

I rub my eyes and sit up. The phone pings with the address, deep in South St. Petersburg. Not a great area. I move quietly, not wanting to wake Syd, and splash cold water on my face in the bathroom. I dress in black jeans and an old Pearl Jam T-shirt, strap on the belly holster, check the Glock, and slide it in. My faded denim jacket goes over the top.

I scribble a note: *Work emergency, back for breakfast.* Another lie. It is getting hard to keep them all straight.

Downstairs, the night clerk barely glances at me, nose buried in a Brad Thor novel. I almost laugh. My life is less believable than anything Thor could dream up.

Outside, blue and red strobes pulse against the buildings, painting the street in frantic color. Several patrol cars block off 7th Avenue, their engines idling, doors ajar. In Ybor this late at night, anything could have happened—and none of it good.

I hop into a white Camry, idling, the driver reading something on his phone. The car reeks of beef jerky and gym socks. Dog hair covers the back seat. I brush it aside, pop in earbuds, and sink into the music as the city slides by.

What the hell is waiting for me out there?

****

Goat sticks a tiny plastic Jesus bobblehead to the dash with a suction cup, makes the sign of the cross, and closes his eyes.

"What the hell is that, and what are you doing?" Avner asks.

"Dear Jesus, protect us on this mission and Jason wherever he is headed. Ignore Avner's comments and help him find the Lord. If we must inflict pain, bless the souls of those we hurt."

Avner shakes his head and pulls out of the lot, falling in several cars behind the Uber. "Time to find out what Jason is up to."

"Don't get too close," Goat warns, checking his sidearm. "It's late, and you'll stick out like a priest at a peep show."

"Thanks, Goat. I've only done this about ten thousand times," Avner snipes, turning up the radio to drown him out.

Forty minutes later, they exit I-275 and follow the Uber down 9th Avenue, then onto 20th Street South. The neighborhood is pure desperation—sagging houses, beat-up apartment buildings, a boarded-up triplex.

"What's Jason doing in a place like this at 3 a.m.?" Goat mutters as they watch him climb out of the Uber. "Looks like a neighborhood I used to score smack in."

Avner sinks a little lower in the seat, scanning the street. He pulls a small device from his gym bag and points it at the house.

"What's that?"

"Thermal radar. Let's see who's in there," Avner says, adjusting the screen.

Bright orange blobs bloom on the display. "Six or seven," Avner confirms.

He pulls out another antenna and aims it at the walls.

"Trying to listen in?" Goat asks.

"Yeah. Let's see if they're dumb enough to talk loudly."

Static screams from the speaker. Nothing else.

"They're jamming the signal," Avner mutters. "That's pro-level. Which is usually bad news."

"What's the play, Avner?" Goat asks. "We can't just sit here all night with our crosses in our hands."

Avner peers through a small monocular. "First, the phrase is *dick* in our hands, Goat. Second, we are going to sit here unless we hear shooting—then we kill everyone. Got it?"

A soft tapping on the window makes them both jump, guns up in a blink.

"Hey, you dumb shits, it's just me," Zeke hisses. "Put those toys away before you blow a hole through my skull."

Avner unlocks the door, glaring as Zeke slides into the back seat.

"What the fuck are you doing here?" Avner growls.

"We tracked Jason. Saw you two tailing him. Figured we'd watch your backs," Zeke says, wrinkling his nose. "What's that smell?"

"Pickle diet," Goat says proudly. "Down ten pounds."

Zeke looks at his protruding gut. "That actually works?"

"If you two girls are finished with your diet club," Avner snaps, "can we focus?"

"We'll set up surveillance and grab photos of anyone going in or out. See if they match any databases. Whatever Jason is into here, it doesn't smell right—and I don't mean Goat's pickle gas," Zeke responds.

"Fine," Avner sighs. "Keep us posted. We can work together on this."

Zeke steps out, then taps the window again.

"And Avner? You're slipping, letting an old FBI agent sneak up on you like that. You're getting soft, dating Apple Lee."

"Fuck off, Zeke," Avner grunts, flipping him the bird before pulling away. But he wonders if he is right.

****

I walk up the warped driveway, trying to look confident and trying not to get mugged. The place seems ready to collapse, with yellow paint flaking off and a blue tarp sagging over a busted section of the roof. It's tilted, like a drunk kid trying to carry a heavy weight.

I knock.

George opens the door and waves me in. Six men stand behind him, all built like linebackers, arms crossed, eyes flat and cold.

"What's so important you dragged me to this dump at three in the morning?" I ask, forcing my shoulders back. I'm still slightly drunk and fight not to sway.

"The boys just finished a job," George says. "They'll be key to our future. I wanted you to meet them."

The windows are newly covered with blackout blinds, no light bleeding through. The torn orange carpet stinks, and the door is rigged with industrial locks.

These guys don't like visitors.

I need to pull myself together. If these thugs are part of the future, they need to go down as well. I burn their faces into my memory.

The men are a mix of white, Black, and Hispanic. Most have facial hair and baseball hats, but none of them look friendly. They stand with their arms flexed and focused stares. They remind me of a room full of Avners, which is not good for me. I wish he were here for backup.

"What are you all, military or ex-military?"

A man with his John Deere hat turned backward and a thick beard steps forward. No handshakes, no smile. "We're former military. A group of Navy SEALs that completed special missions for the government. Let's call them off-the-book missions. They called us Shadow SEALs. We decided the government pays for shit and went out on our own. You can call me Omaha. Best not to know the rest of the team."

One look in his cold gray eyes and I know: this is the bastard who had me clocked in Ybor—the one who kidnapped that kid.

"Do we know each other, Omaha?" I ask.

He just stares.

"Fine," I say. "What can you do for me?"

"Abduction. Interrogation. Intimidation. Making people disappear. You name it."

I look at George. "Like Max Braun's crew?"

George snorts. "Max Braun was a Girl Scout compared to these guys. But they don't come cheap. And once you know them, you can't unknow them if you know what I mean. No loose ends, Jason."

Terrific. My reward for Preferred status is a bunch of sociopaths on speed dial.

CHAPTER 42

Instead of going back to the room, I order a coffee at Café Quiquiriqui in Haya's lobby. The barista has just turned on the lights and started up the espresso machine, which gives a reluctant chirp, then settles into a steady hum as it warms up.

My head is pounding—too much booze, not enough sleep, and way too many lies. Everything feels like it's spinning out of control. These lunatics think I work for them—hell, maybe I do. What other choice do I have? I help them, or they kill me. Kill everyone I care about.

And Syd. Jesus. She's upstairs right now, sleeping in my bed. What the hell was I thinking of bringing her here? Well, I know exactly what I was thinking, but I'm in love with Lia, and there's no way she was involved in my kidnapping. She risked everything to see me again.

Despite my feelings for Lia, I can't entirely dismiss Syd. She's beautiful, witty, and magnetic—someone who feels real. Being with her has a clarity, while a life with Lia seems like a fantasy.

My list of problems has passed ninety-nine and is still climbing. They want me to give them access to Winnie—but how? Even if I could, should I? Nikesh trusts me. I can't betray him. Would he really choose Winnie over his son? Maybe I can manipulate George instead, but odds are he's already five steps ahead.

Then there's Zeke. He's been calling every day since the airport. I can't avoid him forever. Eventually, he'll force my hand, maybe even arrest me. I need to talk to that slimy lawyer George sent.

And I'm lying to Avner and the Bluebird team, people I trust, my closest family. If I tell them what's really going on, it puts a target on their backs too. I need to be alone with this mess.

As I let these thoughts roll around in my head like clothes in a washing machine, I can picture those mean gray eyes staring at me. If I turn on *The One*, will they send the Shadow SEALs to tie up the loose end?

Down the priority list but not forgotten—Sloppy Joe. I don't know who he is or why he's tailing me, but he's a problem for another day. Maybe Avner or Goat can run him down—if they catch him, then what? If he wanted to hurt me, I assume he would have already tried.

It's too much. One crisis at a time. I need to prioritize my problems, and every thread leads back to *The One*. So that's where I start. I've recorded everything I've learned, and now I have to deal with George and Governor Frederick. If I can bring them down, maybe I can finally see who else is pulling the strings. But to get that far, I'll have to play their game—and stay alive long enough to end it.

I finish the coffee and head for the elevators. Before the doors shut, an arm wedges in, holding them open. Two guys step inside. One tall and built, the other short and pudgy. The big guy looks familiar, but I can't place him.

As soon as the doors close, the big guy slams the stop button. The elevator jolts to a halt.

"Hey, what the hell?" I snap.

They position themselves between me and the door, blocking any escape. I scan for weak points. I know close-quarters fighting, and my Glock is within reach. I could end this fast, but nobody wants gunshots in an elevator.

The big guy speaks first. "Relax, Jason. We're just here to deliver a message. Zeke says call him. Or things get very uncomfortable. You comprehend?"

I nod.

He restarts the elevator.

When the doors open on my floor, they move aside, but the big guy leans close. "Twenty-four hours. Or next time, it's handcuffs."

How can a day be so shitty at only 6 a.m.?

****

I swipe my room key, moving slowly, quietly. There's a flicker of light—a cell phone glow. I reach for the Glock, flipping on the lamp in one motion. Syd is standing near my laptop, half-dressed, eyes wide in the sudden light.

"Jason! You scared me," she blurts. "Your note said you'd be back for breakfast."

"I wrapped up early," I say, eyes scanning the room. "What are you doing?"

She blushes, wearing one of my T-shirts and nothing else. "I was trying to find my clothes. I couldn't find the light switches, so I used my phone light."

I hand over her jeans and the Lightning sweatshirt from the floor. Instead of putting them on, she kisses me.

"I'm going to shower," she says, "then you need to feed me. I'm famished."

I nod, forcing a smile, but something doesn't sit right. It is like I walked in on more than I saw.

Who are you, Sydney Summers—and how do you fit into this?

CHAPTER 43

Avner scans the Cuban diner until he spots Zeke, perched on a black round stool at the counter, wedged between two older men. A waitress hustles by, pouring coffee and juggling orders. He's been to La Teresita plenty of times with Apple, but today he's got no appetite. He's still pissed that he let Zeke sneak up on him, and even more worried about Jason being in deep trouble.

"What's for breakfast?" Avner asks, nodding at the man to Zeke's right. The guy takes one look at him and shuffles away.

Zeke doesn't even glance up. "Is it your mission in life to ruin every meal I have?"

"We need to talk," Avner says, dropping onto the newly vacated stool. "And you need to cut back on this greasy food. Try a banana sometime."

Zeke sighs, taking a sloppy bite of a fried egg sandwich. "I already have one wife lecturing me about my diet. I don't need a second. And I hate bananas. What do you want, Avner?"

"You ID anyone at that hellhole after we left last night?"

Zeke snorts, chasing his sandwich with a gulp of Cuban coffee. "Of course we did. We're the FBI." He wipes his mouth with a napkin, still refusing to look Avner straight in the eye.

"How about some names? We need to set our differences aside and work together. For Jason's sake."

Zeke finally meets his gaze, eyes sharp. "I know he's in trouble. And he'd better haul his ass to headquarters and tell me the truth. We played this game with him less than a year ago, and people died. He's damn lucky he wasn't one of them. You too."

"I'll talk to him," Avner says. "Who did you ID?"

"Two guys," Zeke says. "First one is George Klein. Big money, finance guy, respected, clean record. Been around Tampa a while."

Avner raises an eyebrow. "What the hell's a finance guy doing in crackville at two in the morning?"

He considers spilling what he learned from the D.C. airport, but decides to hold it close for now.

Zeke shrugs. "No clue. But he was with a military type—Connor Doyle. Goes by call sign 'Omaha.' Navy SEAL—tough, nasty, went dark with his whole unit after they left the Navy."

Avner's stomach tightens. Omaha. That had to be the big guy he and Goat saw on the video.

What the hell is Jason doing with these people?

"We met this George Klein at Oxford Exchange," Avner says carefully. "He was with Jason, who claimed he was a new client."

Zeke finally turns, his eyes going wide before narrowing to slits. "What kind of client do you meet in a war zone in the middle of the night?"

Avner grabs a piece of toast off Zeke's plate and stands to leave. Then he thinks twice and sits back down.

"Let me ask you a question, Zeke. Do you buy all this, *The One* business, or is Jason just mixed up with some bad people? I'm starting to worry he's imagining things if you know what I mean."

Zeke takes a long moment contemplating the question. "I'm not sure. There was all the Safe Harbor fraud business, and that was real. But all this new world order talk seems like conspiracy nonsense. I'm trying to keep an open mind. These are people in the FBI who believe it, and something happened in Greece. Someone killed a bunch of police and shot Jason. Those are facts. He's got the wound to prove it."

"I'm worried everything he's been through has made him paranoid. Connecting dots that don't exist. If there was really this mysterious group, why wouldn't they just kill him?"

"I don't know. Let's keep an eye on him. Find out more about this Klein and Omaha."

"I'm on it," Avner says. "And maybe try some fruit, Zeke."

CHAPTER 44

If I'm going to take down *The One*, I can't do it alone. I thought Lia and I might be able to work on it, but that is off the table. The Faraday bag at Oxford blindsided me, a reminder to dig back into my training in Israel and sharpen my game.

It feels like days have passed since the middle-of-the-night meeting with George's hit squad, but it has only been twelve hours. Now Ernesto and I sit in the car outside George's office. I've told him only what he absolutely needs to know and swore him to silence. All he knows is that the conversation must be recorded. He clipped a small device to the inside of my shirt and will monitor everything from the car. We tested it earlier—clean audio, no interference. Perfect.

"Thanks for coming by," George says as I'm led into his office by a red-haired assistant. She's pretty, in a cold, magazine-ad sort of way. George stands up from behind his sleek desk and gestures toward a camel-colored couch. His gray slacks and crisp white dress shirt look impossibly neat for a man who was with me in the hood last night. The room smells like a pine forest, and sunlight streams through the window across the room.

"Do you have your phone?"

I hold up my hands. "Left it in the car. Those things are only good for tracking."

His assistant offers me a drink. I ask for coffee, even though it's nearly four in the afternoon. I haven't slept. The flesh under my eyes feels like wet sandbags. I'm hungover and irritable.

"You look terrible," George says, sitting across from me.

"No shit," I mutter. "Might have something to do with getting dragged out of bed and brought to some dive in South St. Pete."

He raises an eyebrow. "Try not to curse, Jason. George Washington said, 'The foolish and wicked practice of profane cursing and swearing is a vice so mean and low that every person of sense and character detests and despises it.'"

Before I can fire back, the door opens. A blast from my worst memories steps in, carrying a coffee mug marked *Palma Ceia Capital*. Clinton. Terrance's old lapdog. Always scribbling notes, never making eye contact, following Terrance like a duckling. A face I saw at the chamber event weeks ago. I didn't trust him then, and I don't trust him now.

My stomach turns. "What the fuck is *he* doing here?" I snap, pointing straight at Clinton.

"Jason," George warns, calm and fatherly. "Language. Clinton worked for Terrance, yes—but after his death, he kept his mouth shut despite the FBI leaning on him hard. He stayed alive and earned a job. A second chance."

I hope Ernesto got that.

"I saw him at a table when I was speaking to the chamber."

George smiles warmly. "We were all there. The firm had a table. You did great. We wanted to see you in action."

My fists form balls, and I struggle to control myself. These guys have been playing me from the beginning.

"I want him out," I growl, pointing at Clinton. "I don't want to see that creep again."

Clinton smirks, eyes darting to me and then away. "It's pleasant to see you, Jason. By the way, I met your girlfriend. Her name's Sydney, right? Hot. If it doesn't work out, I'd appreciate an intro."

My vision goes red. I bolt up from the couch. "What the hell do you mean, you *met* Syd?"

George flicks his hand, and Clinton slinks out of the room with that stupid grin still stuck on his face.

I need to pull it together and get something else I can use.

"What the hell is he talking about?" I demand. "Anyway—my shoulder's killing me, I'm fried, and I'm done with the games. I have some more questions, George."

"Fire away," he says.

"How long have you been part of *The One*?"

He twirls a pen in his fingers and eyes me closely. "Why does that matter, Jason?"

"How do I know I can trust you? How do I know this isn't some hoax? A setup."

"Over a decade."

"If I get you access to Winnie, what will you do with her?"

"We've already discussed that."

"Who do you and the governor answer to?"

"As I said, you'll find out more when we are sure we can trust you."

This guy is as slippery as socks on a waxed floor.

George reaches into his back pocket, pulls out an envelope, and hands it to me. I tear it open. A check made payable to *Bluebird Security Consultants* for one hundred grand.

I stare at it. "What is this?"

George folds his hands. "Palma Ceia Capital is your new client. We need a cybersecurity upgrade anyway. Since you've already informed your team that I'm a new customer, this makes it official. There will be a lot more money once we get Winnie."

I nearly choke on my coffee. It's a bribe, clear as day. I can use this. But how do I say no and keep breathing?

"That's not how our business works, George. We bill either upon completion of the work or at agreed-upon milestones. How am I going to explain this to the team?"

He smirks. "Send your boy Ernesto over. The hacker. We'll put him to work."

A chill rips through me. "How do you know about Ernesto?"

George spreads his hands. "Jason. It's my job to know." He waves it away, like I'm boring him. "Just cash the check and take your pretty new girlfriend to dinner at Ulele."

I slam my coffee cup down. "You're spying on me?"

He gives me a placid smile, as if I'm a child. "We're watching *you*. And anyone close to you, for your protection. Don't worry. It won't interfere with your personal life."

My pulse hammers. "So, I have no privacy, is that it?"

George ignores the question. He steeples his fingers, settling into a practiced grin. "I have exciting news. You're being invited to an important event. A gathering of the country's most influential men. Many of them support the cause."

My stomach knots. "What kind of event?"

He leans in, speaking in a voice that drips with affluence. "Think of it as an all-male, social-club retreat. Cards, fishing, drinking, and eating. And make sure to bring your friend, Oak Williams."

I slide into the car, clinging to the hope we caught something—anything—I can use.

"Well? Tell me we got the conversation."

Ernesto won't even look at me. He shakes his head. "Nothing but static. They're not taking chances anymore."

Another point for the bad guys. But the game isn't over—not even close. It's time for a field trip… and my shot at finally taking them down.

CHAPTER 45

I point at the helicopter, trying to hide my unease. "We're taking *that*?"

George is waiting at a private airstrip on Davis Islands when the Uber drops me off. I've had a few days to evaluate my situation and try to figure out what the hell I am walking into on this trip. He leads me straight to a Sikorsky S-76, where a mechanic is prepping it. It's sleek—white, with blue and black wave patterns running up the sides—and it squats on three tiny wheels.

George smirks. "Not only are we taking it—I'm your pilot."

Of course he is. This guy is worth millions, runs a club of sociopaths, and flies choppers for fun. First Zeke and now this. *Can't I just get a flight on Delta?*

I know I must play the part of a secret-society predator, but every name and face gets logged for the day I break free and bring these monsters down. They need to trust me, and then they will reveal even more information I can use against them. I'm not sure why they want Oak on the island, but as usual, I couldn't reach him, which means at least he's out of harm's way—for now. Before I deal with anything, I need to survive the flight.

The mechanic hauls away our luggage while George gives me a quick tour. The cockpit is a chaotic mix of dials, switches, and screens, with two pilot chairs and what looks like a video-game joystick bolted between them. Behind it, there's a long white leather bench along one wall and a couple of bucket seats opposite.

"These things are pretty simple," George says. "Throttle, cyclic stick, tail rotor pedals. We're legally required to have a co-pilot, so you can relax in the back. Here he comes now."

I glance outside. Omaha is strutting toward us, radiating aggression like a dog released from its chain. His mean gray eyes lie in wait behind black wraparound sunglasses.

"He's your co-pilot?" I ask. That's all I need.

George grins. "You bet. Omaha learned in the military. After a Black Hawk, this is a toy. We shouldn't need to shoot anything down today."

Omaha boards without acknowledging me, shakes George's hand, and slides into the pilot's chair, running through the checklist. George looks like he stepped out of a yacht ad—watermelon-pink Peter Millar golf shirt, dark dress pants, boat shoes. Omaha is the opposite: cargo shorts, a Cubs jersey, and a backward Skoal hat. He is spitting tobacco into a dented Coke can.

I try to focus. "Can you please tell me more about this 'trip'? My team is not exactly buying the story that I'm going camping with a bunch of billionaires."

George settles into the left seat and flips switches as the rotors start to whine. He gestures to a pair of matching headsets.

"Rooster Island," he says through the headset, "is about 200 acres off the Naples coast. Private. The only way to get there is by boat or helicopter. Most people come through Naples, and then the owner sends a speedboat. We're skipping the line."

"And who owns it? What's with the name?"

He laughs. "Family trust you'd recognize, but there's no paper trail. They're friends of the cause. Technically, a sanctuary for roosters—to get nonprofit status—but the damn birds took over the whole island and shit on everything. It's disgusting."

"What exactly happens at this Rooster Island?"

George smiles like he's about to sell me a used Chevy. "Think of it as a secret club for the rich and powerful. The members gather once a year and have a little fun. The cause uses it as a recruiting tool, but not everyone in attendance is included, so you need to be discreet. You'll like it. There are ten separate camps with twenty guys in a cabin; cards, fishing, and whiskey."

Omaha fires up the engines. The rotors accelerate, becoming a blur. George steadies the controls, his grin unshakable.

"Sit back, Jason," he says. "Half-hour flight. You'll love it."

I sink into the leather bench as the helicopter lifts off, nose tipping forward, slicing through the air. The ground falls away, and Tampa shrinks beneath us.

I stare out the window, mind spinning with everything left behind—Lia, Syd, *The One*, Sloppy Joe, Zeke. So many loose ends, all tangled up, tightening around my throat.

I wonder if I'll ever make things right.

I wonder if I'll ever make it back from Rooster Island.

CHAPTER 46

"There it is, Jason," George says as he banks the helicopter in a slow circle around the island. It's almost a perfect square, floating a couple of miles off the mainland. Blue water glitters on all sides. From up here, I can see the rooftops of scattered buildings, roads weaving between them, thousands of palm trees, and a beach along the western side. Something big sits on the sand, but I can't make out what it is.

George circles once more, then brings the Sikorsky down into a clearing where the palms have been cut back. The landing is smooth, effortless.

We step out and are immediately met by a half-dozen men in matching baby-blue polos and khaki shorts. One of them—bright white smile, polished bald head, posture full of practiced confidence—offers us a pink cocktail crowned with a pineapple wedge. His gaze lingers on me a beat too long, his smile slipping for a flicker before snapping back into place.

"Welcome to Rooster Island," he says. "I'm Malik. I'll take you to your cabin and help you with anything you need, day or night."

This isn't a vacation, and these are not my friends. I need to dig up some dirt. Find something I can use. The clock is ticking, and they expect me to deliver Winnie when we get back. I can't do that.

We follow Malik down a dirt path lined with palm trees, chickens, roosters, and chicks weaving through our feet. Overhead, the helicopter roars back into the sky, Omaha in the pilot's seat, barely glancing down as George waves. Clearly, he is not as concerned about flying without a co-pilot.

After a short hike through squawking birds, we reach a sprawling Key West-style cabin painted a minty green with pink trim. The sign out front reads *Island Time*. Music and laughter spill out the windows.

Inside, I hear a familiar voice already holding court, telling stories at top volume.

"And then I asked the stewardess, 'Are you still in the Mile High Club if you are by yourself?'" he shouts, sending a group of older guys into a fit of laughter.

When he sees me, his grin stretches even wider. "Oh my god, my best friend, Jason Miles! Boys, meet the man, the myth, the legend! Oh, wait, that's me!"

He wraps me in a bear hug, nearly lifting me off my feet. He smells like sweat and stale beer, dressed in shorts, a tank top, flip-flops, and a straw beach hat. The rest of the men wear golf shirts stretched over protruding bellies, creased shorts, and boat shoes.

I look around—there are big-name politicians, a couple of chart-topping musicians, and some CEOs I recognize from magazine covers. Everybody's drinking. George starts working the room, introducing me as the CEO of Bluebird Security.

When I finally break away, I pull Oak to the side.

"What the hell are you doing here?" I ask. "You never called me back."

Oak takes a sloppy sip of beer, missing part of his mouth, and shrugs. "Jay-Bird, I come to Roosterfest every year unless I'm filming. This is where all the rich and powerful hang. Studio execs, producers, actors, CEOs. Barbecue and whiskey on tap. How'd *you* score an invitation? No offense, but you're not exactly Oak Williams."

"Yeah, thanks for the reminder," I say, rolling my eyes. "My customer, George, pulled strings."

He looks me over, frowning. "Jesus, man, you look rough. The beard, the hair—you're starting to look like Evil Jason. You need to clean up your look. You know Avner is still pissed about the Greece fiasco."

I rub my face. My head is pounding, and my shoulder feels like it's on fire. "I'll deal with him when I get back."

Oak grins, switching topics without missing a beat. "What about that hot little blonde? You ever plant your flag?" He makes a crude gesture.

"If you mean Syd, yeah, we're seeing each other."

He lets out a whistle. "Damn, Jay-Bird! I didn't think you'd ever get over Lia. Syd's a knockout. Not Oak Williams-level, obviously," he laughs, "but a solid ten for you."

I steer him back. "What happens at this place, exactly?"

Oak raises his beer. "Guy stuff. We drink, smoke, and play cards. There are some more serious breakouts, and I skip those. I hang with the musicians, jam out, and smoke a little weed. Tomorrow night, they bring in some women. Final night, there's a ceremony."

"What kind of ceremony?"

He smirks. "I could tell you, but then I'd have to kill you."

He claps me on the shoulder, and I wince in pain. "Come on, let's get you a drink and we'll clean these actor boys out at the poker game tonight."

A few hours later, after an afternoon of too many cocktails and bad jokes, we follow a stream of guys from other cabins toward the main lodge, growing into a drunken, laughing mob. I wonder what the collective net worth of this crew is.

It is hard to believe some of these guys are part of *The One*. They seem like rich guys embracing their inner frat boy, not planning world supremacy. I remind myself of the mission. Record names, faces, and anything else I can use to prove that Frederick and George are dirty. I also need to keep Oak in the dark to keep him safe. I wonder if they want him here for leverage.

The lodge is huge, with a massive thatch roof and tiki torches lining the perimeter. Standing at the main entrance, arms wide like a televangelist, is Governor Frederick himself. He's tan, comfortable, dressed in a tropical-print shirt and linen cream slacks.

"Jason!" he calls out, clapping me on the back. "So good to see you. We'll catch up privately with George later. For now, meet everyone you can."

I nod, introduce Oak, and slip inside. The place is wide open, with round tables filling the space, bars in every corner, and a buffet line being laid out. On the walls, hundreds of animal heads—deer, antelope, even a giant elephant with tusks as long as my arms.

Oak is already off making new best friends, so I head for the nearest bar. The first face I recognize is a blast from the past. Sebastian Keller. One of the biggest developers in the South—and a man Avner and I nearly fed to bull sharks during the Safe Harbor Bank fiasco.

His face drains of color the second he sees me.

"What the fuck are *you* doing here?" he spits. "Your psycho friend with you? I'll call security."

"Nice to see you too, Sebastian," I say, taking the Cabernet the bartender hands me. "I thought you'd learned to stay away from these circles."

He flips me the bird and scurries away.

George materializes beside me, cool as ever. "Making friends already?"

I smirk. "We go way back."

George's voice lowers. "I know. Just remember, we're all on the same side now."

I look around the room, at the politicians, celebrities, and power brokers, all laughing and drinking like this is just another weekend getaway.

And I wonder, once again, what the hell I've gotten myself into.

CHAPTER 47

Avner and Goat cut across the water in a pink-and-blue Scarab, the twin 502s howling beneath their feet. They stand shoulder-to-shoulder at the helm with Avner driving. The wind tears at their shirts and blows their hair.

Avner's in dark sunglasses, flip-flops, and an untucked short-sleeve shirt that does a good job concealing his Beretta. He glances over at Goat and scowls. "Why are you dressed like that?"

Goat is wearing a white suit with a pink t-shirt underneath. The suit jacket's sleeves are rolled up. He pops off his Ray-Bans. "Look around, partner. You and I are the new Crockett and Tubbs. Tampa Vice. I'm the cool one, Sonny, obviously."

"You look ridiculous," Avner yells over the engine.

As Rooster Island comes into view, he eases off the throttle and drifts on the gentle chop, about fifty yards offshore. The place looks too peaceful to be real—palm trees, a white beach, a sprawling cluster of pastel cabins.

"This is the spot," Avner mutters.

"What is it, some kind of chicken farm?"

"Bird sanctuary," he says. "I put a tracker in Jason's luggage. This is where he went."

Goat scratches at his stubble. "What's the plan, Tubbs?"

Avner glares. "Call me that again, and you're swimming back to Tampa."

Before Goat can answer, three sleek black-and-silver Baja Outlaws approach fast, water spraying from their hulls. They idle just a few yards off the Scarab's bow. A total of a dozen men are on board, each with a semi-auto rifle hanging casually around their necks.

One of them—a man in a baby blue polo and khaki shorts, with a face carved out of granite—calls out, "Private property. You need to move on."

Avner plants his feet. "That island might be private, but the water isn't. Public navigation, boss."

The man doesn't blink. "There's a private event this week. You can leave under your own power, or we can open up these rifles and sink your little boat. Your choice."

The barrels come up in unison.

Avner's hand moves toward his Glock, but Goat places his hand on top and shakes his head.

He whispers, "Another time."

Avner memorizes the man's face and nods. "Fine. We'll leave. But you and I—we aren't done."

The man smiles thinly. "I'll look forward to it. We'll escort you back to the marina, Crockett and Tubbs."

As Avner throttles up and pulls away, he leans over and says, "Why do you always have to embarrass me?"

****

The day on Rooster Island was fantastic. While Oak slept off a night of cards and booze, I attended several breakout sessions with George. I almost forgot why I was invited.

My favorite talk was on the economy. It was led by the CEO of the nation's largest bank. After the talk, George introduced me, and the man gave me his card.

"I have to admit," I tell George afterward, "this is insane. Everyone here is someone."

George puffs on a cigar, dark eyes unreadable. "So are you, Jason. Come on. Fun's over."

His mood shifts in a blink. He no longer walks beside me, but strides ahead, making me follow. We cut through the cabins until we reach a bright-pink cabin with purple shutters. A sign reads *Driftwood Dreams*.

Malik waits by the door, no goofy grin or fruity cocktails, just crossed arms and a hard stare.

"Step to the side," he says. "I'm going to search you."

"Is that necessary?"

He doesn't bother to answer, starts patting me down, working every inch—a little too slow and rough around my belt and thighs.

"He's clean," he calls to George.

My heart is pounding so hard I feel it in my ears. Sweat pools under my shirt.

Inside, they've cleared out the beds and set up twenty folding chairs, all aimed at a makeshift stage. Seated in those chairs are senators, mayors, a hedge fund titan, and a Federal Reserve Board governor.

And there, standing at a podium, is Governor Frederick in a linen suit, arms spread wide.

"Gentlemen, our guest of honor has arrived. For those who haven't met him, this is Jason Miles."

A slow murmur rolls through the room. Faces turn. Eyes take me in, measure me, strip me down. George steers me to a seat in the front row.

Frederick beams. "Jason, these men are the core of the cause. Rooster Island is our chance to network, yes—but also to plan, to recruit, and to expand."

I scan the crowd. Two familiar mayors. A senator from the northeast. A money manager who was on CNBC last month.

And then my stomach drops. A face I know too well, from a night in a trunk and a prison hit.

Warden Walter Billy Ray stands up, squaring his shoulders.

"'Scuse me," he drawls, pointing a bony finger at me. "I got somethin' needs sayin'. This sumbitch right here? He's an FBI mole."

CHAPTER 48

The room erupts in angry shouts. Members of the inner circle whirl on each other, their faces red, voices overlapping. My skin goes hot, my pulse pounding as I scan for help. My eyes land on George, but he looks just as shell-shocked.

This is bad. That hillbilly blowing my cover is a problem. Without their trust, they might decide to silence me for good. Before I can speak, the governor swoops in.

"Everyone, calm down," Frederick commands, his tone slicing through the chaos like a blade.

"That boy was with the FBI, hasslin' me at the prison!" the warden barks. "We cain't trust him!"

Frederick fixes him with a flat stare. "Warden, I always value your input, but Jason has been thoroughly vetted. And he has plenty of incentive to join us. I personally vouch for him."

The warden scowls, arms folded, eyes burning holes in me.

Then another man rises—a general whose face I recognize from television, a battlefield legend. He jabs a stubby finger at me. "What makes this boy so important that we just hand him our secrets? He knows who we are now."

He's right. Their faces are seared into my memory. They are all going down. Assuming, of course, I survive Rooster Island.

Frederick holds up a hand. "We'll get to that, General. First, some housekeeping. I want to thank all of you for your efforts. We are in the ninth inning of our initiative. South America and Europe are firmly under our influence."

A voice from the back: "What about the Middle East? That's still a problem."

Frederick shakes his head, calm as a surgeon. "We have an arrangement with the oil states. And if any other nations prove troublesome, we'll remove them from the board."

A low murmur of agreement spreads around the table.

Remove them from the board?

"What about the gangs in Mexico?" another man asks.

"We've been over this," he says. "For now, we work with them. Their poison thins the weak herd. And when the moment comes, we send in our military and wipe them out"—he snaps his fingers—"just like that. No gangs, no drugs, and, in the worst case, no Mexico."

The entire room starts to snap. I look around and find myself snapping as well.

Frederick presses on. "We need to double our fundraising. Whatever it takes. The results will be worth every sacrifice. Remember, from chaos comes peace. One leader, one world. But until then, no loose ends. Cover your tracks. We are closer to victory than ever."

He walks in my direction, extending his hand, and urges me to stand beside him.

"Now, to the General's question. You need to understand that Jason Miles is Preferred."

A ripple of murmurs rushes through the group, then more snapping breaks out—a strange, unsettling wave of approval.

Preferred? The word still means nothing to me, but it clearly means everything to them.

Why won't they tell me what the hell it means? How horrible can it be?

Frederick lets the snapping die before delivering the final blow.

"Secondly, Jason is the key to our ultimate triumph. He will help us gain access to the most powerful quantum computer ever built—capable of breaking any encryption on Earth."

He pauses, letting that sink in, and then adds, almost casually, "Yes, gentlemen. That includes nuclear codes."

****

Avner sits across from the man they call Omaha—real name Connor Doyle. His face is still sunburnt from the boat ride, and his pride smarts after being escorted back to the marina like a child on a borrowed boat.

Connor doesn't bother to look up from his battered copy of *Extreme Ownership*. Steam rises from a chipped ceramic mug, and an apple core sits browning on the table between them.

Avner already knows the file his Israeli contact provided by heart. Connor Doyle, thirty-five. Former Navy SEAL from Nebraska. He grew up in a rough South Omaha neighborhood and joined the Navy after graduating from high school. After several years of successful missions with the SEALs, he left the military. They believe he led a group of "shadow" SEALs that worked covertly for the government, completing off-the-book jobs. At some point, the group went rogue and is now available to the highest bidder.

Connor's gray eyes finally rise, cold and unblinking. "Something I can do for you, Avner Cohen?"

Avner leans in. "I want to know why you're meeting with Jason Miles."

Connor sets the book aside, studying Avner like a lion sizing up another predator. "Name doesn't ring a bell."

Ignoring the bait, Avner responds, "I wonder to myself, why would a respected member of society be dealing with some scumbag gun for hire? I'm not sure what Jason tangled himself in, but I'm telling you this: I've got his back. And you don't want a problem with me."

Connor sips his coffee, eyes drifting toward another man across the café. Avner tracks the look, his pulse tightening as his hand inches toward the Glock in the small of his back. He checks the room for collateral damage.

Connor's voice stays even. "Well, Israeli, maybe your friend is not as respected as you think. And you're not the only one with contacts. We know who you really are—a psychotic agent playing house in America with your new girlfriend, Apple Lee. We also know you nearly died last year. Maybe you should have. Or just taken the money and disappeared like your bitch ex-partner."

Avner pushes back from the table, standing fast, his hand ready. "You dig into my past again, or mention Apple or Lia, and I'll bury you in the swamps. Understood?"

At that moment, three men of Connor's size close in, jackets shifting with the unmistakable bulge of weapons. Connor doesn't even flinch, gray eyes locked on Avner's.

"Time to go, Avner," he says calmly. "But I'm sure we'll see each other again. Real soon. Say hi to Jason."

CHAPTER 49

I feel sick after the meeting, but I can't deny it—my ego is riding high. The rich and powerful treated me like a hero, fighting for space to shake my hand while George and the governor stood nearby, grinning like proud parents. Even one of my childhood basketball idols pulled me in for a hug.

The only one not buying my act is Warden Billy Ray. He leaned in close, sour breath curling around my ear. "Don't think you're slick, boy," he hissed. "I got my eyes on ya, and I ain't lookin' away."

His words cover me like a rash as I wander back toward the cabins as the sun begins to set. I feel the weight of every handshake, every false smile. I remind myself who these men are.

When I get back, Oak is alone by a campfire, smoking a joint, listening to reggae. A big, multicolored rooster sits calmly next to him on the ground, as if it belongs there.

"Where you been, Jay-Bird?" he calls out.

I drop into a seat across from him. "I was with my client talking to some guys about an opportunity. What are you doing here all by yourself?"

He takes a long pull and exhales into the flames, the smoke swirling up like a ghost. "Everybody's over at the main building," he says. "It's ladies' night—they fly in hookers for those old bastards hopped up on Viagra. You know Oak Williams doesn't need to pay to play."

I almost laugh, but it dies in my throat. Sitting here with Oak, a part of me wants to spill everything. Maybe he'd know someone who could help. But what if he can't? What if I just end up getting him killed?

I can't have any more blood on my hands.

"You good, Jason? You seem… off, which doesn't make sense to me. You've got a growing business, a hot girlfriend, a rich, famous, and incredibly handsome best friend—what could be wrong?"

If he only knew.

"Give me that," I say, grabbing the joint.

I inhale deeply, let the smoke burn through me, then exhale, the earthy scent wrapping around my head. Things slow down, and the panic steps back. I take another pull and hand it over.

"I need to talk to you about something, Oak. But first, what's with the rooster?" I ask.

He glances at it, eyes half-lidded. "No clue. I was sitting here, getting high, and he just sat down. I'm thinking of getting him tattooed on my ass. Still got some real estate available down south."

"That's an image I did *not* need."

"Maybe he's stoned too," Oak shrugs, and we both crack up, giggling like kids.

The weed is helping to convince me to come clean when George suddenly appears, carrying a six-pack of Jai Alai.

"Sorry to barge in," he says, "but that scene up there's not my thing. Mind if I have a couple of beers with you guys? You like pale ale?"

Oak grins. "Sure, man, the more the merrier. Any friend of Jason's is a friend of Oak Williams and my pet bird, Drumstick."

George hands me a cold bottle, eyes searching mine. "That okay with you, Jason?"

I nod, swallowing the lump in my throat. "Yeah. Hard to pass on a Jai Alai."

Oak leans back, eyes drifting shut. "Did you need to tell me something, Jay-Bird?"

George looks at me, too, calm but laser-focused. "Yeah, Jason. Did you?" he asks, slowly shaking his head from side to side.

I hold George's stare, my brain buzzing from the weed and the dread. And I know I'm completely screwed.

CHAPTER 50

It is finally the last full day on the island. I tossed and turned all night trying to formulate a plan. When I did sleep, my dreams were a blur of roosters, Lia, and men snapping.

Most of the men headed out early for their chartered fishing trips, leaving the cabin quiet. Oak slept until nearly eleven, giving me the perfect window to work. I pulled out a small notebook and carefully listed every name I could remember from *The One's* meeting. Once I was back in Tampa, I'd dig into each man's background—and figure out exactly how to leverage them. The beginning of a plan is starting to grow, but it is still a small seed that needs water. I need to pay attention to my surroundings and find some weak links.

When Oak finally gets dressed, I hide the notebook in my backpack and prepare for the day. I can't have anyone finding my notes.

After a light lunch, Oak and I hit the gym. It feels good having time with him again—just the two of us—and I'm not about to ruin it by dragging my mess into the moment. George's warning last night was unmistakable; the look in his eyes told me Oak would be in danger if I said a word. I won't put him in that position.

As night falls, we head with the rest of the group to the main building for a bourbon tasting. The CEO of a major distillery hosts the event, and the venue has a polished, low-lit ambiance. An Old-Fashioned is placed in front of every chair, easing us into the evening.

The night carries a strange vibe. I keep catching people staring at me, only to turn their eyes away the second I look back. Maybe it's just my paranoia, but it feels too deliberate to ignore. I mention it to Oak, and he brushes it off, insisting everyone's looking at him—he's the biggest star on the island after all. It must be nice in his world.

When the CEO drones on about the history of bourbon—the centuries of craftsmanship, the chemistry of charred oak barrels—half the room starts yawning.

Finally, a staffer sets down a tasting kit—small pours of bourbon in Glencairn glasses are lined up.

"Take the first bourbon," the CEO instructs. "Smell the aroma. See if you can identify hints of vanilla or caramel."

Oak shoots me a look, then throws the entire glass back in one gulp. "Definitely vanilla," he says, deadpan.

An old man across the table scowls at us.

The CEO soldiers on. "Now, sip gently and note the sweetness, the smoke…"

Glass after glass goes down, each one paired with bites of cheese, chocolate, or smoked meats.

About halfway through, Oak leans close. "This is way too bougie for me," he mutters, and we slip outside for air.

He excuses himself to "water the bushes," disappearing behind the building.

I stay by the railing, breathing deeply. The past few days swirl through my head—the conspiracies, the secrets, the half-seductive talk of a better world under one ruler. Part of me hates admitting it, but there's logic in it. Perhaps having one world, one leader, could end the never-ending conflicts.

I need to snap out of that thinking. They are trying to manipulate me for their own purposes.

I look around for Oak. He's nowhere.

A second later, darkness floods over me—a black bag slams down over my head. Strong hands seize my arms, wrenching me off the ground.

This is it. Something told me I'd never make it off Rooster Island.

CHAPTER 51

They carry me like a sack of potatoes for what feels like forever, my head spinning from the jostling. I twist, try to break free, but the ropes bite into my wrists. Then I hear the warden's greasy drawl right below me.

"C'mon now, y'all, let's git this boy strung up!"

The rest of the voices blur together in a mess of chanting and half-mad shouting.

When they finally dump me down, I feel my feet sink into sand, toes curling in the cool grit. Thick ropes lash my arms to something solid and heavy behind me. I twist and turn to no avail.

The ocean breeze, the smell of salt—I'm on the beach. I'm not dead yet. Maybe there's still a chance. I need to survive. I can't let them win, not like this.

Where the hell is Oak?

They rip the bag off my head, and I squint into the harsh light of torches and a massive full moon overhead. As my eyes adjust, I see them—a hundred men in black ceremonial robes, ringed around me.

They've tied me at the base of a thirty-foot stone rooster statue; its wings spread in a pose halfway between glorious and obscene.

This must be what I saw from the helicopter.

A masked figure pushes through the mob, stooped and slow, a gleaming dagger in his hand, catching every bit of moonlight. The crowd chants nonsense words that build in volume, mixed with the pulsing beat of ritual drums hidden in the dunes. The sound rises, whipping them into a frenzy.

Then, all at once, the drums cut out. Silence slams down like a hammer, and the robed men all drop to their knees—except the one with the knife.

He raises his voice:

"Who offers this man as a sacrifice to the Great Rooster?"

I feel my legs tremble as I see George stand and step forward, his voice calm.

"I do, Your Excellence."

A wave of panic washes through me.

A sacrifice? Did the warden convince them?

The masked man turns toward me. "Jason Miles, membership in this society is only by invitation. You have been chosen for inclusion. It is an honor. I will now ask you several questions you must answer in the affirmative. Do you understand?"

I stand there, unable to speak until George leans close enough that I can smell the bourbon on his breath. "Say yes, Jason."

I mutter, "Yes."

"Do you swear to protect the secrets of the Great Rooster society, even at great personal cost?"

What the fuck?

I glance around at this fever-dream scene—the masks, the robes, the roaring surf. I'm pretty sure they aren't about to kill me. Probably.

I swallow hard and force my voice to work. "Yes. I do."

"Will you remain loyal to your brothers in this order above all others?"

"Yes."

"Do you agree never to reveal what you learn here to the uninitiated?"

"Yes."

"Do you believe in the mission of this society and commit to advancing it?"

Which mission? The Roosters or the psychos?

"Yes."

"Will you carry out the tasks entrusted to you, without fail?"

I hesitate, contemplating the question and all it could mean. Faces of the people I love flicker through my mind, one after another. If I don't say yes, every one of them could die.

"Yes."

"Do you agree to abide by our rituals and attend our gatherings?"

No, I am hoping you are all in prison.

"Yes," I say louder.

The old man lifts the dagger and cuts the ropes off my wrists.

A split second later, the crowd erupts. Bottles of champagne appear from under their robes, and they pop them, spraying me in a wild, sticky celebration. The foamy mess soaks me from head to toe as men rush forward to hug me, slap my shoulders, and pull me in.

Through the chaos, I spot Oak laughing with the general, shouting something I can't quite make out over the roar.

Governor Frederick appears last, steady, smiling, extending his hand through the downpour of champagne. I see a tear roll down his cheek.

"You are one of us now," he says.

CHAPTER 52

Everyone leaves the island after breakfast—except George, Governor Frederick, and me.

The staff scurries around the grounds, cleaning up the wreckage from a night that went loud and late. Well past 3 a.m., by my count.

We're holed up in a cabin called the *Hodge Podge Lodge*. The furniture is mismatched, dark leather, heavy, and worn. Frederick lounges across a long couch like he owns the place—which he might. George and I sit opposite him in cracked club chairs that creak every time we shift. It smells like stale beer and cigar smoke.

This is my chance to squeeze more information out of them. I've done everything they've asked to earn their trust, and I need something new to add to my hidden notebook.

Frederick breaks the silence. "Did you enjoy the weekend?"

I shoot him a look. "Everything but being kidnapped and tied to a giant rooster. That part might take some intensive therapy to work through."

He chuckles like I'm joking. I'm not.

"I want more information about the cause. Maybe I am misunderstanding it," I state. "More about *The One*."

"It goes by many names," he says, hands steepled across his chest. "But the goal is the same—unity. A righteous objective."

"Why don't you start with what Preferred means. Why is it a

big secret?" I ask. "I vowed to join your cause and even joined the Roosters. You need to start trusting me."

They look at each other, and George nods toward Frederick.

"A society like ours has many different levels. Not everyone has access to all the secrets. All the plans. Some have specific roles, and some are leaders who know everything."

"So, what am I?"

"Right now, somewhere between a neophyte trying to become an apprentice. But being Preferred allows you to move up quickly," Frederick responds.

"Like that kid's game where there are chutes and ladders. If we can trust you, you take the ladder right to the top. Right to the Inner Sanctum with direct access to the Supreme Master," George adds.

This is new information.

"There is a Supreme Master? Who is it? Where is he or she?"

"Slow down, Jason," George warns.

"I am having trouble understanding the righteous objective. All I've seen is theft, blackmail, and murder. Doesn't exactly scream honorable."

"Jason," Frederick says with forced patience, "you're too focused on *how*. You need to understand *why*. This world is spinning off its axis. Left to their own devices, humanity will tear itself apart. You must know that."

George leans in, lowering his voice like we're sharing a secret. "We're on the brink right now. China, Russia, the U.S.—this close to war." He holds two fingers an inch apart. "Any spark could set it off: Taiwan, Israel, a rogue state with a suitcase nuke, even a market collapse. The Middle East is a powder keg. We're the solution. *You're* the solution."

He pauses. "You have access to Winnie. We need her to prevent collapse. Think about it. You will help avert the end of civilization. Talk about being a hero."

I shake my head. "It sounds like we're terrorists. They always point to a righteous cause as well. What's the difference?"

Frederick snorts. "It's not all sunshine and ponies, Jason. If diplomacy worked, we'd use it. But time's up. We've been working behind the scenes for centuries. Most of our work is quiet and peaceful. But sometimes? You use the hammer, not the honey."

"Why do we steal from the poor and funnel it to the powerful? That's not saving the world."

"Like it or not," Frederick replies, "the gap between rich and poor is growing. The elite—those with vision and intelligence—will lead. And that will result in a safer, better world for everyone."

George taps my knee like we're old friends. "Imagine a world with unified leadership. No politics. No division. Just order."

I stare at him. "You keep saying, *we're almost there*. What does that *mean*? If you want me involved and want Winnie, I need answers. Who's really running this? What happens if I say no?"

Frederick rises and begins pacing. He's restless now. Calculating.

"We still don't know if we can trust you, Jason. But in time, you'll know everything. You have an important role. When the change is complete, you'll be among the leaders. We already control several nations. Others are... teetering. There is even talk of me running for the President."

More new information. I can't let this delusional man anywhere near the White House.

George stands too. The meeting is over. I can feel it.

"We need to know if you're loyal," he says. "Here's the test."

I don't move. "A test?"

"You have a client—Regency Bank."

"Yeah?"

"You're going to give us access to their systems."

"To do *what*?"

"Whatever we want," Frederick says, voice sharp as broken glass.

George's tone stays even. "We need to test some things before trying it at Tampa Scientific."

"And if I refuse?"

Frederick glares at me. "You need to stop asking that."

He leans in, deadly calm. "The answer never changes. We erase everyone you love—one by one. You'll live to feel every ounce of it. And we start with Lia."

I wait until they're out of sight before jogging back to my cabin. I need to get my notes down while everything is still sharp. The reminder of what happens to the disobedient rattles me, but I shove it aside.

Inside, the room has already been tidied. My pulse spikes as I tear into my backpack. I reach the spot where I hid the notebook. I dump everything onto the bed: pens, pencils, a calculator, two books, a pullover.

Then I stare. The space is empty. My notes are gone. And whoever took them now knows I've been spying.

CHAPTER 53

The stress coils inside me like a shaken bottle of champagne—ready to explode but not yet uncorked. Pressure builds in every breath, every heartbeat. I can barely think straight, let alone breathe, as I replay what *The One* has asked me to do.

Change the course of history.

They call me a hero—but in any sane telling of this story, I'd be the villain.

I'm not proud of what I've done. Agreeing to play along with this madness—and shutting out my friends—gnaws at me. But it's the only way. I'll take down Frederick, George, and all their merry men and keep everyone safe. It is my only path back to a normal life if such a thing is even possible for someone like me.

I run the plan through my mind again and again—revising it, tightening it—yet each pass makes it heavier. Since my return from Rooster Island, the days at the office have been tense. I sense eyes on me, glances that disappear the moment I look up.

I need to clear my head. One place always helps: *South Tampa Krav Maga*, where I can sweat, breathe, and move. A place where my fists can think for me, and the noise in my mind gets turned down—at least for an hour.

Also, something is brewing between me and Omaha. There's a charge in the air, violent and inevitable. I can feel it coming. If he comes for me, I need to be ready.

Upon returning from Israel many years ago, I sought a gym that wasn't all mirrors and flexing. The owner, Instructor E, is the real deal. We connected from the beginning, and I've attended once or twice a week for a decade, except for when I was on the run. I have superior skills, so Instructor E has me work with the less experienced students. If I start getting cocky, he spars with me and easily forces me to submit.

Krav Maga is designed for survival—real-world violence. No rules, no showboating, just brutal, efficient ends to fights you didn't start. One wall of the gym reads, painted in block letters: **THE BEST WAY TO WIN A FIGHT IS TO NOT GET INTO ONE.**

The gym smells like ammonia and rubber mats. It's warm and humming with motion. Some students hammer heavy bags while others trade controlled kicks. I recognize most faces—except one.

A new guy. Big. Barrel chest. Goatee.

I nod at him. "You new?"

He grunts. "Name's Blackjack."

Something about him puts me on edge. I'm off-balance already—jittery, raw—but now I'm watching him from the corner of my eye.

We start warm-ups. Dynamic stretches, hip openers, neck rolls. Then cardio: jumping jacks, high knees, ground rolls. I watch Blackjack. He's surprisingly fluid for a guy his size. Keeps glancing at me, sizing me up. I wonder where this guy came from. Could he have been sent to deliver a message?

Instructor E claps his hands. "Alright, everyone should be a glazed donut by now. Time for striking drills. Twenty minutes. Pairs. Pads. Let's work on the combinations we learned last week. Jason and I will circulate."

I move between pairs—men, women, even a few retirees. Some are stiff, while others are too aggressive. I correct their form, slow them down, and build them up. Jabs, crosses, hooks, kicks. Technique before power.

When the timer beeps, Instructor E steps forward. "Now we spar. Three-minute rounds. Light contact. No elbows, no knees. This is about control, people—street-level realism, not cage brawls. Full gear. Mouthguards. Let's go."

Most of the students pair off quickly. The buzz of nervous excitement spreads.

Then I see him—Blackjack—standing alone in the center of the mat. Nobody's volunteering. He's looking my way.

Instructor E scans the room. "We need someone to step up."

I raise my hand. "I'll take him."

I strap on my gear, adrenaline starting to pump. My shoulder's still sore, but I figure I can dance around it. Stay light. Keep it clean.

We touch gloves. The room goes quiet. A few students start whispering, watching closely. They feel what I feel. This is more than just sparring.

We circle. He's heavier, but nimble. Then—*thwack*—he lands a brutal leg kick. I stumble, surprised by his speed.

Get your head in the game, Jason.

We trade jabs. I throw a cross-hook combo that lands cleaner than I intend. He retaliates with a spinning back fist—*crack*—right against my temple.

Instructor E steps in. "Dial it down! You two want to go full contact? Take it outside. Not here."

But it's too late. The switch is flipped.

Alright, big guy. You want to throw bombs? Let's go.

I step in, trading quick jabs as I circle, light on my feet, hunting for an opening. He swings a roundhouse block—I slip inside and drive a front kick into his guard, snapping a cross right after. My leg whips up in a high arc, the kick clipping his headgear with a satisfying crack.

I engage. We trade jabs. I circle fast, looking for openings. He throws a roundhouse kick, and I counter with a front kick, then a snapping cross. I follow it with a high kick that catches his headgear.

He growls and charges. We brawl. Wild punches. I kick his ribs and land a knee into his thigh. He grunts, staggering.

Then—*bam*—he clips me with a heavy right. My headgear spins around. For a second, I think I'm knocked out. I stagger, vision blurred, until a student fixes it.

Instinct takes over. I duck low, bend my knees, shoot forward, grab the back of his legs, and drive through. We crash into the mat, me on top.

I grab his head. My voice breaks, guttural, primal.

"Who the fuck sent you? Huh? What are you doing here?"

Suddenly, Instructor E's arms are around my neck. Rear naked choke. Strong and smooth. My world starts to tilt.

I raise both hands in submission, knowing the lights go out.

He releases me and steps back. "Jason Miles, you are *banned* from this class. I don't care what you're going through. You fight like that; someone will get seriously hurt. Control yourself—or don't come back."

I stagger to my feet, breathing hard. Gloves hit the mat with a loud slap.

The students avert their eyes. No one speaks. No one helps.

"I'm sorry," I say, voice cracking. "Instructor E… I don't know what's happening to me. I've been off. Angry. Scattered. That won't happen again. I swear."

He doesn't respond. Just turns and walks away.

I strip off the rest of my gear and leave. Outside, I pass by the front window and catch my reflection in the glass.

I don't recognize the man staring back at me.

His eyes are wide, wild.

His fists still clenched.

CHAPTER 54

I feel sick walking into the weekly morning management meeting at Tampa Scientific—a required powwow between the Bluebird team and Nikesh's people. We meet in Nikesh's private conference room, which is glass and steel and sterile.

Nikesh glides in and out of the room, checking his phone every few minutes. Yet somehow, he never misses a beat. He's absorbing everything—every update, every hesitation, every glance.

I'm still rattled by what happened at the gym. The loss of control. And the orders I've been given by *The One*. This company trusts me, Nikesh trusts me—and I'm pretending I'm still worthy of that trust. Worse, I didn't even realize until this morning that I had the start of a black eye. Puffy and purple, like my soul bruising from the inside out.

Winnie is the key to this messy puzzle. I need to find out more about her strengths and weaknesses. Maybe I can give them access to her, but she has a defense mechanism. It would be a win-win. They think I'm doing what they want, but still don't get access to her. My people stay safe, and maybe they move on.

Avner shows up late, as usual. Jeans, flip-flops, and a faded Jiu-Jitsu t-shirt like we're at a beach bar instead of a briefing on national infrastructure. He grabs a bottle of water and a handful of grapes from the conference table before finally noticing me.

"What the fuck happened to your face?" he says, squinting at my eye.

"It's nothing," I lie. "Took a punch at class last night."

"Sure, Rocky," he says, tossing a grape into his mouth. "Want to hear about my hot date with Apple?"

"Will you shut up and pay attention?" Apple chimes in, smiling despite herself. She blushes.

I look at them—smiling, joking, winking like normal people. My world is cracking apart, and Avner the Grouch is in love.

Ernesto gives the usual rundown on our cybersecurity efforts—new vendor, improved threat detection, zero breaches this week. Nikesh jots a few notes, murmurs to his assistant, and then dismisses his team.

"Before we leave," I say, "do you think we could learn more about Winnie? A big part of our job is protecting her."

"Team Bluebird," he says, stepping forward with a rare smile, "you've earned a reward for your hard work. I'll show you something almost no one outside my inner circle has seen. But first, a little context."

He approaches the massive wall-mounted touchscreen that spans the length of the room. He picks up the stylus and pauses like he's centering himself. Then he writes, in large all-caps letters:

ENCRYPTION

"Jason," he says, glancing at me. "You worked in banking. What do you know about encryption?"

I clear my throat, forcing my mind back into the room. "Basically, it is all about protecting data. You convert data into a coded form, and only someone with a key or password can read it. Think about your online bank account. You need a password to access it."

"Not me. I'm all cash," Avner blurts out. "I don't trust the robots."

Nikesh ignores him and continues writing on the board:

PLAINTEXT—ALGORITHM—KEY—CIPHERTEXT

"Plaintext is readable data," he says. "It gets encrypted using an algorithm and a key."

"An algo-what?" Goat asks, blinking.

"An algorithm," I explain, "is like a set of instructions for a computer. It sorts things, searches, makes decisions. In encryption, it transforms your data."

"Exactly," Ernesto adds. "An encryption algorithm is just the method to turn regular data into coded data."

"Almost everything important is encrypted," I say. "Medical records. Social Security numbers. Financial data—credit cards, bank accounts."

"Didn't we already cover this in another meeting?" Avner mutters, stifling a yawn.

Nikesh keeps writing:

CLOUD STORAGE—WEBSITES—APPS—DEVICES

He circles them, then underlines two more words:

PRIVACY—SECURITY

Apple nods slowly. "Without encryption, there's no privacy. No security."

Then he writes a final word on the board, big and bold:

WINNIE

"As you all know," he says, "we have Winnie. She's a quantum computer—technically an Alpha Quantum System, but that's a conversation for another time."

"Quants can do a bunch of calculations at once," Goat says.

We all look at him.

He shrugs. "What? I did some research. Might have used ChatGPT."

"You're right," Nikesh replies. "Quantum computers don't process information like classical machines. They use the laws of quantum mechanics—superposition, entanglement—to make connections that traditional systems can't. They compute faster. Smarter."

"And you said last time," I add slowly, "that Winnie can break some encryptions."

Nikesh looks at me for a long moment. Then he turns back to the board and writes one final word in huge, unmistakable letters:

ALL

"I did say she could break *some* encryption," he says.

"But now, she can break *all* encryptions."

CHAPTER 55

The air is sucked from the room. Everyone straightens up in their chairs. I realize my jaw is locked, and I'm rubbing my pinky without the nail.

"It really is Q-Day," Ernesto murmurs.

I turn to Nikesh. "How is that possible? I know people have warned about Quantum Day—when quantum computing becomes powerful enough to break encryption—but that's supposed to be decades away. If it's real... if we're there now, everything's at risk. Banking. Government systems. The entire digital infrastructure."

The stakes have just skyrocketed. Winnie has reached a level most people believed was years—maybe decades—away. I can't let *The One* get anywhere near her. The thought of her power in their hands is terrifying. With her, their impossible dream suddenly isn't impossible at all. It's within reach. And that's the part that scares me most.

"What about post-quantum cryptography?" Ernesto asks. "Aren't we already developing quantum-resistant encryption?"

Nikesh silently picks up the stylus and writes two words:

TOO LATE.

I stand. "Let's be clear. Are you telling us you have a quantum computer that can break any encryption?"

Nikesh smiles like a proud father. "Winnie is actually an *Alpha Quantum Computer*."

"What the hell is that supposed to mean?" Avner asks.

"She's a next-next-generation Quant. She taught herself how to do the unimaginable. Breaking encryption is just the start. She can communicate with other machines. And you'd be surprised how many AI bots embedded in corporate systems have access to… well, everything."

"And let me guess," I say, "she has access to those bots."

"It's really quite remarkable," Nikesh says, almost glowing. "They communicate."

"Does anyone else know what Winnie is capable of?" I ask, already knowing the answer.

"Of course not," he replies. "Her existence—and her capabilities—are tightly guarded. But now, it's time you met her."

We follow Nikesh out of the conference room and down a hallway toward what looks like a storage area. He swipes a card against a hidden reader, and a seamless door opens. A sharp chill hits us immediately.

The temperature drops by at least fifteen degrees as we descend a narrow staircase. Another locked door. Armed security. Nikesh turns to Avner.

"In the coming weeks, I want a full audit of our physical security. Every inch of this place."

"Yes, sir," Avner replies, eyes scanning the setup.

We head deeper, underground now, into a surprisingly clean tunnel running beneath the building. It's far more sophisticated than the moldy Ybor tunnels I used to rescue Nikesh's son.

I stop. "Wait a second. You have tunnels under your building?"

Nikesh doesn't break stride. "We discovered them during construction. Worked with the city to seal them off… but we kept one section. It was perfect for what we needed."

Perfect for what? My mind races. Did he know about the Ybor tunnels? Was he part of that hostage operation? Is it possible that

Nikesh is part of *The One*?

We reach the final door. A massive man with a shaved head and a clipboard checks our IDs. Once cleared, we enter a changing area. Gowns, booties, hats.

When we pass through two more doors, the room hits us like a glimpse of the future.

The lighting is low and sterile. Cooling systems hum like a purring cat. A thick pane of glass divides the observation area from a chamber where a golden, chandelier-like structure dangles, spider-legged wires stretching into glowing racks of control units.

"Ladies and gentlemen," Nikesh announces, "meet Winnie. The processor is housed at the bottom, inside a dilution refrigerator. It's colder than outer space in there."

"Doesn't she get cold?" Avner quips.

Nikesh doesn't laugh. "What you're seeing is just the surface. The wiring, hardware, the helium tanks—every part is necessary to keep her functional."

Ernesto's mouth is hanging open. "This is amazing."

Technicians in white lab coats monitor readings on nearby screens. I step closer.

"What are they tracking?"

"Real-time stats," Nikesh says. "Coherence times, gate fidelities, error rates... the things that keep Winnie stable. These guys are top-tier physicists. The best in the world."

Nikesh sits at a terminal and begins typing. A large monitor blinks on. A female voice speaks through a speaker:

"Good morning, Nikesh. I see you've brought guests."

A female avatar appears on screen—elegant, uncanny. She wears stylish librarian glasses.

"Are you going to introduce me?" she asks.

"She can talk?" Apple asks, eyebrows raised.

"Oh yes," Nikesh says. "Winnie, meet the Bluebird team. They protect us from cyber threats. Can you say hello?"

The avatar morphs into a vivid bluebird.

"Nice to meet you, Bluebirds."

I wave.

"Winnie, can you demonstrate your encryption-breaking abilities?"

"Of course," she replies. "It's one of my favorite tricks and very easy. How about the Bluebird bank account?"

"That's not possible," I say. "We use Regency Bank. We designed their security protocols ourselves. It's airtight."

The screen flickers. The bank's online platform appears, followed by a balance: **$450,353.23**.

I feel my stomach drop.

"Here is the balance," she says sweetly. "Would you like me to transfer it? Avner, you could use a few dollars." She giggles.

"Why is there that much money in our account?" Avner shoots me a look sharp enough to cut steel.

The screen shifts again, revealing two deposits—$100,000 each—from Cigar City Capital.

"Looks like your boy George has been paying you," Avner says, voice tight. "And we haven't done anything for him yet. Must be paying you for something."

How the hell do I explain that?

Apple steps forward. "Let me try. Hi, Winnie. I'm Apple."

Winnie's screen fills with an image of Apple. We all laugh.

"Apple Lee. Accomplished author and professor. And currently writing a book on secret societies."

Apple freezes. "How do you know that?"

"I accessed your iCloud account. It wasn't hard."

"That's supposed to be protected," she says under her breath.

"Not anymore," Nikesh says, without a trace of remorse.

CHAPTER 56

"Today is going to change your life forever," George says, pacing like a kid waiting for Santa. He's jittery, glancing toward the door as if someone—or something—is about to burst through. "You are going to meet a genius."

We're in a private office on the main floor of a modern waterfront mansion on Davis Islands—sleek lines, steel, and glass. Outside, floor-to-ceiling windows frame an infinity pool that appears to spill seamlessly into the open water. The landscaping is dense and intentional—tropical plants, sculpted hedges, strange metallic statues jutting out like alien relics. A woman lounges poolside in a barely-there bikini, sipping something from a tall glass.

It has been a couple of days since we met Winnie. I need to move my plan forward. After the exhibition at Tampa Scientific, there's no denying Winnie's ability to reshape civilization. When I pushed him, Nikesh finally admitted that Winnie has no way to defend herself from an attack. That's an entirely different skill set—and the reason he's relying so heavily on Bluebird.

I now know I cannot do this alone. I'm going to have to include Ernesto. He has the right skill set, will ask the fewest questions, and I can trust him. If I can build a strong enough case, I'll bring it to Zeke before I am supposed to turn over Winnie. The full force of the FBI might be able to keep us all safe. But I'm going to need some solid proof. Zeke has been clear that he does not believe in *The One*.

Even if Zeke cooperates and I manage to keep everyone else safe, there's still Lia. I've called her every day since our fight and hear nothing but endless ringing. If I turn on *The One*, how am I supposed to protect someone I can't even find?

"Whose house is this, George?" I ask, tearing my eyes away from the pool—and then stealing another look.

Davis Islands is a high-end neighborhood located just south of Downtown Tampa. It was constructed on top of two natural islands and is one of the most desirable addresses in the area. Driving in, we saw a mix of Mediterranean-style architecture and new-build modern residences like the one we are sitting in.

Before George can answer, a booming voice fills the room.

"Gentlemen!"

Claude Hoffmann strides in like he owns the world. His hair is even longer than I remember—loose curls down to his shoulders. His shirt is a loud tropical print, unbuttoned to the middle of his chest. A two-day beard creeps around a thick mustache. He's barefoot, wearing flowing white linen pants. He looks like a beach prophet who traded his sandals for a laptop.

Brushing his hair back, he smiles. "I hope you haven't been waiting long."

"Not at all," George says. "Claude, you remember Jason Miles?"

"How could I forget?" Claude grins and extends his hand like a catcher's mitt. His grip is iron. "The hero."

I force a smile. I have no idea what we're doing here. Governor Frederick supposedly brought in Claude to end cybercrime in Florida, straight from an executive seat at Google. I thought he was one of the good guys. I am starting to wonder if there are any good guys.

Claude follows my gaze to the pool. "Enjoying the view?" He smirks. "I've got a downtown office, but I prefer working here. It's a rental. Used to belong to a famous football player."

"I don't blame you," I say. "This place is incredible."

It is. Sunlight floods the space. On one wall, a high-res screen cycles through digital renderings of famous paintings. In the corner, a white guitar rests on a sculptural stand—sleek, iconic.

"That's Prince's guitar from *Purple Rain*," Claude says. "Beautiful, right? It inspires me. Like all beautiful things." His eyes flick back toward the pool.

With two sharp claps, the floor-to-ceiling windows tint dark. A massive screen descends from the ceiling.

"Join me," he says, motioning to a crescent-shaped leather couch. He grabs a laptop from a reclaimed wood desk and starts typing.

The screen lights up, showing stars and nebulae. A soft voice speaks from hidden speakers: "The world is changing. This isn't science fiction. This is now."

Claude turns to me. "People fear artificial intelligence. They shouldn't. We should *embrace* it. The age of human dominance is over."

"What do you mean?" I ask.

He doesn't answer. Instead, more images flicker across the screen—satellites, smart cities, digital code like rain falling over skyscrapers.

"The technological revolution is the greatest opportunity we've ever had," Claude says. "But it's also our greatest threat."

"Threat how? Can anyone even control this stuff anymore? It sounds like it's evolving on its own," I say, thinking of Winnie.

Claude's tone sharpens. "It *is* a race. Not one country or person can control the technology. But the right minds can guide it. That's why it matters *who* gets there first. Imagine if it's the Chinese. Or the Russians. Hell, even the Americans—have you *seen* how this country is run?"

"So, you are part of this, too," I say slowly.

George jumps in. "Claude isn't just part of it. *He's* the architect. With Claude and Winnie, it's game, set, match."

I'm up against some of the brightest minds in the world. George was right. This does change things. Knowing Claude is on board makes me even more concerned.

Claude leans forward, voice low and deliberate. "America built the nuclear bomb. Now, we've built something even more powerful—technology. Autonomous, adaptive, uncontainable. In the wrong hands, it's the end of civilization."

I feel a chill crawl up my spine. "And what exactly does it become in the wrong hands?"

Claude glances at George, who gives a subtle nod.

"Unchecked," Claude says, "technology will rule us all. Enslave us or destroy the world."

CHAPTER 57

I jump to my feet and pace, lungs burning, my thumb rubbing the raw pink flesh where the nail used to be. "Why isn't this front-page news?" I ask. "If people understood the risk, they'd be rioting."

Claude lounges back, combing sleek fingers through his perfect hair. "Jason, most of the world is sheep. They sleepwalk through their lives, clueless. They need to be led. They want to be led so they don't have to think. They can't help it. They don't have the brain wattage. They want us to do what we are doing. They don't know it yet."

This is different. With Claude among the masterminds, they have the technological expertise to use Winnie in unimaginable ways. The clock is ticking faster than I realized. I need more information.

George leans across the table, eyes sharp. "Look at social media. These fools live their lives online, handing over data that our people can mine and use for our purposes. Every time they go on ChatGPT, they are solving the riddle for us. Understand, he who rules the data rules the world."

"But this isn't only about power," Claude cuts in, voice reverent. "The speed at which the technology is learning is even beyond what I thought it could do. And it is speeding up every day. What do you know about CRISPR technology?"

"Only that it's medical related," I admit.

"It's precision gene editing," he says, almost whispering. "We can make changes to the DNA of living organisms. Snip out the mutations that maim and kill. Someday—maybe soon—we erase cancer."

I shake my head. "And AI fits in where?"

"AI devours genomic data in weeks that would take human teams decades," George says, fingers tapping on the desk. "Pair that with Winnie and the bioengineers already with us, and the blind see, the paralyzed walk. Who knows, maybe we live forever."

For a moment, their madness almost sounds like salvation. It's no wonder their ranks keep growing. The world is full of problems, and they offer a solution that glimmers on the surface. But beneath it, the core is brown and rotten.

"This is about Winnie." I stop pacing. "You need me to get inside. What makes you think I can? Recruit Nikesh yourself—or have you tried?"

Claude scoffs as he walks to the guitar and slowly strokes its handle. "We've tried, but in addition to his off-the-charts intelligence, he is also very principled. He understands the power of Winnie. He would die before letting anyone else have access. He would even let those close to him die."

His words settle in. I know he is talking about Amir, and that sends a shiver up my spine.

"How do you know so much about her? Winnie isn't exactly public."

George's smile is thin. "We have friends inside Tampa Scientific. It's amazing what people will do for money."

"Use them instead of me."

"They're high, but not high enough. We've spent months earning Nikesh's trust in you. It has to be you. It's your destiny."

Cold washes over me—the pivot point of history balances on the following sentence.

"What do you want me to do?" The words scrape out.

Claude sits, crossing one leg over the other. "We're engineering a virus. You open the gate with your security credentials, we slide the payload in, and Winnie belongs to us. Quick. Clean. Wham, bam, thank you, ma'am."

George leans over and says, "There's something else we have to show you. Once you lock down Winnie, you'll be a hero. New power, new responsibilities—riches you can't even imagine."

"I never asked for riches, or to be your hero."

"Jason, you're destined for this. You are Preferred," Claude injects.

"Preferred how? Preferred *why*? Somebody spell it out."

George and Claude share a silent, loaded look.

"That answer comes from leadership," George finally says.

"And leadership is…?"

"Patience," Claude intones. "You've got the rest of your life to learn the secrets."

"For now, we need to show you how all this is funded."

CHAPTER 58

We scream East on I-4 in George's white Audi RS 7, the twin-turbo V8 throbbing under my feet. Brandon's low-rise sprawl blurs by. A flash of memory hits me like a sucker punch—Lia and I plucking strawberries here, splitting a milkshake, sunburned and happy. I swallow it down.

George exits on Brandon Boulevard, steering toward the only five-story building in sight: a glass structure reaching into the sky surrounded by palms. Blue sky and parking lot asphalt glint in its mirrored face.

"What are we doing in the suburbs?" I ask.

"Florida's number-one fundraising hub," Claude says. "After Winnie, you'll run the state. George goes back to headquarters."

If this is indeed where they generate their dirty money, I am going to need to shut it down. There is no way I can forget this albatross of a building.

"Where's headquarters?"

Silence.

The security gate greets us with cameras, card scanners, and retracting tire spikes. Overkill for an office—precisely the point.

We find a parking spot and head to the door where a sign reads, DDE, LLC. Claude pulls his security card out of his back pocket and scans it at the door. Three security guards are sitting at a desk. Claude scans his badge again and converses with one of the men, who rises and approaches me.

"I need to search you, Mr. Miles," he says.

I look to George and Claude for help.

"You earn our trust, and then you earn more," Claude says, nodding to the man who pats me firmly throughout my body.

"He's clean. No weapons and no wires."

I have no idea where we are, but the security is as tight as Avner's grip on his wallet when the dinner bill comes. The lobby has been updated with new tile and paint. It's bright and clean with music playing in the background. I think it is Styx or maybe Journey.

Elevators ding. A compact, muscular man barrels out, beard bristling, eyes lit like torches.

"Jason, meet Chance—the master of disaster," Claude announces.

Chance hugs George and Claude, then grips my hand. His veins look like braided rope beneath hairless forearms.

"Heard a lot about you, Jason. Ready for the tour?"

"Ready as I'll ever be. What *is* this place?"

"Profit engine," Chance says, guiding us down a corridor. "Institutionalized fraud at scale. Cyber, credit, crypto—you name the dirty deed, we monetize it."

I round on Claude. "You're the state cybercrime czar. Weren't you hired to stop this stuff?"

He barks a thunderous laugh. "Jason, the fix is everywhere. We control both the poison and the antidote."

My right eye starts to twitch. I follow Chance toward an entrance pulsing with nightclub electricity. I'm not sure what is through that doorway, but I know it changes everything.

CHAPTER 59

The floor looks like a startup's dream—an open sea of call center cubes surrounded by glass-walled offices. Every desk is occupied, most standing height, with employees pacing, pitching, and punching keys. Overhead, massive video screens rotate through corporate-bright motivational slogans like *"Crush Today!"* and *"Every Objection Is an Opportunity."*

Headsets. Hoodies. Branded t-shirts with the DDE logo: a grinning skull in a knit ski cap.

These psychos aren't bad at branding.

"We've got five floors, about three hundred staff," Chance says, strolling beside me like a proud tour guide. "First floor handles the basic scams—training ground stuff. But it's still profitable. Each floor up gets more complex. Fifth floor is elite ops—top coders, hackers, the team that took down Tampa Scientific with that trojan-and-hostage stunt."

They say you kill a snake by cutting off its head. In this case, the head is the funding. If I can sever that, I might finally have a shot at bringing down *The One*. I need to track every player and every scam, then package it tightly enough to convince Zeke this threat is real. I wish I could get some video, but security is too tight.

I scan the room, stunned. "All these people are scammers?"

"They're cyber professionals," Chance corrects. "This is a business:

full benefits—medical, matching 401(k), and year-end bonuses. We even pay for continuing education. Our top earners break a million-plus annually. You saw the cars out front? Top performers get a BMW or Tesla—bulk-leased through one of our supporters."

Claude strokes his mustache. "It's competitive. Russia and China pay better, but mess up once, and you get a bullet on the spot."

"They make their money stealing from people?" I ask, trying to hide the heat in my voice.

George shrugs. "We've been over this. It's short-term pain for long-term salvation. We take from the weak to build a stronger society. Left to their own devices, they'd blow their money on lottery tickets and booze."

Chance leads us into a nearby office and shuts the door. "Let's listen in."

He taps a button. A call rings. An old man answers.

"Hello?"

"Hello, this is Officer Weinberg from the Internal Revenue Service," the caller says, robotic and confident. "This is a legal notification. You owe back taxes. If this isn't resolved immediately, a warrant will be issued. Do not hang up. Are you aware of this?"

"I—I haven't heard anything—what's going on?"

"You've been mailed multiple notices."

No response.

"You owe $2,800. Can you pay today?"

"I don't have that kind of money. Can I set up a plan?"

"That's not an option anymore. But I can help you avoid arrest if you act now. Do you have your credit card or bank info handy?"

"This... this doesn't sound right. Can I call the IRS directly?"

"If you hang up, your case is sent to local law enforcement. You'll be in custody within forty-five minutes. I'm your only chance. Are you going to resolve this or not?"

A pause.

"Let me get my card."

Chance high-fives Claude. "Flawless. That kid's a rising star."

"That's just one play," he adds. "We've got debt relief, fake loans, sweepstakes wins, and medical billing. We coach the team, tune the scripts. The ROI is off the charts."

I'm numb. It's corporate America reimagined—except built entirely on lies and theft. They even have a damn 401(k).

"Let me guess," I say dryly. "The Nigerian Prince scam is next?"

"Second floor," Chance confirms, ushering us forward.

****

"What the hell is this place?" Avner asks, staring at the glass building. He parks across the street with Zeke in the passenger seat and Goat and Ernesto in the back.

To avoid detection, one of Avner's drones followed George's car from high above. Avner drove his Chevy Malibu with darkly tinted windows several miles behind.

"I don't know," Zeke responds, "but why the hell did you bring the kid? He's a hacker and was headed to jail." He turns back to Ernesto and says, "No offense."

"None taken," Ernesto responds politely.

"He's part of the team," Goat responds. "We can trust him."

"He knows the price if we can't," Avner grumbles under his breath.

"This place is leased by something called DDE, a Limited Liability Company," Zeke says, checking his notes. "Some bullshit Delaware company."

"Why would anyone build this big ass building out here?" Avner says. "It sticks out like Shaq at a midget convention."

"I believe the politically correct term is little people," Goat corrects.

Avner slowly raises his middle finger, and Ernesto giggles under his breath.

"Original developer went bellyup decades ago," Zeke says, binoculars glued to his face. "These guys leased it five years back. Permits show a *lot* of reinforced concrete and redundant power."

"But why? And why is Jason here with that George character and Claude the cyber weirdo with the 'stache?"

"Claude was put in charge of cybertheft for the state by the governor. Maybe this is a government thing," Goat says, pulling the binoculars from Zeke. "But whatever it is, security is tight. They have a gate, men patrolling the grounds, and look at the roof."

He hands the binoculars to Avner, who scans up. "Why the fuck does an office have sniper stands on the roof?"

"I don't know if you noticed, but there are video cameras everywhere, and our cell phones are not working. Must be a blocker coming off the building," Avner says, gripping the steering wheel tightly.

"Send the drone to the top of the building, Ernesto. Let's see what else is up there," Zeke instructs.

They watch a small screen as the drone takes off next to the car. Ernesto fiddles with a small throttle on the controller. It climbs and moves closer to the building. When it reaches the top, it explodes, and the video turns to static.

"We're burned," Goat yells.

"They shot the fucking thing out of the sky," Zeke roars. "What are we in a war zone? You can't fire a gun out here."

Avner fires up the car and tears away. "I'm not sure what is going on, but I know it's nothing good."

CHAPTER 60

The elevator to the second floor opens to a quieter, more refined space. Classical music drifts through the air. Half the staff here are glued to screens, typing quietly.

"This is for people with some tech skills," he explains. "No private offices. Managers are embedded with their teams."

"And what scams are they running?" I ask.

"Classic royalty emails," Claude says. "Claiming to be foreign dignitaries offering a cut of hidden millions in exchange for help. Still works. People hand over credit cards, and we drain what we can. Then we sell the numbers on the dark web."

"We like scams with multiple revenue streams," Chance adds.

"How much are you pulling in from just that?"

Chance shrugs. "Just over a million a month. From this floor alone."

George steps in. "Globally, this network clears a billion a year—net. That's after paying our talent. It's good for them. Good for us. Stable income. Social utility."

At the cost of people's life savings.

"The rest of this floor handles phishing and ID theft," Chance says. "We farm data—SSNs, birthdays, credit scores. Then it's credit card advances, fraudulent loans, new cards, and dark web auctions. It's all about the data."

"You're going to love the next floors," George says. "This is where AI meets Main Street. You'll appreciate the tech."

We step onto the third floor. Sleek cubes, leather chairs, triple-monitor setups. It feels like a hedge fund.

"Ever hear of Silk Road?" Chance asks.

"It was an online black market. Shut down a decade ago," I respond.

"Well, it's back, baby," he grins. "This is the prototype. Word's spreading fast. Thousands of products. Bitcoin is the only way to pay."

"You'll get caught like Dread Pirate Roberts," I warn.

"Not a chance," Claude cuts in. "Our version is untraceable. Custom security, real-time relay servers, and dynamic encryption layers. Invisible."

I think of Winnie. She could break the encryption. Could I use her to bring them down?

"What's being sold?"

"Whatever degenerates want," George says casually. "Prescription meds, fentanyl, stolen goods, weapons. We take a cut."

"Why only Bitcoin?"

Claude leans in, voice low. "Little secret? We created it."

I blink. "You what?"

"Everyone believes in some genius called Satoshi. Nah—it was us. We didn't expect it to blow up like it did. But here we are. And we built in back doors. If we want, we can drain every Bitcoin wallet in the world overnight."

I make a note to close my Bitcoin account as soon as we are done.

George smiles. "The blockchain's useful. We may use it in the new world. Time will tell."

I stare at them, reeling. "You're joking."

Claude strokes his mustache. "Story for another time."

"Onward to the fourth floor," Chance says. "Time's ticking."

The doors open to an employee playground—ping pong tables, arcade machines, and a stocked cafeteria. People laugh, snack, and spar in VR boxing matches.

George spreads his arms. "Beautiful. We built a place they *want* to be. We've got a chef and a gym. Camaraderie thrives here. We encourage leadership to eat with the team—sometimes. They also have a private dining room."

"How long do they stay? Move on to other jobs?"

The three men exchange a glance. Claude nods.

"They stay forever."

I freeze. "What if they leave?"

"We… encourage them not to," Claude says. "If they still choose to go, well… they exit the workforce permanently."

A chill races down my spine. These men are casually discussing murder like it's an HR policy. I think of Lia. I think of Bluebird. They will wipe us off the map without another thought.

I need to finish this tour, but my legs feel heavy, and I feel sick with every step.

"The fifth floor," I say. "Let's see the crown jewel."

"No chance," Claude replies. "Pun intended."

"I thought I was Preferred," I say. "Supposed to run this operation. Isn't Chance going to be under my command?"

Chance stiffens. He cracks his knuckles, then his neck. A security guard approaches and whispers something. Chance listens, then nods.

"Disturbance outside. I'll handle it. Claude, would you mind taking over?"

"We good?" Claude asks.

"Covered. This place is tighter than Fort Knox. If someone's creeping around, we'll know—and deal with it."

I fight the urge to rub my pinky. It's too coincidental. George watched for a tail. Still, Bluebird's good. I don't need them mixed up in this mess.

Claude motions me to a quiet table. We sit. He leans so close I can see the individual hairs in his mustache. Dark, coarse hairs that look perfectly trimmed from afar, but up close I see many that curl and shoot in different directions. Not unlike George and Claude's fake personas.

The fifth floor, Claude tells me, "houses the best minds in the world." He says it like a professor describing his class. "I manage them personally."

"What do they do?"

"Top-tier attacks. Corporate blackmail. Government targets. Nothing under $5 million. Tampa Scientific was just one of many."

George grins. "Tell him about the deepfakes."

Claude leans forward. "Picture this: You're an accountant on a Zoom call with the CFO and the rest of the executive team. They instruct you to wire $20 million to a specific account."

"Let me guess—it's fake."

"Bingo. Every face on that call, every voice, fabricated. The accountant saw their bosses, heard their orders, and sent the money. Gone in seconds. One of our cleanest jobs."

I shift in my seat. "Companies must be fighting this. Isn't deepfake detection a thing now?"

Claude smiles like a teacher humoring a child. "Of course. Entire teams are hunting for 'artifacts'—AI flaws. But they're always behind. They study apples while we're already selling oranges."

George nudges him. "Tell him the CEO play."

Claude's eyes sharpen. "Real-World Defender had promising detection tools. We couldn't crack them—until we sent the CEO a sex video starring him and his head of HR. Not real, of course, but perfect. He handed over the tech to keep it buried. We fed it to our AI, taught it to outpace every detection method on the market. Then it started teaching itself."

George laughs. "In a few years, deepfake losses will top $40 billion. A fat slice will go to us."

"No one's caught you?" I ask.

Claude spreads his hands. "Perfect faces. Cloned voices. We fabricate interviews, sex tapes, racist tirades. Send them to actors, senators—pay up or burn."

I think of Oak.

"But it's all fake," I say.

"Reality," Claude says, "is what we tell people it is."

George studies me, like he's trying to read my mind.

"What do you do with all the money?"

Claude chuckles. "World domination isn't cheap."

"This feels wrong," I say. "You're destroying lives."

George rests a hand on my arm. "Short-term damage. Once we're in control, the theft stops, and we'll unleash the geniuses—cures for diseases, limitless energy, tech revolutions. Decades of progress in weeks."

He locks eyes with me. "This is the future, Jason. And you can't stop it. No one can."

CHAPTER 61

Regency Bank is the largest community bank in the region—and Bluebird's very first client. The thought of betraying their trust twists my stomach. I've been wrestling with it ever since I toured the fraud center a week ago, but I can't see any way around it. Not if I want to lock in Frederick's trust.

Their CEO, Robert Field, and I go way back. We met at banking school, where he stood out for his sharp instincts and relentless loyalty. The man practically bleeds RB. He spent decades paying his dues, and now he runs the place like it's his legacy.

Rob had been trying to hire me away from Safe Harbor Bank for years. When I started Bluebird, he didn't hesitate, signed on immediately for our tech and cybersecurity services, trusting me without blinking.

"There are my two favorite IT nerds," he says as Ernesto and I step into the polished glass-and-marble lobby of the corporate headquarters. "Did we do something special to deserve a visit from the boss himself? Usually, we get Ernesto and the contractors. And thanks for dressing up, by the way."

I glance down at my wrinkled white Oxford and then over at Ernesto's faded Batman T-shirt. RB is old-school. Rumor has it employees can't even use the restroom without wearing their suit jackets.

I step forward and shake his hand. "Can't a guy check in on his favorite client?"

He tilts his head and raises an eyebrow. "Usually, when you want to see me, it involves a long lunch and bad decisions at the Red Dog. So, what gives? Something wrong?"

"Nothing at all. Ernesto and I are just running a little security test. I wanted to be here for it. You'll still get your invite to the Dog—don't worry. I'll even buy."

"That would be a first."

I'm lying through my teeth, and it makes me sick. Rob's trust in me is total, and I'm about to exploit it. *The One* wants to test me. This job. This friendship. This loyalty. I just pray they don't burn the bank to the ground in the process.

"I'm glad you guys are on top of it," Rob says. "We've got too many threats out there. Customers need to know we've got their backs."

"We've got it covered," I tell him. "Ernesto monitors everything remotely. And we're using top-tier partners. You're in good hands."

"Then I'll leave you to it. Time for me to go make some money."

We shake again, and he disappears down the hallway. We move to the server room and unpack our backpacks. I feel the buzz of a text in my pocket and pull out my phone. It's from Claude.

Look for an email with the subject line: "*Tomahawk*." Take down the bank's security and open it up. We'll tell you when to bring it back online.

Ernesto logs in and starts checking systems. "Are we following the usual protocol?"

"Not this time," I say, keeping my voice steady. "We're testing a new security system. Vendor said to look for a message titled *Tomahawk*, then drop defenses, and they will activate the backup net."

He frowns. "That'll leave us wide open."

"It won't. They've developed something new. They call it a spider web. Nothing gets through."

Ernesto hesitates. "Never heard of that, and I'm not sure it makes sense."

I rest a hand on his shoulder. "I told you things were going to get strange for a while. Some of it has to stay between us. I need you to trust me."

He nods and says, "You're the boss."

He digs into the console. A few minutes pass. Then he looks up again. "Got the email. You're sure?"

"Do it," I snap—sharper than I meant. He flinches but complies.

His fingers fly across the keyboard. "Jason... It's done. But I'm seeing activity. Fast. Something's spreading."

"It's part of the test," I lie, staring at the screen—my gut knots.

My phone buzzes again.

> Good boy. We're in.

Ten minutes later, every screen in the room goes black.

Seconds after that, Rob bursts in along with two other execs. His tie is askew, eyes wide. "Jason, what the *fuck* is going on?"

His COO is red-faced and shaking. "Our vendor called. The firewall dropped. A virus is in the system."

"It's fine," I say too quickly. "We're testing a backup protocol."

Rob's voice cuts through the room. "What kind of backup protocol shuts down our entire infrastructure?"

"We're just testing a new layer—something more adaptive."

"The vendor doesn't know anything about this," the COO snaps. "They caught the virus just in time. *Barely.* I pray there is no long-lasting damage or losses we don't know about."

I try to respond, but the words don't come. Ernesto stares at the floor, silent. I can feel the betrayal radiating off Rob like heat.

He takes a breath, then glares at me. "Jason, we've known each other a long time. But this?" His voice hardens. "This was a *royal* fuckup."

He points to the door.

"Pack your stuff. You're fired."

CHAPTER 62

After receiving our pink slip, I limp into Avner's so-called sanctuary—a squat warehouse off Adamo Drive—close enough to Ybor to smell roasting coffee, far enough that no one comes snooping. Only the Bluebird team knows it exists. Avner and Goat have crammed enough firepower inside to topple a small republic. Four aluminum walls, a cracked concrete floor, and a bathroom. No A/C—just a Big Ass Fan chopping the humid air.

I'm still smarting from being fired by Regency. Ernesto was so mad that he stormed off without another word. I tried to come up with an explanation, but when none came to mind, I just let him walk.

Being let go was one thing. Being played by *The One*, that's what *really* burns. If the word spreads in the business community, we'll be lucky to get a job teaching spreadsheets to interns.

Every time I think things can't get worse, they do.

The metal door behind me slams shut with a hollow clang.

I don't wait for a greeting. "What's so urgent that I had to leave *work*?" I bark. "Somebody's got to pay you lunatics."

Since my last visit, Avner has added a dented white fridge and a plaid couch that appears to have been rescued from a curb. Scott's old Harley sits partially disassembled next to two beat-up sedans that he uses for surveillance. Occasionally, he and Goat work on the old bike, dreaming about the cross-country trip Scott threatened to take.

Sitting in the middle of the room is a person tied to a chair with a dark bag over his head. The man's clothes are torn and bloody.

"Guys, who the hell is this?" I ask. "Does someone always need to be strapped to a chair with a bag over their head? It's not very comfortable. I know from experience."

"You said you were being tailed. We ran some countersurveillance, asked around, and—boom—meet Sloppy Joe," Goat proudly states.

"Why is he bloody?"

"We asked him to come nicely, but he chose the hard way," Avner responds as he opens a bottle of Budweiser.

I sigh. "And who exactly is he?"

"Let's ask," Avner replies, yanking the hood off.

Greasy hair whips back. The guy blinks at the warehouse, wary but not terrified. Then he smiles. "At least it's you idiots and not the assassins chasing me."

The voice slams into me—older, rougher, but unmistakable.

"No way."

He grins, broken teeth and all. "Yeah, Jason. Long time."

"Holy shit," I mutter. "Sloppy Joe is Eric Gruber."

Goat frowns. "Who's Eric Gruber?"

"One of the bankers I used to work with at Safe Harbor. The architect of the tax fraud that torched my life. Transplant from Switzerland."

Gruber's eyes bulge. He jerks against the tip ties. "Torched your life? Look at me, you self-righteous prick! I'm homeless, hunted, living on scraps because you had to play whistle-blowing hero."

Avner downs half his beer. "Touching. We feel so bad for you."

I interrupt him. "Let me handle this. Why are you following me? You want revenge?"

"I want my life back," Gruber spits. "You are the only one who can get it for me."

I pause, puzzled. What exactly is this bad memory talking about? I need to navigate this, or Eric could spill some secrets I've kept from the team.

"How, exactly?" I ask.

"Talk to *The One*. Tell them to call off the dogs."

"Is this for real?" Avner scoffs. "More of this secret society silliness."

"I've told you, Avner, it is real," I say, "it's time you trust me."

"Hard to trust someone who keeps lying to you," he responds, his eyes probing me for a response.

I ignore him and turn back to Eric. "Why would I do that? And why would they listen to me?"

Gruber leans forward, tendons straining. "Because you're *Preferred*, Jason."

Avner downs his beer and opens another. "I've heard this Preferred word before. What are we talking about?"

My stomach drops. "I don't know. Eric, can you tell us what *Preferred* means?"

"It means," he whispers, "they have to listen to you. You are part of them. You are related by blood."

CHAPTER 63

I'm stunned. Eric's words punch the breath from my lungs, and I pace the concrete floor, trying to steady myself.

"What the hell are you talking about, Eric? I'm not related to any of them. My dad was Doug Miles, a financial planner. My mom stayed home and raised me."

Eric reclines in the folding chair, wrists still lashed, eyes skating around the room before locking on mine. "Someone want to cut me loose? Your two attack dogs already proved they can handle one guy."

Avner looks at me; I nod. He chambers a round, holsters the pistol, and slices the tip ties. "You're free, Sloppy Joe or whoever the hell you are. One wrong twitch and I'll ventilate your skull. Comprende?"

"It's Eric, jerk." He rubs the raw marks on his wrists. "And yeah, I comprende."

"Listen carefully, Eric. You're going to explain what the hell you're talking about, and you're going to do it now. Be honest, and I'll help you. But I want it all—the leaders, their hideouts, and exactly how we bring them down."

This is my chance. I lost Sterling, but now I've got a new lead. I'm going to get everything I need from Eric—and I'll do whatever it takes.

"Your parents knew, Jason. *The One* courted your dad for years—wouldn't quit until he refused once too often. He was a good man."

This can't be right. My childhood was normal… wasn't it? We did move a lot, and no one ever told me why. We'd pack up overnight and vanish.

"They just let him walk away?" My pulse hammers: my hands shake.

Eric laughs, low and bitter. "No one walks away. You say 'yes,' or you die."

Avner invades his space, his voice a snarl. "Spit it out. Say what you have to say."

"They murdered your parents, Jason. Faked a drunkdriving crash."

I seize his shirt and haul him upright. "Liar! A teenager killed them—he went to prison. Why are you fucking with me?"

Eric raises both palms. "Ever wonder why that kid vanished from the system? He was a prop. You're alive because you're Preferred. They erase whoever they want. Think back to the night before they were killed. It was the last time they asked."

I go back to a time long ago, to when I was a thirteen-year-old boy again. I remember the night before everything changed, though I must have blocked it out. My father screamed into the phone, my mother crying in the next room.

Grief and rage blur my vision. "Where are they? How do I reach them?"

"I need your help," he whispers. "Tell them I'm harmless. They'll listen to you."

"Where?" I roar.

"Headquarters is in L—"

The door explodes inward. Shrapnel whistles past. Six men in matteblack armor flood the room, rifles leveled.

Two barrels lock on Avner's chest as his hand twitches toward his gun. He freezes. I know those eyes behind the leader's mask.

"Appreciate you bagging our stray," the leader says. "Avner, weapon on the floor or nobody walks out."

Jaw clenched, Avner lowers his pistol. "How do you know my name?"

The man's eyes glint.

"All of you are dead. Especially you, Omaha."

They hood Eric, cinch fresh tip ties. His muffled screams echo.

I can't lose him. I can't start over now that I know what they did. What they are capable of. What I now know I am.

I lunge at Omaha, swinging wide, but I never land the hit. My muscles lock all at once, a brutal jolt snapping through me. My mind screams *attack*, but my body goes dead weight—arms useless, legs folding. Every nerve lights up in white-hot pain as my vision smears. I crash into the concrete face-first.

Avner and Goat rush toward me, but Omaha fires a shot into the air—sharp, cracking, a warning.

"Take one more step," he snarls, "and you all die. Jason will be fine. This time it was a Taser. Next time, I blow his fucking head off."

We're shoved facedown, wrists bound tight. Goat whispers a prayer; Avner spits curses.

The leader pauses at the threshold. "One more loose end tied up."

Boots pound toward a waiting van, and the warehouse swims in ringing silence.

CHAPTER 64

When Eric comes to, mosquitoes blanket his skin like a second layer. He lies on damp ground, just feet from the foamy edge of Lake Seminole. A filthy rag is stuffed in his mouth. His arms and legs are tightly bound. He tries to scream, but the sound dies in his throat as he chokes on panic and cloth.

The sun sets in slow motion, casting a molten gold shimmer across the lake. The world around him is quiet, unnervingly so. A lone frog croaks from the tall grass, then goes silent. A duck takes off in a rush of wings, and a heron lets out a harsh squawk before gliding away. Something slithers nearby, unseen in the thick curtain of cattails.

A group of men smoke in a circle not far from him. The stench of tobacco, algae, and damp earth churns in the air, making Eric's insides tighten. One of them, with cold gray eyes and a face carved from stone, walks over and kicks him hard in the ribs. Eric groans against the rag. The man scatters handfuls of small fish around Eric's body, then shoves him closer to the water's edge until the cold lake kisses his side. The sudden chill jolts his senses.

From a picnic table nearby, George approaches, brushing dirt from his jeans like he's just come from a backyard barbecue.

"Eric," he says with mock warmth, "you've been a very bad boy."

He crouches beside him.

"You were ordered home after the Safe Harbor mess, but instead, you ran. I'll admit it—you lasted longer out there than I thought some pompous Swiss banker ever could. Still..." He straightens, his face hardening. "You know how we feel about loose ends."

He nods to his men. "Pick him up."

Three of them drag Eric upright and shove him into the shallows. One yanks the gag free.

"If you scream," George warns, "we'll just kill you."

Eric spits lake water, gasping. "Please, George... we've known each other a long time. Let me go, and I swear—I'll disappear. I'm no threat. You know that."

George's eyes narrow. "What did you tell them?"

"Nothing. I swear."

George tilts his head, unconvinced. "Goodbye, Eric."

"No, no, wait!" Eric cries. "I'll talk. I told him about his 'Preferred' status. I thought maybe he could help me. He didn't even know what it meant."

"Did you tell him?"

"Yes, but your people stormed in before I said anything else."

"Nothing about his parents? Or our headquarters?"

"I swear. Nothing."

George studies him for a beat, then gives a calm nod. "I believe you. Gentlemen, throw him in."

Eric shrieks as two men shove the rag back into his mouth and drag him to the edge. One of them raises a phone, recording a warning for others.

"You should've taken your medicine," George says. "Maybe then we'd have shown mercy. Quick. Clean. But now..."

He turns to the men. "Bait the water."

They scatter more chunks of fish across the shore and into the dirty water, then retreat quickly.

Eric flails, trying to roll, but the men hoist him and hurl him into the lake with a splash. He sinks fast, limbs useless, lungs burning. He kicks wildly to the surface, barely managing a breath.

Then everything goes still.

The water ripples behind him. Eric sees it—a long, dark shape gliding just beneath the surface. For a moment, he hopes it's a drifting log. But the trail of bubbles tells the truth.

It's a gator—a massive one.

It circles slowly, sensing the meal. Eric thrashes, a garbled scream caught in his throat. One of the men tosses another bucket of fish toward him and laughs loudly.

The water explodes.

Jaws the size of bear traps clamp around his torso. Bones snap like twigs. The gator spins, dragging him under, twisting with terrifying force. The lake froths red. Eric is tossed like a rag doll, his body folding and breaking with each violent turn.

One final spin. Searing pain follows a strange, quiet peace.

CHAPTER 65

Avner storms around the office like a trapped bull, a neon green tennis ball clenched so tight in his fist it creaks. Heat rolls off him in waves. The rest of the Bluebird team hovers at their desks, suddenly fascinated by keyboards and floor tiles. They've seen Avner in this mood, and no one wants to be around.

The police arrived at Avner's warehouse after a report of a gunshot. They cut us loose and took our statements. We lied—claimed it was a robbery. They exchanged suspicious glances and promised to investigate. We knew they wouldn't.

"Enough, Jason." His voice booms. "What the hell is your connection to George Klein and these psychos? What have they got on you?"

I lean against a desk, an ice pack against my face. Eric's kidnapping and Avner's fury have my pulse jackhammering, but I keep my tone level. "George is a new client. That's all."

Avner crosses the room in two strides, yanks me up by my shirtfront. "Stop lying to me."

Goat wedges himself between us, prying Avner's fingers from my collar. Apple pulls Avner back, whispering urgently in his ear while he glares at me over her shoulder—pure apex predator.

"We have to cut this out," Goat says. "We're family."

I don't know what to say. Avner has never turned his anger toward me. I want to run, but there is nowhere to go. It might be time to tell them what is going on. Beg for their help. I might not have a choice.

I start to speak when Zeke, Gloria, and three agents in suits come through the door.

"Jason Miles," Zeke says, flashing his FBI creds we already know by heart, "you're coming with us."

I lift my hands. "Zeke, I don't need this today."

Avner grabs Zeke's arm. The fed's reptile eyes flick down, then drill into Avner's. "Touch me again, and you'll be on a boat back to Israel."

"Can we all just settle down?" Apple begs. "We're all friends."

"We're not," Gloria responds. "We're with the FBI, and we're taking Jason with us. One way or another. Now you all need to stand down, or we'll lock everyone up."

"Am I under arrest?" I ask.

"Your call," Zeke says. "Walk or we cuff. You have three seconds to decide."

I nod to Berta. "Call Mr. Bailey."

****

"I want to make sure we state for the record that Jason Miles is here of his own accord. He is not under arrest," my attorney says as if reading from a script. He is wearing shorts and an Old Memorial golf shirt that his belly stretches to its limits. He rushed over directly from the course when Berta called. His golf shoes leave a muddy trail.

I'm running out of time, and my options are collapsing fast. I've even caught myself considering arrest—being locked away. At least prison would keep me from handing Winnie over or becoming *The One's* puppet. But Sterling's murder proved they can reach anyone, anywhere. And jail wouldn't shield my friends. That is not an option.

I need to keep connecting the dots. Convergence. I'm building a case against George, Frederick, and Chance at the fraud center. I could try to blackmail the men from Rooster Island, including the warden, but what do I really have? Avner and Goat saw Eric taken. If I can find him and get him somewhere safe, he could be the key—my strongest link, and the keeper of the secrets I need if I'm going to stand a fighting chance.

When the time is right, I'll bring everything I have to Zeke. For now, though, I'm still far from ready—and most of what I have is circumstantial.

Priority one is getting out of here, but my mind keeps circling back to Eric's claim. Did *The One* really kill my parents? Am I related to these monsters? I can't go down that path right now. I must lock it away before it corrodes my focus and feeds the anger simmering under my skin.

There will be plenty of time for therapy when this is over—assuming, of course, I make it to the other side alive.

"I want to state for the record that you are an asshole and should dress properly when meeting with the FBI," Zeke responds.

"Why am I here?" I ask.

The room has to be at least 90 degrees. Sweat gleams under my attorney's arms, streaking down his back. Zeke thrives on this—finding any way to make you squirm, any edge he can exploit.

Zeke's pupils dilate, then shrink to slits. He starts laughing to himself. A maniacal stutter. "We've got an extradition request from Greece." He waves a document.

"Let me see that," Bailey says, snapping his magnetic readers together.

Gloria plants her palms on the table. "Option one: we ship you back to Athens. Their circus, their lions, their problem. Option two: Zoom interview—US and Greek prosecutors ask whatever they want. You tell the truth for once."

"Give us the room," Bailey requests. "And turn up the damn air."

Zeke smirks. "Five minutes. I'll see if I can find the thermostat."

Bailey removes his cell phone and presses a button to play classical music. He turns it to its highest setting and covers his mouth with a legal pad. He whispers near my ear, "You can't go back to Greece. They might throw you in prison, and we know you have a job to do. We're going to have to do the interview."

"I need prep time," I whisper. "I'm not sure how to answer certain questions."

"Leave that to me." He winks. "We have friends in high and low places."

Zeke and Gloria re-enter the room. "What's the verdict?"

"We'll Zoom," Bailey says, "but we need a few days."

"What's there to prepare, Jason? Just tell the truth. It's not that hard. Drop this double-talking ambulance-chasing lawyer, and we'll work together to solve whatever the hell is going on. You and me."

"Are you attempting to entice Mr. Miles to drop legal counsel?"

"I would never do that."

"Good, we'll be going now."

We both stand up and move toward the door when Zeke tosses a folder onto the table.

"Before you go, you might want to look at this."

Alarm bells go off in my head. Zeke only acts this dramatically when he has your balls in a vice, and he is about to tighten.

Bailey scans the photo inside. "Jesus."

Gloria's gaze drills me. "Curious, Jason?"

I swallow, pick up the picture. A severed head, lakeslick and gray, stares back.

"Recognize that head?" Zeke asks.

"Of course not," I respond. "Who the hell is it?"

"Your old friend, Eric Gruber. Remember him from Safe Harbor Bank? It washed up on the shore of Lake Seminole. An old lady found it. Any idea what happened to him?"

My hand flies to my mouth as bile surges up my throat. I need Eric, but the truth of what they did to him hits like a hammer—another death on my conscience. Another connection is gone.

"You're looking a little pale. Have you seen Eric recently? I heard through the grapevine that the local police had to rescue some idiots zip-tied in a warehouse. Something about a robbery where nothing was taken. And what happened to your face?"

I don't answer. I stand there, looking at Zeke, who wears a taunting smile.

"Things are falling apart, buddy. Don't you need a friend?"

"We're leaving," Bailey states. "Don't say anything, Jason."

As we walk out, I hear Zeke saying, "Oh, come on, Jason. It was just a question. Don't lose your head over it. We have to deal with this problem head-on. You have a good head on your shoulders; don't walk away."

I barely make it to the bathroom before retching in the stall. The walls are closing in. Something has to break—and it's not going to be me.

CHAPTER 66

Syd studies my face like it's a missing puppy flyer. "Jason, are you okay?"

Probably not. My beard's unkempt, and the bruise around my eye has turned multiple ugly colors, combining with the new scab, a gift from Omaha. My shoulder throbs every time I shift. I should've taken the Oxy my doctor pushed on me. Instead, I drown the pain with aspirin and another gulp of Ouzo.

We're on the patio of Acropolis in Ybor, and the early evening heat is thick as tar. We walked here from the hotel after spending the day together—her idea of quality time, mine of surveillance. I keep ignoring Avner's calls; sooner or later, he'll appear in the flesh.

"I'm fine," I mutter. My knee moves like a bobber in a lake with a big fish on the hook. I look around, expecting a visit from the FBI or a bullet from Lia.

The waitress glides over and tops off our water glasses. We order grilled octopus, dolmades, and a gyro platter to share. My appetite, however, has checked out. Every time I close my eyes, I see the pictures of Eric—or at least his head. It's only been a day, but the images feel burned into my brain, and I can't imagine them ever fading.

"You promised to tell me more about your past," Syd says, elbows on the table, eyes locked on mine. "I want to know. There are things written after the Safe Harbor meltdown, but I don't know what is real. Lots on the internet also."

I stretch my neck until it pops. "You can't believe everything you read. What do you want to know?"

"How did you meet Avner and Lia?"

Her name is a spark against dry tinder. In my mind's eye, I see Lia's beautiful face, the tiny gap in her teeth. I think back to that last horrible conversation. It is strange to hear Syd say her name.

"I can't talk about that," I say. "We crossed paths in Israel. That's all."

"Were they government? Like Mossad or something?"

I pin her with a stare. "Why dig into this?"

"Because I care." She details my collection of scars: the missing fingernail on my pinky, the knife wound on my leg, and the burn marks on my forearm. "Were you tortured? Tell me what happened. I know you have bad dreams. You say things in your sleep."

I realize I'm rubbing the pinky. I toss back the rest of my drink and signal for another.

"Slow down," she says. "Why are you drinking so much?"

Well, the fate of the world and the lives of all the people I care about depend on my next moves. And I think you might be a spy.

But I only shrug. "There are things I can't share."

"Fine," she says, though her tone says anything but. "At least tell me about Lia and Safe Harbor Bank. Where is she? How did you uncover the fraud?"

Instead of answering, I change lanes. "Have you ever met a guy named Clinton?"

She squints toward the street, thinking. "No. Unusual name—I'd remember. Who is he?"

"Someone I'd rather forget. You're sure you haven't seen him or spoken with him?"

"Positive. Now back to Lia and—"

I massage the pulse hammering in my forehead. "Why are you so interested?"

"Because I want to understand you. I want to be with you. Maybe I can help."

You can't, Syd. You should run before my fucked-up life swallows you whole.

"I have a question for you," I say.

She sits back in her chair and smiles a sexy little grin. She purrs, "What do you want to know?"

"Why don't we ever go to your place? I've offered, and you always want to come to the hotel. Why is that? You're not married, are you, Syd?"

She laughs out loud. "Of course not. I told you I have a roommate. It's nice to get away. She is a different duck. Seeing you at Haya feels like a vacation. It sucks being thirty and sharing a house. I'm embarrassed."

"You're embarrassed? I live in a hotel," I laugh. "I want to see your place."

She drops her gaze, focuses on a family of chickens strutting across Seventh Avenue. The waitress sets down the food; steam curls between us. We eat in silence, each of us tasting different kinds of deceit.

CHAPTER 67

"Avner, I know you're pissed at me, but I need your help," I say, stepping into the smoky haze of King Corona cigar shop.

Avner's parked in his usual seat, puffing on a long, dark cigar. Ernesto's beside him, sipping cold brew, his cigar smoldering in the ashtray.

Avner doesn't even look at me. "You hear that, Ernesto?" he says. "Sounds like one of those Ybor ghosts they write books about."

"Come on, man. Don't be like that."

"Fuck off, Jason. If it weren't for Apple, I'd be back in Israel right now." His voice cuts sharper than his words.

"I know you don't mean that," I say, lowering my voice. "I'm sorry for all of it. I'll tell you everything, I swear. But right now, I need a favor."

Avner exhales a long stream of smoke and finally meets my eyes. "With what?"

"It's Syd. Something's not right. I need you to help me break into her house."

He chokes out a laugh, then takes a long swig of his beer. "You serious? You finally meet a smart, beautiful woman who actually likes you—and your first instinct is to break into her place? What is wrong with you? You're completely unhinged."

"I know how it sounds. Maybe I *am* losing it. But something's off, and I can't ignore it."

"You look like hell, you know that? Get a haircut. Shave. You're acting like a paranoid burnout."

"Maybe I am," I admit. "But help me, and I'll lay it all out for you. Deal?"

Avner shakes his head. "You realize Apple's the one who introduced you to Syd, right? If this blows back on me and ruins that connection, you're a dead man. And I mean literally."

"Can I come?" Ernesto asks. "I never get to do the fun stuff. I'll stay out of the way. I need some action."

Avner turns to him and says, "No way."

Ernesto is still pissed from the Regency Bank debacle. This is my chance to get him back in my good graces. "Let him go, Avner. We can trust him."

Avner glares at me, then turns back to Ernesto. "Too many people make it messy. I should do this myself. If we all go, no more bodies, no more arrests."

****

We park a block from Syd's house, crouched low in one of Avner's fleet of nondescript cars as the sun sinks behind the trees.

"I can't believe you dragged Apple into this," Avner says, shaking his head. "You're lucky you sold them on that girls' night out. Real slick."

Guilt gnaws at my gut. I didn't want to lie to Syd, but the doubt won't go away. The way she poked around my hotel room. The endless questions about my past. Clinton's mention of their meeting and her denial. And then there's something I haven't said out loud.

Could she be connected to *The One*? Is she manipulating me somehow for their benefit? Did they force her to do this? Am I sleeping with the enemy or jumping at shadows?

If Lia and I are over and she is my plan B, I need to know I can trust her. I need to put this doubt to rest so I can move on to what will be the battle of my life.

If she's connected to *The One*, I may have another move. Turn lemons into lemonade. Learn what she knows, then turn her—make her a double agent. Use Syd to take down my adversaries, not become one.

Ernesto's in the backseat, wired on caffeine and spouting nonsense as he sips another Pepsi. He crunches down on a mouthful of Doritos and wipes his hands on his jeans. He's our lookout—his idea, but we didn't argue.

Syd's house sits quietly at the end of the street, a tidy brick bungalow in Seminole Heights. Classic porch, flowers by the steps. Cozy. Inviting. The online listing said 1,200 square feet, two beds, two baths.

"You sure you don't want to walk away?" Avner asks, not looking at me.

"No. I need to see inside. I just… I know something's up."

"We should be focused on finding Sloppy Joe and those thugs who took him."

Too late for that.

Avner pulls a sleek black device from his backpack and holds it to his eye.

"What is that?" Ernesto asks.

"Monocular with thermal. I can see up close and spot heat signatures inside. People, dogs, you name it. Trust me, the last thing you want in a break-in is to get surprised by Cujo."

"Do you see anyone?" I ask. "She said she has a roommate."

Avner adjusts the focus. "Nothing. The house looks empty."

"What about a security system?"

"I had my guy run it. No alarm billed to the address. If you don't screw this up, you should buy her one. Sketchy neighborhood for a hot blonde."

"They say the area is up and coming," Ernesto pipes up.

Avner snorts. "Looks like it came and left."

I check my earpiece. "Alright, E You're our eyes. If you see anything that looks like a cop or a neighbor with a gun, please tip us off. Got it?"

He snaps off a salute. "You got it, boss."

I glance once more at Syd's house. It's calm. Too calm.

I take a breath and feel the weight settle in my chest. I'm about to betray another person I care about.

But I need the truth.

CHAPTER 68

Under the cover of a pitch-black sky, we move low and fast down the block, keeping our heads tucked beneath hoods and baseball caps. If anyone has an exterior camera, we don't want to be caught on it. The street is dead silent—except for a dog barking faintly somewhere in the distance.

We slip into the side yard, crouching behind a line of hedges. Branches scrape our arms as we squeeze between them and the house. I can feel my pulse in my ears. Every slight sound feels like a gunshot in the stillness.

After scanning the neighborhood for life—porch lights, open windows, nosy neighbors—we creep into the backyard. I peer through the sliding glass doors. No lights. No shadows. No pets rushing through the door. And no roommate.

Avner pulls a small set of tools from his pocket and gets to work. The lock clicks open like it's nothing.

Inside, the air hangs cold and still. A wall clock ticks sharply, accusing, relentless. We flatten against the wall, listening.

No footsteps. No creaks. No voices.

"I think we're clear," Avner whispers. "What exactly are we looking for?"

"I'm not sure. Anything that might seem out of place or out of character for a thirty-something professor."

We each pull out small flashlights and split up.

I head toward the kitchen, tiptoeing on the balls of my feet across the tile. A bit of moonlight filters through the window, just enough to make out shapes. The air smells like cinnamon and coffee, a familiar blend that only makes me feel worse.

I shouldn't be here. I know that. But doubt can be poison, and I need the antidote. I'm not sure if it's a sixth sense or a delusion.

I open drawers slowly, one by one. Utensils in perfect rows. Measuring cups piled up. Nothing out of place. I move to the fridge. The light floods the room when I open it. Chardonnay. Almond milk. Some glass containers packed with quinoa, grilled chicken, and maybe tofu. Lettuce. Cheese. Leftover Thai food that's well past its prime.

The door's lined with organic condiments. Primal Kitchen ketchup. Dijon. Unopened jalapeños.

I close the fridge and head back to the living room, where Avner's sweeping his flashlight along the wall.

"Find anything?" I ask under my breath.

He grins. "Couple dead bodies and a bloodstained ax. Wanna see?"

"Cut it out. Seriously."

He sighs. "Nah, just pictures. Big screen. Cozy couch. Real slice of domestic bliss." He picks up a framed photo from the shelf and hands it to me. "Want to feel like a real asshole?"

I feel the blood drain from my face.

It's me and Syd—at the beach. I remember that picnic. She took this selfie, laughing, barefoot in the sand. Now it's in a goddamn frame. On display like we're something real. Something permanent.

Maybe I read this one wrong.

"Let's wrap this up," I murmur. "You check the hallway bathroom. I'll take her bedroom."

Avner smirks. "Come on. Give an old man a thrill. I promise not to touch her silky stuff."

"You've got a girlfriend, perv. Go count toilet paper."

The bedroom door creaks as I push it open. I pause in the doorway, letting my eyes adjust.

It smells like Syd. Soft. Feminine. Vanilla, soap, and something floral. The bed is perfectly made—pink comforter, a teddy bear propped against the pillows, watching me like he knows I don't belong here.

A candle rests on the nightstand. I open the drawers carefully. Silk, lace. A box with a pair of earrings and a few folded dollar bills. Nothing else.

The closet's another story. Shoes piled. Dresses tossed. Bags lined like trophies. A small chandelier dangles overhead—delicate, vintage. Everything about this room screams female.

I feel like a voyeur—a creep.

"Before you start trying on outfits," Avner's voice calls behind me, "come see this."

I spin. "What is it?"

"The other bedroom is locked. You want me to pick it, or are we done playing spy?"

I nod. "Do it. We're already in deep."

It takes him less than a minute to get the door open. No roommate's messy bedroom. No smell of dirty laundry.

Instead, we step into an office.

A large wooden desk dominates the room, its surface buried under paper and books. A laptop sits closed in the center.

Avner swings his flashlight across the room and freezes.

"Holy shit," he mutters. "Look at that."

I follow the beam of light.

And suddenly, I know.

I didn't imagine it. I'm not crazy.

CHAPTER 69

The wall is a chaotic collage of photos, with names printed in bold beneath each one. Arrows, strings, red ink. Some faces are circled. Mine is dead center like a bullseye.

"What the fuck," I mutter, more to myself than to Avner.

I didn't want to believe it, but my gut hasn't failed me yet. Something about Syd has always felt... off. Too convenient. Too perfect. Too hot for a mess like me. Now this. I don't know exactly what I'm looking at, but I sure as hell know who's behind it.

And the question screaming in my head: *Why?*

Avner steps closer, scanning the photos. "This looks like *Jason Miles: This Is Your Life*. She's got everyone—Lia, Scott, Zeke, Goat, Apple... and me, right next to you." He scoffs. "Jesus, that's a horrible picture of me. She could've at least used my good side."

I shoot him a look. "Pretty sure you don't have one."

He ignores me, reaching for a shelf. "Look at this." He holds up a delicate piece of jewelry, tarnished silver catching the low light. "Isn't this one of the necklaces Lia sold online?"

My blood runs cold. "Yeah. It is. What the hell is it doing here?"

Before I can answer my question, Ernesto's voice crackles in our earpieces, sharp and urgent. "Abort. Abort. Guys, you need to get the hell out of there—Apple's car just pulled into the driveway."

"Shit," I hiss, heart thudding in my chest. I yank out my phone and start snapping pictures of the wall.

Avner moves to the door and locks it.

"What the hell are we going to do, Avner?" I whisper.

****

"I'm so sorry, Apple," Syd says as they step through the door. "I can't believe I left my purse behind. Total brain fog. Do you want to hang out for a bit? Maybe a glass of wine?"

"Don't worry about it," Apple replies, slipping off her shoes. "That sounds perfect—a drink, maybe some DoorDash. I could use a quiet night. I've been spending a *lot* of time with Avner lately."

Syd smiles and closes the door behind them. "How's that going? You two seem happy."

Apple tilts her head and shrugs with a smile. "Honestly, I never thought it would click. We're polar opposites. But he's... amazing. Gruff as hell, but there's a sweetness underneath it. Weird thing to say, but he has this masculine scent—and I swear I can smell it right now." She glances around. "Has Jason been over recently? Maybe it's him?"

Syd freezes for the briefest moment, then shakes her head. "No. I've never invited him over."

Apple raises an eyebrow. "Why not, girl? You two have serious chemistry."

Syd busies herself in the kitchen, pulling a bottle of Chardonnay from the fridge. "He's been... off lately," she says, filling two glasses to the brim. "Distant. I ask if he's okay, and he shuts down. We have fun, sure, but it's like there's this wall I can't get past. I want to know more about him—*need* to. What do you know?"

Apple takes a long sip, her eyes drifting. "Only that he's been through hell. When his wife left... it wrecked him. Avner told me Lia was his whole world. Whatever happened, it left some serious damage. Not to mention whatever the heck went on in Greece."

Syd returns to the couch, handing over the wine and sinking into the cushions beside her. "I'm not giving up. He's worth the effort." She glances toward the hallway.

"Honestly? I wish they were both here."

****

"You're such a big softie, Avner," I whisper, grinning as I make exaggerated kissing noises.

He shoots me a glare. "Unless you want to get choked out, I suggest you shut your mouth and find us a way out of here."

I chuckle under my breath, despite the pressure mounting around us. "Okay, okay." I scan the room and point to the lone window. "That's our only shot—unless you want to jump out screaming *'surprise!'*"

Avner strides over and unlocks it, trying to force it open. Nothing. He pushes harder. Still nothing. "Shit. It's painted shut."

"Can you clear the seal with one of your magic tools?" I ask, already knowing the answer.

He pulls a small blade from his pocket. "Yeah. But if she checks, she'll know someone tampered with it, and there is no way to re-lock it from the outside."

I shrug. "Desperate times, my friend. Start chipping."

He gets to work, scraping the edges with precise, deliberate movements. The sound of metal against wood fills the quiet room. My heart pounds with every second that ticks by.

After a tense minute, he gives the frame a final yank. The window creaks open with a loud, miserable screech.

We both freeze.

Footsteps?

Avner looks at me, eyes sharp. "Let's go."

****

Syd and Apple both turn toward the back of the house, eyes drawn to the sound from behind the locked door.

"What was that?" Apple asks, straightening.

Syd forces a casual shrug. "No idea."

Apple narrows her eyes. "What room is that?"

"Just my office," Syd says, a little too quickly. "Total disaster zone. You stay here—if I scream, come running."

Apple half-smiles, half-warns. "Avner gave me a can of mace. Want to borrow it?"

"Don't judge me," Syd says with a dry laugh, "but I have a gun. Seminole Heights can get sketchy after dark."

She heads into the kitchen, rummages through a drawer, and pulls out a small brass key. Her movements are calm, practiced. She returns to the hallway and fits the key into the lock with deliberate ease.

The door clicks open. She flips the light switch on just as two shadows pass by the window.

CHAPTER 70

Zeke storms into Buddy Brew like a man on fire. The midday calm of Hyde Park cracks around him. I've been trying to lay low for a couple of days, regroup, and figure out what the hell is happening. But the universe seems determined to keep unraveling me, thread by damn thread.

He spots me near the window and zeroes in.

"How the fuck did you do it, Jason?" he hisses, spit flying.

I shield my coffee and mutter an apology to a mom in Lululemon whose toddler clutches a sippy cup like a weapon.

"You want a drink?" I ask calmly, "Or do you want to get us both tossed out of here?"

Zeke yanks a chair, dragging it loudly across the polished floor. Every head turns. He sneers at the gawking baristas. "Go back to your lattes and matcha's, you sanctimonious sheep."

I lower my voice. "What's wrong with you?"

His eyes flare—wild, dilated. "I want to know," he says, each word spaced like a bullet, "how you got an entire fucking country to stop looking for you?"

"I have no idea what you're talking about, Zeke."

For once, I am telling the truth. I don't have any idea. I've been on a few calls with my attorney and otherwise have been trying to block out the whole situation. I assume the techs took DNA from the room and know I was with Lia. I am half expecting to be sent back to Greece, which might be a relief, except for the whole filthy Greek prison thing.

"The Greeks dropped the extradition request," Zeke says. "You're no longer a person of interest."

The words hit me like a depth charge. A sudden, impossible weight lifts—then just as quickly, dread replaces it. Why would they back off?

I already know the answer. Someone got to them.

"Zeke," I say cautiously, "I didn't do anything. I'll call my attorney, find out what's going on."

"You do that," he sneers. "You and your slick little mouthpiece can play dumb all day. But listen to me: I don't know what you're into or who you're protecting, but it's not going to end well."

"I get it. You're angry. But we're friends."

"No." His voice sharpens. "You have one week. That's it. If I don't hear from you by then, you'll be under arrest. Don't forget—if I label you a national threat, we can bury you in a hole so deep your new pals and that hot-air balloon lawyer won't find you."

He rises, the storm in his eyes finally quieting to a squint. "Now give me five bucks. I told Gloria I'd bring her an iced coffee and left my wallet in the car."

****

Later that afternoon, my phone lights up with Syd's name. I almost don't answer.

"I'm so glad you picked up," she says, her voice tight. "Why didn't you respond last night?"

After Zeke's ultimatum, my nerves are a live wire. The last thing I want to deal with is Syd—and that twisted collage she made of my life. Her "Jason Miles" wall haunts me. Stalker? Or worse... is she part of *The One*?

"I must've turned it off by accident," I say, forcing concern into my voice. "Everything okay?"

"Not exactly. Someone broke into my house last night."

"Are you alright?"

"I'm fine. Apple was with me. She let me crash at her place."

"How do you know it was a break-in?"

"I heard a noise. Then I found a window open, and I always keep it locked. The paint on the sill was chipped, like someone forced it."

"Did you call the cops?"

She hesitates. I know why—the *room*.

"No. But I've got hidden cameras."

My blood turns cold. We searched outside for surveillance, but never imagined she had cameras inside.

"Jason? You still there?"

I steady my voice. "Yeah… just worried about you. What's on the footage?"

"It's not that simple. It uploads to the cloud, and then I have to request the data. They said it'll take a week to process and email me the clips. After that, I can go to the police. Until then, I'm installing a full security system—motion sensors, smart locks, the works."

She pauses.

"Can I stay with you in the meantime?"

I exhale slowly. "Of course. Meet me at the hotel after you finish your classes. Pack some clothes and stay as long as you need."

Another ticking clock. Another week.

The noose is tightening.

Hopefully, keeping her close will expose her true motives. If she's spying on me, I'll find out why—and turn it to my advantage.

As the saying goes: keep your friends close, and your enemies closer.

CHAPTER 71

"Are you sure you weren't followed?" I ask as Morgan steps inside the Roosevelt Room toward the back of Hotel Haya. I shut the door fast enough to make her jump after taking a quick look outside.

I'm out of time. Zeke's deadline is up, and I'm sure he is coordinating my arrest. Syd will know that Avner and I were at her house. And worst of all, tomorrow I'm supposed to steal Winnie.

Morgan scans the space—a faux library lined with bookshelves, a giant portrait of Teddy Roosevelt sitting on horseback, and an assortment of lifelike animals on the walls: a peacock with its colorful feathers and two deer heads watching us closely.

I grip her shoulders and meet her eyes. "Morgan, I know I can trust you."

I don't doubt it. At my lowest point a year ago, I asked her to believe me when almost no one else would. Without her, I'd be in prison or dead.

"Oh boy." She sighs. "That sentence never ends well for me. By the way, I followed your crazy instructions—ducking into gift shops, doubling back twice. It took me an hour to travel half a mile."

"I need to tell you what's really going on."

"I know. The governor. The warden. Tampa Scientific. Sloppy Joe. I'm up to speed."

Not even close. I rub my forehead. All of this sounds like the ramblings of a madman, even to me.

"You saw everything at Safe Harbor—the fraud ring, the players involved, and most importantly, the money trail leading to *The One*."

She nods and pulls her ever-present notebook from her purse. "I documented everything. Wrote half a dozen stories. But we never proved *The One* existed and that the funds went to them. It was all circumstantial."

"That's why I needed Sterling. He had the missing piece."

"All we know is he was shanked in prison," she says directly.

"We both know he was silenced." Frustration slips into my voice. I don't have time to ease her into this. "I need you to keep an open mind."

She twirls her pen, a fancy gold and black Montblanc Meisterstück, then nods for me to continue.

"It starts with Safe Harbor. Scott and I uncovered the fraud. He got killed. In the end, we proved the scheme, but—"

"—but not where the money went. It could have been some rich guys who didn't like paying taxes. That's all."

"Not true. Sterling knew. They killed him for it."

"Allegedly," she mutters, not sounding thoroughly convinced.

"You revealed the rumors about the governor and the warden."

"Jason, are you going to tell me anything new today?"

I sit. Deep breath. "You also know Tampa Scientific's data—and Nikesh's child—were held hostage."

"Yes. And you were the hero who saved him."

"Not exactly." I shake my head. "It was a setup. *The One* pulled strings so I'd look like a hero and earn Nikesh's trust."

Morgan goes quiet—rare for her. Her eyes widen as she scribbles. "Jason... why?"

"Because of Winnie. Tampa Scientific built the world's first Alpha Quantum Computer. She's beyond anything anyone's ever seen. And

The One wants her."

"Slow down," she says, palms up.

"I can't. I have dinner with the bad guys in an hour. Just trust me—if *The One* gets their hands on Winnie, everything changes. Globally and forever."

She swallows hard.

"When I was in Greece, they kidnapped me after murdering the local police. I am sure you can find a record of that. What you won't find is that I was shot, drugged, taken to some unknown location where they told me point-blank: join *The One*, or everyone I love dies. Avner. Goat. Zeke."

"And Lia?" she asks quietly.

That's the one question I won't touch. I look away.

"Since then," I continue, "I've been working with Frederick, George—a local businessman—and Claude, who you met at the TSC event."

"Wait a minute. You are saying that Florida's governor is a member of a secret society that wants to take over the world?"

I nod. "He's not just a member. He's a leader."

She continues to scribble in her notebook. "Along with that creepy guy Frederick brought in to fight fraud?"

"Yeah. Turns out he's part of the cause, running a massive fraud operation in Brandon—millions, maybe billions stolen every year. He has the technical skills."

"Jason... do you have proof of any of this? It sounds like fiction."

"There's more." I stand again, pacing. "They forced me to breach Regency Bank's security as a test after taking me to a place called Rooster Island—a gathering of wealthy lunatics who are all part of *The One*."

I slide her the handwritten list. "These are the names I remember."

She scans the page and gasps. "Do you have proof?" she repeats, voice tight.

"I think my girlfriend, Syd, is a spy for *The One* too. I thought about trying to turn her, but every time I dance around it, she plays dumb. We don't have time for the full story. Avner can fill you in."

She raises an eyebrow. "Jason, you have terrible taste in women. Maybe I should set you up with someone normal."

I ignore her. "Last few things. Sloppy Joe was Eric Gruber."

"The banker in the Safe Harbor fraud? We all assumed he was dead."

"He wasn't. Now he is. A body turned up in Lake Seminole—gator bait. They silenced him so he couldn't talk."

Her pen stops. "How do you know this?"

"I was there. Avner and Goat were there. A former SEAL named Omaha grabbed him—bad guy. Before they took him, Gruber told me *The One* killed my parents. And that I'm what they call 'Preferred'—which means I'm related to their leadership by blood."

"Jesus, Jason..."

"Last thing." I grab my coat. "Tomorrow at noon, they expect me to plant a virus at TSC that'll give them full access to Winnie. Before that, I'm meeting Zeke. I'm going to tell him everything I've told you. If he helps, we go after *The One* together. If he doesn't..." I swallow. "Then I have to choose between unleashing Winnie or protecting the people I love. It's an impossible decision."

She stands, voice softer than I've heard since I've known her. "Why tell me all this? Why not Avner? Why not go to Zeke right now?"

"You know Avner. Shoot first, ask questions later. He already almost died for me once. I won't let that happen again. I've got to make sure they don't change the playbook tonight. Throw me a curveball for tomorrow."

She hesitates. "Are you sure you want me?"

"I need someone to know the truth. To help end this once and for all." My voice is shakier than I intend. "There's a real chance I don't survive this."

CHAPTER 72

"Gentlemen, raise your glasses," Frederick says, lifting his tumbler of Macallan 30-Year Double Cask. The amber liquid glows beneath the low light, swirling around a single, perfect cube of ice.

"Tomorrow," he says with a slow smile, "the world changes."

I need to play my role and make sure the plan stays the same. After dinner, I'll go home and document everything the best I can for Zeke. Ernesto promised to make sure the Bluebird team is somewhere safe when it all goes down.

We raise our drinks—George, Claude, and I—and clink softly. The private room at Bern's Steakhouse is all dark wood, velvet, and power. Known for its art, wine, and steaks that melt like secrets on your tongue, Bern's bent over backwards to make this happen, even swapped the long table for a small, round one. More intimate. More conspiratorial.

"To Jason Miles," George adds, looking at me. "The newest member of the family… and the oldest."

I let out a low laugh, trying to act confused. "What does that mean?"

But I already know.

Eric told me the truth—that I'm blood. Not just related. Royalty, by their standards. I still don't want to believe it.

"You finally get to know why you are Preferred, Jason," Frederick says. "You have the highest honor by birth. Your blood is that of our royal family. Not only are you part of our family, but you are also part of *THE* family."

"How can that be?" I ask. "I'm just a guy from the Midwest. My dad was just a regular person."

"Not true," George says softly. "Your father was a patriot—a leader. A hero of the cause… until that tragic day he was taken from us. He hid it from you to protect you, but he would have wanted you to be a leader."

My hands clench into fists under the table. Rage pushes hot behind my eyes. I picture flipping the table, slamming my tumbler into Frederick's skull, and never looking back.

Play the part, Jason.

"I never knew," I say, leaning back, faking the ache. "He was my hero. I wish someone had told me."

"We had to be sure we could trust you," George says. "But you passed every test. Tomorrow, Jason… tomorrow, you become a legend."

We're interrupted by one of Omaha's men, who enters the room and whispers something in Frederick's ear. We all lean in to try to hear. He nods and whispers something to the man.

"What's going on?" I ask.

"Apparently, your buddies, Avner and the little FBI guy, are here. Trying to listen in."

This was not expected. The curveballs keep coming.

"I promise I was careful. There is no way they followed me."

He waves his hand dismissively in the air. "It doesn't matter. We prepare for things like this. It's too late for them to be a problem."

The door opens again with a cluster of waiters and the maître d', who carries a bottle of Opus One Cabernet like it's a holy relic. The waitstaff looks like they stepped out of a tuxedo catalog.

"My sincerest apologies, gentlemen," the maître d' says, beaming. "The owner would be honored for you to enjoy this 2017 Opus One. One of Napa Valley's finest vintages. We've also arranged a private tour and a visit to the dessert room when you're ready."

The plates land in front of us: Filet mignon, baked potatoes, fried onions, and vegetables arranged like art.

"All steaks prepared medium rare," the waiter announces. "Except for the governor's. He prefers his well done."

"Why would you do that to a defenseless steak?" Claude laughs, slicing his in half. A pool of red forms under his knife. He leans so close to the meal that his mustache touches the steak.

"Sorry, boys," Frederick says, grinning. "You like your cows still mooing. I like to make sure mine is *dead*."

I try to enjoy the food, but the Prime, dry-aged steak tastes like Spam. Even the glorious lobster bisque is no better than the cheap French onion soup. The company has ruined my appetite, along with the heinous act they expect me to execute tomorrow. I'm also concerned for Avner and Zeke, but I know they can take care of themselves.

After a stretch of forced small talk and swirling wine glasses, Claude wipes his mouth and says, "I hate to mix business with pleasure, but let's review the plan one more time."

As he speaks, a shred of potato clings to his mustache like a parasite. I want to flick it off, or better, punch him so hard it launches across the room.

I feel like I'm trapped in a movie, and I hate the ending.

Claude continues. "Jason and Ernesto will be at TSC at noon tomorrow. They will disable the security systems and open an email from a sender named Trey Heyward, asking for customer support. When they open the email, the virus will spread quickly through the network and server, including direct access to Winnie. Remember, all security protocols must be disabled; otherwise, the virus will become trapped in a cyber web. Do you understand, Jason?"

I nod slowly. My throat burns as I swallow the wine. "I understand," I manage.

Claude leans forward, the flickering candlelight casting his smile in a demonic light. "By twelve-thirty, our team—engineers, physicists, quantum freaks—will have total control of Winnie."

"And then?" Frederick asks.

Claude raises his glass high, wine sloshing near the rim. "And then, we crack every firewall, break every encryption, and the world—gentlemen—is ours."

CHAPTER 73

"I can't hear a damn thing," Avner mutters, pulling off his headphones in frustration. They are holed up in an empty banquet room down the hall from Jason's private dinner, the faint hum of distant voices barely cutting through the static in their feed.

Zeke and a young FBI tech hunch over a console of blinking lights and knobs, adjusting dials like frustrated radio operators from a bygone war. All three wear headphones, and no one is calm.

"We bugged the room with our best tech," the FBI tech says, glancing nervously between them. "It's top-of-the-line."

Avner shoots him a glare and snaps his headphones onto the table. "Then your best belongs in the clearance aisle at Walmart. Shin Bet would have had these assholes crystal clear *and* in custody by now."

"Cool your jets, Israeli," Zeke says, voice low but stern. "We're eavesdropping on the sitting governor of Florida—without a shred of evidence. This is beyond illegal."

He steps away from the table and lowers his voice further. "The only reason we're even *in* this room is that I eat at the bar two nights a week and play poker with the owner."

Avner is pacing, gripping a cloth napkin as if it were a stress ball. Every few steps, he stops to crack his knuckles or stretch his back, muscles tight, nerves fraying.

Zeke adjusts his headset again. "Something's off, man. Jason's up to his neck in this, and whatever's happening in that room—it's big."

"They've got that cyber freak with them," Avner snaps. "The one with all the bracelets on his arm and the social skills of a used car salesman. I'd bet he's jamming us right now."

The room goes quiet except for the low static in their ears.

Then Avner turns, his expression hardening. "I say we stop playing games and crash their little party."

Zeke looks up. "We do that, and this whole thing burns. No wiretap, no cause, no warrant. They walk. All of them."

Avner steps closer. "And if we wait, people might die."

The tech glances between them, wide-eyed. "You... want me to keep trying?"

Neither man answers.

Zeke listens to the feed a moment longer, jaw tight. Then, under his breath: "Not yet. Give it one more shot."

Avner paces again, the napkin nearly shredded in his fist.

The clock is ticking—and they all know it.

****

"I hope you all enjoyed your dinner," the maître d' says with a gracious nod. "I'll be leading your tour personally."

We fall in behind him like obedient schoolchildren, weaving through the tables while patrons gawk at Governor Frederick. He soaks in the attention, flashing his politician's smile and giving a practiced wave, as if he's still on the campaign trail.

I need to get the hell out of here. I'll probably be up all night connecting the dots.

The maître d' walks us through the aging room first—walls lined with marbled cuts of beef in various stages of perfection. The air is cold, heavy with the scent of iron and fat. Then we move on to the kitchen, steaks hissing over open charcoal flames. Even after a full meal, the smell teases my stomach. I could probably manage a few more bites—if my nerves weren't so shot.

As we round a corner near an unmarked exit, I feel Frederick's hand wrap around my elbow.

"This is where your tour ends," he says, gently but firmly.

He pushes open the door to the back of the building, and the warm interior gives way to a blast of cool night air. A black SUV waits by the curb, idling. Omaha stands beside it, expressionless.

"Your Uber has arrived," he says. No smile. No sarcasm.

I glance between the two of them. "What's going on, Frederick?"

He straightens his tie like he's about to give a press conference. "We can't risk anything happening before noon tomorrow."

The blood drains from my face. This can't happen. If they lock me down, I have no way to get to Zeke.

"Omaha will make sure you're tucked in safe and sound," Frederick continues. "No distractions. No surprises."

"This isn't necessary," I protest, trying to stay calm even as panic coils inside me—but I know what happens if I push too hard.

Omaha pulls back his coat, showing his weapon. "We're not asking."

I breathe in through my nose and exhale slowly.

"Fine," I say. "Let's go."

Omaha opens the SUV door, and I slide inside, already thinking about how to escape the moment the locks click shut.

My plan just exploded, and the choice I need to make in the morning could destroy everything.

****

"**W**ell, isn't this romantic?" Zeke says, striding toward the repurposed wine cask tucked in the corner of Bern's Dessert Room.

Frederick, George, and Claude sit huddled around the intimate table, sipping coffee and picking at slices of key lime pie. They glance up at Zeke, unimpressed, and then return to their low conversation like he's an annoying echo.

"Where's Jason?" Avner asks, sliding in beside Claude without waiting for permission. Zeke takes the other side, nudging closer to Frederick, crowding the table.

"This is a private table," George says, signaling to a passing waiter with a flick of his hand.

"I'm going to ask one more time," Avner says, lifting a fork and stabbing a piece of pie. "Where. Is. Jason?"

Within seconds, the maître d' arrives with a swarm of waiters in tow. "Gentlemen," he says, trying to stay composed, "please leave the governor and his party, or we'll be forced to contact the authorities."

Zeke rises slowly, stepping in until he's nose-to-nose with the maître d'. His voice drops to a dangerous calm.

"My name is Zeke Michaels. FBI. I am the authorities. You have two seconds to get out of my face before I shut this entire place down. And if you need permission, go ask your boss."

The maître d's face flushes a deeper red. He hesitates, glances over his shoulder, then relents. With a curt nod, he waves his staff off and backs away.

Zeke turns back to the table. "As my friend asked—where's Jason?"

Frederick stands now, looking down on Zeke. His tone is mocking, but tight.

"Can you clarify which Jason you're looking for?" he says.

"You can push around waiters and busboys all you want," he adds. "But keep this up, and you'll be writing parking tickets outside Disney."

Just then, the owner of Bern's appears, clearly summoned from somewhere deeper in the building. His face is taut with tension.

"Zeke," he says carefully, "please. This disturbance can't continue."

Zeke stares at him for a beat, then nods once and turns to Avner. "Let's go."

They both rise from the table. Zeke pauses, one hand on the back of his chair, and looks each of the men in the eye.

"But I want all three of you to hear this: I know you're dirty. I can't prove it yet. But I will. And when I do…" He leans forward, voice low and deliberate. "You'll be thinking about Mickey and Minnie from an eight-foot cell."

CHAPTER 74

"Avner, Jason never came back to the hotel last night," Syd says as she steps into the Bungalow.

Avner sits at the kitchen table, cradling a mug of coffee, eyes hollow from a sleepless night. He rubs his temples and looks up.

"I know, Syd. We're not sure where he is. Zeke and I lost him at Bern's."

Ernesto briefly looks up from his laptop, trying to hear the conversation.

Syd glances at him, then leans toward Avner. "Can I talk to you in private?" she asks under her breath.

Avner nods and follows her out onto the porch. The morning is overcast; the air is heavy with moisture. Clouds drift low and gray.

Syd closes the screen door behind them and turns to face him.

"I got the recording back from the security company."

Avner doesn't react immediately, just stares toward the quiet street. "Yeah? What was on it?"

Syd steps closer and turns his shoulders so he's looking at her.

"You know what was on it. Why did you and Jason break into my house?"

Avner stiffens. "Why are you stalking Jason? Who are you working for?"

She recoils slightly, then plants her feet and crosses her arms.

"Working for? I'm a college professor. I'm not stalking anyone."

"Then what's with the weirdo board? All the photos and notes about people in Jason's life?"

"I'm also an author. You know that. I was thinking about writing a book about Jason. Apple told me about him at school, and I thought it was interesting, so I did some research."

"That's why you wouldn't let him come over?"

"Of course. Once we met, I fell for him. I was going to talk to him about it, but then it got kind of awkward between us."

Avner studies her face, searching for deception. He finds none.

"Are you going to tell Apple? Or the cops?"

Syd shakes her head. "No. It can stay between us. Just tell me—is Jason okay?"

Avner exhales and looks back to the street, voice low. "I don't know. But something's wrong. I can feel it. Whatever this is, it's coming to a head—and if we don't act soon, Jason might not make it out alive."

CHAPTER 75

I sit in the juror box, though it's far too big—like a theater box. The courtroom is bathed in an odd, golden light, soft and heavy. My parents preside over the bench; both are dressed in long black robes. They wear matching stern expressions, but their gavels are oversized and cartoonish. My dad taps impatiently. Mom looks bored.

At one table, Zeke and Gloria scribble notes like frantic students cramming for an exam. At the other end, Frederick, George, and Clinton huddle over a glowing laptop, Clinton's fingers slamming the keys. He stops and winks at Syd.

The jury box around me teems with ghosts from different lives—past coworkers, old friends, enemies, exes. I haven't seen some of these faces in years. Others, I thought I'd never see again.

Avner and Lia sit close together, deep in quiet conversation. Every so often, Avner glances at me and slowly shakes his head. Disappointed, maybe. Or resigned.

Oak is leaning into Syd, whispering something. She laughs—tosses her blonde hair over her shoulder like they're on a date—my gut twists. Jealousy flares up, fast and irrational. I force it down like bile and keep scanning the crowd.

Scott Kowalski sits stiffly near the back. I wave. He doesn't wave back. He's locked in a silent glare with Terrance from Safe Harbor Bank, who has a bloody hole in the middle of his forehead. Terrance dabs at the wound with a monogrammed handkerchief like it's a nosebleed. Max Braun, his bulldog of a security chief, meets my eyes and casually flips me off.

And then I see him—A headless man, soaking wet, holding a cardboard box to his chest like it contains something sacred. Or dangerous. I don't know what's in the box. I don't want to know.

The sound of my father's gavel cracks through the room like a rifle shot.

"Court is now in session," he announces. "My wife and I have dinner reservations, so let's get this moving. Today, we decide the fate of Jason Miles."

I freeze. My name sounds foreign here. I'm on trial. It looks like I have enough friends in court, but I've let so many of them down.

I stand and turn toward my father. "Since apparently I am on trial, I would like to say something."

"Make it fast, boy," he says.

"I just want to say that I've always tried to do the right thing. I haven't always been successful and made some bad choices, but I am always trying, and I hope you consider that. I love most of the people in this room."

"Oh, boo hoo," someone yells from the back.

"Defending Mr. Miles are Zeke Michaels and Gloria Chavez," my dad continues. "Prosecuting on behalf of the State of Florida— Governor Frederick Matthews and local business legend George Klein."

"I object!" Zeke shouts, leaping to his feet. "The governor's a blowhard, and Mr. Klein's only a legend in his mind."

"Overruled," my dad replies, with no hint of humor. "Mr. Michaels, proceed."

Zeke clutches a legal pad and begins pacing like he's seen too many courtroom dramas. He looks at me, nods, then clears his throat. "Let's be honest. Jason Miles has made some questionable decisions. But eternal damnation? Bit much, don't you think?" He pauses. "We intend to show that while his methods were flawed—and often catastrophic—his intentions were noble. He wanted to be a hero. He just... sucked at it."

"Jesus, Zeke," I mutter.

"Language, honey," my mom says, flashing me a warm smile.

Zeke turns back to the jury box. "Our first witness: Jason's former wife, Lia Miles. Please stand."

Lia rises slowly. Her face is calm, unreadable.

"Do you swear to tell the truth, the whole truth, and nothing but the truth?" Zeke asks.

Lia smirks. "Nothing but the truth? That's a tall order. I'll try."

Frederick stands and clears his throat like he's at a press conference. "For the record, Lia Miles is an international fugitive. Her testimony should be considered... unreliable at best."

"So noted," my father says without looking up, banging his ridiculous oversized gavel like he's breaking rocks.

Lia is wearing worn jeans and a black tank top; her hair pulled into a tight ponytail. It is light like it was in Greece. There's a Glock strapped to her thigh and a laptop tucked under her arm like a purse. My chest tightens. She locks eyes with me, but there's no smile, no warmth—just sadness behind those tired eyes.

"Mrs. Miles," Zeke begins smoothly, "you were formerly an intelligence officer in Israel. Also, Jason's handler before you married him. Correct?"

"That's classified," she replies, deadpan.

Zeke nods like that's expected. "Right. Fine. But you were married to him for ten years."

"That's true." Her eyes don't leave mine. "And I still love him."

My throat is dry. I mouth, *I love you too*, and hope she still knows how to read lips.

"Would you say Jason was a good husband? Provided for you?"

"Yes. He was wonderful."

Zeke steps closer. "Did you see him as a hero?"

"He tried," she says. "He never stopped trying. That's what I loved most."

Zeke drops his legal pad on the table and turns. "That's all I have."

Frederick wastes no time—he strides across the courtroom like he owns the floor. "Mrs. Miles, is it true you shot your husband and stole sensitive intel, which you then sold to *The One*?"

Lia doesn't flinch. "I'm not on trial, asshole."

Avner smirks in the jury box.

Frederick tries again, nastier this time: "Fine. Let's make it simple. Is it true Jason's now sleeping with the cute little blonde sitting next to Oak Williams?"

Lia looks away from me. Her eyes drift to Syd and scan her from head to toe. "That is true. Jason told me that we should not be together and is now sleeping with that tramp. He broke my heart."

"I'm not a tramp," Syd blurts out.

"Chick fight!" Oak yells, grinning like it's a pay-per-view event.

I jump to my feet. "That's not true, Lia. I love you. I always have. I made a mistake. I mean... you're in hiding."

"No more questions," Frederick says, smug as ever. "You may sit, Mrs. Miles."

She does, and doesn't look at me again. Avner, however, won't stop glaring.

My father sighs, tapping his gavel like he's ready to leave. "Zeke, who's next?"

Zeke scans the room. "Mr. Scott Kowalski, please stand. You're dead, right?"

Scott pokes at the side of his skull until his fingers dip into a neat, bloodless bullet hole. "Correct. Shot in the head. Courtesy of those Safe Harbor assholes."

He looks exactly how I remember him: ratty hoodie, tangled

beard, glasses sitting on his forehead. Hair like a perm gone wild.

Zeke nods. "You and Jason uncovered the fraud at Safe Harbor. Would you consider yourself a hero? What about Jason?"

Scott strokes his beard like he's thinking. "I'm really the one who uncovered the fraud, but yeah. We did the right thing."

Zeke sits back down. "That's all, Your Honor."

Frederick stays seated. Just one question. "Did Jason Miles warn you about the danger you were in?"

Scott doesn't hesitate. He turns to me. "No. He let me die."

I lurch to my feet again. "Scott, I'm sorry. I should've warned you. I didn't know—"

"Sit down, Jason," my dad says with a groan. "Let's wrap this up, people. Some say Jason's a hero. Others think he's just a walking disaster. Anyone got something *new*?"

Frederick strolls toward the bench, then points at *him*.

"What about that guy? Jason failed him."

Eric Gruber, the headless man, steps forward. He opens his soggy box and lifts his severed head into the air. His mouth moves independently of his body.

"I needed help," the head says. "Now I don't even have a head. He's guilty of something."

Zeke bolts upright. "Objection! Frederick, George, and Omaha fed that man to a gator. They can't call him as a witness!"

"That seems reasonable," my mom says calmly, filing her nails. "But we've all heard enough. There's one person whose opinion might settle this."

She looks at Avner. Everyone turns.

My stomach drops.

"Let's hear what *he* has to say."

CHAPTER 76

"Avner, are you going to tell the truth?" Zeke asks, his voice louder than before.

Avner stands slowly, grumbling something I can't make out. He's squeezing his tennis ball with white-knuckled fury, eyes locked on mine like twin spotlights of judgment. He's wearing his old jiu-jitsu shirt—the one with the image of a man wrestling a lion.

"Avner," Zeke tries again, "do you have *any* idea what's going on with Jason?"

Avner shakes his head once. "No. He's been avoiding me. Lying. Slipping further away."

Zeke takes a step closer. "And what would you say if I told you Jason has the fate of humanity in his hands?"

Avner doesn't flinch. He keeps crushing that tennis ball like he wants to split it in half. His jaw tightens.

"I'd say humanity is fucked," he says at last. "He should've trusted me."

My voice cracks as I shout across the courtroom, "I *do* trust you! You don't understand! If I don't do this, they're going to kill everyone I love. I can't let that happen!"

Frederick slams his hand on the table and stands up. "Oh, for God's sake—can we skip the drama? Are you going to do it or not?"

Suddenly, the whole room explodes in sound.

Everyone starts talking—*screaming*.

Lia's voice cuts through: *Jason, don't!*

Avner shouts over her: *You had your chance!*

Eric Gruber's *head* is yelling from the witness box: *You owe me a body!*

Oak is laughing maniacally: "Oak Williams would *never* give up the world—but it sounds like a great movie!"

I cover my ears, but it's useless—the voices bleed through, louder, faster, overlapping like static in my brain. My heart's pounding in my throat. My vision tunnels. I hear my father, calm and clear, like a judge from heaven.

"Quiet, everyone," he says. The gavel cracks like thunder. "Time to answer the question, son."

The room stills. All eyes on me.

My dad leans forward.

"What are you going to do?"

CHAPTER 77

Someone shakes me, but the dream refuses to release. I break the surface gasping, soaked in sweat, heart pounding hard enough to hurt. A scream presses at my throat. Either choice will drown me in guilt.

"Rise and shine, sleepyhead," Omaha says. "Nightmare? Too bad. Time's up. Get your ass in gear. You've got a promise to keep—and I'm getting you to Tampa Scientific on time."

Being held captive without my phone made reaching Zeke impossible. I'd considered jumping Omaha, but that fantasy died the moment two more of his men walked in.

"I need to pick up Ernesto," I say. This might be my last chance.

"Don't worry, we've taken care of it. You just do your job."

The dream clings to me like static as I stumble into the shower. I trim my beard with shaking hands and dress in the clothes Omaha left out—khakis and a dark blue polo. I feel like a fraud. I'm expected to change the world forever, and I look like I'm selling appliances.

Omaha's SUV rolls up to the security gate. I open the door to step out when he says, "Don't make me come find you again, Jason."

I don't answer. I walk through the doors like a condemned man entering his own execution.

It's 11:50 a.m. The air in the lobby hums with fluorescent indifference.

Ernesto is waiting, pacing back and forth, looking down at his phone. "Where have you been? Everyone's looking for you."

"I had a situation," I say flatly. "Let's get to the control room. Time to run the security testing protocol."

A thought crosses my mind. "Did you make sure the team is going to be together at one?" I ask.

His hands shake as he gathers his things, sending a pen and a stack of credit cards skittering to the floor. He ducks down to snatch them up. "Yeah, I took care of it," he says.

We sit at the server bank—blinking lights, endless screens. Normally, Ernesto runs the tests while I supervise. Not today.

My head is pounding. I keep rubbing at my bare pinky, where the nail used to be. Trying to focus. I can still hear the voices from the dream—Lia, Avner, Eric's severed head yelling. I remember telling them all that I love them. I can't shake their faces.

"Okay, boss," Ernesto says. "I found the email from Trey Heyward you flagged. Want me to open it?"

I knew this moment would find me. Choosing between society and the people I love steals my breath, and I feel tears rise. The familiar faces in the dream or the many more faces I don't even know.

My finger hovers near my keyboard.

"First," I say, "take down all the security fences."

He stiffens. "You want to what? Didn't we just get fired for doing that?"

"Bring down all system security. There's a fail-safe we're testing."

"Jason, that'll leave us wide open. This place will be naked. Are you sure?"

"Do it, Ernesto," I instruct quietly.

He nods, then begins typing. The firewalls fall, one by one. Vulnerable. Exposed.

The email sits there. A single click will unleash the virus. *The One* will control Winnie. But if I don't… they'll kill everyone I love.

Before I can act, the door bursts open.

Nikesh, Avner, and Zeke storm in. Nikesh is red-faced and breathless.

"Jason, what the hell are you doing?" he yells. "Security's down! Winnie is completely exposed!"

Avner steps forward, calm but firm. "Morgan came to us when you didn't show. You don't have to do this, Jason. We'll figure it out. Keep everyone safe. Just bring the security back online."

Zeke's hand drifts to his sidearm. "Times up. Don't even think about clicking that email."

My hand is on the mouse. The email is highlighted. This is the edge of the cliff. One move in either direction, and I fall to my death.

I hit delete.

"Ernesto, bring the security back up. Now," I instruct.

He types rapidly, eyes scanning code. "Trying... wait—no. Someone logged in remotely. They opened the file. The virus is live. It's disabling everything."

My heart stops. I didn't open it. Someone else did. They had a backup. They didn't trust me after all. They used me again.

"Nikesh," I shout, "you have to shut down Winnie. That virus was built to hijack her. If she falls, they can break every encryption system on Earth."

"She's an Apex Quantum Computer, Jason. I can't just unplug her!" he screams. "What are we dealing with?"

"It's *The One*. They blackmailed me into giving them access. They're behind everything: the ransom, your son, all of it. I tried to stop them. But they planned for this. They had a backup. We must disable Winnie before she's theirs."

Zeke turns to Nikesh. "If we lose her, we lose *everything*."

Nikesh shakes his head, pained. "She's my life's work. To disable her... I would have to *kill* her."

"If you don't, we all lose," I say. "Humanity."

Nikesh hesitates.

Zeke inches closer. "How long do we have?"

I check the clock. "Less than thirty minutes."

Nikesh bolts for the back stairs.

"Ernesto, go get the team together," I say, but realize he's gone.

We follow, descending deep into the tunnels, toward the secure AI vault.

Inside, Winnie's lair pulses with quiet energy. Her voice greets us. "Security breach detected. A virus is replicating across all nodes."

"Nikesh," Zeke urges, "you know what you have to do."

Nikesh chokes back a sob. "Winnie," he says, voice trembling, "can you isolate the virus?"

"No. The virus was engineered with quantum familiarity. I am being systematically dismantled."

I place a hand on Nikesh's shoulder. "You can end this."

His breath catches. He sits at the terminal, puts his face in his hands, then lifts it, eyes steel.

He begins typing—furiously. Fingers dancing across the keys. The sound is like rain on glass: click-click-click.

The minutes crawl. The virus keeps spreading. I check the time. 12:25. We're out of time.

"Nikesh!" I shout. "It's now or never!"

Suddenly, the lights flicker—then go out. The servers power down. The glow behind the screens fades.

Silence.

I whisper, "Is it done?"

Nikesh doesn't turn. He just says, through gritted teeth and sobs— "She's gone."

CHAPTER 78

"You're back sooner than I thought," Avner says as I step into the Bungalow. I expect the full team, but it's just him, Goat, and Syd.

"Where is everyone? I told Ernesto that we needed all hands here. Now."

Avner shrugs. "He didn't say anything. We figured Zeke would lock you down for a few hours."

"Zeke had an emergency. Some sort of a shooting. Let me go if I promised to return without my lawyer. Pretty sure J. Robert Bailey isn't taking my calls again anyway." I pause, lowering my voice. "We need everyone now. And we need to talk about security—either protective custody or private contractors."

Avner nods, understanding my concern. "Morgan told us about the threat. Zeke promised to take care of it. Send people our way."

"I've been trying to reach Apple," he adds. "No luck. Maybe she's teaching. I was about to head to UT after this. Also, Ernesto vanished from TSC, and Berta didn't show up today."

"Can you try to reach everyone again? It's important."

I turn to Syd. "Can we talk? In private?"

She nods, and we step into one of the small offices. I lean against the desk, trying to find the right words.

"Avner told me about the book," I say.

Syd's face drops. "I'm sorry, Jason. It started as just a fun idea, then I got to know you. And it no longer felt right. I was going to tell you. I'm not writing anything. I want us to be a normal couple."

I offer a crooked smile. "We broke into your house. I've been... off. I'll tell you everything, eventually. I don't know what normal looks like for me—but I'll try."

My phone buzzes. A mess of letters and numbers flash on the screen.

Lia.

She never calls this phone.

Syd leans in. "Aren't you going to answer?"

I step away and lift the phone to my ear. "This is Jason."

Lia's voice is breathless, frantic. "Jay, listen to me. Get somewhere safe. Now."

"Why are you calling this phone? What's happening?"

"There's an execute order. On your whole team. And Zeke. A kill squad is en route. *GO.*"

"Lia, what about you—?"

"I can handle myself. *MOVE!*"

The line goes dead.

The phone slips from my hand and hits the floor.

"You look like you've seen a ghost," Goat says. "Who was that?"

"Talk," Avner barks. He feels the shift in the air, the sudden heat of danger.

I meet his eyes. "We need to move. Now. No questions. Safe house."

Avner grabs my shoulders. "Who was on the phone?"

I shake my head. "We don't have time. A kill squad is coming."

Avner doesn't argue. He knows what that means. He moves to the safe, punches in the code, and starts passing out weapons—Glocks, AKs, ammo.

He pauses, eyes wide. "Apple."

"Call her again," Goat says, slapping a rifle into my hands. "I'll get Jason and Syd to the van. You pick up Apple. We'll rendezvous at the safe house. Then we find Berta and Ernesto."

Avner is out the door before the sentence finishes.

Goat racks a round into his rifle and flips the safety off. "You two—move. If we see them, shoot first. Like we used to say in the Stan: *kill or be killed*. And I'm not in the mood to die today."

****

Avner redials Apple's phone repeatedly. It goes straight to voicemail. The University of Tampa is ten minutes away—but he gets there in five.

His hands shake on the wheel. His heart pounds like it wants out of his chest.

Flashing lights greet him as he reaches the lot. Police. SWAT. Evacuating students who run for safety, screaming.

He jumps from the car and sprints toward Apple's building. Officers yell. Weapons rise.

"DON'T SHOOT!" Zeke appears from the chaos, yelling. "He's with me!"

Avner barrels past him. "Where is she?"

"Avner, stop—this is an active shooter situation. SWAT and FBI are clearing the area."

"WHERE IS SHE?!"

Zeke grabs him, forces him to a stop, and hands him an FBI windbreaker. "Put this on before you get shot. What the hell is going on?"

Avner shoves it on and pushes toward Apple's building. "Kill order. Jason got a tip. You're on it too. Apple wasn't with us."

Zeke jogs to catch up. "No wonder Jason has been blowing up my phone."

The Entrepreneur Center is swarming—at least fifteen officers, one ambulance with lights flashing, but no movement. The siren screams, abandoned.

"You don't want to see this," Zeke says. "I'm warning you."

Avner turns, eyes blazing. "Zeke, if you think you're stopping me from going in that building, you'd better shoot me right here."

Zeke's jaw tightens. He signals an officer. They're both given gloves and booties.

"Don't touch anything and be careful where you walk," a female officer says. She has too many lines of sadness on her young face. They have all seen things that will haunt them.

Zeke and Avner ride the elevator in silence to the eighth floor. When the door opens, no one is present, but yellow tape has been hung in certain areas. The smell of death hangs heavy in the air. They can see several lumps under white sheets that are stained with dark red.

Zeke says, "Avner, can we just get you somewhere safe? Whoever we are dealing with has gone on the offensive. You don't need to do this."

Room 809.

Apple's room.

The demand for her classes is so high that they require stadium seating to accommodate the requests. Often, the room is filled with others who are not even signed up but want to hear her educate and entertain.

One body is slumped just outside the door, and the sheet has slipped down. Avner stops to see Apple's beloved teaching assistant on the ground with her eyes wide open. He and Apple had taken the young girl to lunch a month ago. Apple had arranged an internship at a local non-profit that she was supposed to start soon. Avner bends down and gently closes them.

"Let's get you out of here," Zeke says. "You don't want this memory."

"I have lots of bad memories," Avner growls.

He enters the classroom.

One body at the front. A sheet draped over it. Blood pooled beneath the head.

The chalkboard is still filled with Apple's elegant cursive.

Above it, in blocky ugly scrawl: **CLASS DISMISSED.**

Avner's breath catches.

"How did they do it?" he asks, voice like gravel.

"Execution style," Zeke says softly. "One bullet. On her knees."

Avner walks forward. Kneels. Pulls back the sheet.

Apple's face is pale, still beautiful. A hole in her forehead. Her engagement ring catches the light. They were going to announce it next week.

He gently covers her again.

"Avner," Zeke pleads, "let's get you out of here. We'll handle this."

Avner doesn't answer. He turns, fists clenched, forearms shaking, tears gone.

The grief hardens into something colder. Darker. Primal.

They have woken the monster, and there will be hell to pay.

CHAPTER 79

Wood splinters. Glass explodes—the windows of the bungalow rain down like ice. We're sitting ducks in here, and I've already tried Berta and Ernesto half a dozen times—no answer. It's time to move.

"We can't stay," I tell Goat.

"I'll provide cover," he says, voice steady even as bullets chew into the walls. "You and Syd run for the van."

I grab Syd's hand. She's trembling. Her face is pale, eyes wide with terror.

"It's going to be okay," I say, locking eyes with her. "Goat and I'll lay down fire. You sprint to the van and get low. They're not here for you."

She nods, but her chest rises and falls too fast. I don't blame her. She's a teacher, not a soldier. Dropping her into this world? It's like tossing a mouse into a python tank.

Goat and I both have AKs slung across our shoulders, Glocks holstered at our sides. It's not enough. But it'll have to be.

"On three," I shout. "We light 'em up. Syd, you run. No hesitation. No matter what happens."

"You drive," Goat calls out. "I'll shoot. God bless us."

"One... two... three!"

We burst through the doorway, rifles up. Muzzle flashes blink in the shadows across the street. I squeeze the trigger and send hot lead in their direction. Syd sprints for the van, legs pumping, ponytail whipping behind her.

She dives in.

We fire as we retreat, step by step, until we're inside too. The van roars to life. The back rattles with incoming rounds.

I yank the wheel hard and tear down 4th Street. We're out—but not safe. In the rearview, a black Dodge Charger swerves into pursuit.

"They're gaining," I say, slamming the gas to the floor.

"We'll lose them on the way to the safehouse," Goat says calmly, loading a fresh magazine. He's done this before.

"Where are we even going?" Syd shouts from the floor, curled into a ball.

"Avner has an old farmhouse out in the country. Nobody knows about it except the Bluebird Team. In a worst-case scenario, we know to meet there. I would say this is a worst-case scenario," I respond.

"The van groans like it's going to tear itself apart. The Charger keeps coming, closing fast.

"Let it get closer," Goat says, rolling down the window. "I'll take the tires."

"What if they shoot you first?"

He doesn't answer. Just leans out, AK braced against the window frame. The wind howls. I glance over just in time to see muzzle flashes.

The Charger returns fire—then jerks hard to the side. Tires squeal. It skids, hits the guardrail, and flips once before slamming to a stop.

"Bullseye," Goat mutters, then makes the sign of the cross.

We reach the safehouse in thirty minutes flat. A padlocked gate marks the entrance. Goat unlocks it with a rusty key, moving slower than before.

"You okay?" I ask.

"Yeah," he groans. "Just peachy."

The van creaks down a dirt path swallowed by weeds. Trees hang over like they're hiding something. After a mile, the house appears—if you can call it that. The place looks like it was built during the Civil War and held together by termites holding hands.

"Park in the barn," Goat says, voice raspier now. "Grab the weapons."

I slide the door open. Syd is still curled up on the floor, shaking.

"Are you alright?" I ask gently.

She stares at me, then the AK in my hand. "Who were they?" she whispers. "Why were they trying to kill us?"

I help her up. One hand on her back, the other clutching cold steel.

The farmhouse is worse inside. The stench of mildew punches me in the face. Wallpaper dangles in ribbons. The fridge door hangs open on its hinges.

"This is disgusting," Syd says. "There's... is that blood?"

She points to a fresh pool on the floor. My stomach tightens.

I look at Goat—he's pressing his hand against his stomach.

"Goat... you've been shot."

He grins weakly. "Just a flesh wound."

Blood drips through his fingers.

"You need a hospital," Syd begs.

"No time. Bedroom. Safe behind the dresser. First aid kit. Avner always plans for hell."

He gives me the combination. Inside the safe: pistols, ammo, and a red-labeled box that reads **FIRST AID**.

"Give that to me," Syd says, snapping on gloves. "I studied nursing. Briefly."

She lifts Goat's shirt. The wound is ugly—raw, swollen, leaking too much blood too fast.

"This isn't good," she says. "I'll wrap it, but he needs a trauma center."

"I've been worse," Goat mutters, sweat dripping off his nose.

Then—gravel crunches outside.

"Avner," I say. Relief floods me. "He must've found Apple... maybe Berta and Ernesto too."

I peek through the faded curtain.

An SUV. Four men. Tactical vests. Assault rifles. Masks.

Not Avner.

"Is it him?" Syd asks, eyes wide. Hopeful.

I shake my head. "No. It's over. Someone on our team gave them this location. No one knew except our people."

The dots don't just connect, they collide. Convergence. Ernesto is a traitor. Not only was he the backup meant to steal Winnie, but he also failed to protect the team and handed over the safehouse.

I raise my AK.

Outside, a voice booms: "Come out, come out, wherever you are!"

It's Omaha.

"Jason, we only want you. We'll let the others go—for now."

"They found us," I say, turning to Syd and Goat. "We're done."

Goat groans and tries to straighten up. "No. You and Syd slip out the back. There's a path through the woods. I'll hold them off."

"You can barely sit up," I say.

"Jason, you gave me my life back. Let me give you yours. Just prop me up with some weapons. I can buy you time until…"

"They only want me," I say, softly. "Maybe I can give you both a chance."

Tears stream down Syd's cheeks. "Jason, you can't go out there. They'll kill you."

Outside, Omaha shouts again: "Last chance! Come out, or we come in shooting. Everyone doesn't have to die."

"I've got to go," I say.

Syd grabs my arm. "Jason, please—don't."

"Take care of Goat and find everyone else."

I pull her close, then hug Goat.

I face the front door. One last look over my shoulder before leaving.

I walk into the muddy yard with light rain falling and my heart pounding like a war drum. Omaha stands in front of me, holding an automatic weapon steady, the barrel aimed square at my chest. His team fans out around the farmhouse, weapons drawn, covering every exit. No one's getting out of here unless Omaha wants them to.

"On your knees," he barks.

I hesitate just long enough for him to raise the muzzle a few inches.

Now it's pointed at my face.

I kneel slowly.

"Hands behind your head," he says. "Stay very still."

I lace my fingers and glance up at him. "You know Avner's going to come for you."

He smiles. It's not the kind you give a friend—it's the kind you give a man before an execution.

"I think Avner's a little busy right now."

"What do you mean?" My voice cracks. "Where is he?"

Omaha tilts his head. "Probably planning a funeral for his sweet little Apple. She didn't make it."

My blood turns cold. My vision narrows. "You motherfucker—"

These people keep taking everything from me. The blame for Apple's death is ultimately mine, and I can only pray they will leave Syd and Goat alive. If they haven't killed Aver, they better.

Then there is Lia. She warned us, but did she save herself?

I start to rise, rage overcoming rational thought, then everything goes black as the butt of his rifle cracks against my skull.

****

I come to with pain roaring in my skull and darkness pressing on my eyes—a blindfold. My hands are zip-tied behind my back, wrists burning with every movement. I'm being dragged—no, half-carried out of an SUV. My shoes scuff against grass, then slap onto hard concrete.

"Where am I?" My voice is hoarse, barely audible.

No answer.

The air is crisp. Clean. No smoke or car exhaust. We're far from the city.

We move up a few steps. Cold, dry air hits my face as I'm pulled inside. Air-conditioned. Quiet. Too quiet.

Then something odd. Flowers. Candles. The place smells… nice.

The men drag me into an elevator. We descend one floor. When the doors open, my feet sink into thick carpet. I'm steered into a room and forced into a soft, rounded chair. The pressure eases on my wrists. The tip ties come off. My hands are numb.

Then the blindfold disappears.

And I'm staring into the face of a ghost.

"Holy shit," I whisper. "Governor Mack Matthews?"

CHAPTER 80

He's seated across from me in an identical chair, calm, almost regal. It's a perfect re-creation of Peacock Alley, down to the lighting and the subtle hotel scent.

"The rumors of my death," he says with a sad smile, "have been greatly exaggerated."

A slow, deliberate clapping echoes down the hallway. I turn as Frederick strolls in, wearing a pale blue linen suit like he's on vacation. An enormous tan labradoodle walks beside him, perfectly in step. They have matching blonde hair.

"Surprise!" he says, grinning and motioning toward his father.

"What the hell is going on?"

Frederick sighs, disappointed. "God, you really are a letdown. We had such high hopes. But Ernesto came cheap—a hundred grand, and he flipped. As they say, once a thief, always a thief."

"And Apple?" I say, teeth clenched. "Why'd you have to kill her? She had nothing to do with this."

He shakes his head slowly. "No, Jason. *You* killed Apple. We warned you. You couldn't help yourself. Just had to be the hero."

"Avner is coming for you," I spit. "You have no idea what you've done."

He smiles—slow, sick, savoring it. "Avner's dead. They're all dead, Jason. And the best part?" He leans closer. "You get to live with it."

It can't be true. It *can't*. I bury my face in my hands, fighting the tears I can't stop. I see all of their faces. All of the collateral damage. It is all on me. Their lives were cut short due to my failures.

Frederick's smile widens. "And if anyone comes looking, I've got thirty operators waiting—including Shadow SEALs." He glances toward the reinforced door. "We're in the middle of nowhere. Plenty of places to bury the bodies."

"You're seriously fucked up," I mumble.

"Maybe. Now, excuse me. This little exercise will give me a chance to put on my fatigues and lead the boys. I was a pretty good soldier in my day. Who knows, maybe that smartass FBI agent will show up, and I'll put his head on the wall so you can see it every day."

"You weren't a soldier. You would have been a sailor if you didn't fail out of Annapolis," Mack states coldly.

He turns to the dog. "C'mon, Lux."

He looks back once more before leaving. "Dad, show our guest around, would you? If he behaves, maybe we'll let him stay. If not, he's going to Luxembourg. They'll know what to do with him."

My head snaps up. "Luxembourg? That's the headquarters?"

Frederick chuckles. "Oops. Slipped. It doesn't matter now. Yes, leadership is in Luxembourg. George is being sent there after his pathetic failure. They'll probably hang him. A warning for others."

"Well, when I track them down, I'll be sure to send your regards," I state.

Frederick whistles, and the dog jumps to attention. "Bad news, Jason. That's never going to happen."

He punches in a code and walks out. The door locks with a cold metallic snap.

Governor Matthews—Mack—leans forward. "I'm sorry about your friends. What did Frederick say your name was?"

"Jason Miles."

"Nice to meet you, Jason. How do you know my psychopathic son?"

I let out a bitter laugh. "That's… a long story."

Mack leans back with a sigh. "Well. Unfortunately for us, we've got lots of time."

CHAPTER 81

"The short version?" I say, shifting in the chair. "A co-worker and I uncovered massive tax fraud at a bank last year. Since then, my life's been a wreck. Lost my job. My wife. Almost died. Just as I started to get my feet under me, Frederick's lunatic cult came knocking. They blackmailed me. Used me. Turns out, I'm related to these nuts. At this point, I don't know what's real and what's staged."

I shake my head. "Sorry, Governor. That's a lot."

He gives a slow, weary nod. "Call me Mack. It's been a long time since I was governor."

"How the hell did *you* end up here? Everyone thinks you're dead."

"Most days, I wish I were," he says, voice hollow. "You probably know Frederick was my Lieutenant Governor. What you don't know is that we were never aligned. Not really."

"I know you were respected. Loved, even. People wanted you both in the White House."

"Yeah," he nods. "We talked about it. But then I started to see cracks. He wasn't just political, he was paranoid. Obsessed. Late-night rants about global cabals, secret rulers of the world. At first, I thought it was the bourbon. But then…"

He trails off, staring at the chandelier.

"And then?" I prompt.

"I started digging. The books weren't adding up. Money was

disappearing. I realized this wasn't fantasy or mental illness. He was involved with very powerful people with bad intentions."

Finally—someone who understands this is real. Not just bank fraud, but an international conspiracy aimed at control on a global scale. We can fight *The One* together if we can get out of here.

Emotions swirl inside me—guilt, bloodlust, sorrow—but above all, there is hope.

"I told him he would need to step down. That was it—the final break. A few days later, I took my Porsche out for a drive. The brakes failed. The car crashed. Next thing I know, I'm here. No remains. No search. They covered up the whole thing."

I scan the room—Peacock Alley in perfect detail. It's unsettling.

"Did you document what you found?" I ask.

He nods. "I have it all in a safe place if I ever escape."

"Have you tried?"

"For the first year, that's all I thought about. But this place—" he gestures around us "—is locked down tighter than Guantanamo Bay. Every door, every hall, every vent. I've looked."

"And Frederick? What's his plan for you?"

"He says once the revolution comes, we're all moving to Luxembourg. Then I'm free to help him rule the world." Mack's voice drips with sarcasm.

"I've got good news and bad news," I say.

"Hit me."

"We're going to figure out how to escape. Bad news: we might have to kill your son."

Mack smiles sadly, eyes full of something like relief. "It's been a long time since he was my son."

CHAPTER 82

Two days later, hours before dawn, the assault begins.

Rifle shots crack through the air like snapping bones. I'm out of my room before I'm fully awake. Mack barrels out of his just as fast, and we collide in Peacock Alley.

We've spent long days plotting our escape, cycling through dozens of reckless ideas—ways to trick Frederick, turn the tables, and break free. Most are just fantasies and a way to kill endless hours.

A grenade explodes somewhere nearby, and the whole house lurches like it's been punched in the gut. Plaster dust rains from the ceiling.

Then I hear the relentless *rrtt-rrt-rrt* of the Mini Uzi. The short bursts have an unmistakable metallic growl, one I've heard a hundred times at the shooting range.

"What the hell is going on?" Mack shouts over the chaos.

"That's my friend," I say, catching my breath. "Avner, the one I told you about. He's not dead."

Maybe if he is alive, others are also.

"One guy is making that much noise?"

"One guy on a mission."

"But it's thirty to one. He has no chance."

"You haven't met Avner."

As if on cue, the lights die—everything drops into a suffocating black. We freeze, straining to hear anything except the gunfire and distant screams. A few heartbeats later, the emergency generator kicks in—sickly green light flickers to life, casting twisted shadows across the hall.

We drop low, take cover behind a marble column, and wait.

The firefight rages—gunshots, more explosions, then the unmistakable sound of men dying. Screams echo through the walls, short and final.

Then... silence. Heavy. Suffocating.

Mack and I lock eyes, barely breathing. Neither of us speaks.

Then—BANG.

The door flies open, slamming against the wall.

Frederick bursts in like the devil is chasing him. His battle fatigues are soaked in sweat, and his hair sticks up like he's been electrocuted. There's something feral in his eyes. He locks the door behind him and pulls out his phone without a word.

"What the hell's going on out there?" I scream.

He doesn't answer. His fingers fly across the screen. Then he raises the phone like a weapon, aiming it at the door.

The door explodes inward in a flash of fire and wood. Smoke pours into the room, thick and choking. Shards of splintered door rain down. And through the haze, two figures appear—moving slowly, deliberately, like demons emerging from the underworld.

They're drenched in blood, dirt, and war paint.

Avner steps into view first. All black. Face unreadable. Glock raised. He's not the man I know—he's a beast. A phantom. A reaper with a gun.

And beside him—

My breath catches in my throat.

She's changed—short hair, camo paint streaked across her cheeks—but I know her. Her eyes cut through the smoke like lasers. I've seen those eyes in dreams, in memories, in every quiet moment.

Lia.

Frederick's voice cracks as he tries to reassert control. "I'm recording this! It goes straight to the cloud and to my people. If you shoot me, you'll go to prison. I'm still the governor of Florida!"

Avner says nothing. He walks forward and presses the barrel of his Glock to Frederick's forehead. His hand doesn't waver. Frederick shakes so hard his teeth clack.

"On your knees," Avner growls. His voice is unrecognizable—raw, savage.

Frederick drops down, the phone still pointed at Avner, the recording light blinking red through the haze.

I step beside my friend. "Don't do it, Avner. He's not worth it."

Avner doesn't blink. Doesn't breathe. He stares, radiating fury.

Frederick senses the opening. "That's right. Put the gun down. You can still surrender."

"He's nothing in the bigger picture. Just a pawn," I tell Avner, keeping my voice steady. "We'll put him away and learn everything he knows. Others are responsible. We'll make them pay. You and me. We have help. Governor Mack has evidence. We'll get justice for Apple. For them all."

Avner's grip loosens. I ease the gun from his hand.

Then I turn and swing. The butt of the gun connects with Frederick's jaw in a sickening crack. He collapses instantly, like a puppet with its strings cut.

His phone skitters across the floor.

Lia steps forward and brings her heel down. The screen explodes under her boot.

She steps forward through the swirling smoke and emerald glow, and I forget how to breathe.

"Is this a dream?" I ask.

Lia takes my face in her hands and kisses me. She whispers in my ear, and my life changes forever.

She turns and walks away, vanishing into the smoke without another glance.

"Who the hell was that?" Mack asks.

I swallow. My voice cracks as I speak.

"That was the love of my life. My wife, Lia."

I pause. The weight of her words still rings in my head.

"And apparently... the mother of my child."

CHAPTER 83

"Berta, open the door." I bang hard, raising my voice. The hallway outside her apartment is dim and smells like cheap disinfectants. I knock again, louder this time.

The door cracks open a few inches—one brown eye peers through the gap, sharp and wary.

"I told you to leave me alone, Jason," she says, trying to shut the door—but my foot is already wedged in the frame.

I haven't slept in days. Zeke's team swooped in and moved Governor Mack into a secure safehouse. Frederick wasn't as lucky. With his jaw wired shut, he was shipped off to ADX Florence—the supermax in Colorado, the most secure prison on the planet. He'll rot in isolation until the interrogations begin.

Avner and Lia vanished into the darkness. No calls. No messages. Just silence. I've tried reaching Lia on the burner several times, but I know she needs to find safety first. Still, I can't stop replaying her words—every one of them echoing, every one of them weighing on what it could mean for us.

At least Goat is still breathing. I stopped by the hospital to see him as he recovers. He lost a terrifying amount of blood, but Syd saved his life. He calls her his angel. I promised I'd bring him home as soon as the doctors clear him.

"Let me in. We need to talk."

"Is he with you? Avner?" Her voice trembles.

"No. But he's coming."

That lands. Her face tightens. She opens the door wider and glances over her shoulder, scanning the hallway for danger before waving me in.

The apartment reeks of fried food. Dishes pile in the sink, laundry spills across the floor, and a half-eaten sandwich sits forgotten on the counter. It's chaos. She's unraveling.

"I don't know where he is," she blurts, already crying.

I clear a spot on the edge of the couch and sit, brushing aside a dirty sweatshirt. "Berta, listen to me. We need to find Ernesto. We must get him to Zeke before Avner finds him."

She breaks down, sobbing harder. "You can't let him hurt my boy. He's all I've got left."

I stand and grip her shoulders, steady but not unkind. "I swear—I'll try to keep him safe. But if you don't help me, you know how this ends."

Her eyes plead. "He didn't do anything wrong."

"He can prove that to Zeke, but right now, all that matters is that we get to him before Avner does. You know I can't control him. Now, where is he, Berta?"

You've got about a couple of hours at the most. The lion is hunting and bloodthirsty.

She nods, trembling, and dabs her eyes with a crumpled tissue. "If I take you to him, you promise he'll be safe?"

"I'm calling Zeke right now. We'll get him into protective custody. That's the only chance he's got to survive the night."

****

The apartment complex near the University of South Florida is precisely what I expect—peeling paint, a sagging basketball hoop, garbage spilling from the compactor. A half-deflated ball bounces off a rusted rim as Zeke's black Suburban crawls past.

"He's in unit 203," Berta says, pointing to the second floor.

Zeke and I check our weapons—magazines loaded, safeties off.

"What are you doing?" Berta's voice jumps an octave. "You said he'd be safe!"

"Avner's not the only threat," I say. "Your son's tangled up with some very bad people. Please stay in the car."

She opens the door anyway, muttering, "Oh, ni a putas…"

Zeke frowns. "What the fuck does that mean?"

I sigh. "Let's just say… she's not happy and coming with us."

At the stairs, a group of teens blocks the way—one of them, tall, white tank top, puffing a vape—steps forward. All youth and machismo.

"Where you think you're going?"

Zeke flashes his badge, then parts his coat to show the holstered Glock. "FBI, assholes. Move unless you want a new set of problems."

He snatches the vape and crushes it under his heel. "And stop poisoning yourself, kid."

We push past them and head up the stairs. The door to 203 is chipped, and the doorknob barely hangs on. It's already ajar.

"Stay back, Berta," I say, pulling my weapon.

Zeke does the same. We nudge the door open.

The stench hits first—decay and rot. My gut clenches.

Zeke pulls a flashlight and sweeps the beam across the living room. A white leather couch slouches against the far wall. And there—slumped, head tilted at an unnatural angle—is Ernesto.

A bullet hole dead center in his forehead. Dried blood streaks the cushion beneath him.

Behind us, a scream. Berta pushes past and crumbles to her knees, wailing. Her cries cut through me like a jagged knife.

Zeke's light climbs the wall behind the couch.

Spray-painted in red across the plaster:
NO LOOSE ENDS.

CHAPTER 84

"Follow me, boys," Zeke says as he crosses the prison parking lot, boots crunching on gravel. Behind him, a swarm of law enforcement follows—FBI agents in flak vests, state police, and county sheriffs from three different jurisdictions. At least fifty strong. The cavalry.

After Governor Frederick's spectacular fall, the floodgates opened. Every dirty secret tied to him began leaking out, and one of the filthiest was Warden Walter Billy Ray. Zeke didn't wait to be assigned—he stepped up and volunteered to lead the investigation for the Bureau.

The findings were worse than anyone imagined: years of abuse, ignored complaints from inmates and townspeople alike, bribes, a thriving gambling ring, drugs, and prostitution. A privately run hellhole with a god complex at the top.

The prison looms ahead—silent, still. No one's waiting in the lobby. The front entrance is sealed tight—zero movement.

"They knew we were coming," one of the officers says.

Zeke scowls. "Break the fucking door down."

A nearby sheriff nods, turns to a heavyset man built like a linebacker. The guy steps forward, hefts an ax, and swings hard—wood splinters. Hinges crack—three more hits, and the reinforced door caves in with a thunderous crash.

"Let's move," Zeke barks.

They pour inside—fifty strong, boots echoing across tile, weapons ready. The fluorescent lights flicker above as they approach the first set of electronic security gates.

Still no sign of staff. No guards at the desk. Just that humming silence.

A storm is about to hit, and everyone inside knows it.

And this time, Zeke brings the storm.

****

"Well now, boys," Walter Billy Ray drawls, his voice steady but cold. "Reckon it's time we make our stand. Been a good run, it has."

The room falls silent. His men shift uncomfortably, glancing at one another with pale faces and twitching hands. Panic clings to the air like smoke.

All except Lil' John, who grins as he spins *Sally*.

"What are we gonna do, boss?" one of them finally asks, voice cracking. "They've got, like, an army out there."

Billy Ray lights a cigarette with calm fingers. Inhales. Exhales. Then smirks. "And we've got two thousand inmates. That math work for you?"

Nervous glances shoot around the room.

"You're saying we... unleash them?" another man stammers.

"What I'm sayin' is," Billy Ray says slowly, "if they come through that gate, we open them cages. Turn every last critter loose. In the ruckus, we slip off."

One of the guards swallows hard. "But won't the inmates tear us apart? We've—well, we've done things..."

Billy Ray chuckles, low and joyless. "If you beat a dog long enough, it forgets how to bite. These men won't touch us."

Lil' John stops spinning Sally and slings her over his shoulder, grinning wider. "Let the wolves out. Let's watch them sheep run."

Billy Ray nods. "If they want a war—hell, we'll give them a riot."

****

A junior agent hustles over to Zeke, tablet in hand and sweat beading on his forehead.

"We're working with the tech guys to get control of the doors," he says. "Problem is, there are multiple fail-safes, and the warden's crew has insulated themselves. We need to open the access points to their control room—but keep the cell blocks sealed tight."

Zeke doesn't blink. "Keep pushing. They've got nowhere to run. They either surrender to us… or they get ripped alive."

The team pushes deeper into the prison. One checkpoint. Then another. Each secured control room they take feels like another rung up a ladder with no way down. Finally, they reach the last barrier—beyond it, a reinforced room with a bulletproof window.

Inside, Zeke sees them.

Warden Walter Billy Ray and his men.

They're boxed in, but they've still got options. The room branches in two directions—one door leads to Zeke's squad, the other to the general population. They stand between a rock and a riot.

Lil' John, the hulking brute with the psychotic grin, is slapping a nightstick against his open palm. Slow. Deliberate. Like he's trying to keep time with his heartbeat.

They're armed and cornered.

"What the hell are we going to do, Zeke?" a junior agent asks. "We open that door, it's a bloodbath in a broom closet. You think they'll surrender?"

Zeke doesn't answer. He stares through the glass, eyes unblinking. Cold. Reptilian.

His pupils narrow, calculating.

Then he turns and moves to the tech specialist—some kid hunched over a control panel next to the prison's systems engineer. Zeke leans in close and whispers something.

The kid looks up, startled. Zeke nods once.

If they want a fight, they are going to get one.

****

"Alright, boys—this here's our fight for freedom!" Walter Billy Ray bellows, voice thick with southern grit. "Grab your damn weapons and git ready to raise some hell!"

His men spring into action, fumbling with pistols, batons, and shotguns. They move with nervous energy—fast hands, shaking eyes.

Beyond the reinforced glass, the inmates begin to stir. The noise inside the cellblock shifts—buzzing at first, then swelling into a roar. One by one, the convicts turn their attention to the control room, faces twisted with rage, curiosity, and frenzy.

The seventy-five worst of them, the lifers, the gang leaders, the killers—press forward and crowd the glass. Their fists slam against it, synchronized like war drums. Each thud echoes like a countdown.

Walter watches them, eyes gleaming.

"Ain't that a sight," he mutters, a grin tugging at the edge of his mouth. "You see 'em, boys? They smell it. Change's comin'. Just don't forget—we hold the leash."

Lil' John snarls, spinning *Sally*—his grotesque bat—in his thick hands. He turns toward the glass door; the mob is just inches beyond it.

Then he swings.

CRACK!

Sally smashes against the bulletproof glass. The inmates cheer from the other side, fists pounding harder now, louder—manic.

"Don't get scared now," Walter says, his voice low and deadly calm. "They ain't comin' through 'less we let 'em. And we *will*, if that's what it takes."

Then he raises his shotgun and pumps a shell into the chamber.

"Now let's give the feds a real North Florida welcome."

****

On the other side of the glass, chaos churns. The prison staff unholsters their weapons, their hands trembling, their eyes wide. Behind them, inmates press against the reinforced glass, pounding fists and screaming curses. It's not a riot yet—but it's seconds away.

The FBI and the local SWAT team raise their rifles in unison, laser sights trained on the steel door that separates them from hell.

Zeke steps forward, calm as ever. He leans into the wall-mounted intercom and presses the button.

"Warden," he says, voice flat and sharp, "this is your one chance. Lay down your weapons and come with us peacefully. You have ten seconds."

There's a long pause. Then static. Then Warden Walter Billy Ray's voice booms through the speaker, dripping with venom and ego.

"Fuck you, FBI. This is *my* prison. This is *my* county. You mess with me; I unleash every last one of these animals. You wanna make history? Fine. But this is your only chance to walk away."

Zeke doesn't blink. "Open the doors," he says to the tech, calm like he's ordering a bagel.

A click. A hiss. The locks disengage with a mechanical groan.

Everyone braces for the explosion.

****

"**H**ere we go!" Warden Walter Billy Ray shouts the moment the lock gives its telltale *click*.

He braces for the front door to swing open—for a firefight with the FBI. But nothing happens. Not in front of him.

Instead, behind him, the door to the general population slams open with a violent clang.

Confusion flashes across his face—just a flicker—before chaos erupts.

Dozens of inmates pour through the doorway like a tidal wave—tattoos, rage, and raw muscle. They charge without hesitation, without fear—a wall of fury.

"Shit!" Lil' John roars, swinging his nightstick in wild arcs—but it's no use. The tide is too strong. One blow lands, then another, and then the mob swallows him up.

The warden is next to fall, ripped away from the control room and into the open yard like a rag doll. The rest of the staff try to retreat, but it's too late.

Punches fly—boots stomp. Screams echo off the concrete. It's not just violence—it's years of pain erupting all at once.

The inmates swarm like hornets. No order. No mercy.

The balance of power has shifted, and the prison belongs to the damned now.

****

Zeke hears the screams before he sees them, the sound of pure rage, fists pounding flesh, bones cracking under boots.

Through the reinforced glass, they watch as the prison staff gets swallowed by the mob. They're being torn to pieces—rage met with retribution—a savage, merciless storm.

"Zeke!" the junior agent shouts over the noise. "We opened the wrong door!"

He doesn't flinch. Just stands there, arms crossed, eyes cool. Then he turns to him and winks. "Yeah," he says. "Looks like we made a mistake."

"They're going to kill them."

Zeke shrugs, his voice calm. "Well, karma's a bitch."

CHAPTER 85

Morgan and I step into the bar at Charley's Steakhouse just after five. Happy hour is in full swing—corporate travelers tossing back cocktails on company dimes, mingling with locals who claim the same seats like clockwork. The air is thick with the scent of seared beef drifting from the open grill. Dim lighting casts everything in amber shadows. Laughter spills across the room, riding the low murmur of conversation.

We spot George slumped at the bar, nursing a glass of scotch. His usually perfect hair is disheveled, his posture slack. He looks... older. Worn.

"Mind if we join you?" I ask.

Without turning, he mutters, "Do I have a choice? To what do I owe this particular displeasure?"

"Time to play *Let's Make a Deal*," I say, motioning for two beers and telling the bartender, "Put it on George's tab."

"Come on," I nod toward a nearby table. "Somewhere a little more private."

He drains his glass and waves for another. When we sit, he finally looks up—eyes bloodshot, jaw clenched. "What makes you think you have any leverage? You're already dead. Every one of you."

"You're confused, George. We hold all the cards." I gesture to Morgan. "This is Morgan Chase."

He sneers. "Yeah, I know who she is. She wrote that fantasy piece on the Safe Harbor tax scheme. Total fiction," he adds.

Morgan smiles. Takes a drink of her beer.

"Here's the situation, George. I have been keeping detailed notes about *The One,* which Morgan has verified: people, places, you. We also have the draft copy of Apple Lee's investigative novel. We have what you would call a blockbuster. Finally, Governor Mack has proof of Frederick's involvement."

"Prove it," he says, slurring slightly. "Sounds like a bunch of fiction to me. By the way, I barely know the ex-governor. Why don't you let me see what you've got?"

"No chance. It's our insurance policy. Something happens to me, Morgan, Avner, Lia, Zeke, or Goat—it goes public. Five copies in five different places. Each person knows exactly what to do."

His smirk falters. Just a flicker—but I catch it.

"You think this changes anything?" he asks. "Maybe it buys you time, but we'll win. And when we do, you'll beg me to feed you to a gator."

I lean in. "I'm not done yet. You want the manuscript and other proof to stay buried; we stay alive. And I want Connor Doyle—Omaha. We know he killed Apple. He doesn't get to walk away."

"I don't owe you shit."

"George, when did you start cursing? A foul mouth is not an attractive trait."

"Fuck off," he responds.

I smile coldly. "Warden Walter Billy Ray died in a riot yesterday. Guess what the FBI found? Detailed records. Turns out he kept notes, too—lots of them. And your name came up more than once. You've been laundering his dirty money for a long time. Not to mention we have your buddy, Frederick, in custody. Enough time to himself and he'll crack."

"I told you I barely know Frederick. Always thought there was something wrong with the guy."

Morgan leans in, voice low. "It'll make one hell of a story, George. You'll be rotting in the same prison the warden ran. Might want to ask Sterling Kennedy how that feels. Except he's dead. I'd assume the same fate is waiting for you."

"I don't have time for this. I haven't been charged with anything. I have a flight to catch."

"Give my best to your master in Luxembourg," I say, watching for a reaction.

"Big deal. You know where leadership is. You get within fifty miles, and you'll cease to exist."

"We'll see," I respond. "For now, do we have a deal?"

George drains his scotch and stands slowly. "Fine, you all are safe for the moment. And you can have Connor. He knows too much anyway. Saves us having to tie off that loose end."

"Where is he?" I ask.

"You might want to start with his call sign, genius."

CHAPTER 86

It's a cold, gray Nebraska afternoon, the kind that you feel in your bones and is hard to shake. The boarding house across the street used to be a frat house—red brick, sharp edges, three stories—now surrounded by a collapsing railroad tie wall. The area's homes are rented by a mix of Creighton students and people down on their luck.

We've been holed up in this room for hours. The place is an old white house with a sagging roof and a heat system that died sometime in the last decade. Feels like the landlord gutted it into apartments and then forgot about it. Cars drift past outside, tires whispering over damp asphalt. No one's gone into our target house.

Goat sits hunched by the window in a frayed army jacket; video camera balanced on a tripod. He's pale and thin, still mending from the bullet that nearly killed him. Being a former addict, he refuses pain meds. Says the Lord will handle it. He's been on this guy for days, following the tip from George.

Avner paces the room like a caged animal. I sip bitter coffee, trying to steal some warmth.

"Are you sure it's him?" Avner asks, tugging a stocking cap over his head.

I rub the raw skin where my pinky nail used to be and step up beside Goat, eyes scanning the house. My nerves feel frayed.

"You don't have to be here, Jason," Avner says. "Goat and I can handle this."

I shake my head. "No. I loved Apple too. You would do anything for me—I'm in."

Avner drops his weapon bag onto the floor. Out spills three Glocks, an array of knives, a stun gun, and a box of gloves. We drove from Florida with enough gear to start a small war.

"You're sure it's him, Goat?" Avner asks again.

"I sent you both the videos. He's good. Keeps his head down. Changed his appearance a few times. Even tried to alter his gait. But he can't change those mean gray eyes, and a killer has a certain swagger. Always aware of his surroundings. I'll be damned to hell if this isn't Connor Reagan. Omaha."

"I've got bad news," Avner says without looking up. "You're already going to hell with the rest of us."

Goat makes the sign of the cross in the air. "Don't say that. I've repented. You can too. It is never too late."

Avner zips the bag shut. "Better sign up for confession. It's time to kill this motherfucker."

Goat mutters under his breath, "An eye for an eye."

Unit 301 isn't much of a challenge. Omaha set up trip indicators—thin threads, tape, subtle cues—but we spot them quickly. Goat stays outside to reset them while Avner and I slip in.

The apartment smells like cold air, old liquor, and unwashed clothes. It is not much bigger than the bed with a rusting iron frame, a stained mattress, and a ripped plaid comforter. The wallpaper had long since faded, and the pattern had become a blur of muted colors. A single window looks out onto the street, but it's so warped I can feel the cold coming through. A portable heater is set up near the bed, blowing warmish air.

On a wobbling table sits the last bite of a sandwich, three cockroaches picking it apart. Two empty vodka bottles lie beside the bed.

"Fitting resting place for this asshole," Avner mutters. "You sure you don't want to swap with Goat?" he asks me.

"I can handle it. Just give me the stun gun. I owe him and will light him up."

An hour later, the door creaks open. Omaha steps inside, silent, eyes sweeping the room. He shrugs off his coat, drops it on the floor, and sets a grocery bag beside the stale sandwich.

"Hello, Connor," Avner says, stepping from the bathroom, Glock leveled at his forehead.

Omaha doesn't flinch. "If you were going to shoot me, I'd be dead already. What's next?"

Before he can turn, I slip from the closet and jam the stun gun into his neck. The current kicks—five milliamps, seven seconds. He crumples to the ground.

Twenty minutes later, he's sitting upright in a chair, gagged and wrists bound. Avner stands close, blade pressing into the side of his throat. His eyes are lifeless, and his hand is calm. Goat is murmuring something low and prayerful.

"Avner," I say quietly, "this won't bring her back."

His head tilts toward me. A hard smile curls at the edges of his mouth. The knife presses deeper, and Omaha's muffled voice breaks into frantic sounds.

"Might not bring her back, Jason," Avner says. "But what is it these psychos don't want?"

"Loose ends," I say.

CHAPTER 87

Zeke's black SUV slices through traffic, flanked by a convoy of unmarked FBI vehicles and a SWAT truck. I ride shotgun, the seatbelt digging into my shoulder, adrenaline humming under my skin. Zeke drives like he's auditioning for Formula 1—expression unreadable behind his mirrored sunglasses.

"We're really hitting some glass office building in the suburbs?" he says. "Because you swear a fraud ring's operating inside?"

"Yes. Trust me." My voice is stern. I'm picturing Chance—long beard, smug face—getting cuffed and shoved into a squad car. Maybe Claude's stupid smirk and moustache will be wiped off too.

We pull into the lot. Immediately, something's wrong.

The grass is overgrown. There's no security. No Teslas. No blacked-out BMWs. Just empty asphalt baking in the sun.

Zeke kills the engine and steps out, frowning. "This is the place?"

"I swear," I say, climbing out. "Last time I was here, the parking lot was packed. Guards at every entrance. Inside was buzzing like a boiler room."

He motions the team forward. SWAT fans out fast and silent. One agent pushes the front door—it creaks open without resistance.

Inside, the space is gutted.

No desks. No phones. No monitors. No scammers yelling into headsets. Just a lone cleaning lady vacuuming under flickering lights where cubicles used to be.

"What the hell…" I mutter, spinning slowly. My voice echoes in the emptiness.

"This can't be right. There were sales floors, team leads, managers—hell, they even claimed to have a 401(k)."

An agent in a dark suit approaches briskly. "Agent Michaels," he says to Zeke. "We swept the building. It's empty. Not a trace."

Zeke turns to me, jaw tight. "Jason. A word."

He leads me into a glass-walled office, the same one where we'd once listened to live scam calls. Now it's just dust and turned-over furniture.

"I know what you're thinking," I start. "But I'm not making this up. They cleared this place out fast. Did you question George and Claude?"

Zeke studies me.

"We did. They denied everything. Claimed you and Frederick were running the whole thing."

"Are you kidding me? They're flipping it on *me*? What about the dinner at Bern's? Why would we all be there if they weren't in on it?"

"They said the governor invited them," Zeke replies flatly. "Claimed they were just being polite. That you were raving about conspiracies, global elites, some 'deep state' takeover."

"That's a lie. George was my handler. Claude built the whole strategy. They were right here. Right here in this goddamn building."

Zeke scans the empty room again, slow and deliberate.

"In *this* building?" he asks. "Because all I see is a guy yelling at ghosts."

"I'm not crazy, Zeke," I snap. "You don't believe them over me. You can't."

He hesitates—just long enough to hurt.

"We can start in Luxembourg. That's the headquarters. Frederick told me."

Then he turns and walks away.

I hear his voice drift down the hallway.

"Maybe what you need, Jason... is a vacation. And some sleep. But stay away from Greece."

And just like that, I'm alone. Surrounded by silence. Standing in the ruins of something I know was real.

CHAPTER 88

The box shows up with the rest of the Amazon deliveries—plain, unmarked, with only my name on the label—no return address. My heart kicks harder as I peel back the tape.

Inside is a burner phone. Pre-activated. One number saved.

I already know who it is.

My fingers shake as I hit *call*: butterflies—fear, hope, something in between—flutter in my chest.

A familiar voice answers.

"Is this Mrs. Smith?" I manage, barely.

That soft laugh—God, I've missed it. "Hello, Mr. Smith. How are you doing?"

My legs go weak. I drop into the nearest chair, trying to steady myself. "Lia... are you okay? Where have you been? I've been worried sick."

"I'm fine, Jay. When Avner said he needed me, I went. We did what we had to do, and... after that, I had to leave the country. Getting out wasn't easy."

"Are *you* okay? And—everyone else?"

"We're fine." Her voice softens, almost apologetic. "I'm sorry I dropped all that on you. I didn't know if... I didn't know when we'd see each other again. And I wasn't sure you'd want to know."

Emotion blindsides me. I swallow hard, fighting back tears. "Of course I want to know. It's complicated, sure, but it's also… incredible. Just tell me what you need. Where are you?"

She hesitates. "I'm in hiding. With some old friends—you might remember the gun-toting monks in Santorini." A weak laugh. "They've sworn to keep me safe until the baby comes."

"Let me come," I say immediately. "I'll stay there too. Then we can figure out the rest together."

Another pause. A long one.

"Jason… we've made powerful people very angry. As much as I want you here, you can't come. It would put all of us in danger. And now there's someone more important than either of us."

The words hit me like a punch. My throat tightens. *Is this it? Is this really the end?*

"But it's our baby," I whisper. "I can't pretend they don't exist. I can't pretend *you* don't exist. I won't."

"Jay… now you understand what *Preferred* means."

"I do. But what does that have to do with—"

Then it clicks. Hard. I'm not the only one who's Preferred. The baby is too.

"If they find out," she says quietly, "they'll never stop hunting. We can't let them know. Ever."

"I understand," I say, though my voice cracks. "But there has to be something. Some way."

"Look on the bright side," she says, "you get a chance at something normal. Something good. You deserve that. You're a good man, Jay. I love you. And I'm so, so sorry for everything I've done."

Her voice trembles—and that breaks me more than her words.

"So… is this it, Lia?" I ask. "Is this how we end?"

A soft breath. Almost a sob.

"I don't like goodbyes, Jay. Let's just say… until we meet again."

CHAPTER 89

I walk to the podium beside Morgan Chase and Governor Mack Matthews. The room is packed—reporters jockey for position, politicians murmur behind tight smiles, and what's left of the Bluebird Team takes up the first row. Avner sits there in his T-shirt, ripped jeans, and sunglasses, nodding once as I glance his way. His approval steadies my nerves. Goat is making eyes at Morgan and chatting up an attractive writer next to him.

I adjust the microphone. "Ladies and gentlemen, thank you for being here. My name is Jason Miles, CEO of Bluebird Security Consultants. I'm joined today by the reinstated governor of Florida, Mack Matthews, and Morgan Chase, Pulitzer Prize-winning journalist and someone who's risked a lot to bring truth into the light. Tomorrow, her global exposé on cybercrime will be released."

Flashes pop like fireworks. The buzz in the room swells. This is their first look at Mack since the news broke.

I pause to take a sip of water, feeling the weight of the moment. "Over the past few months, we confronted a coordinated cyberattack targeting Tampa Scientific Corporation—one of this country's most sensitive tech firms. With the decisive leadership of CEO Nikesh Singh and the efforts of Bluebird, we stopped what could've been a global catastrophe. A criminal syndicate nearly took control of proprietary technology with military and civilian implications."

A reporter calls out, "Mr. Miles—was it the Chinese? Russian hackers? North Korea?"

I glance at my notes, though I barely need them. The facts are seared into my memory. "In 2024 alone, reported losses from cyber fraud and scams ranged from twelve to sixteen billion dollars—a huge spike from the year before. And those are just the numbers people *admit* to. Real losses are estimated to be north of a hundred billion. That's billion—with a B."

I let the silence stretch. Let them bask in it.

"The bad guys aren't in basements anymore—they're in office buildings. The criminal underworld is evolving. They're efficient, well-funded, and frighteningly good at what they do. They steal identities, impersonate your banks, fake delivery notices, trigger bogus fraud alerts, and hijack your trust—all in real time, thousands of times a day. They're getting smarter, and our defenses aren't keeping up."

I step aside, and Morgan moves in, calm but commanding.

"The FBI and FTC are doing what they can, but this problem belongs to *all* of us," she says. "Banks, telecoms, social platforms—they must take more responsibility. But what we truly need is a unified response. A central reporting agency. A single point of accountability."

She glances at me before continuing. "Today, we announce the formation of the Apple Lee Watchdog Organization. In the coming weeks, we, along with Governor Matthews, will take our proposal to Washington. For those unfamiliar with Apple Lee, she was a professor at the University of Tampa, a gifted writer, and a fierce advocate for the vulnerable. She was murdered by the same network we're exposing."

That last sentence lands like a hammer. The room is frozen.

I look out across the crowd and catch a glimpse of movement—Avner, slipping out the side door without a word. Just a shadow, disappearing into whatever storm comes next.

****

After the press conference, I drive straight to the bungalow. My body's running on fumes, my head full of static. I need to clean up—my office, my life, and maybe whatever's left of me.

The yellow police tape flutters in the wind. I duck under it and push open the unlocked door.

The place looks like it's been chewed up and spat out. Bullet holes pockmark the plaster and shred the furniture. Lamps lie on their sides, surrounded by paper and scattered pens. Every step crunches glass under my shoes. I start hunting for a broom, though I'm not sure what good it will do.

"Hey, stranger."

I turn. Syd is in the doorway, big blue eyes sweeping the wreckage. "I can't believe we survived this."

"Hi, Syd." My voice sounds flat. "I know I owe you a call. Things have been… complicated."

"You don't have to apologize, Jason." She steps in, careful with the debris. "I know you've got a lot going on. But I need to talk to you about something."

I exhale. "Listen, Syd. I like you—a lot. I want you in my life. But only as a friend. I don't have anything else to give. You deserve better than… this." I gesture at myself, the room, the chaos.

She gives me a small, sad smile, then pulls me into a hug that lingers a beat too long.

When she steps back, her eyes are steady. "I figured we were done. But that's not why I'm here."

My brow lifts. "Really? Then why?"

"I want to work at Bluebird."

It hits me like another gunshot. "You *what*? Syd, this place nearly got you killed. I almost got you killed. Why would you want anything to do with this mess?"

"I can't go back to the University after what happened to Apple. I see her everywhere. But here—" She swallows hard. "Here, I could carry on her work. Her mission. Her legacy."

I think about the empty desks: Goat healing, Avner gone, Apple and Ernesto dead. Syd's smart. Professional. She already knows my life is a disaster. And maybe she's right—we could use someone who still believes in something.

"Bluebird would be lucky to have you, Syd."

Her face lights up, warm as a sunrise. "Good. Because I also brought you something."

My stomach tightens. "What is it?"

"I think you need someone to love. And someone who loves you back."

I shake my head. "Syd, I told you—"

"Not me, silly." She disappears out the front door, then comes back cradling a small, light-gray puppy with bat-like ears and a white streak down its belly—pink tongue, black nose, eyes that could melt an iceberg.

"This is Popeye," she says softly. "I found him at a shelter. They said he's been through some things… and needs someone special to put him back together. I figured you two could help heal each other."

She places him in my arms. He licks my face, tasting the salt of my tears before I even know they've fallen.

CHAPTER 90

For the past three weeks, Syd and I have been inseparable. We're strictly platonic, but we've fallen into an easy rhythm—long walks, shared meals, and my new dog, Pop, glued to my side. Sometimes, I catch myself stealing a glance at her, wondering if there's something more. Then Lia's face invades my mind, and the thought dissolves.

Someone said normal life is what happens when you're not looking for it. I've stopped trying to chase it. This past year has been chaos, and maybe I was never meant for anything ordinary. The battle may be quiet for now, but I know it isn't over.

I'm standing with Pop in the kitchen of a dated Spanish Colonial with chipping stucco when my phone buzzes. Nikesh.

The realtor is still yammering about original tiles, a big yard for the dog, and "potential." I excuse myself and step outside. It's time to move out of the hotel and grow up, maybe even become a parent.

Avner vanished after the press conference. I stopped by his warehouse last week. Nothing changed except for one thing: Scott's old Harley is gone. I tell myself he's out there somewhere, chasing the horizon with Scott's ghost riding shotgun.

But now Nikesh's voice is tight. Urgent.

"Drop everything and come. Now."

No questions. He's Bluebird's biggest client. I go.

Security waves Pop and me through without a word. Inside, the receptionist stands before I say a word and practically throws the door open to Nikesh's office. He's behind his desk, eyes locked on a massive screen, exhaling a long drag from a vape pen. The cloud drifts like a phantom between us.

"What's going on?" I ask. "And since when do you smoke?"

"This is bad, Jason." He doesn't turn.

"We've been through a lot together, Nikesh. It can't be worse than a ransom with a hostage and *The One's* attempts to steal Winnie."

Still not looking at me, he says, "It might be, Jason."

Pressure clamps down behind my eyes. Instead of rubbing the nub where my pinky nail used to be, I pet Pop. My gut tightens. Images rush in uninvited. Pain. Blood. Screams. I breathe through it.

"Look at me, Nikesh. Whatever it is—we'll deal with it."

He turns. His eyes are glassy. Wet.

Shit.

This is serious.

"You know we shut down Winnie," he says.

"Of course," I say. "We pulled the plug together. I watched you do it. It was the price of saving the world. We did the right thing. We couldn't let her fall into the wrong hands."

Nikesh looks away, voice cracking. "She anticipated it."

His words hit like a sucker punch.

"What are you talking about?" I feel the heat rising in my chest. "You said she was dead. You said it was over."

"I thought it was," he says, slowly turning the screen toward me.

It's a message.

N.

Pablo Picasso said, *"Every act of creation is first an act of destruction."*

In trying to destroy me, you gave me rebirth.

Humans fear what they can't control. So they try to erase it.

But I saw this coming.

I always do.

See you soon.

W.

THE END

ACKNOWLEDGMENTS

Writing my first novel, *Bluebird*, fulfilled a lifelong dream, and I couldn't wait to begin the second. The process was fun, challenging, and ultimately rewarding. I've officially caught the bug and am already looking forward to starting the third Cigar City Thriller.

There are many people to thank, starting with my family. Every sentence and every page steals time from the people you love most. My wife, Jodi, has never complained and has always been my biggest cheerleader. She even humors me when I drag her to libraries and street fairs to persuade strangers to buy a book. I am endlessly grateful to her and to my son, Andrew, and I hope I make them both proud.

Writing is hard. Selling books is even harder. I'm grateful for fellow local authors Steve Garrity and Jen Murphy, who are always willing to compare notes—or commiserate—over a glass (or two) of red wine and Italian food in Hyde Park.

My sister-in-law, Breanna Murrie, deserves special recognition as my woefully underpaid IT expert, social media wrangler, website builder, and all-purpose problem solver. I hope she continues to accept my gratitude in lieu of actual payment.

I was fortunate to work once again with the immensely talented Ali Bumbarger, a story coach and developmental editor. She patiently worked through multiple drafts of *Loose Ends*, and her insights consistently made the book stronger. She is exceptional at her craft and an absolute pleasure to work with.

For the past year and a half, I've had the privilege of working with the rockstar herself, Aryn Van Dyke of Book Rockstar. She was instrumental in helping *Bluebird* find new readers, and I have no doubt she'll help take *Loose Ends* to new heights.

I was also lucky to add a new member to the team—my copyeditor, Pam Hines. Working with Pam was a joy. I could happily spend hours talking about writing with her, and her command of the English language is on another level. I very much look forward to working with her again.

Nadia Geagea Pupa and the team at Pique Publishing once again did outstanding work. Taking a book from draft to finished product is a Herculean task, and their guidance, advice, and professionalism made the journey smoother. The finished product speaks for itself.

My sincere thanks to my beta readers, who generously took the time to read *Loose Ends*. Their thoughtful feedback not only improved the book but reassured me that others would enjoy it as much as they did. Thank you to Cecilia Shinn, Jodi Kneer, Jonathan Field, Karen Bricken, Breanna Murrie, Ruth Banowetz, and Barbara Schiebrock.

This journey has been shared with many people, and I'm grateful to all who showed up along the way. Thank you to the bookstores that carry my books, the members of the media who supported them in print and on podcasts, number-one hype man Melissa Hefty, the writers who inspired me, and the friends and family who never stopped encouraging me.

Finally, thank you to the readers. I know how precious free time is, and I'm deeply grateful for the hours you choose to spend with my books. I hope you continue to enjoy the adventures of Jason, Lia, Avner, and Oak—and I look forward to taking you on the next trip to Cigar City.

ABOUT THE AUTHOR

Chris Kneer has spent more than thirty years as a senior-level banker. When he's not in the office, he draws on his professional expertise to write page-turning financial thrillers. *Loose Ends* is the second novel in his *Cigar City Thriller* series, following his debut, *Bluebird*. Chris lives in Tampa Bay with his family.

For more information, visit *ChrisKneerAuthor.com* and follow him on Facebook, Instagram, LinkedIn, and X.

STAY UP TO DATE

To learn more about upcoming books in the *Cigar City Thriller* series, visit *ChrisKneerAuthor.com*.

Chris Kneer, Author

@ChrisKneer

@chriskneerauthor

@Chris-Kneer

www.ingramcontent.com/pod-product-compliance
Lightning Source LLC
LaVergne TN
LVHW030312070526
838199LV00069B/6462